Praise for Christine Wells

"Royalty, secrets, diamonds, and courtesans all come together in this riveting tale. . . . A sweeping novel about love, ambition, and what family really means."

— Natasha Lester, *New York Times* bestselling author of *The Paris Orphan*

"*The Royal Windsor Secret* is a thrilling historical fiction brimming with adventure, mystery, romance, and a willful, independent heroine you will root for, all wrapped up in a scintillating secret."

— Madeline Martin, *New York Times* and internationally bestselling author

"In *The Royal Windsor Secret*, Christine Wells takes a fascinating chapter in the Duke of Windsor's early life and gives it an equally fascinating coda in the form of a love child, who shares all of the duke's passion and impulsivity, and yearns for a life beyond what she already knows. The truth of Cleo's parentage will have you turning pages until the very end, while Cleo's search for fulfillment—creative, professional, social, and romantic—results in a beautifully told tale."

— Bryn Turnbull, author of *The Paris Deception*

"From the exotic hotels of pre-war Cairo to the glittering jewelry ateliers of Paris, Christine Wells has written a richly layered tale of intrigue in *The Royal Windsor Secret*. Fans of *The Crown* will delight in the familiar faces of Wallis Simpson and the Duke of Windsor even as they revel in this story of dreams and ambitions, love and war."

— Stephanie Marie Thornton, *USA Today* bestselling author of *Her Lost Words*

THE
ROYAL
WINDSOR
SECRET

ALSO BY CHRISTINE WELLS

One Woman's War
Sisters of the Resistance

October 11, 2023

THE
ROYAL
WINDSOR
SECRET

A Novel

CHRISTINE WELLS

WM

WILLIAM MORROW

An Imprint of HarperCollins*Publishers*

HarperCollins books may be purchased for educational, business, or sales promotional use. For information, please email the Special Markets Department at SPsales@harpercollins.com.

FIRST EDITION

Designed by Diahann Sturge
Page break ornaments throughout © Made by Made/The Noun Project
Illustration on pages 1, 34, 51, 99, 119, 129, 143, 154, 171, 267, 297, 311 © Alena
   Artemova/The Noun Project
Illustration on pages 7, 182, 234, 259, 282, 325 © Olga/The Noun Project
Illustration on pages 87 and 285 © SAHAS2015
Illustration on pages 210 and 225 © PATILPIVART/Shutterstock
Illustration on pages 63, 73, 193, 250 © IR Stone/Shutterstock

Library of Congress Cataloging-in-Publication Data has been applied for.

ISBN 978-0-06-326824-1

23 24 25 26 27 LBC 5 4 3 2 1

To my nanna, Maisie Robe, who loved books, and who made her home an enchanted place

Prologue

MARGUERITE

Paris, France
Spring 1914

"Jewels, *ma chère*. Jewels are the only things that matter."

Twenty-three-year-old Marguerite Meller sat at a small marble-and-gilt table, watching as her employer and mentor went to a cabinet in the corner of the room. This piece was draped in a pretty cloth, printed with swirls of pale blue and taupe paisley and fringed with silk tassels. Lifting the cloth and draping it over the carriage clock that sat on top of the cabinet, Madame revealed what was in fact a dark green safe. The statuesque form of the *maîtresse* blocked Marguerite's view of the dial as she bent to open her repository of treasures.

The *maison de rendezvous* at 3 rue Galilée was as elegantly furnished as any grand Parisian town house, and Marguerite loved to be invited into Madame Denart's private domain. Marguerite was learning to become a first-class courtesan. Not only was she schooled in the arts of the boudoir, she'd been instructed in a range of disciplines: horse riding, singing, playing the piano, Italian and German, elocution and etiquette, current events, history, and politics.

Her morning lessons with Madame smacked of special privilege; the *maîtresse* did not give private instruction to just any of the women who graced her books.

Today, jewels. The tips of Marguerite's fingers warmed and tingled with anticipation.

Much as she longed to jump up and sneak a glimpse of the safe's contents over Madame's shoulder, Marguerite forced herself to remain where she was and wait. After a few moments, the older woman closed the safe and let down the shawl. She returned to the table and set a black lacquered box between them. Its mirror-glaze surface was punctuated by a central motif: a jungle cat made of inlaid mother-of-pearl.

Madame Denart opened the box and lifted out two red satin-covered beds that glittered with precious stones.

Marguerite gasped. "Magnificent! Madame, these are fit for a queen. How I should love to wear such pieces."

Madame fixed Marguerite with a reproving gaze. "These are not mere decorative baubles, *ma fille*. Jewels—the *right* jewels—are the lifeblood of a courtesan. More stable in value than paper money, and infinitely more portable. Easily converted to currency wherever one happens to be yet bestowing upon the woman who wears them a cachet which the mere possession of money never could. They are the first items a woman sews into her petticoats when she makes her escape—whether from a revolution, a war, or a marriage." Madame smiled thinly. "For courtesans and queens alike, jewels are *always* better than money." She jerked her chin. "Hold out your hand."

Eagerly, Marguerite complied. Madame plucked diamond bracelets from their plush setting, one by one, and clasped them around Marguerite's slender forearm.

The bracelets were cold and hard against Marguerite's bare skin. One was too tight and pinched her flesh, but she ignored the discomfort. She angled her arm so that the gems caught the sunlight, dazzling her.

Not for the first time, Marguerite wondered about Madame Denart's past. She was a handsome woman who took such excellent care of her skin that she might have been aged more than a decade younger than her seventy years. She had been a courtesan at a time when the profession was at its height, when luminaries such as La Belle Otero, Blanche d'Antigny, and Cora Pearl had enchanted all of Paris with their extravagance and their style. Legends abounded telling of the lengths to which the *grandes horizontales* drove their admirers—to folly, to madness, to financial ruin, and even to suicide.

Well, what did these men expect? If they did not have the sense to hold on to their fortunes, more fool they. Men had not treated Marguerite so well that she had an ounce of pity to spare for them.

Her husky voice warming to her theme, Madame took Marguerite's hand and pushed the diamond bracelets together so that they formed a dazzling gauntlet from elbow to wrist, then added one more.

"Jewels are a currency that gentlemen may use to purchase our company without the nasty taint of the transaction. For the courtesan, jewelry is a status symbol, an advertisement of her worth, the standard which other men must match or exceed if they expect to win her favors." She held up a finger. "But remember this, Marguerite. Let no man own you. Courtesans are not mistresses; we do not confine ourselves to one lover. When a man has exclusive possession of a woman, he becomes complacent, and that diminishes her value. No matter how charming or handsome or rich he might be, if a gentleman does not make the appropriate gift to show his appreciation, you must drop him. Immediately."

"Of course." Dreamily, Marguerite wondered if she could ever hope to command a collection to rival Madame's. Marguerite was no beauty. Her mouth was too small, her nose a trifle too large and her eyebrows straight and thick, tapering toward the temples, like strokes of a calligrapher's brush. Her stature was small, but she did have an excellent figure and she took the utmost pains to play up her attractions: a pair of large, melancholy grey-green eyes, a beauty spot on her left cheek, and masses of auburn hair.

She could be charming when she wished, but she had a devilishly bad temper that sometimes got her into trouble. She had learned to curb that tendency—at least until a conquest was firmly ensnared. But like an active volcano, sooner or later, the pressure would build inside her. She would erupt.

Regardless of this undoubted flaw, Madame must have seen something in Marguerite that merited cultivation. For her part, Marguerite meant to grab every opportunity presented to her, while the grabbing was good.

The older woman selected a large ruby pendant and held it up between her finger and thumb, angling it so that it caught the gentle sunlight that streamed between the pale blue velvet curtains of her boudoir. Captivated, Marguerite gazed at the stone. Encased in a plain gold setting, it was smooth and rounded, as dull as oxblood until the light filtered through.

The diamond bracelets encircling Marguerite's wrist glittered and flashed as coldly as Madame's smile. But despite its comparative dullness, it was the ruby that held Marguerite entranced. The interior of the stone seemed to flicker and dance with wicked shadows of devils and hell-bound souls. It seemed to beckon her to enter.

Marguerite shivered, shaking off the unwonted fancy, and asked, "How much did that one cost, then?"

The *maîtresse* frowned at this lapse into vulgarity and Marguerite bit her lip. Her conversational style had improved under Madame's careful tutelage but sometimes she slipped.

"You will learn how to quickly and discreetly appraise any gift," said Madame, disregarding the gauche impertinence and replacing the pendant. "You must never allow yourself to be taken in by inferior stones, or—heaven forbid!—fake gems made of paste. A courtesan's jewel collection is her security and her pension fund." She narrowed her eyes. "Too many times, I have seen a woman build up tremendous wealth, only to squander it at the gaming tables. Once the toast of Paris, she ends her days old, unwanted, and destitute. Do *not* let that happen to you."

Of course, everyone in their circle had heard those stories. "No fear of that," said Marguerite. She only gambled with other people's money.

A convent girl, then a servant, turned off without a character after falling pregnant to the master's son at fifteen, Marguerite knew what it was to be vulnerable, hungry, and alone in the world, subject to all kinds of degradations in the doorways and back alleys of Paris. She had given up her daughter to her mother to raise but it was Marguerite's work on the streets that kept the child clothed and fed.

Sheer determination and smarts—and a hard-won stint at the Folies Bergère—had lifted her out of that existence. She took a rich lover or two, one of whom she falsely claimed to have married, thereby gaining a certain status among the Parisian demimonde. Madame Denart had discovered Marguerite through a mutual acquaintance and invited her to be part of her select list of *poules de luxe,* elevating her to even greater heights.

Madame's clientele included many wealthy and important men. With the older lady's connections as well as her expert guidance, Marguerite would never, *ever,* suffer poverty and humiliation again.

And if the possession of jewels was the way to make sure of that, she would do anything and everything to get as many of those precious baubles as she could.

Chapter One

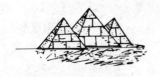

Cairo, Egypt
Autumn 1935

$\mathcal{B}$reathless and exhilarated and furious, sixteen-year-old Cleo Davenport reined in her grey mare and turned to glare at the approaching rider. Brodie had let her win. *Again.* Impatiently, she shoved away the strand of curly gold hair that had whipped into her mouth during their desert race. Brodie was only one year older than she was and the best horseman she knew. She wanted desperately to beat him fair and square.

"You beast!" Her words were lost on the wind. The slow dawn had begun with a soft, spiced glow and a pink mist rising over the desert, but now the tangerine disk of the sun was high in the sky, bathing the timeless peaks of the pyramids in shimmering light.

Brodie grinned. He cupped his ear, shrugged, and shook his head. In spite of herself, Cleo smiled back as he cantered toward her. Brodie moved easily in the saddle, his shaggy black hair swept away from his angular face by the strong breeze. He needed a haircut but he'd refused to let her near him with Fifi's sewing shears after the last time.

His mount, still frisky from the race, danced and sidled. "Come on." Brodie jerked his head toward the city. "They'll be looking for you."

As they entered the city and slowed to a more sedate pace, Cleo slid a glance at her companion. Brodie was Scottish by birth. He'd grown up in France but when his parents had died, his uncle, Mr. Gordon, had brought him back to Shepheard's Hotel with him.

Mr. Gordon was the zookeeper at Shepheard's and a bachelor, and his adoption of his nephew was begrudging at best. He'd only warmed to his new charge when he witnessed Brodie's almost mystical affinity with animals. But Mr. Gordon had died two years ago of a fever. The new director spent most of his time traveling the world in search of new inmates for the zoo and conducting his own research, so Brodie had taken on most of his responsibilities in addition to his own work.

Cleo, too, was an orphan, and she also resided at Shepheard's Hotel. But while Brodie lived in the zoo director's cramped quarters, Cleo slept in luxury in the hotel itself.

As they rode through the labyrinthine Cairo streets, the smells of dung and donkey, of incense and spices and refuse filled Cleo's nostrils. They passed a greengrocer with giant cauliflowers and cabbages, oranges and dates piled high in wicker baskets.

The workers were watering the dusty road, and Brodie urged his horse to a fast trot. He was responsible for the day-to-day running of the zoo: feeding and watering the animals and checking on their welfare. The zoo was not large but it held a pair of camels, some young Arabian horses, a handful of tame gazelles that delighted the hotel's children, and even two pandas all the way from China.

They reached Ibrahim Pasha Street with its pretty gardens and approached the wide sweep of Shepheard's Hotel. It was a four-storied stone building with arched windows and colonnades and tiny French balconies—a grand edifice that might have been a museum plucked from any European capital.

Wrought iron railings girded a square, raised terrace that dominated the expansive frontage. The terrace was furnished with marble-topped tables, rattan armchairs, and lush potted palms. The waiters, called *safragi,* were smartly clad in crimson-and-gold embroidered jackets, baggy white *sirwal* trousers, and red tarbooshes. Even if visitors to Cairo preferred to stay at Mena House or one of the other fine hotels in the city, sooner or later, everyone who was anyone—from Mark Twain and Noël Coward to royalty of every nation—came to tea on the terrace at Shepheard's.

Forbidden from coming upstairs to harass the guests, hawkers gathered in the street below to sell their wares to the wealthy patrons. Everything from fans, fruits, and fly whisks, stuffed snakes and crocodiles to live chickens could be purchased from these vendors and handed up to the buyer. Cleo and Brodie picked their way through the crowd, firmly refusing assistance from the dragomen hoping to sell their services as tour guides. The pair continued around to the stables, where Brodie slid from the saddle, tethered his animal, then reached up, lifting Cleo by the waist to swing her down.

"I can get down by myself, you know," she said. "I'm not a child." He was so big and she was so small, she often felt the need to assert herself.

"Don't I know it." Grinning at her puzzled look, he took her mare's bridle. "I'll take her. Fifi will not be pleased."

Cleo rolled her eyes. Her French governess, Mademoiselle Faubert, was as lazy as a pasha. "I don't care for one of her scolds."

"Well, we'll both be in trouble if anyone sees you helping with my chores," said Brodie. "Or me riding out with you, for that matter."

"Then we must make sure no one catches us. I'll do my share."

When he still hesitated as if they hadn't had this conversation many times before, she stamped her foot. "*Brodie.*"

He sighed. "Yes, Your Highness." He pretended to tug a forelock and held out Starlight's reins to her. "Whatever you say, Your Majesty."

Usually he spoke with only the slightest Scottish burr, but whenever he mocked what he called Cleo's "hoity-toity ways" he adopted a thick brogue. *Yerr Maejesty.* She scowled, then laughed and snatched up Starlight's reins.

When they had dealt with the tack, they set to work in companionable silence, rubbing down the horses and brushing their coats. Brodie was right. She ought to be getting back. But this was the best part of her day and she wanted to stretch it out as long as she could.

After a while, she said, "Do you want to leave Egypt one day? Go home, I mean?"

"My parents left Scotland shortly after I was born. They were poor and hated France every second we lived there, so there aren't a lot of good memories to go home to." He shrugged. "I've never even met my Scottish kin."

Surprised that he'd said so much about his family, whom he rarely mentioned, Cleo was emboldened to ask, "Has none of your family ever written to you?" Cleo waited as Starlight tossed her head and snorted, then she ran the currycomb through the mare's pale mane.

As she worked, her own long, golden curls, which had tumbled free of their ribbon during that glorious ride, mingled now and then with the mare's coarse hair. With a grimace, Cleo pushed her hair back and tucked it behind her ear. Realizing Brodie had not answered her question, she looked up.

His gaze cut away.

"My grandfather," he said at last. "Once." His face turned grim. "Informing me he'd disinherited my father, who disgraced him, and considered my uncle a blithering fool, but if I'd like to prove myself worthy, he would be prepared to consider reinstating me as his heir."

"Is that why you've been studying so hard?"

He shook his head. "I don't want the old curmudgeon's money. I'll make my own way."

Cleo's honorary aunt and guardian had recognized Brodie's quick intelligence and hectored Mr. Gordon into letting Brodie share Cleo's lessons. Serafina had even deigned to tutor Brodie herself when his thirst for knowledge surpassed the French governess's ability to quench it.

Sometimes Cleo envied the way Brodie so effortlessly engaged Serafina's attention. He was a keen student of Egyptology and Serafina seemed to enjoy tutoring him, whereas she was liable to forget Cleo's existence for days at a time when deeply involved in research and writing. Serafina was not an easy person to love.

"Will you become an Egyptologist like Serafina, then?"

He shrugged. "I don't see much future in Egypt for someone like me. They want the British out, and I don't blame them. No, I want to travel to remote places and study wildlife like my uncle did. There are a lot of things I want to see and do, but . . . it's hard to imagine I'll ever get to do them." He gave a final pat to his horse's flank. "All done." Done with the horse, and done with the subject, too. She knew this mood, so she didn't say any more.

She longed to travel, too. Not to far-flung destinations like Brodie but to Paris, the most brilliant and cultured city in the world. She didn't like much about her governess, but she could sit and listen to her stories about the City of Light for hours.

Cleo went with Brodie to the zoo, to pet and cosset her particular friend, Daisy, a gazelle whose limpid brown eyes had the power to quiet the restlessness in Cleo's soul. Stroking the suede softness of her neck, Cleo whispered greetings and made little clicking noises with her tongue. She was about to fetch the gazelles their feed when the high-pitched trill of her governess's voice made Daisy startle and flick her ears. "Cleo? *Peste!* Where is that dreadful girl?"

"Oops!" With a kiss on the gazelle's nose and a wave to Brodie, Cleo slipped away, hurrying across the courtyard in which so many lavish parties were held. Parties to which she, not yet having made her debut, was rarely invited. But Serafina's suite overlooked the gardens, and Cleo had often sat by the window dreamily watching these enchanted evenings filled with beautiful gowns and glittering jewels. She skirted the Carrara marble dance floor and ducked into the hotel through a servant entrance.

A tunnel beneath the hotel ran diagonally from the laundry and pantry to the kitchens. Cleo headed through the laundry, feeling the steam from the copper cauldrons cloud about her face. She entered the comparative cool of the narrow subterranean corridor, where dry, musty air filled her lungs. She used to play in that tunnel as a little girl, pretending to be Howard Carter excavating Tutankhamun's tomb. Now she sped along in the semidarkness toward the light up ahead, ignoring the furtive rustles of rats as she went. Surfacing in the kitchens, Cleo slipped past the bustle of chefs and waiters, all of whom were too busy with the breakfast orders to notice her. She darted out into the lobby, ignoring the lure of Mansoor's Jewelry and Antiques, hurried past the sinuous ebony caryatids that flanked the staircase, and up the stairs to her floor.

Cleo eased inside her guardian's suite and paused to listen.

Aunt Serafina was in her bedroom with the door closed, talking to someone—most probably to her sister, Lady Grayson. So, they were awake. Too much to hope they hadn't noticed Cleo's absence. Cleo made a face. She was due for a scold, then. Mainly because Lady Grayson had strict notions of propriety and expected Serafina to discipline Cleo accordingly. Serafina herself rarely cared what Cleo did, as long as it didn't interfere with her scholarly work. Cleo much preferred it that way.

Still, she liked Lady Grayson, who despite her proper notions had a distinct twinkle in her eye and took more interest in Cleo than Serafina ever had. Lord Grayson was kind, too. However, there was no denying that whenever they were in Cairo on holiday, Cleo was obliged to mind her p's and q's to a degree she never had before. Well, perhaps if she washed and changed into something feminine and charming, she might avoid another lecture.

The sitting room, which doubled as Serafina's study, was littered with stacks of papers and papyri, books and maps, not to mention the odd artefact: an ushabti here, a faience scarab beetle there. Cleo's own corner of the room was scarcely any tidier. Her desk was stacked high with sketches of the fabulous jewelry she loved to design and scrapbooks full of inspiration. Cleo was picking her way around the detritus when she heard her name spoken.

She stopped. Not only were the sisters talking about her, the discussion seemed heated.

Cleo hesitated. Eavesdropping was not really cricket, she knew that. On the other hand, when one's very origins were shrouded in mystery, one developed the habit of gleaning any and all information about oneself in whatever manner possible. When Cleo's name was mentioned again, she tiptoed over to the closed door and bent to listen.

Lady Grayson was saying, "She's growing up wild. You must see this can't go on."

"Cleo is *perfect*!" The rejoinder from Serafina made Cleo's eyes pop open in shock. "She is the opposite of insipid." Cleo clapped a hand over her mouth to stifle a chuckle. *Really*? Serafina never would have dreamed of saying such a thing to Cleo's face.

"She is a beauty, I'll grant you," said Lady Grayson. "But far from perfect. Why, even now she is running about the desert with that strapping stable boy—"

Cleo's hot cry of indignation nearly gave her away but Serafina cut in before Cleo could storm in and leap to Brodie's defense. "I won't hear a word against him! That young man has a fine mind. He's going to make something of himself one day. Mark my words."

"That may be, but he ought not to be hobnobbing unchaperoned with a sixteen-year-old girl." At a snort from Serafina, Lady Grayson continued, "Saffy, you have no notion of responsibility. Why, Mademoiselle Faubert told me you left that child on her own in the hotel for two months last winter while you went off on one of your digs."

Cleo rolled her eyes. Between Taaleb, the enormous Nubian who stood guard outside their room each night, the hotel staff, *and* the permanent guests—not to mention Fifi herself—so very many people had kept an eye on Cleo in Serafina's absence that Cleo had felt far more restricted than when her guardian was there.

"She was hardly alone." This came in a mumble Cleo had to strain to catch. "Besides, *our* parents left us for months on end and we didn't suffer."

"We were at home in England with Nanny and a staff of old retainers, not at a hotel in Cairo!" After a pause, Lady Grayson added gently, "There is no future for her here, Saffy. Surely you must see that. Her birth alone entitles her—"

"*Birth?*" Serafina gave a crack of laughter. "Did someone turn back the clock a few centuries while I wasn't looking?"

Goodness, what did *that* mean? Cleo frowned but she didn't have time to mull it over. She was too eager to hear what came next.

"Saffy." The gentle reproach was followed by something Cleo couldn't quite catch. She strained to hear more.

Then: "Oh, why did I even start all this?" Serafina's voice rang with despair. "I never *wanted* a child."

Cleo swallowed hard. Her throat burned strangely, as if she was coming down with a cold, but she lifted her chin and glared defiantly at the door. She'd known she wasn't wanted, hadn't she? Where was the surprise in that?

"You did it because you're a good-hearted woman," said Lady Grayson. "And because everyone needs their own person to love. But loving that child means doing what's best for her, even if that means letting her go."

Silence greeted this statement. Cleo waited for what seemed like an age. Then Serafina sighed. "Very well, then. Take her."

The blood drummed in Cleo's ears so hard that she felt lightheaded, and missed the next few sentences. Serafina was giving in? Just like that? Surrendering Cleo to her sister as if she were a dog or a horse. How *could* she?

No one ever made Serafina do what she didn't want to do. She must have some reason—certainly not the selfless sort of love Lady Grayson described. The tender emotions were completely alien to the Honorable Serafina Davenport.

Cleo was about to barge into the room to plead her case when she heard Serafina add, "Promise me two things, Lydia."

"Hmm. Why do I feel a sudden *terrific* apprehension?"

Serafina hurried on. "Cleo is . . . oh, 'spirited' is the polite euphemism, I believe. Don't try to iron that out of her, will you, Lyddy? Don't let anyone crush her the way Mama tried to crush me."

"All right, I promise," said Lady Grayson. "Though from what I've seen of Cleo, I shouldn't think anyone could." She paused. "And the second thing?"

Cleo burst into the room. "You can't! You simply can't send me away!" Serafina was seated across from her sister at the breakfast table by the window. Delicate china teacups rattled in their saucers as Cleo strode over to her in her heavy riding boots. She dropped to her knees and stared beseechingly into Serafina's eyes. "*Please!* Don't make me go with them. I . . . I'll run away." She shot a reproachful glare at Lady Grayson, who only smiled faintly in response.

"Eavesdropping, Cleo?" said Serafina, ignoring the threat. Then in her brisk way, she caught Cleo's hands in hers and gripped them tightly. "What I was about to ask my sister before you so rudely interrupted was whether she would take Brodie back to England with her, too."

"*What?*" Lady Grayson and Cleo cried at once.

"I couldn't possibly . . ." said Lady Grayson, her pretty face drawn with shock.

"Brodie? In England?" said Cleo. "He would never go there. Not in a *thousand years*."

"Well, then, it will be up to us to persuade him, won't it?" Serafina leaned forward, her expression avid. "Think about it, Cleo. Here, Brodie has very little future. In England, as the protégé of Lord and Lady Grayson, he would be given the best education money could buy. Oxford, or Cambridge, perhaps . . . There are scholarships he can apply for, too. I'm sure he'll get one. Only think what he might become."

Abruptly Cleo shut her mouth and thought. Brodie, with access to the best equipment and laboratories, professors, and tutors, unlimited opportunities for research. Was she going to stand in his way? How *could* she stand in his way?

"You are diabolical," she whispered to Serafina with grudging admiration. Cleo couldn't even begin to comprehend what life in England would mean for her, personally, but she didn't have to. She would do anything for Brodie and her guardian knew it.

"Now, just one moment . . ." Lady Grayson began in a baleful tone.

Serafina smiled at her sister. "You heard Cleo. If you take her without him, she will run away. She's perfectly capable of it, you know."

"So I'm to hold this boy hostage to her good behavior, is that it?" Lady Grayson threw back her head and laughed. "Cleo's right, Saffy. You *are* diabolical."

WHEN THE PLAN was disclosed to Brodie, his dark eyes burned with a strange mix of emotions that made Cleo hot and uncertain and slightly afraid. It was a look of fiery yearning, as if he wanted to go very badly but was angry about it. At himself for wanting it? Or at Serafina for having it so easily within her power to give? But when he met Cleo's pleading gaze, the expression in those deep brown eyes softened, and she knew in her heart then and there that she could never bear to be parted from him. Not ever.

If she had to learn to be a lady in England, she would jolly well do it. She would beat those proper English misses at their own game. And she might finally discover who she was, and who her parents were. Lady Grayson knew something—perhaps everything—and she would be an easier nut to crack than Serafina, who steadfastly and blandly claimed ignorance whenever Cleo questioned her on the subject.

Her birth alone entitles her. What on earth did that mean?

"REALLY! IT'S THE outside of enough," said Lady Grayson to her husband as Cleo helped her pack up the dahabeeyah she and her husband had rented for the season. "I can't imagine how I let Serafina talk me into this. What do I know about raising a young man, much less one of—" she waved a hand "—of his background."

Scowling, Cleo was about to make a hot retort, when Lord Grayson said, "It's an excellent plan. I rather wonder why I did not think of it myself."

"*What?*" Both Lady G and Cleo stared at him.

"I've had my eye on that young man ever since Serafina took an interest in him. He has a remarkable brain and a quick wit. And he is a Gordon, after all."

Lady Grayson sniffed. "That side of the family are all dirty dishes. His father ran off with a peasant girl, not to mention the rest . . ." She broke off, probably realizing that Cleo was in the room, listening to every word.

Lord Grayson smiled at his wife. "Let's hear no more against the idea, Lyddy. I promise that you won't be sorry for sponsoring him."

Cleo chuckled to herself at the way Lady Grayson visibly melted under her husband's smile. "Well, if you're sure he won't disgrace us . . ."

"I see no reason why he should." Lord Grayson glanced at Cleo and there was a twinkle in his eye. "We ought to keep a close eye on *this* one, however. She's always been trouble with a capital 'T.'"

Cleo grinned back at him. "I can't imagine what you mean."

Her fears in abeyance, if not completely eradicated, Lady Grayson turned into a whirlwind, making travel arrangements, writing letters, and paying calls on everyone in Cairo who might feel slighted if she left Egypt without bidding them a proper goodbye.

She stared aghast at the practical garments that populated Cleo's wardrobe and declared that they must travel first to Paris to outfit Cleo properly for her London debut.

Paris! Cleo could hardly believe it. She had always wanted to see the city—for its monuments and cafés and museums, yes—but most particularly to visit the home of jewelers like Cartier and Boucheron. She hoped she would have the chance to see these famous ateliers while she was there.

Cleo loved beautiful clothes as much as the next girl—it was just that generally she preferred comfort and practicality in her dress. One never knew what adventures might be afoot in and around the hotel. It was horrifically easy to ruin one's best tea gown when exploring the cellars, feeding the tame birds in the gardens, or consuming as many *friandises* in the kitchens as Monsieur Martin would allow.

The plan, after Paris, was to spend the spring and early summer months making her debut in England, then to travel to the Riviera to recover from the social whirl. Cleo did not see what there was to recover *from,* exactly, but Lady Grayson was adamant; they would not return to Egypt for at least another year.

Excited but already missing her friends around the hotel, Cleo visited them all in the week before their departure. The only person she wouldn't miss was her governess, Mademoiselle Faubert, who, upon being told her services wouldn't be needed any longer, promptly decamped to the household of a wealthy Cairene family. *Good riddance,* Cleo thought. Fifi had never quite let Cleo forget that she was an orphan, and an illegitimate one at that.

The question of her true parentage had never troubled Cleo as much as it did now that she was about to leave Shepheard's Hotel, the only home she'd ever known—perhaps permanently.

The future was something Serafina had never discussed. Despite her towering intellect, Serafina was not a very practical sort of person, and probably expected Cleo to live out her days at Shepheard's, this timeless bastion of British imperialism, like an insect preserved in amber. Like one of those mummies Serafina always hoped to dig up.

Now Cleo was going to London—via Paris—and Brodie was coming with her. If her life was about to change, his was on the precipice of a revolution. She couldn't help feeling anxious at the idea of his attending a prestigious university among a set of people who might taunt him for his poor origins and rough manners. Perhaps she ought to have insisted on going to Oxford, too.

But despite her facility for languages, Cleo was no scholar. What Cleo wanted was to use her talents for jewelry design—working for Cartier, Boucheron, or Van Cleef & Arpels, perhaps. But the ultimate prize—her own brand, her own business. Marriage? She didn't feel ready for that, and despite having agreed to a London season, she rather guessed she wouldn't feel ready for many years yet. She pressed her lips together. One thing at a time.

Before she left Cairo, Cleo meant to find out all she could about the circumstances that had brought her into Serafina's care. If her guardian wouldn't tell her, perhaps someone else might.

Taaleb had been employed at the hotel after Cleo's arrival, so he might not know the details. Then again, perhaps the general gossip had reached him. The world of Shepheard's was rarefied and small, after all.

Taaleb was a guard, footman, and an occasional partner in crime for Cleo. When she was a child, he would sneak little treats to her from the kitchens during a grand dinner or reception—petits fours, cheeses, exotic fruits, which she had insisted he share. Cleo popped her head out of the room and saw him at his usual station, guarding the door to their suite.

"Good evening, princess." Taaleb smiled down at her.

With a quick glance either way down the corridor to make sure no one saw, she beckoned him inside. Serafina and the Graysons had gone out for the evening, so the coast was clear.

Taaleb had the stature and the initiation scars of a warrior, and his presence seemed to make their sitting room shrink to the size of a doll's house. Cleo wanted to invite him to sit but knew he would decline, so she stood also, rocking a bit on her heels, biting her lip, wondering how to approach such a delicate and foreign subject.

"I'm leaving soon," said Cleo, plaiting her fingers together. "I suppose you knew that."

"Yes, princess. It is very sad."

Suddenly Cleo wanted to hug his solid, utterly dependable form and hold on tight. She fought back the urge. "Oh, I shall miss you all! And I don't even know when I'll be back. That's why I wanted to ask you . . ." She sighed. What was the use? She had asked everyone repeatedly when she was younger and all had claimed ignorance.

He folded his arms. "Ask."

She drew a deep breath. "When I was a baby. When I was brought here . . . I know you weren't even working at the hotel at the time, but did you ever hear any gossip about my parents? Or about who left me at the hotel?"

He smiled and shook his head. "No, princess. No one would dare gossip about you. Not to me."

"Oh." Such loyalty was commendable but not what she needed. "Well, thank you. You have always been so good to me."

He turned to go, but she said, "Taaleb, why do you call me 'princess'? Is it . . ." No, that was silly. Of course it was just a term of affection. Hadn't he assured her he did not know any gossip about her parentage? Then again, with so many real princesses visiting the hotel, wasn't it odd and a little confusing to call Cleo that?

He turned, clearly surprised, then he frowned. "I don't know. I picked it up from somewhere, maybe."

He couldn't remember from whom and Cleo suspected it might have been the Nubian rais, who would have assigned Taaleb the task of guarding Serafina all those years ago. But Soleiman al Nubi had retired and returned to his village a wealthy man. She sighed. Well, it probably wasn't worth pursuing that line of inquiry anyway. Many of the staff called her "princess." The reason might be as simple as the fact that she had long blond hair. Or it might be because of that silly rumor about her father being the Prince of Wales.

When the rumor had come to Cleo's ears many years ago, she had immediately asked Serafina about it, and she had said it was nonsense.

Cleo believed her. While Serafina might refuse to speak of certain subjects, Cleo had never known her to tell an outright lie. Besides, Cleo had followed up this clue years before and discovered that, far from being in Egypt at the approximate time of her conception, the heir to the British throne had been off fighting in France.

The prince had visited Egypt when Cleo was little and she had even met him, or so she'd been told, but that meant nothing at all.

Taaleb might not be able to help, but Cleo wasn't about to give up. The following morning, she went down to the lobby to investigate further.

The lobby of Shepheard's was like a small village in itself, with its own post and telegram offices. It even boasted an antique shop decorated like a souk in the Muski, full of valuable antiquities, jewels from Cartier, Van Cleef & Arpels, and Fabergé, carved alabaster statues, fine Egyptian gold filigree work—every rare luxury the hotel guests might desire.

The proprietor of the antique shop was polishing his jeweler's loupe with a soft cloth when Cleo approached his domain, calling out a cheery good morning. Mr. Mansoor looked up and his eyes lit. "Ah! I have something special to show you today, Cleo. Wait while I fetch it."

Distracted from her mission, Cleo held her breath while he went out to the back room of his little shop. Mr. Mansoor often let her sit in his shop and sketch the exquisite pieces in his collection before they were snapped up by his voracious clientele.

With a magician's flourish, Mr. Mansoor produced an unusual yellow gold ring. "A star ruby, you see. Clasped on either side by a panther." The panthers' tails curved around and met to form the circle of the ring.

"Oh, it's beautiful!" said Cleo. She ached to touch it, to slide the chic, utterly modern ring onto her own finger, but she knew Mr. Mansoor well enough not to ask. "The panthers are so lifelike. What are their black spots made of? Enamel?"

"Lacquer," said Mr. Mansoor. He tilted it to the light. "See?"

"And *yellow* gold. So unusual! You will have all the ladies fighting over this one," said Cleo.

Mr. Mansoor shook his head and tapped his nose. "This I bring out only for those who have the soul to appreciate."

Cleo flushed at the implied compliment. "How I wish I could afford to buy it."

"One day you will," said Mr. Mansoor, chuckling. "Of that I have no doubt."

She thanked Mr. Mansoor and headed for the stairs. Presided over by Mr. Costas, the basement at Shepheard's was full of left luggage, neatly labeled and waiting, safe and sound, for whenever their owners might return. It could be weeks or months or decades— Mr. Costas would find the item in minutes when its owner came to claim it.

As a child, Cleo would lose herself in this Aladdin's cave of treasures. The steamer trunks and suitcases it contained were plastered with labels from all over the world, and Cleo loved imagining the exotic places they had been. But the storeroom did not house only conventional luggage. There were artefacts of all kinds, statues and taxidermy, rugs and birdcages, lamps, tents, tools, swords, tennis rackets, bicycles, even a pair of skis.

But the best part of all was watching Mr. Costas in the little workshop that adjoined the storeroom, where he and his wife made silver cigarette boxes, which they would sell to the tourists who passed through the hotel.

The craft and artistry involved in making these boxes entranced Cleo. As she grew older, Mr. and Mrs. Costas let Cleo design some of the patterns that would be engraved or pressed into the shining sheets of silver. She learned quite a bit of Greek from the couple, too, although they tended to get excited easily and then they spoke too quickly for her to follow.

"The night you arrived here? Yes, yes, I remember," said Mr. Costas, glancing at the number on the ticket in his hand as he moved through the passage between steamer trunks and random paraphernalia. Cleo trailed after him, noting cricket bats and golf clubs, volumes of poetry and Egyptian pharaonic statuettes that looked quite valuable but might have been fakes, elephant tusks and panther skins (horrid!), parcels wrapped in brown paper and string.

"Could you tell me about it?" Cleo asked. "I'm sixteen, I'm leaving Egypt soon—perhaps forever—and I think I have a right to know."

"Well, I'll tell you what little I can," Mr. Costas said, absently.

Cleo's heart lifted. Perhaps Serafina had not thought to warn him against speaking of the subject.

"What? What's that you're saying?" The *pat-pat-pat* of Mrs. Costas's footsteps came toward them along the neighboring aisle. The lady herself was so tiny, Cleo could not see her above the piles of luggage until she rounded the corner and came toward them.

"Ears as sharp as a hound," muttered Mr. Costas but he smiled beatifically at his wife. "Hello, my dearest love. What are you—"

"Tell her what?" The little woman jabbed a silver-handled fly whisk she happened to be carrying in her husband's direction. "What were you going to tell her?"

"Nothing, nothing, my dove," murmured Mr. Costas.

"Yes, he was," said Cleo, capturing the older woman's work-worn hands in hers, fly whisk and all. "Don't be cross, dear Mrs. Costas. I need to hear whatever it is the two of you know about my parentage, about how I came to be here. I need to know before I leave."

Mrs. Costas exchanged a long glance with her husband. Three

deep creases lined her brow beneath its widow's peak. She tucked a strand of shining black hair behind her ear. "Miss Davenport forbade us to speak of it."

"Well, what right had she to do that?" demanded Cleo. "She's not even my blood relation."

"She said it was for your own good," replied Mrs. Costas, but from her disapproving expression, Cleo could tell Mrs. Costas did not agree.

Her resolve seemed to be wavering, so Cleo jumped in. "How can it be good for me not to know where I came from or how I got here? I need to find out the truth. Nothing will change between Aunt Serafina and me, but it's like I have a big space . . . a—a hole in my heart where my real family should be. Even if my parents are both dead, at least I might find out where they are buried, discover a little about my background. I don't even know what nationality I am!"

"Now, now, there's no need to be so tragic about it," said Mrs. Costas, freeing a hand to pat her arm. "As for nationality, with that talent for drama, one might almost think you were Greek!"

There was a pause while husband and wife locked gazes, discussing the subject without speaking, as married couples often do. "Well," said Mr. Costas at last, "I'm sure you'll be disappointed for it's little enough we do know. Come, sit with us and drink a little coffee and we will tell you the story."

He prepared a carafe of coffee and poured it into small china cups. Cleo sipped the strong black brew and listened to Mr. Costas tell his tale.

It was a night on which the stars seemed to have fallen from the heavens to scatter among the palm trees, bathing Shepheard's Hotel in an unearthly glow. Patrons with cocktails and brandies stayed out on the terrace until the small hours, basking in the magical star shine, their conversations and laughter weaving in and out of the strains from the orchestra in the gardens below.

On a night such as this, there is enchantment in the air, and it was on that same night that a small soul came to Shepheard's. The hour was very late—or early the next day, as one might call it—when a figure, furtive and shrouded in black, left a small bundle next to one of the service entrances out of sight of the people on the terrace. The figure, only glimpsed briefly by the maid who found the child, darted off and melted into the shadows of the night.

The maid herself had been stealthy, returning from some assignation she did not wish to be known. But she took pity on the little bundle—how could she not?—and brought it into the hotel to see what might be done about the child.

"How old was I then?" Cleo asked.

"Oh, no more than a couple of months," said Mrs. Costas. "Had we known, we would have taken you. But . . ." She shrugged.

"Aunt Serafina got there first," said Cleo. Grateful as she was to Serafina, she couldn't help but wonder what it would have been like to have this warm and wonderful couple as parents. But Serafina had come across the small crowd that had gathered in the foyer around the maid and her discovery, and immediately taken charge of the situation.

"You have every comfort you could desire, my dear," said Mr. Costas, gently reproving.

Yes, she has given me everything, thought Cleo. Everything except . . . "So it was my real mother who left me at the doorstep, presumably. I wonder why."

Mr. Costas spread his hands. "Who can tell? She might have been unmarried, too poor to raise a child . . ."

"Yes, of course. But why Shepheard's? It seems an odd place to choose. And using a side door at night. What if no one went through it for a day or more?"

"Perhaps she was familiar with the routines. She might have worked here once," said Mrs. Costas.

"Maybe she hoped things would turn out much as they have done," said her husband. "After all, she couldn't have asked for better: an affluent, respectable woman took you under her wing. You are healthy, wealthy, and . . . Well, perhaps I'll stop there." His eyes twinkled.

Cleo laughed, then sobered, frowning. "I might not be *wise* but I do find this story a bit implausible." She tilted her head. "Or is 'implausible' the word I'm looking for? I don't know. It doesn't ring true, somehow. It sounds like a fairy tale."

"I hope you're not accusing us of making it up!" said Mrs. Costas.

"Of course not." Cleo smiled at her. "You don't happen to remember the name of this maid who found me? Her address? Or her employer's address, I suppose it would have to be."

"Wait a moment." Mr. Costas went to his office and returned with a large ledger. He had a remarkable memory for guests of the hotel and the dates of their stay, so it did not surprise Cleo at all when he quickly found the relevant entry for that year. "Hmm," he said. "It seems there are some items left here by the maid's employer. A French woman by the name of Madame Meller. She stayed here often. Well, she did in the years before . . . Ahem! But I believe she remarried and her name is Fahmy now." A sharp dig in the ribs from his wife cut off that train of speech. "The maid was Aimée Pain. I'll write down the address for you, though I expect she has moved on since then."

Cleo decided not to pursue whatever secret Mrs. Costas did not want her husband to reveal, nor was she particularly interested in Madame Fahmy. She did not remember meeting that lady, nor Se-rafina ever mentioning her. But now she had a name and address; that was a start. Aimée Pain might know no more than Mr. Costas had told Cleo but at least she was an eyewitness. And her employer lived in Paris. Or at least, she had lived there at the time of Cleo's birth. That was a lucky chance.

Cleo thanked the couple and hugged each of them in turn. She returned to her room and resumed her packing with renewed vigor. Between buying a wardrobe for her debut, visiting Parisian jew-elry stores and museums for inspiration, and tracking down Aimée Pain, Cleo was going to be very busy in the City of Light.

ON THE EVE of Cleo's departure, Serafina called her into her bedroom and invited her to sit.

Warily, Cleo perched on the window seat and tucked her bare feet up beneath her. "Aren't you going to the opera tonight?"

"Later. First, I want to talk to you about your future, Cleo." She hesitated, smoothing her skirt, as if she didn't know how to begin.

The sun was sinking; the muezzins were calling the faithful to prayer. Cleo gazed out of the window, into the pink-and-purple dusk, and the setting sun that touched the streets of Cairo with golden fire. She was excited to go to Paris but she would miss her home quite dreadfully. She would miss Serafina, too.

"Will you write?" said Cleo when it didn't seem as if Serafina would ever tell her what was on her mind.

Serafina's eyebrows shot up. "If you like. But you'll be too busy to—"

"No. I won't be too busy," said Cleo. She wanted to express her gratitude to Serafina but she didn't know how to do it without sounding maudlin. That would only draw her guardian's mockery.

Serafina cleared her throat. "Well. You know I'm not much for idle chitchat but I'll do my best." She licked her lips, took off her spectacles and set them aside. Then she jumped up and thrust her fingers through the thick dark mass of her hair, until her carelessly pinned bun began to sprout ringlets like springs from an old sofa.

"What's the matter, Aunt?" Cleo hugged her knees and rested her chin on top. "Will you miss me?"

A faint smile at that. "I rather expect I shall."

"Really?"

"Oh, don't look so shocked." The older woman sniffed. "Anyway, with all of that swanning around to balls and parties I doubt you'll miss life here at all."

Cleo blinked. Was that a wistful note in her guardian's voice? She was too stunned to think of a reply.

"But I want to have a serious talk with you before you go." Serafina flicked a hand. "Now that you'll be meeting young men, you ought to know about . . . uh . . . you know . . . *relations,* I suppose you might say."

"Rela— Ohhh. No, really, it's not nec—"

"Please, Cleo. This is not easy for me but I feel it must be done." Serafina heaved out a breath, then launched into a clinical and thorough explanation of where babies came from, facts Cleo knew all about already. The governess who had taught Cleo before Fifi arrived had given her quite the education on that subject in whispered confidences, before eloping with one of the guests from the hotel.

"You are shocked," said Serafina when she finished. "It *is* shocking, I know. And it sounds thoroughly disgusting, of course, but with the right man, I—I'm *told* it can be rather lovely."

Cleo ducked her head and buried it in her folded arms. Honestly! She was beginning to feel queasy.

"But that is precisely why I must warn you against it," continued Serafina. "When I was a girl, we had no notion of such things. My mother insisted the stork was responsible for all the newborns in the world, and we believed her. Lydia had quite a rude shock on her wedding night, let me tell you!"

"*Please* don't." Cleo's head was still buried, so her voice came out muffled. She was sure she could never look Lady Grayson in the eye again. Or Lord Grayson, for that matter.

Cleo peeked between her fringe to see that her guardian was pacing the floor now, hands clasped behind her back, a diminutive professor in full lecturing mode. It was an attitude she often adopted when holding forth on Egyptology or berating her British compatriots for their appalling treatment of the Egyptian people. Now Cleo would give much to be lectured on ancient embalming tools and procedures or the imperative for true Egyptian independence. Anything but this.

"Just remember that some men—men who seem to be gentlemen on the surface—can be dangerous," Serafina continued. "You will have the protection of the Graysons, of course, but you are such a headstrong girl, one never knows . . ." The pacing stopped. "Are you *laughing,* Cleo?"

Cleo's head shot up. "Me? Of course not." She was closer to tears of embarrassment. "But really, Aunt, there's no need to worry. I can take care of myself." She had cajoled Brodie into teaching her self-defense and had a few neat tricks up her sleeve to repel unwanted advances.

"Is that so?" Serafina looked skeptical. "Well, if you don't have any questions, that's all there is to say on the subject. I know the Graysons will take good care of you. But, Cleo, do *try* not to become one of those empty-headed society debs, won't you? I couldn't bear it if you did."

"I can safely promise you I won't," said Cleo, relieved at the change of subject. "But you're acting as if this is our final farewell. I'll be back at Shepheard's in no time." She wished she felt as confident as she sounded.

"One never knows what life holds in store," said Serafina. "Far be it from me to encourage you to think only of marriage, but that's what a London season is for, after all." Her face fell, then she brightened. "But you can come back for visits, or I will come to see you. I haven't been home for an age."

"Of course." Impulsively, Cleo slid off the window seat and went to put her arms around Serafina. The older woman froze, as if she'd never been embraced before. Refusing to be put off, Cleo hugged her tighter. "I *shall* miss you," Cleo whispered. "And I shall miss Shepheard's, as well."

She left Serafina's chamber and found Brodie waiting in the sitting room outside. "Oh! I didn't know you were here."

He set down the book he'd been studying, a text on ancient hieroglyphs. "Miss Davenport asked to see me," he said.

"Hmm. She's in a strange mood." With a grin, Cleo leaned toward him and lowered her voice. "If she starts talking about the birds and the bees, I recommend that you back away quietly."

A gleam lit his eyes. "Why would I do that? I would rather ask her many, many questions."

Cleo laughed. "I wonder why I didn't think of that! It would certainly have made her sorry she raised the subject."

He lifted an eyebrow. "Warning you off, was she? I suppose that was wise. Most girls don't know a thing worth knowing until it's too late."

"That's what Serafina said." Cleo shrugged. "She is all for women's education. I suppose that extends to the facts of life, as well."

"Well, I imagine she will have something quite different to say to me," Brodie replied as Serafina's door opened once more. Under his breath, he added, "Wish me luck."

Chapter Two

*P*aris! Cleo couldn't believe it. She was finally here. Thick grey clouds hung low over the city and a sharp wind kicked the dead leaves along the cobblestones, but Cleo was enchanted. She tried to catch Brodie's eye to share her delight but his gaze was fixed on the scenery passing by. How much did he remember? She didn't like to raise the subject, since the childhood he spent in Paris didn't seem to have been a happy one.

"We are staying near the Bois de Boulogne at the *hôtel particulier* of a dear family friend," said Lady Grayson as their taxicab nosed through the traffic. "Madame Santerre is a widow with two sons, although I don't know if they'll be in residence at the moment." She glanced at Brodie. "Miss Davenport told me you speak French?"

"Like a Parisian," Cleo answered for him, earning her a withering look from her friend.

"Cleo is the one with the ear for languages," said Brodie. "She even speaks a little Arabic."

"Does she?" Lady G seemed unimpressed. "In that case, you will endear yourselves to our hosts. There is nothing more ignorant than going to a foreign country and expecting the inhabitants to speak English."

Brodie regarded Lady G for a long moment, then returned his gaze to the scenery. "Very true."

They swung into the Champs-Élysées, and Cleo leaned forward to peer up at the Arc de Triomphe. The monument was just as she had seen it depicted in the books Fifi had shown her, and yet the scale of it was somehow unexpected. "It's like being inside a film," she said. "Paris hardly seems real." She turned eagerly to Lady Grayson. "Might we go out sightseeing this afternoon?"

"Sightseeing?" Lady Grayson pronounced the word as if it were foreign, then gave a slight shrug. "It's beastly weather. Paris is much prettier in the spring. We'll come back then and you can explore properly. On this visit, our mission is shopping!"

The cab pulled up outside a magnificent villa surrounded by a small park. Servants dashed out to carry bags and usher Lady Grayson's party inside. They found themselves in an echoing, lofty hall with a flowing marble staircase winding upward and classical paintings, tapestries, and alabaster busts on plinths lining the wall. There was gilding and *glaces* everywhere, all arranged with delicate restraint, very fine and very Parisian. It was so formal, and so different from the exotic richness of Shepheard's Hotel, that Cleo gazed around her in wonder, until Brodie's fingertips beneath her chin shut her mouth for her. "You are staring like a colonial."

Lady Grayson laughed. "Yes, do try to cultivate a little sangfroid, Cleo." She glanced at Brodie and gave a small nod of approval.

Despite being unaccustomed to such riches, Brodie was unimpressed by displays of wealth. He had listened politely to Lady Grayson's many instructions on etiquette on their journey to Paris, but her vigilance over his table manners had been unnecessary. He quickly adapted, paying more attention to Lady G's instructions on which fork to use than Cleo did. Brodie even allowed Lady G to tell him what to wear. Cleo had been astonished at his docility, but her ladyship had warmed considerably to her unexpected charge, so Cleo supposed it was all to the good.

Brodie might feign indifference to his surroundings but Cleo didn't see the point of acting as if she were unimpressed. While Lady Grayson spoke with the housekeeper, Cleo became absorbed in studying a magnificent portrait—perhaps of one of the Santerre ancestors—a lady in an elaborate gown with the most stunning collar of diamonds and pearls at her throat.

Lady Grayson exclaimed, "Ah, Hippolyte! *Ça fait trop long-temps!*"

A tall young man not many years older than Cleo jogged lightly down the stairs. "Lady Grayson. How do you do? I must apologize on behalf of Maman. She has been delayed and will arrive home from Juan-les-Pins in the next few days." His cool blue eyes snagged on Cleo and he smiled. "This must be your new protégée."

Lady Grayson introduced Cleo and Brodie. Hippolyte Santerre's gaze turned assessing as he eyed the other young man, but Cleo was pleased to see that Brodie took this in stride, responding politely to Hippolyte's greeting.

"You all speak French so well," said Hippolyte with a strong inflection of surprise in his voice. "Splendid! The housekeeper will see you to your rooms."

"First things first," said Lady G when they had freshened up and met back in her suite. "I want to undertake your court presentation next year, Cleo."

"*Court* presentation?" Cleo gasped. "But—"

"The sooner the better," said Lady Grayson cryptically. With a quick glance at Brodie, who wore his Sunday best, she added, "Brodie, Lord G will take you to his Savile Row tailor the instant you set foot in London. He maintains that no Frenchman can make a well-cut coat. In the meantime . . ." From the drawer of her escritoire, the lady drew a fat envelope and handed it to the young man. "This is for sundries. I have accounts at the major department stores, where you may purchase the essentials. Don't forget a hat, good boots, gloves, and a winter coat." She crossed to the mantelpiece and pressed the electric bell next to it to summon a servant. "Monsieur Santerre's valet will assist you."

The valet was a large man with a mouth like India rubber, his expression lugubrious under the brilliantined wings of his salt-and-pepper hair. When Lady Grayson explained his mission, his thick eyebrows lifted. He inspected Brodie from head to toe in one swift glance. "One shall endeavor." He bowed to Lady Grayson and ushered Brodie from the room.

"We'll begin our work tomorrow," Lady Grayson told Cleo, flipping through her appointment book and laying it flat before her. She turned to scrutinize her young charge. "You are thin, which is good. Petite, not much of a bust, not fond of frills and fuss . . . I think for you, Chanel will be a most suitable choice. We'll go there first."

Chanel! Serafina had never bothered about physical appearance and she had always discouraged any hint of vanity in Cleo. But in Paris, Cleo could indulge herself. Lady Grayson clearly intended that she should. She could hardly wait until morning.

She must not lose sight of her true objective in coming to Paris, however. She needed to speak with Aimée Pain, the servant who had found her on the doorstep of Shepheard's sixteen years ago. When Cleo returned to her room, she took out the address Mr. Costas had given her and found the place on the map in her little guidebook.

Good. She could walk there. She would try to slip away tomorrow. She debated whether to tell Brodie the story and ask him to come with her, but he might try to stop her, telling her that that she was chasing rainbows. He didn't know anything about her quest to find her parents. She decided to keep it that way for now.

WHEN SHE ARRIVED in the Santerres' drawing room before dinner, Cleo saw a stranger: a tall, broad-shouldered young man with neatly barbered hair. His back was to her; it must be Madame Santerre's other son. "Monsieur . . ." Her greeting faltered and died as the gentleman turned to face her.

Brodie! Gone was the shaggy hair, the ill-fitting jacket and frayed tie. He wore a dinner suit with shiny lapels that even she knew could not have come ready-made from a department store. And his hair! He—or rather, his coiffeur—had used some sort of pomade, so that it shone like black lacquer. The new style revealed the chiseled beauty of his cheekbones. He seemed older, somehow, more masculine. He wasn't her childhood friend anymore.

A stab of betrayal pierced her chest. How *could* he?

"Mademoiselle, you look pretty this evening." The soft voice of Monsieur Santerre came from behind her. She whipped around to fix him with an accusing stare. "Did you do this?" She gestured at Brodie.

"I?" Santerre shot his left cuff and adjusted his tie. "Certainly not."

Brodie spoke. "Good of you to lend me your valet." He indicated his person. "And your wardrobe."

Their host laughed. "The clothes are yours, my dear fellow. But if you try to steal my valet, I will shoot you."

Cleo rather thought Brodie might have objected strenuously to receiving castoffs. However, Santerre possessed a charming air of self-deprecation and gave no indication at all that he considered Brodie beneath him in status. In fact, the two young men seemed to have become well acquainted in the space of an afternoon.

"Ah! You're down before me. Am I late?" said Lady Grayson, smiling at Santerre. When she saw Brodie, she gave a start and put one gloved hand to her breast. "My dear boy! *What* a transformation. Doesn't he look handsome, Cleo?"

Cleo did not reply.

As dinner progressed, she realized her concern on Brodie's behalf had never been necessary. Despite being unaccustomed to moving in such exalted circles, his manners were good. He hesitated less over which piece of cutlery to use than Cleo did—the rule about working from the outside in seemed to have a bewildering number of exceptions.

She stole yet another glance at Brodie. He looked so . . . confident. She would never have guessed in a million years that the rough lad from the Shepheard's Hotel zoo would have turned into this urbane sophisticate. He made her, even dressed in one of her best tea gowns, feel like the shabby one.

Cleo was torn between admiration, envy, and some other, less identifiable emotion. A sense of imminent loss might be the best way to describe it. Brodie had always been *her* secret. Well, hers and Serafina's, at least. Now it seemed she must share him.

She was on tenterhooks to get him alone and make plans for the next day. She wanted to explain all about her quest to find her parents and ask him to go with her to visit Aimée Pain. However, after dinner in the drawing room, Santerre turned to Brodie. "I'm meet-ing some friends this evening. Would you like to join us?"

Cleo, in the act of sipping her tea, choked on a scorching mouth-ful and coughed.

Brodie smiled, ignoring her. "Thank you. I'd like that very much."

IT WAS EARLY the next morning when Cleo slipped out of the San-terres' villa and set out alone for the address Mr. Costas had given her. Servants were always up well before their employers, and she wanted to escape questioning by Lady Grayson. She would go to the service entrance and ask for Mademoiselle Pain there.

The walk took longer than she'd expected and the sun's rays were struggling through the mist as she arrived at her destination. A ma-ture housemaid in a highly starched white apron and cap answered her knock, but when Cleo inquired about Mademoiselle Pain, the woman shook her head.

"Her mistress doesn't live here anymore. Hasn't for years," said the maid.

That was a disappointment, but not altogether unexpected. More than sixteen years had elapsed since Aimée Pain's employer had given Shepheard's her details. "Do you happen to have that lady's current address or know how I can find her?"

The maid shrugged. "All I know is she calls herself a princess these days. *Pfft!*" She rolled her eyes. "Some princess!"

Cleo's eyes widened. That was news to her. "Was her new name Fahmy?"

The maid shrugged. "Foreign, that's all I know."

Cleo thanked her and hurried back to the Santerres'. What should she do next? Surely if Princess Fahmy lived in Paris still, someone would know where to find her. Royalty—even obscure royalty—did not usually pass unnoticed in society.

As Cleo slipped back into the house by a side door, a voice called her name.

She froze, then whipped around, clutching her chest. "Brodie! You scared me."

He was fully dressed, so he must have been up early, too. His eyebrows were drawn together. "What do you think you're doing, sneaking out like that? Have you been wandering around Paris on your own?"

She lifted her chin. "I don't see why I shouldn't. You were out until all hours, after all."

But Brodie wasn't about to let her distract him. "What were you doing?"

She darted a glance around, then took his arm and drew him into the library and closed the door. "I'm trying to find out about my parents."

"I don't understand."

Cleo related the story Mr. Costas had told her and her efforts that morning to find Aimée Pain.

Brodie thought this over. "But if this maid found you on the doorstep it seems she wouldn't know any more than Mr. Costas already told you."

"It's the best lead I have," said Cleo. "And if nothing else, I would like to hear firsthand how it all came about." She hesitated, but decided not to tell him about the rumor that her father was the Prince of Wales.

"You're clutching at straws."

"Well, what if I am?" She threw her shoulders back, but her voice shook. "It's nobody's business but mine."

He took a step toward her, his hand stretched out, then he stopped. "I don't want to see you hurt, Cleo."

Her throat swelled up, but she managed to answer, "I want to know where I come from. I want to know who my real parents are."

"But isn't it more important to focus on where you're going than where you've come from?" He glanced away. "If I didn't believe that, I wouldn't have left Cairo."

She frowned. "What do you mean?"

He sighed. "You're so blind sometimes, Cleo. *You* see me as an equal and you believe that's how everyone else must see me, too."

She wasn't stupid. She knew people could be terrible snobs—particularly in Cairo, where the British expatriate community was so small. But if he had suffered slights from anyone in their household, she'd have something to say about it. "Has Lady G been horrid to you? I thought—"

"No, that's not it. And don't start interrogating me about the particulars. I don't need you to defend me. There's nothing for you to fix. Nothing you *can* fix."

"But—"

"Anyway, we're talking about you," Brodie interrupted. "What real difference will it make to know who your parents are?"

They didn't want you then. They haven't sought you out since. Why would they want you now?

The implication of his words struck her like a blow to the chest. She couldn't explain this deep yearning. She simply knew that nothing would ease it but the truth. "You knew your parents," she said. "Of course you wouldn't understand." Before she made a complete fool of herself and burst into tears, she pushed past him and ran from the room.

The conversation left Cleo feeling utterly alone. Even Brodie, her best friend in the world, didn't understand her deepest desire. Well, he might be right that the most important thing was her future, rather than her past, but Cleo couldn't help it. She needed to know her parents. She wouldn't mention the matter again to him, however. She'd pursue it on her own.

Hippolyte. Perhaps he might know where she could find Madame Fahmy. But over the next few days, Cleo didn't have an opportunity to speak with their host alone. He was out most nights, and by day, she was occupied fully with an exhausting whirl of shopping in exclusive *maisons de couture*. As Lady Grayson had predicted, Cleo's favorite designer was Coco Chanel—she preferred the clean, plain lines of the costumes, the practical elegance of jersey trousers, the hint of contrasting femininity in the corsage blouses, worn with a slim, three-quarter-length skirt.

Price was never discussed and Cleo wondered precisely what sum was being spent on her wardrobe. Lady Grayson wanted to outfit her not just for the winter, but for the forthcoming London season, which would span the spring and reach into the summer months, before everyone left for the Continent or their country estates.

In between these shopping stints, Cleo pursued her investigations into Princess Fahmy's whereabouts, even trying the telephone directory without success. She worked up the courage to ask Hippolyte about Madame Fahmy but he knew nothing about her or how to find her and made no offer to inquire on her behalf. She was rather in awe of his suave sophistication and his manner seemed chilly when she asked about the princess, so she let the matter rest. Perhaps she might broach the subject with Madame Santerre when she returned.

Their hostess arrived home amid a mountain of luggage and a flurry of scampering white lapdogs. A tall, dark sliver of a person, Madame Santerre regarded Cleo with snapping black eyes, then cast an approving glance over Brodie. "Come, my dears," she said, tucking a hand of each of them beneath a thin, Schiaparelli-clad arm. "You *cannot* visit Paris without going to Angelina!"

As it turned out, Angelina was not a person but a tearoom that resided on the rue de Rivoli. Cleo followed their hostess inside and couldn't help staring about her—like a yokel, Lady Grayson would have said. The interior of the *salon de thé* was a splendid blend of art nouveau and art deco styles, with ornate moldings and cornices, square arches with rounded corners, the same shape echoed in the beautiful painted landscape on the wall. Polished beveled mirrors and a vast expanse of square skylights added a sense of light and space.

The three of them sat at one of the white-clothed tables and Madame Santerre leaned forward to murmur, "Over there is Coco Chanel. She comes here every day for hot chocolate."

Cleo's gaze flicked to a table where two women sat. One, an extremely thin, dark woman dressed in black and the other wearing a leopard-print coat.

"With her is Jeanne Toussaint, from Cartier," said Madame. She addressed Cleo. "I hear you are interested in jewels, my dear."

"More than interested," said Brodie. "She's obsessed."

"Really?" Madame laughed. "Where did you get that from? Not Serafina."

"Well . . ." Cleo flushed. The truth—that she had fallen in love with jewels the day she had sat on the floor at Abdeen Palace with Princess Fawzia of Egypt, poring over the younger girl's spectacular jewel collection—would sound like terrible bragging. Besides, Serafina despised the Egyptian royal family and had been furious at Cleo for making friends with the princess. "I saw many fine pieces at Shepheard's Hotel and . . . and I like to sketch, so eventually I made up pieces of my own." She twisted her fingers together. "It's just a hobby, really."

Brodie raised his eyebrows at her. "Cleo is being modest. Princess Fawzia herself commissioned the design of a—what was it? A necklace? A bracelet?—from her a few months ago."

Madame's eyes widened. "*Vraiment?* Then you must meet Mademoiselle Toussaint. I shall make an appointment before you leave Paris. We'll visit Cartier and you may view their collection." Madame's eyes gleamed like jet at the prospect.

Cleo lit up. "Really? Oh, but you must not go to such trouble on my account."

"Trouble?" Madame scoffed. "Nonsense." She grinned and in her gamine face Cleo caught the shadow of a much younger woman. "One can always have more jewels, *n'est-ce pas?*"

Cleo's heart soared to the square-paned ceiling. Finally she would have the chance to see the principal atelier of the famous jewelers who had made many of the pieces in the Egyptian royal family's collection. And to meet the famous Jeanne Toussaint . . . Cleo hadn't dared to dream of such an opportunity.

Madame ordered for them—a hot chocolate each for herself and Cleo and a Mont Blanc—Angelina's signature pâtisserie—for Brodie.

The hot chocolate, topped with billowy dollops of whipped cream, was thick and dark. Cleo stirred in the cream, then sipped cautiously. A rush of pure bliss flooded her senses. She'd never had much of a sweet tooth but she had a weakness for chocolate, and this was extraordinary. She stole a glance at Brodie as he dipped his spoon into the small hillock of his dessert. Brodie *did* have a sweet tooth, and his eyes briefly closed as he savored the confection.

"Good, yes?" said Madame with the suggestion of a girlish simper. Cleo didn't blame her. Brodie seemed to grow more handsome with every passing day. The thought gave her an odd squirm in the stomach, as if she was about to speak in public or show her work to someone whose good opinion she craved.

"Thought I'd look in at the Louvre while we're here," said Brodie, touching a napkin to his lips. "Would you ladies like to accompany me?"

"Oh, yes!" Cleo turned to their hostess. "If that's all right with you, madame."

"The Louvre can wait," said Madame Santerre. "We have shopping to do. You will escort us, Brodie."

Cleo nearly burst into incredulous laughter at the thought of Brodie carrying their shopping bags and waiting by idly while she and Madame Santerre browsed the boutiques.

"Madame, I'm afraid I have a previous engagement," said Brodie.

"But you said you were going to the Louvre," Cleo pointed out, purely to make trouble.

"Yes, but that was before I recollected an appointment elsewhere," responded Brodie, his face bland as cream.

He wasn't going to get away with that. "Oh?" She smiled and batted her eyelashes at him. "Where are you going?"

"Anywhere that does not involve shopping." With an unrepentant grin directed at Madame that was awfully attractive, drat him, he added, "Your pardon, madame."

Madame Santerre laughed, unoffended and perhaps even charmed by his audacity. "Make sure you are back in time for dinner, *mon chèr*. We have guests tonight."

Brodie reassured her and rose from the table. Despite the promised shopping spree, Cleo wished she could have gone with him. He seemed to be drawing away from her, these days, even though they were living in the same house. Far from being a fish out of water, he seemed to have taken to this sophisticated life with remarkable ease.

As Cleo watched Brodie's tall form saunter from the *salon de thé,* she realized many other feminine gazes followed him, too. Fear clutched at her heart, which annoyed her. She gulped down the cooling, intensely sweet dregs of her hot chocolate and said brightly, "Will you help me find something special, madame? I should like to look ravishing tonight."

THE PROMISED VISIT to Cartier took place the following week. The rue de la Paix showroom was just as much of a treasure trove as Mr. Mansoor's bazaar at Shepheard's Hotel, if more formally arranged. The establishment consisted of a set of salons such as one might find in a private home, carpeted and high ceilinged, its rooms sparsely furnished with vitrines and counters filled with expensive knickknacks.

Enameled and bejeweled vanity cases, cigarette boxes and lighters, wristwatches, and gold-clasped evening bags met her interested gaze. A delightful ladybird brooch in black-and-red lacquer with diamond spots caught her eye. "How sweet!"

But Madame was uninterested in what she termed mere

"trinkets." They were ushered into a private room and offered refreshment, which they both declined. Then an elegant woman dressed in a black sheath and knee-high Russian boots came out to greet them.

"Ah, Pan-Pan!" Madame jumped up to meet her and they kissed cheeks. The two women seemed like old friends.

Madame introduced Cleo but Mademoiselle Toussaint's gaze barely grazed her before she turned back to Madame and invited them to sit on a Louis XVI settee. "I am glad you have come to see us today, because I have just the piece for you. I've been keeping it safe." A wave of the hand conjured up a male assistant, who bustled forward to place a bed of black velvet on the coffee table in front of them. On the velvet bed was laid a wide bib necklace, intricately designed, and distinctive because of its unique combination of gems.

"We call this style *pierres de couleur*. Monsieur Cartier brought the stones back from India on one of his trips."

Cleo shifted closer to Madame on the sofa and craned her neck to get a better view. Forgetting her shyness, she exclaimed, "Diamonds, rubies, emeralds, *and* sapphires. May I see?"

With a fond laugh, Madame slid the jewel box over to her, saying to Mademoiselle Toussaint, "You will forgive the indulgence. Cleo is mad about jewelry. She is a keen designer herself, you know. I've seen her work. It's remarkable."

"Really?" The response could not have been less interested, but Mademoiselle permitted herself a small smile. "Then you will appreciate the artistry in this piece."

Indeed, the bib necklace was a miraculous piece of workmanship, and so unusual. The stones did not have the dark, multifaceted dazzle one might expect from such an arrangement of precious gems. There was a lightness to it, almost a playful air. The emeralds were a lucent, jade green, the sapphires light blue, the rubies a deep, rich pink. All of them carved and fluted, arranged like embroidered beads on a lace fretwork. In the wrong hands, putting all of these gems together would have been too much, but in this arrangement, it was perfect.

Madame laughed and Cleo realized she had babbled her thoughts aloud.

"Shall I have it, then?" said Madame in a teasing voice.

"Oh, you must! You simply must!" said Cleo. "With this piece, you will make every other woman in the room feel old-fashioned and shabby." She turned to Mademoiselle Toussaint. "What did you say it was called again?"

For the first time, the *directrice* looked at her with approval. *"Pierres de couleur."*

"Well, I will take it," said Madame. She nodded at Cleo. "And a gift for my charming young friend here, too, I think. She is to make her debut this year. Something to suit *la jeune fille.*"

Cleo protested. "No, really, madame, you must not. I would never have asked to come along if I'd thought—"

"Nonsense! I insist. I have no daughter of my own, after all, and Serafina and Lydia are very dear to me."

To protest further would be ungracious, so Cleo meekly submitted. As a young, unmarried woman, it was considered poor taste for her to wear elaborate jewels, and Serafina had given her a very fine pearl necklace to wear for her presentation. She was delighted to accept an exquisite pearl-and-diamond bracelet from Madame.

"You are a *very* lucky girl," said Mademoiselle Toussaint as she clasped the bracelet around Cleo's wrist.

Cleo took a deep breath. It was now or never. She stared Mademoiselle dead in the eye. "I should count myself the most fortunate girl in the world if you would agree to take a look at my designs."

Toussaint laughed and shook her head. She started to say, "I'm afraid—"

"Oh, please!" Cleo begged. "Please say I may visit again and show you my sketches. I won't take too much of your time."

"I am afraid that I am leaving tomorrow for Biarritz," said Mademoiselle. She eyed Cleo for a moment. "But here is what I will do." She took a card and scribbled an address on the back of it. "You may visit Monsieur Lemarchand and tell him I sent you. But be warned. He will not spare your feelings. He will soon tell you if your designs are up to scratch."

Chapter Three

Paris, France
Winter 1935

Cleo awoke, shivering. What had happened to the radiator overnight? The Santerre house, though beautiful, was old, and amenities
like plumbing and heating could be unreliable. It was so freezing,
Cleo was tempted to pull the covers over her head.

Her time in Paris was drawing to a close. Despite her resolu-
tion, she had not had much success in tracking down Aimée Pain
or her mistress, Madame Meller. Or no, it was Princess Fahmy,
now, wasn't it? Cleo recognized the Fahmy name as belonging to
a wealthy Egyptian family but she didn't know of any princes in
that clan. How had *that* marriage come about? When she'd asked
Madame Santerre if she knew the princess or her whereabouts,
Madame had raised her finely plucked eyebrows and said with a
touch of hauteur, "*Comment?* I'm afraid I am not acquainted with
anyone of that name."

With a sigh, Cleo launched out of bed and threw open the
curtains. When she looked out, the sparkle of sunlight on snow
made her cry out in wonder. Flurries of snowflakes fell, whirling
and dancing past her window. The trees were frosted with icicles,

clumps of snow caught in the forks of their bare branches. In the garden below, she spied drifts and blankets of white.

Cleo threw on her warmest winter clothes and scrabbled about for the deliciously soft mittens Lady Grayson had bought her. She bolted along the corridor to Brodie's room and rapped on the door. "Brodie, it's me! Open up!"

She pounded again, but there was no answer. She yelled through the door, "Come on, the sun's out. It might melt if you don't hurry!"

The door was wrenched open and Brodie stood there in an emerald green silk dressing gown, his hair disheveled, eyes bleary and unfocused. "Cleo . . . What?"

"*Snow*! It's snowing, Brodie. Come quickly!"

He winced as if she'd clubbed him over the head. Then he shut the door in her face.

Cleo blinked. How could he fail to be as excited as she was? He had never seen snow, either. Well, she couldn't wait for him to catch up. She turned and clattered down the marble steps, racing through to the back garden.

The cold was unlike anything she'd experienced before. It had an apple-crispness to it, a clean, fresh scent. Her boots squeaked on the freshly laid snow and she wiggled her toes, which were starting to freeze, even through her boots and stockings. She held out her hands, palms flattened and turned upward, catching the tiny flakes, lifting her face to the sky.

"A snowman," she decided. She had always read about English children who went toboggan-riding and built snowmen and thought it sounded like tremendous fun. As Cleo swept up snow with her hands and clumped it together, she panted out misted puffs of air. Ambitious, as ever, she decided this snowman would be fully human-sized and set to work with gusto.

The drifts covered the ground prettily but they weren't very deep, so it took some time to gather up the snow and shape it. Cleo gave a wry smile. As usual, her ambition outstripped her patience. Of course, it would have been more fun if Brodie had deigned to join her, but perversity forced her to carry through with her grand plan and make herself enjoy it, if only to spite him.

Cleo's mittens were sodden and her cheeks were stiff with cold, and crossing her eyes to view her nose, she thought it looked very pink. But finally, she got the body of the snowman looking rotund and perfect. She was about to begin on the head, when one of the doors to the house opened and she heard footsteps.

From the shelter of the terrace, Brodie stood, watching her. He was dressed for going out, not for playing in the snow.

She smiled brightly and waved. "Hello! Don't you want to come out? This is such fun!"

He lifted one eyebrow. "So I see."

She put her hands on her hips. "You needn't be so sniffy about it. When was the last time you saw snow?"

"I've seen a lot of sand but it doesn't prompt me to build castles." He stifled a yawn.

Cleo narrowed her eyes. "Were you out late last night?"

"I was, as it happens."

"Were you *drinking*?" she demanded.

His eyes gleamed. "And if I was? Do you disapprove?"

Were there women there? she wanted to ask, but didn't. "You know, you're only one year older than I am. I'm sure Lady Grayson wouldn't like you—"

"Lady Grayson is a kind woman and I hope I wouldn't do anything to embarrass her. But she's not my keeper, you know, Cleo. And neither are you."

Cleo's fists clenched around two great handfuls of snow. As Brodie turned to leave, she hurled a snowball at his retreating back. The first one fell short. The second hit him square between the shoulder blades.

"Hey!" Brodie swung back around. Another snowball spatted his waistcoated stomach. "Ye wee scoundrel!" In three strides, he was on the ground, scooping up snow in his bare hands and shaping it into a ball.

Laughing, Cleo allowed herself to be hit by the first missile, then ducked behind her snowman, mercilessly plundering its defenseless body for ammunition.

Brodie chased her, one leg sliding outward as he lost his footing and slipped on the wet ground. Cleo's next projectile hit him in the back of the head, and within seconds, he'd caught her hands in his, crushing snow between their palms. "Stop, stop! You win. I surrender," he said, still laughing and out of breath.

Cleo stared up at him, and knew a sudden, soul-deep longing. To kiss the snowflakes from his thick black eyelashes, to trace that beautiful warm mouth with cold fingertips . . . Gosh! Where had those thoughts come from? Despite the cold, she felt warmth rush to her cheeks.

Please let us stay like this, as we are, forever, she thought. *Please don't ever leave me.*

But as Brodie stared down at her, both of them panting, the smile faded from his face. Abruptly, he released her and stepped back, dusting the snow from his bare hands and blowing on them, rubbing them together for warmth.

"Brodie, I—"

"I have to go. I'm late." With a frown, he indicated his wet coat.

"And now I'll have to change and be even later." He turned on his heel and stalked back into the house.

CONFUSED AND EMBARRASSED by their unsettling encounter in the snow, Cleo did her best to avoid Brodie for the rest of their stay in Paris. That wasn't too difficult; he was hardly ever home. Between Madame's and Lady G's social calendars and her own creative work, Cleo managed to keep busy herself.

In Paris, Cleo found much inspiration for her jewelry designs in the art and artefacts housed in the Louvre, but also in the world around her. The lacy design of an individual snowflake turned into a filigree brooch encrusted with crystals, diamonds, and pearls. A rose-tinted sunset over the Seine became a stunning necklace of pink opals set in gold.

Would her own sketches ever be turned into real jewelry? Excited to have won Mademoiselle Toussaint's personal introduction, she had telephoned to make an appointment with the Cartier designer, Pierre Lemarchand, but she had not been able to reach him. Cleo was due to leave for London tomorrow, so it looked like she'd lost her chance.

She stared at the card Mademoiselle Toussaint had given her. Monsieur Lemarchand's studio was in Montparnasse. Would it be too bold of her simply to turn up and knock on his door? She was desperate enough to try.

She studied a map of Paris to see if she might walk there but it was too far. Other than her attempt to locate Aimée Pain, she hadn't been anywhere by herself since she'd arrived in the City of Light.

She could try the Métro but she didn't quite understand the intricacies of the Paris subway, so a taxi it must be. It would be foolhardy to sneak out at night, but might she slip away while Madame and Lady Grayson took their early afternoon naps? Not that Madame would mind, but Lady Grayson would probably try to stop her.

Cleo dressed warmly, tucked her sketchbook under her arm, and walked in the general direction of the Seine until she spied a taxi and hailed it. Even accustomed to Paris as she was by now, having been there for more than a month, the sight of the Eiffel Tower in the distance still sent a pleasurable shiver down her spine. Both Lady Grayson and Madame Santerre scoffed at what they termed a monstrosity and a tourist trap but Cleo loved the elegant spire; she imagined a flat, elongated triangular pendant sparkling with a fretwork of pavé yellow diamonds. Or perhaps a three-dimensional piece carved from carnelian and edged with yellow gold. She couldn't wait to sketch her ideas when she got home.

They crossed the Seine to the Left Bank, and Cleo stared about her eagerly. She had tried and failed to persuade Brodie and Hippolyte Santerre to take her out to a club or to one of the cafés they frequented in Saint-Germain-des-Prés. She'd gathered Hippolyte ran with a bohemian set of people who liked jazz music and absinthe—not that she was quite certain what absinthe was, although the "sin" part made it sound delightfully wicked. But whatever wickedness this district contained must be carried on indoors or at a different time of day. She couldn't see any evidence of debauchery as the taxi's wheels hushed along slick, icy streets.

Alighting at the address Mademoiselle Toussaint had given her, Cleo walked up to the entrance, which was guarded by a door the color of verdigris with an ornate grille at the top. She pushed open the door and found herself in a small, enclosed courtyard, with a staircase that branched off in two different directions. She went up the stone steps, the cold deepening the farther into darkness she went. By the time she had climbed to the jeweler's studio on the top floor, Cleo had warmed up, however, and was somewhat short of breath.

She knocked softly. After waiting a moment, she knocked harder. Movement came from within. She heard a crash, a curse, then the door opened. A tall man with a long face and a nose to match it peered out at her. His eyebrows were thick lines, now inverted in a V of displeasure. "What?"

"Uh, good afternoon, Monsieur Lemarchand. My name is Cleo Davenport. Mademoiselle Toussaint sent me. Perhaps she has mentioned my name to you?"

The designer's eyebrows separated. With a grunt, he took the card Cleo proffered.

He handed it back to her. "So? What do you think I can do for you?" His tone was gruff but no longer belligerent. It gave her an inkling of hope.

Still, Lemarchand was a formidable man, in both physical stature and talent, if the Cartier catalogs Cleo had pored over were anything to judge by. Cleo hesitated, clutching her portfolio to her chest. All of a sudden, her intention of asking an artisan at the pinnacle of his profession to look at her schoolgirl sketches seemed like the most amazing cheek.

"Well?" he snapped. "*Écoutez bien, ma fille,* I don't have all day."

Cleo felt her hackles rise, and with it, her determination. She'd come all this way. She was going back to England tomorrow. After Christmas, her schedule would be packed to the brim with elocution lessons and dancing lessons and music lessons and all sorts of activities designed to make up for "living like a savage" in Cairo as

Lady Grayson would have said. This was her one chance to get a few pointers and advance her craft before she left Paris.

The shortest route to getting there would be to show Lemarchand her designs and prove she was serious.

"All right, I will!" She slipped under the man's arm and darted inside. "Oh!" She stopped short, then made a slow turn, her mouth slightly open, her eyes wide.

Winter light filled the attic room, slanting down from the sloping glass ceiling, flooding the drafting table that was placed on a platform by the window. For an instant, it seemed as if all of God's angels sang a chorus as the light formed a nimbus over the artist's tools.

Surely that was a sign. "I *promise* I am not here to waste your time." She hurried over to the drafting table and placed her portfolio on a clear space. She untied the leather thong that held the portfolio together and opened it.

Lemarchand stomped after her. "Now see here—"

"Please! Please just look and tell me how I may do better." All fingers and thumbs in her excitement, she spread out her best designs for him to see.

"I don't know what you expect me to . . ." Lemarchand trailed off as something among her pen and watercolor sketches seemed to catch his eye. He cocked one of those bushy eyebrows and glanced at her sideways, then bent his gaze to her work. He picked up one design—a ruby parure Princess Fawzia had once admired—then tossed it down.

Cleo held her breath, not wanting to move or make a sound that might distract or annoy him.

"You have talent, but no technique." He shifted several designs to the side. "These are impractical." Another few designs. "These are derivative. But this . . ." He held up her sketch of a monkey ring with sapphire eyes and a curling tail. "This has something."

She let out a breath. "Truly?"

He shrugged. "Don't get excited. I don't know what you want from me." He eyed her up and down, perhaps appraising her clothing. "Not an apprenticeship, I'll wager."

If only! But that would take years and she had this single afternoon.

"I want to know how I might learn to do what you do," she said. "May I watch you work for a while?" He would say no, she was sure of it, but instead, he grunted. "You'll find the tea things over there."

With shaking hands, Cleo made them each a tisane. As the plumes of fragrant steam spiraled upward, the artist showed her how to measure and mark out her designs using a special template with holes cut out in different shapes and sizes. After a hunt through his studio with attendant grumbling, Lemarchand came up with a template for her to take away. It was scarred and ink-marked and chipped in a couple of places, which only made it more precious to Cleo.

The designer showed her the types of inks and paints and paper he favored, and finally, he revealed his colorful, sinuous designs, carefully labeled with the size and cut of the stones he intended to feature, the pages and pages of notes and sketches of wildlife he used for inspiration—flowers, berries, leaves and birds, jungle animals and insects. He lent her a book called *La Science de la Peinture,* by Vilbert, and waved away her promise to return it to him by post when she'd finished.

"But all of this is pointless," said Lemarchand, with an impatient shake of his head. "A firm like Cartier would never hire a female designer."

"But what about Mademoiselle Toussaint?"

"She is not a designer. Besides, Mademoiselle is a special case."

He refused to explain what he meant by this, so Cleo said, "Well, I'll just go into business for myself, then."

"*Pah!*" Lemarchand gestured at his work. "Do you think all of this comes cheap? To make the kind of jewelry you wish to create, you need capital and contacts, money to buy the best gems from the most trusted sources. And you need a master jeweler to make the pieces you design. Not to mention clients who will buy them when you're done. No, no, you are just a little girl with a big fantasy. It's impossible."

Then why had he wasted so much time teaching her? "Perhaps," said Cleo. "But I won't know if I don't try."

Lemarchand stared hard at her and she wondered if her stubbornness annoyed him. After a moment, he gave a curt nod, as if satisfied of something. Abruptly, he said, "I'm not really a jewelry designer, you know."

Cleo looked around her, at the canvases that leaned, three or four deep, against every wall, and thought she understood. "You are an artist."

He shrugged. "Designing for Cartier pays the bills. I go to one meeting a week with Toussaint, fewer if I can get away with it, and I work on Cartier designs for two days a week. The rest . . ." He made a sweeping gesture. "The rest of the time I devote to my first love. To painting." He nodded at her. "You should do the same."

"Do you think so?" Cleo had never dared to hope she might have talent beyond the decorative arts. "Then I will. I mean I'll try."

"I could teach you if you like," said Lemarchand in an offhand manner. "I give lessons to Marion Cartier, after all."

"Oh, how wonderful that would be!" said Cleo. "But I'm afraid, monsieur, that it's my last day in Paris. We leave for London to-morrow."

"Do you? That is a pity," said Lemarchand.

"I will come back as soon as I can," Cleo promised herself as much as him. Thinking of the London season that stood between her and her ambition, she growled in frustration. "There's so much to learn and I haven't even begun."

Lemarchand's thin mouth quirked up at one corner. "Well, mademoiselle, do not despair. With your determination, and a little luck, I have no doubt we will meet again. Perhaps sooner than you think."

Cleo stayed on in the artist's studio until the light began to fade and her third cup of tea grew cold. "I must go or they will send out a search party." Suddenly she wanted to cry. She'd found this magical place and its attendant wizard on her very last day in Paris. If only she'd mustered the courage sooner to climb up to Lemarchand's eyrie and knock on his door.

She hadn't achieved her principal aim in Paris, either: to find Princess Fahmy's maid. A thought occurred to her. "Monsieur Lemarchand, do you know a woman called Princess Fahmy? Perhaps you've made jewels for her before?"

"Fahmy?" He sat back and stared at her hard. "Yes, of course. Everyone knows Madame Fahmy."

A surge of excitement ran through her. "Do you know where she lives, by any chance?"

Lemarchand's brows drew together. "I don't. And if I did, I couldn't tell you. Client records are strictly confidential, you understand."

"Well, can you tell me *about* her, then? Why did you look shocked when I mentioned her name?"

It was the first time she'd seen Lemarchand at a loss for words. After a bit of sputtering, he said, "She is not the sort of woman a *jeune fille* like you should know."

"Oh! Is she a . . ." But Cleo didn't know the word in French for "scarlet woman."

He refused to expand upon this statement and it was past time for Cleo to leave.

Despite his earlier discouragement, the artist loaded her up with instructions, books, and spare materials, until she wondered if she could manage to carry it all down those many flights of steps.

Cleo came away from Lemarchand's studio fired with a new determination, and so many ideas, she would need weeks to get them all down on paper. One day, as soon as she could manage it, she would return to Paris. And she would become a star pupil of Monsieur Lemarchand.

The new information about Princess Fahmy was intriguing but it would hardly help Cleo to find her or her maid. She would have to leave Paris without getting any closer to that goal.

Chapter Four

London, England
Spring 1936

$\mathcal{H}$is Majesty, the King of England, died without warning in January of 1936. The sepulchral tolling of Great Tom, one of the bells at St. Paul's Cathedral, marked the sadness of the occasion on the morning after his death. Union Jacks everywhere flew at half-mast, and despite the palace having issued no directive about mourning, within hours, the shops sold out of black ties, coats, and hats.

The Prince of Wales succeeded his father to the throne and became Edward VIII. With his accession, the golden prince Cleo had dreamed about meeting one day in London became a more remote figure than ever. It seemed incredible that anyone had ever believed he might be her father.

She had little leisure for pursuing the matter of her parentage in those months leading up to her presentation. Every evening was filled with engagements. Once or twice while at a ball, she glimpsed the King, but there was no getting near him. He invariably arrived later than anyone else to great fanfare and left soon afterward.

Despite his movie star looks and scintillating presence, which made all of the debutantes swoon, it was said the King preferred small, intimate parties to balls: cozy weekends spent at Fort Belvedere in the company of his friends, including his American mistress, Wallis Simpson.

Cleo would be presented to him formally later in the season. She was both elated and terrified at the prospect of seeing him up close.

"Come on, Cleo. Hurry!" The Honorable Madeline Bowe, a tall redhead who was older and infinitely more worldly than Cleo despite never having set foot out of England, slid along the seat of the taxi and gestured for Cleo to get in. They were ditching a very dull and overcrowded party in favor of spending a slice of the evening at the Café de Paris. Cleo had agreed to go because Madeline had promised faithfully they'd be back at the party before Madeline's mother, who was chaperoning them, thought to leave the bridge tables to seek them out.

As Cleo and Madeline entered the shadowy nightclub and checked their coats, a frisson at the prospect of illicit fun skittered down Cleo's spine. She behaved herself most of the time out of consideration and fondness for the Graysons, but tonight, she felt reckless and thrillingly alive.

There were one or two young men who were sweet on her who might be here tonight, and much as she hated to admit it, their eager attentions were a balm to her injured amour propre. Brodie seemed to have grown completely indifferent to her since his startling transformation. The new persona he had cultivated in Paris had blossomed as he pursued an Oxford education. To everyone's surprise, Brodie had made friends quickly among his peers, and spent his holidays at one or another of their estates instead of with the Graysons. Instead of with Cleo.

"What on earth was that sigh for?" Madeline yelled over the jazz band's trumpet solo and the noise of the club. "One might think you were going to a funeral or something. Oh, look! There's Gerry."

Madeline dragged Cleo with her upstairs to the gallery, where a group of young people crowded around one of the tables.

Jonathan Shaw touched Cleo's shoulder and she turned to smile up at him. "Hold up!" he said. "I'll get you a chair." Though she didn't know him well, Jonathan seemed a decent sort, if a little stuffy. She was reassured by his presence in what she had feared might be a raffish crowd. The group made a space for her and she was just about to sit down when she saw Brodie.

Dressed in formal white tie, Brodie was leaning against the gallery rail. He held a martini glass by the stem, and was smiling down at a girl Cleo knew slightly and realized now that she had never liked. When he looked up and saw Cleo, his smile faded. He detached himself from his admirer without breaking eye contact with Cleo.

"What are you doing still in London?" Cleo beamed up at him. "Where are you staying? You might have telephoned!"

"Never mind that," he said, frowning. "What do you think you're doing here, Cleo?"

Cleo felt as if he had dumped her headfirst into the ice bucket. She stared at him.

He blew out a breath, as if exasperated with the unruly antics of a child. "Get your coat. I'll take you home."

That made her find her voice. "Don't trouble yourself!"

She would have turned away but he gripped her wrist and seemed likely to remove her physically. She was torn between anger at his high-handedness and curiosity at what he might do next, when Jonathan Shaw, who had risen when Cleo did, intervened. "Now, see here. I don't think there's any call for you to—" But the glare Brodie sent him made him stutter to a stop.

"Let me go," snapped Cleo, yanking free. She turned to Jonathan.

"It's all right," she told him. "This gentleman and I grew up together. He's like a brother to me. A very *annoying* brother."

Brodie's gaze pinned her like a butterfly. She bit her lip, flushing. She'd wanted to assert her independence; she hadn't meant to wound him.

She longed to let Brodie escort her home so they could talk properly. But she had her pride and her heart still smarted from the way he seemed to have left her behind without a backward glance. She'd thought he'd need her as much as she needed him. She'd been very wrong about that.

The band struck up a slow tune. Cleo turned her back on Brodie. "Jonathan?" She gave him a blinding smile. "I think they're playing our song."

Cleo tried not to look over her shoulder as Jonathan led her to the floor, but she couldn't help it. She caught the sardonic smile on Brodie's face before he resumed his conversation with that girl she really rather detested, and who had poor taste in clothing, into the bargain.

She tried to look like she was enjoying herself but the contretemps with Brodie had turned the evening sour. Time after time, Cleo caught herself squinting through the smoky haze, searching every group of revelers for him.

He didn't approach her again. After a seemingly endless interval, which was in reality only two hours, it was time to return to the dull party and find Madeline's mama.

BY THE TIME the Graysons gave a birthday ball in Cleo's honor at their house in Grosvenor Square, the London season was in full swing. She wore her favorite creation from Mainbocher in Paris, a silk gown in shades of blue, from almost white to a soft cerulean panel that crossed her body like a sash from her shoulder to the high, belted waist, then fell to the floor. Mindful of Lady Grayson's rules of good taste, she wore Serafina's pearls and the bracelet Madame Santerre had given her, even if secretly she would have loved to pair the gown with more avant-garde pieces.

She couldn't help exclaiming with envy over the diamond drop necklace that complemented the V-neck of Lady Grayson's pale green gown.

"When you are married, dear Cleo, you may have all this and more," said Lady Grayson. "I've invited every eligible young man I could lay hands on this evening. I trust at least one will take your fancy."

Excitement coursed through Cleo's veins. Not at the prospect of the promised legion of young men, but at the expectation that tonight, Brodie would be there and see her at her best. Finally he might sit up and take notice. She was a woman now. He could no longer treat her like a little sister.

Cleo hadn't set eyes on Brodie since that dreadful night at the Café de Paris. He rarely wrote. When he did, the letters were addressed to the Graysons and any mention of Cleo seemed to be an afterthought.

In no time at all, the Graysons had become fond of Brodie. Lord Grayson was no scholar but he was highly intelligent and his deep appreciation of the antiquities and artefacts he had collected in his travels had given these two very different men common ground over which to enthuse and debate. Besides which, any man who handled a horse as well as Brodie did was bound to receive Lord Grayson's stamp of approval.

Cleo craned her neck to look for Brodie. He had to come to her ball, didn't he? He wouldn't miss her special night. But as the evening wore on, Cleo danced with many young men, but her childhood friend was nowhere to be seen.

She sought out Lady Grayson between dances. "Have you seen Brodie?" she asked without preamble.

"Oh, I quite forgot," said Lady Grayson. "He sent word he was unavoidably detained. I do hope he won't miss it altogether."

"What's that, my dear?" said Lord Grayson, joining them and handing his wife a glass of champagne. "Brodie still not here?" He turned to Cleo. "Why aren't you dancing, Cleo?"

She smiled at him through her disappointment. "I was waiting for you."

A short time into their foxtrot, a man came up behind Lord Grayson and tapped him on the shoulder. "Do you mind?" Releasing Cleo, Lord Grayson turned and a delighted smile broke over his face. "Dear boy!" He reached for Brodie's hand and shook it. "We'd almost given you up."

Brodie smiled and apologized but his gaze never left Cleo. "May I?"

Cleo was tempted to send him packing for nearly ruining her evening by turning up so late, but Lord Grayson said, "Of course," and bowed out gracefully.

The strangest feeling came over Cleo as Brodie stood there, about to take her in his arms. Nerves knotted in her stomach; she felt the most curious desire to scream and laugh and cry, all at the same time.

What was this sensation? It felt like the prelude to something dangerous.

His gloved hand clasped hers. His arm stole around her waist.

For the first time, she became acutely aware of the vast difference between them physically. Brodie was a man now, and even the formal dress of a British gentleman could not conceal the raw power of his frame. His hold made her feel delicate and unsure, when she wanted to feel bold and strong. Ugh, what was the matter with her tonight?

As she hesitated, he remarked, "You do know how to dance the foxtrot, don't you, Cleo? I saw you doing it perfectly well just now."

He knew very well that she could dance. They'd taken an intensive course together with a dancing master Lady Grayson had hired before Brodie left for Oxford.

But the amused mockery in his tone snapped her into action. She put her hand on his shoulder and tried not to think about how solid it felt. Her feet shuffled as he drew her closer and she tried to make herself relax as they began to dance. He'd improved since they'd last danced together. That led her to wonder about his other dancing partners, which put her in a worse mood.

"Happy birthday, princess," murmured Brodie. His warm breath tickled her ear.

She gave a start and jerked her head back. "Thank you. I, um . . . It was good of you to come."

She'd imagined this moment so often but now she was tongue-tied, behaving like an insipid bore. After a pause, she managed, "How have you been? We never see you anymore." She hadn't meant to sound so wistful and wanted to kick herself. Before he could answer, she added, "But I've met some lovely people. I'll introduce you if you like."

The prospect of Brodie's meeting her friends made her review them critically, as if through his eyes. They were all rich and rather frivolous. Maybe that wasn't a good idea.

"You look beautiful tonight, Cleo," said Brodie. His voice seemed a little strained. "I bet the chaps are falling over themselves to dance with you."

I hadn't noticed, she thought. *I was waiting for you.*

The old Cleo would have blurted it out. The new and oddly frozen version said tightly, "I am enjoying the party very much. Thank you."

"If Serafina could see us now," he murmured, eyes crinkling at the corners.

"Yes." She laughed, the constraint lifting a touch. "She would be so smug. It has all gone exactly to plan, drat her."

The band segued into a soft, slow number. She sensed Brodie hesitate, and in that hesitation, awkwardness returned. Cleo's mouth went dry. He made as if to draw her closer, but she stood her ground with a nervous smile. "Do you mind if we sit this one out?"

He regarded her quizzically, as if he guessed why she'd made the suggestion, and the agony of it made her want to shrivel to a husk and be blown away. If only she could wipe this encounter from their history and begin again.

He glanced around. "Maybe a spot of supper, then?"

"Yes, please."

As they headed toward the dining room, Jonathan Shaw sauntered up to them. Despite having encountered Brodie before under circumstances he could hardly have forgotten, he stared rudely. "And who might this be?"

Wishing he'd go away, Cleo introduced the two men. "Brodie and I grew up together at Shepheard's Hotel."

"Ah, that's right," drawled Jonathan, raising an eyebrow. "I've heard about Grayson's new protégé. A groom or something, weren't you?" Before Brodie could reply, Jonathan turned his back, cutting

Brodie out of the conversation and drawing Cleo apart. "Cleo, you *must* come and settle this dispute. Bucky says there are six verses in 'God Save the King' and Portia insists there are only two."

Cleo was too stunned to react to Jonathan's rudeness before Brodie sketched an ironic bow in her direction and walked away.

"You are a complete ass, Jonathan," Cleo said, and hurried after Brodie.

She found him in Lord Grayson's private study, a book in his hand. It was the only room on this floor that had not been opened for the ball. She didn't blame him for seeking refuge.

"I was beginning to think you'd left." Cleo closed the door behind her and stood with her back to it, as if she might draw courage from the solid oak.

He closed the book and reached up to shelve it, the pristine whiteness of his shirt cuff stark against the black sleeve of his tailcoat.

"About Jonathan . . ." she began.

"Yes, about Jonathan," he said. "What are you doing being friends with a prat like that?"

"I shall certainly snub him now. I'm sorry, Brodie. I had no idea he was so horrid."

"Forget it," said Brodie. "Do you think it's the first time I've had my background thrown in my face?"

"Is it very bad at Oxford?" She'd asked Lord Grayson about it and he'd said Brodie only needed a few good friends around him. And to fight the first bully and win.

"It was at the start." He smiled grimly. "But not for long. Anyway, I'd suffer a hundred fools like Shaw to be there. You cannot imagine, Cleo, what it's like." He threw out a hand, his face alight with the kind of zeal Cleo used to see in Serafina. "The greatest minds, the best equipment and laboratories. People who are interested in *ideas,* not just knowledge. It's been a revelation."

Perhaps she couldn't imagine Oxford, but Cleo well recalled the exhilaration she'd felt when she spent that afternoon with Lemarchand. The opportunity to indulge one's talents to the full was something so few people were granted in this life. "I am so happy to hear that." She hesitated. "We are both indebted to the Graysons."

He nodded. "I might have a scholarship but that's only the half of it. And I intend to pay them back. Every penny."

"Is . . . is that why you've stayed away from me?" She fought to keep her voice even but she heard the tremor in it. "Did Lady Grayson say something to you? Did Serafina?"

His jaw tightened. "I've been busy, that's all."

"Not too busy to chat up girls at the Café de Paris," muttered Cleo.

He had the utter temerity to grin and she could have flayed herself for betraying such petty jealousy. He eyed her and rubbed his jaw with his thumb. "I don't see what difference it makes to you. I'm like a brother to you, after all."

So that had rankled, had it? Good! They stared at each other, before Brodie blew out a long breath. "I'm trying to make something of myself, Cleo."

But you're perfect as you are! She didn't say it. She was too hurt and angry. "Let me know when you're done, won't you? Although I might not wait around that long." She turned on her heel and strode out, slamming the door behind her.

Chapter Five

Cleo did not see Brodie after the night of her ball. He didn't stay with the Graysons while in London and knowing he was in the same city but never came to see her hurt. She didn't have the heart to enjoy anything, but out of gratitude to the Graysons, she attended every function and pretended to be happy.

She'd been feeling particularly out of sorts and homesick for Cairo one afternoon when the note came.

"Come visit me at three in my studio. The King's coronation is set for next May and all the world and her daughter must have a tiara for the occasion. Lemarchand."

The address he gave her was in London, as was the address of Cartier, engraved on the note card. *What?* Lemarchand in London and she hadn't heard? No wonder her recent letter to his address in Paris had not been answered.

Cleo glanced at the clock. It was already past three P.M. She scrambled up, grabbed her purse, and headed for the door.

"Where are you going?" cried Lady Grayson, as she whizzed past her on the stairs. "The Petershams are coming to tea at four."

Cleo halted so quickly, she had to grip the balustrade to keep her balance. "Please send my apologies, Lady G. I'll ask Miss Trent to cancel all my engagements for the foreseeable future. So sorry, must dash!"

"Not without a hat!" Lady Grayson called after her.

"Oh, right. Hat." Grabbing an old straw boater that hung on the hall stand, Cleo jammed it on her head and fled.

The taxi ride to Lemarchand's studio in Chelsea conjured the same anticipation as her journey through the streets of Montparnasse on her last day in Paris, but the two cities were very different. London was not as exquisite as Paris, true, but while its architecture was less harmonious, the lack of uniformity made it interesting. Cleo loved the surprises she discovered around every corner. In every nook and cranny of London, there was history, layer upon layer of it, and that history gave character and charm to each building and square.

She liked to think about the character of each piece of jewelry she designed, and to imagine its future life with the woman who ultimately possessed it. How wonderful to be Lemarchand and know that your creations would be worn, admired, and treasured, passed down through generations . . .

Cleo paid the taxi driver and got out at the address Lemarchand had given her.

"You're late. Come in and shut the door."

Cleo obeyed. Garrets were meant to be cold, but this one was hot, its functioning windows too small to allow any breeze through them and the glazed panels that formed part of the roof only seeming to magnify the sunshine streaming through.

Lemarchand seemed not to notice the heat and, having ushered her inside, he went back to his work. Cleo took off her hat and her jacket and scarf and laid them on an overstuffed chintz sofa by the wall that was draped with brightly patterned cashmere shawls. Noticing a small table with a carafe of water in the corner of the room, she found two mugs—one of them chipped, neither of them clean—washed them both thoroughly, and poured cool water into them. She put one on a bench by Lemarchand where it would not be knocked over or cause damage to his precious drawings if it were. Then she perched on a stool opposite his desk and sipped at her own mug.

Cleo watched in silence for almost an hour before Lemarchand sat back and jerked his chin at her. "Come see."

Cleo came to stand behind him. She gasped as her gaze alighted on his design. "Who is this for?"

He tapped his nose with a paint-stained fingertip. "Ah, that is top secret, you understand."

"It is . . . sublime."

Personally, Cleo had never liked tiaras. They were uncomfortable to wear, often lugubrious in design, and to the younger generation they seemed fusty and old-fashioned. But this piece was delicate and intricate, so ethereal it might have been made of spun sugar.

"For a young woman," Lemarchand explained. "She is slight—*gamine,* you understand—so her family tiaras are far too heavy."

"Yes, I see," said Cleo. Outlined in ink, with shadings of graphite pencil to add depth and dimension, filled in with gouache and fine touches of watercolor, Lemarchand's drawing of the tiara was, in itself, a work of art.

This piece was unlike any Cleo had seen. It was a kokoshnik shape, like a peaked bandeau, composed of three narrow bands of diamonds, surmounted by fine filigree work of leaves and vines. What made the piece utterly unique was that the small, heart-shaped leaves and undulating vines were picked out in onyx, not diamonds or some colored stone, and they made a bold yet delicate contrast with the pavé diamond background. The effect reminded her of the elegant wrought iron balustrade at Madame Santerre's house in Paris. Along the top of the tiara ran another thin band of tiny diamonds alternating with onyx. The entire piece was surmounted by a handful of perfect pearls, spaced along the top.

Lemarchand's drawing was carefully annotated in ink with specifications and measurements.

"It reminds me of a tree of life," said Cleo, studying the design. "Like the ones you see on beautiful carpets in the Muski."

"I hadn't thought of that. For me, the influence was Indian." He gestured to the pinboard on the wall next to his desk, which was papered in reference materials and sketches.

They pored over his work together, discussing the layers of inspiration behind it, quite as if they had been doing so for many years. Hours flew by like minutes, just as they had on that wintry Parisian afternoon. Cleo felt creativity burgeoning inside her, flourishing like the intricate branches of Lemarchand's onyx-leaved tree.

For the first time since her fight with Brodie on the night of her presentation ball, Cleo felt hopeful.

Hopeful and alive.

"I DON'T BELIEVE it!" Lady G looked up from the Court Circular in *The Times,* her fine grey eyes sparkling with indignation. "The King has decreed that court presentations will take place at a *garden party,* if you please."

They were sitting in the breakfast parlor, a room delightfully positioned to catch the morning sunshine. Unfortunately on that particular morning, the rain poured down, splashing on the coping stones on the terrace outside and dripping from urns filled with spring flowers. It was on damply miserable days like this that Cleo most longed for the dry heat of the desert.

"What?" When his wife passed him the offending announcement, Lord Grayson frowned over it. "No, that won't do. That won't do at all."

"I suppose it's because there's no court this year on account of mourning for King George," suggested Cleo.

"It's *That Woman,*" said Lady Grayson. "I'd wager my best tiara that she's behind this." Cleo imagined the words in capitals whenever Lady Grayson referred thus to Wallis Simpson, Edward VIII's mistress and the root of all the ills in the universe—or at least, all the ills of the present monarchy.

Lady G threw up her hands. "No beautiful gowns, no ostrich feathers in the hair, no jewels to speak of. Hundreds of years of tradition down the drain. And over *two days,* as well. It all seems very pointed, almost designed to make people feel like second-class citizens if they're not presented on the first day."

Cleo hid a smile. The idea that anyone with the means and connections to be presented to the King could consider themselves second-class citizens struck her as comical. The Graysons would be there on the first day, of course, because the girls were presented in order of the precedence of their sponsors. Lord Grayson was a marquess, related to half the nobility in England and the royal family besides, so he was high up in the chain.

"It's all of a piece," said Lord Grayson. "What will be next? Selling off the crown jewels? A boogie-woogie version of 'God Save the King'?"

Unlike most British citizens, the Graysons seemed exasperated by Edward VIII, though Cleo couldn't quite understand why. King Edward's film star looks, style, and charm—not to mention his liking for the modern—had seemed to her to breathe fresh air into the stuffy royal family.

"I suppose the question now is, what to wear," mused Lady Grayson. "It is all very disappointing."

Cleo made sympathetic noises but she wasn't sorry at all to hear the news. Madeline had told her about what happened at court presentations. They sounded perfectly dire. A garden party would be infinitely more enjoyable than an elaborate evening reception. No fussy court gown with a long train designed to trip you up when you had to walk backward away from the throne because, apparently, one must not turn one's back on the monarch. No uncomfortable headdress of massive ostrich feathers to stick into the scalp and give one a headache with its terrible weight. No standing around for hours and hours in a stuffy reception room . . . Well, with about four hundred or so debutantes to be presented each day, there *would* be standing about for hours, of course—no getting around that—but at least she could do the standing about in the fresh air. Cleo rather liked this new King. She couldn't help feeling . . . proud of him. Which was ridiculous, of course.

A jolt of nerves set her pulse racing. The Graysons were not part of the Windsors' charmed inner circle but Lord Grayson was related to the royal family, and the King seemed to ask his advice on occasion. As the year of Edward VIII's reign progressed and the vexed question of Mrs. Wallis became increasingly urgent, the Graysons saw more of the King than ever before.

Despite angling for an introduction, Cleo had yet to persuade the Graysons to include her in any occasion that the King might be attending. At her presentation, she would finally see the monarch up close and judge for herself whether he might indeed be her father. If she concluded there was a likeness between them beyond their coloring, she would lay the matter before Lord Grayson and beg him to arrange a proper meeting between her and the King.

When the day of her presentation finally arrived in late July, Cleo realized she'd failed to take into account the additional hours sitting in the family Rolls while they processed slowly toward Buckingham Palace, with the onlookers lining the streets gawking at her through the car window. Twelve-year-old Cleo would have pulled a ghastly face at them; the young lady inside Lord Grayson's gleaming black Rolls waved and smiled.

When Lord Grayson's party finally arrived at the palace, it seemed Lady Grayson's misgivings had been justified: it was a lackluster affair. King Edward looked almost tragically bored in his somber tailcoat and black tie, his grey top hat resting on a table beside him. Rather incongruously given their sylvan surroundings, the King sat on a throne beneath a golden canopy set on an enormous oriental carpet. Seated around him were various courtiers and members of the royal family, including the Duke and Duchess of York and the Duke and Duchess of Kent. The rest of the company was obliged to stand in the open air.

Looking about her, Cleo decided she had scrubbed up rather well. Lady Grayson had chosen for her a simple white gown of figured organza with a high-waisted pale green sash and a matching green hat that dipped fetchingly over one eye. Cleo was glad of the block heel on her pretty green shoes. Many of the other ladies' slender heels were spiking the soft turf like golf tees as they picked their way toward the King's marquee.

As the afternoon wore on, and debutante after debutante made her curtsey to a King who patently wished he was somewhere—*anywhere*—else, Cleo commented to Lady Grayson, "I met him once." Speaking the words aloud made her stomach thrum with anxiety. Would she somehow recognize him when she came close? Would he magically see something of himself in her?

"Oh?" said her chaperone absently. "Who?"

Cleo gestured up at the dais. "The King."

Lady Grayson's head snapped around. She stared at Cleo, the feathers on her hat quivering. "What? When? I'm sure you never mentioned it before."

"Well, it was in Cairo and I was only a little girl. I suppose he must have been visiting for the Independence celebrations." It had not been true independence, of course. The British didn't relinquish control of such a strategically important country as Egypt so easily. Cleo wrinkled her brow. "It's funny, isn't it? How does anyone know whether they truly recall the details of an event or simply *think* they remember it because people have told them about it?"

"Who told you?" demanded Lady Grayson. "Not Serafina."

Cleo shrugged—a gesture her mentor had failed to eradicate from her repertoire. "A few people. My governess . . . other guests at the hotel. I had my photograph taken with him and everything. Aunt Serafina had a copy framed and put it on the mantel. He smelled nice and everyone made a big fuss because he stopped to talk to me. I *think* I remember that."

The wind picked up, and dark clouds rolled overhead; despite the season, Cleo shivered in her light gown.

"Oh, dear!" said Lady Grayson, clutching at her hat as the wind gusted over them. "It's going to rain at any moment."

Cleo squinted up at the sky. Lady Grayson was right. Would Cleo have her chance to meet the King before the heavens opened?

Just as she was about to give up hope, Cleo was directed to queue for her formal presentation. The first tiny sprinkles of rain settled on her skin just as the Lord Chamberlain called her name.

Head high, Cleo moved into position, made her low, low curtsey, and looked up into the blue, indifferent eyes of His Majesty the King. He had long since given up nodding at each girl and was clearly waiting for her to pass on.

But when he heard her name, he smiled, running his approving gaze over her ensemble. "Charming."

"Thank you, Your Majesty." She stared into his eyes, *willing* him to recognize her, the same way she used to stare at Serafina when her aunt was absorbed in her work, longing for even a sliver of her attention.

"I . . ." Suddenly Cleo had to speak, to recount her childhood memory of the golden prince who had crouched down to chat with her in a faraway land. She felt a mad, foolish urge to blurt out, *Everyone at Shepheard's thinks I'm your daughter!* Imagine the furor that would cause.

As Cleo hesitated, an expression of annoyance flitted across the King's face. It was gone in a moment, but it struck her like a blow to the chest. Fighting down the hurt, she closed her lips and made herself move back to her place in the crowd.

As if nature had been waiting for just that moment, the thunderclouds released their grip and the rain poured down, all over the elegantly dressed assembly. Umbrellas popped, women clutched their hats and fled on the arms of their escorts as the wind flurried their skirts. Lord Grayson held his umbrella up to protect his womenfolk, and Cleo and Lady G huddled together underneath, as they all struck out for shelter. It seemed to set the seal on a truly miserable day.

Cleo glanced back, but the King and all of the other dignitaries had vanished, the throne disappeared, the golden canopy dismantled and taken away. As if the King and his court had been no more than a desert mirage, a collective dream.

"So the rest of today's debs miss out?" Lady Grayson exclaimed. "I do call that shabby."

"It's all of a piece," muttered Lord Grayson as he shepherded them to the Rolls, dignified as ever, despite the rain that soaked his coat and drummed on the crown of his grey Ascot topper. "He'll be the death of the monarchy. Mark my words."

As they left Buckingham Palace, Cleo rested her flaming cheek against the cool window. She hadn't expected a miracle, or anything at all, really, but in a mere split second with that flicker of an expression, King Edward had dealt her a terrible blow.

CLEO COULD NOT seem to fall asleep the night after the garden party at the palace. She couldn't banish from her mind the image of King Edward staring down at her with those blue eyes, so like her own, from that opulent throne.

She had not felt the longed-for jolt of recognition, and nor, clearly, had he. Yet his impatience to be rid of her had hurt as if he had indeed been her long-lost father.

She'd been putting off raising the issue with the Graysons but now that it seemed unlikely she would have the opportunity to discover the truth another way, she decided to broach the subject of her parentage with Lady Grayson.

The next morning, the sun shone brightly, as if in defiance of the weather the day before. Cleo found Lady Grayson in the garden, snipping pink peonies and laying them in a basket, their pretty, blowsy heads together like gossiping girls snuggling in a big feather bed. Bees made their busy rounds, their drone a somnolent murmur among hollyhocks and snapdragons. Soon the Graysons would go to Scotland for deer stalking season. Lord Grayson was champing at the bit to be away.

"There you are! Hold this, will you?" Smiling, Lady Grayson handed Cleo the flower basket with its dizzying scents as she leaned forward to nip another long stem with her secateurs.

Cleo tried to think of a diplomatic way to lead into her question but her head was buzzing louder than the bee-riddled flower beds. She blurted out, "You know, don't you, Lady G? You know who my natural parents are."

Lady Grayson's head snapped around. She straightened and her shoulders dropped, hands falling to her sides as if she'd been caught in wrongdoing. Her face, framed by the gauzy lemon scarf that tied her straw hat in place, was creased with concern. "Cleo, I *don't*. Truly, I don't. That is to say, I thought I did, but it turned out not to be the case."

"What do you mean by that?"

Lady Grayson darted a quick look around. "This is hardly the appropriate time or place to discuss this."

"You mean the rumor that I'm King Edward's love child."

"*What?*"

"You know, Edward the Eighth—although of course, he would have been the Prince of Wales when it happened." She tried to sound nonchalant but she knew her voice was shaking. "It's what everyone at Shepheard's thought."

Lady Grayson shook her head in wonder. "All this time, you knew. Even at your presentation, you knew this! And you never said a word."

"My governess told me." On a day when her charge had greatly tried her patience, Fifi had wielded that piece of gossip like a switch. The memory of her cutting remarks about Cleo's illegitimacy still had the power to sting. Cleo took a deep breath and let it out in a shaky exhale. "But it's not true, is it? I mean, Aunt Serafina told me it wasn't."

Lady Grayson sighed. "I don't know who your parents are, Cleo. Serafina said that when the rumor spread after you had your photograph taken with the prince, she allowed everyone to think he was your father because it made them treat you with respect. But she told me before we left Cairo that it was no such thing, and that if ever you went on some zany quest to find your real parents you should be firmly dissuaded." She hesitated. "My sister has cared for you since you were an infant, my dear—"

"That's debatable," muttered Cleo, thinking of the nurses and nannies and governesses employed to ensure Serafina was at liberty to forget all about Cleo for days at a time.

Lady Grayson held up a hand. "She's not a demonstrative woman, but I know Serafina. In her own way, she loves you very much."

Then why had she been so quick to let Cleo go? And why did she never write? Cleo forced herself to smile. "I have received more affection from you and Lord Grayson in the past months than I ever received from Serafina. But of course, I *am* grateful. To Serafina for raising me, and to you and Lord G for taking such pains to see that I'm launched properly . . ." She swallowed hard. "But most of all for what you've done for Brodie. Truly, I . . ." Her voice suspended as she fought a sudden rush of tears. Ugh, where had these come from?

Bitterly though she resented her recent estrangement from Brodie, she could still be thankful that his prospects had improved a thousandfold due to the education Serafina and the Graysons were giving him.

"It has been our pleasure," said Lady Grayson. "You have both become very dear to us, you know." Her voice soft, she added, "Would it be so bad to accept things as they are, Cleo? Find a nice young man to marry. Someone who will give you a comfortable, happy life." She smiled impishly. "Then you may have all of the jewels your heart desires instead of designing them for other people."

"Aunt Lydia!" Cleo frowned at her. "I'm going to pay for my own jewels, thank you very much."

Perhaps due to the Victorian novels she'd read growing up, Cleo had always assumed that being an orphan meant she was destitute and would need to make her own way in the world when she came of age. As is the habit of children who want for nothing, it had not occurred to her that Serafina met every expense of her small existence. Serafina's benign neglect in less material ways had led to the ever-present fear that she would grow tired of Cleo one day and turn her out onto the street.

It had never occurred to Cleo to marry for money. Serafina had been so fiercely independent, the attitude must have rubbed off. Cleo was given an allowance now that she was officially "out," but she'd always assumed that once the season was over, she'd need to make her own way in the world. In the Graysons' milieu, no one ever spoke of money, and particularly not to young ladies like Cleo.

She came away from the conversation no wiser about her parentage. Serafina had told Lady Grayson the same thing she'd told Cleo about the King. But just for the sake of argument, what if there were fire beneath the smoke of rumor at Shepheard's Hotel? What if Serafina hadn't been telling the truth about Cleo's paternity? She couldn't see herself bowling up to King Edward and asking him if he remembered conceiving a child nine months before her birth. She'd probably be arrested for treason or something. And even if he was her father, he probably had not the slightest idea she existed.

Of course she couldn't ask the King. But was there a way to find out which woman he might have been romancing at the time of Cleo's conception? That seemed like it might be a more accessible line of inquiry. According to the spiteful Fifi, the King had former lovers scattered throughout the Commonwealth, but he had been stationed in France during the period Cleo might have been conceived—that she knew because he had been touted in the newspapers as a war hero, the details of his war service meticulously documented.

King Edward had been young at that time, but certainly old enough to have enjoyed some amorous adventures. Perhaps he had been in Paris on leave and taken a mistress there, as so many other British officers had done? In that case, Cleo's mother might well be a prostitute.

But if her mother had been a Parisian prostitute, how had Cleo ended up in Cairo?

It seemed more and more as if all reasonable avenues of inquiry led to Paris. And she still had to find Aimée Pain.

Chapter Six

London-Scotland
Autumn-Winter 1936

He'll abdicate. He's got to. He's gone and proposed to the woman!" Lord Grayson strode into the parlor where his wife sat embroidering and Cleo, wrapped in a thick woolen shawl, worked at her designs. The weather was bleak and freezing. She'd been drawn to the parlor because it was small and cozy, warmed by the fire that crackled and snapped in the grate.

The promised jaunt to the French Riviera had been postponed indefinitely, and it was all King Edward's fault. Lord Grayson was too occupied with the current crisis to leave the country at this pivotal moment. He and other men of influence had tried desperately to persuade the King that marrying Mrs. Simpson was utterly out of the question. Parliament wouldn't stand for it, and nor would His Majesty's dominions, much less the British people. Not only was That Woman an American, she was a divorcée twice over, and possessed a questionable reputation besides. Such a woman was barely acceptable as a mistress; she could never become Queen. Nor could Edward expect to remain King if he was determined to marry her.

"She must be an extraordinary creature," said Cleo. "And he must truly love her to give all that up." She had seen Mrs. Simpson a few times and been struck by her elegance—and by her fabulous jewels. But there was a brittle quality to her perfection that made Cleo feel strangely sorry for her, though she couldn't quite explain why.

"Humph!" said Lord Grayson. "I don't know about all that, but if you ask me, the fellow doesn't seem to *want* to be King."

"He did look dreadfully bored that day of the garden party presentation," said Cleo. "I suppose the life of a monarch is filled with tedious engagements like that."

"Tedious or not, the man has a duty," said Lord G. He sighed. "Although having said that, he's made a complete dog's breakfast of his reign so far. Perhaps we're better off without him. Tommy Lascelles certainly thinks so."

"Well, the alternative isn't spectacular, either," Aunt Lydia pointed out. "Bertie simply doesn't have the charisma."

"Solid sort, though," said Lord Grayson. He waved a hand. "Oh, he'd be nothing without the Duchess of York, of course. Now there's a woman with backbone, and charm enough for them both."

Cleo listened with half an ear as the discussion went on. She sifted through her drawings and surveyed the sketch she had made of Wallis Simpson's engagement ring.

Monsieur Lemarchand had told her with a touch of smugness that he'd known all about the King's intentions long before the British public, or even the cabinet, because Cartier had been commissioned to design Mrs. Simpson's engagement ring. The King had been ushered into a private room through a back entrance to the London premises, where he had disclosed news of the happy event.

The ring was made from an emerald that a Cartier salesman had gone all the way to India to purchase in secret. The original stone was the size of a bird's egg and had once belonged to the Great

Mughal. That gem had been deemed too large for any of Cartier's clientele to afford, so reluctantly, Monsieur Jacques Cartier had ordered it to be cut in two. Wallis's half—all 19.77 carats of it—was cut into a rectangular shape, set in platinum, and surrounded by diamonds, with two more diamonds on each shoulder. It was modern, elegant, and horrendously expensive, a jewel befitting a queen. The King had requested that the ring be engraved with the inscription, *WE are ours now 27X36.*

Cleo tilted her head. The inscription did rather imply that King Edward thought the world well lost for love. Had he always intended to retire with Wallis into private life? Was abdication all part of the plan?

A thought occurred to her. If the King abdicated, might he be free—or at least more willing—to acknowledge an illegitimate child?

Cleo pressed her lips together and shook her head. There she went again, spinning silly daydreams. From the improbable to the utterly impossible.

"What's that, my dear?" Lord Grayson came to look over her shoulder.

"It's *the ring*," replied Cleo. "The one the King gave Mrs. Simpson. Didn't I tell you it's a Cartier design?"

"Oh, I see. And what's this?" Lord G indicated the inscription, which Cleo had noted at the foot of the page.

"'W' for Wallis, 'E' for Edward . . ." Cleo paused. "And I understand the numbers represent the day he proposed. If the 'X' is ten, then it makes sense: the twenty-seventh day of the tenth month, nineteen thirty-six."

"The very day Mrs. Simpson's divorce became final." Lord Grayson visibly shuddered. "Nauseating."

Cleo thought the King's gesture quite romantic but she didn't argue with his lordship. She stood up and kissed his lean cheek. "I am sorry this has been such a rough crossing for you, Lord G. I hope it's all over and done with soon."

But it wasn't until mid-December that the Graysons managed to leave London. The Riviera trip abandoned, the family elected to spend Christmas at their Scottish estate in the Highlands.

It was rugged, beautiful countryside, and Cleo's first Scottish Christmas was a jolly affair with many parties held on neighboring estates. There were quiet afternoons spent sketching her designs by the massive open hearth with its bright log fire, and Doris, one of Lord G's springer spaniels, warming her feet.

Still, without the bustle of town life and the constant stimulation of new people and places, not to mention her lessons with Monsieur Lemarchand, Cleo noticed her sketches starting to look the same. She missed Cairo and the hotel, where every day brought new people to meet and observe. She missed all of her friends there—and yes, she missed Serafina, too, although she always seemed too busy to write. She missed Brodie, who was spending the winter at the Zoological Station in Naples studying marine life. Naples! Cleo was beside herself with envy. After two months in Scotland, she was heartily bored. She was definitely a city girl at heart.

Now she broached the subject that had been uppermost in her mind for the past few months. It was the excuse she needed to return to Paris and resume her search for Aimée Pain. "Monsieur Lemarchand told me that if I'm serious about being a jewelry designer, I must study at the École Boulle in Paris."

"Really?" Aunt Lydia did not seem terribly interested. "Well, I'm sure something can be arranged. How long is the course?"

"Three years."

"*Three years?*" Now she had Lady G's full attention. "But you'll be past twenty by the time you're finished. What about getting married?"

"Oh, there's no hurry for that," said Cleo, smiling extra brightly. She had absolutely no intention of getting married. She'd never met anyone she cared for as much as she cared for Brodie.

Lady Grayson said, "Well, if you're determined to have a career, why not take a secretarial course or something? Plenty of jobs for nice girls in that, and the courses take no time at all."

"Typing and answering the phone and such?" Cleo wasn't terribly interested in being a secretary. On the other hand, she was mindful of Lemarchand's advice that an artist needed a way to support herself while she built her portfolio. A secretarial course couldn't hurt, and it would help keep her busy until she began school in September. "All right, but I'm still applying for Boulle." Not to mention tracking down Princess Fahmy and her maid.

"You can do a six-week secretarial course in London before we leave for Paris," said Lady G, following her own train of thought. "I did promise you Paris in the spring, didn't I? I'll write to Madame Santerre immediately."

Paris, France
Spring 1937

WHEN CLEO FIRST set eyes on Hippolyte Santerre's younger brother, Philippe, she knew they would be friends. He was of medium height, with a mobile mouth, black hair, heavy eyebrows, and intense blue-green eyes.

Philippe stared at Cleo, then transferred an accusatory gaze to his elder brother. "You told me she was a child."

Hippolyte shrugged and lit a cigarette.

"That was over a year ago!" said Cleo. "I have become quite sophisticated since then." She chuckled, not really believing it, but the admiration on Philippe's face seemed to tell her otherwise.

She said to him, "Perhaps you will show me a bit of the Paris nightlife while I'm here. Your brother refuses to take me anywhere."

"That I certainly have," said Hippolyte. He gestured with his cigarette. "Don't let her youth fool you. This one is nothing but trouble."

Philippe laughed. "Then we shall get on famously."

His prediction came true. The two of them spent almost every day together when Cleo was not shopping with Lady Grayson or working on her designs. Philippe showed her all the tourist sites in Paris, marveling to himself that he had never paid much attention to these monuments and historical edifices before. "I'm beginning to see what all of the fuss is about this city." They had spent some time admiring the Degas retrospective at the Orangerie and were strolling arm in arm toward the exit.

"Ha!" said Cleo. "I've never met a native Parisian who doesn't think Paris is the best city in the world."

He shrugged. "It is indisputable, of course."

"I like London better."

She only said it to tease him, but Philippe's expression grew mournful. "It seems I was wrong about you, *ma petite*. Clearly you have no soul."

They were about to leave the museum when a young woman about Cleo's age came toward them, an older woman Cleo took to be her maid trailing two steps behind. "Philippe!"

Philippe muttered something under his breath. Abruptly, he unlinked arms with Cleo and ran an index finger between his collar and throat. Cleo observed the newcomer with interest. Adoration for Philippe glowed in her eyes. Whatever he might feel for this girl, he seemed discomfited that she'd discovered him arm in arm with Cleo.

Philippe introduced the girl as Mirabelle Fontenac. Mirabelle was attractive in that quintessential Parisian way Cleo envied, and she exchanged with Philippe some amusing, frivolous banter that shot back and forth between them without making a detour to Cleo.

Mirabelle might not have included Cleo in the conversation, but the girl's gaze was watchful, darting from Philippe to Cleo and back again several times throughout. Surprised and a little shocked, Cleo realized Mirabelle perceived her as a threat. She wanted to reassure her, but of course that would have been unwelcome.

Did Philippe have an understanding with this girl? Best to leave the two of them to speak privately. "Please excuse me for a moment. I must take one more look at the ballerinas before I go."

She spent some time roaming the gallery and returned to see the pair in a combative attitude. Philippe, hair ruffled and arms folded across his chest, seemed devoid of his usual humor. Bright tinges of color along Mirabelle's high cheekbones indicated anger.

Cleo wondered if she should perhaps slip away and leave them altogether. But as she hesitated, Philippe caught sight of her. He seemed to welcome her approach with relief.

"We must be going," he said to Mirabelle. "I'll see you at dinner this evening."

As they moved away, Cleo nudged him. "What have you done, Philippe? Mirabelle seemed extremely put out to see you here with me. I hope you explained—"

He cut her off with an unhappy laugh. "She is my fiancée."

"Really?" Cleo tried to look back but he took her arm and propelled her forward. Cleo drew free of his hold but kept walking. "I didn't know you were engaged."

"I'm not sure that I am anymore," he muttered. "We shall see what happens tonight." He turned to look at her and smiled, but this time it was not the dazzling grin of the fun-loving dilettante but a smile that contained a real, unsettling warmth. He flicked her cheek lightly. "Don't look so worried. All things considered, that encounter was probably for the best."

It did not take a genius to fathom what he meant. Philippe seemed to have developed serious feelings for Cleo, which his jokes and frivolity had masked until now.

The idea made Cleo's stomach twist. She had only offered Philippe friendship but she ought to have remembered from her experience during the London season that sometimes men mistook friendship for amorous intent. She needed to clear this up immediately, but the fact that Philippe had never actually declared his feelings for her made it awkward to raise the subject. She supposed that if his attachment to Mirabelle was so weak as to suffer irreparable damage by Cleo's mere presence in his company, perhaps Mirabelle was not the woman for Philippe anyway.

What a shame! Cleo didn't have any female friends in Paris and Mirabelle seemed lively and amusing company. Still, whether or not he broke off his engagement, Cleo resolved to keep Philippe at arm's length for the rest of her stay in Paris.

Soon, Cleo and Lady Grayson would join Lord Grayson at the Hotel du Cap on the Riviera, and with the Santerres staying at their own villa, perhaps she wouldn't see him so often. She had enjoyed Philippe's company and she rather resented having to forgo it. But she simply didn't feel any kind of deeper affection for him. He lived life too much for pleasure, his outlook too light and breezy. Attractive he might be, and under different circumstances, she might have been happy to have explored that attraction a little, but now that she'd become aware of his feelings, it wouldn't be fair.

With the knowledge that Philippe was engaged but taking more than a passing interest in her, the delightful rose-tinted bubble around those early days in Paris had burst. Cleo decided to turn her attention to finding Aimée Pain—or at least the maid's mistress. Feeling they were on good enough terms to broach the question that was always nagging at her, Cleo asked Philippe about Marguerite Fahmy.

Philippe's expressive face registered shock. "Why on earth should you want to visit that woman?"

"Do you know her?" Had the answer to her quest been right beside her?

Philippe shrugged. "She's notorious, my dear Cleo. *Not* the sort of woman an innocent young girl like you should associate with."

"And yet I am sure she is the sort of woman that *you* associate with often," retorted Cleo with narrowed eyes.

"It is the way of the world," said Philippe with typical masculine smugness. Then he grinned ruefully as if he knew very well how annoying he was. "But seriously, why do you want to know where she lives? You don't want to visit her, do you?"

"Not the lady herself. I need to speak with her maid." Briefly she explained how she had come to be in Serafina's care as an infant.

"Still . . . I don't know," said Philippe. "I think at the least, I should come with you. That way, you won't come to any harm."

"You make it sound like Princess Fahmy is some sort of gorgon."

"Well, you simply never know with a woman like that." He

regarded her with a softening gaze that set off alarm bells in the back of her mind. "You are still very much a babe in the woods, Cleo."

That smarted. "Please give me the address, Philippe. This is something I must do alone. And besides, I probably won't even cross paths with the princess. I'll inquire for the maid, and if she's not there, I'll leave. Surely nothing so very terrible can happen to me if I do that."

He tilted his head, still reluctant. "I am sure my mother would box my ears for helping you with this."

That was almost certainly true, but Cleo put her hand on his arm and said with quiet earnestness, "Please, Philippe. I can't tell you how much this means to me."

He stared at her for a few moments. Then he placed his hand over hers and gave a wry smile. "All right, then, I'll find out. But any trouble, you come to me, yes?"

COINCIDENTALLY PRINCESS FAHMY'S apartment was situated above the famous jeweler Van Cleef & Arpels at 22 Place Vendôme, opposite the Ritz. When Cleo inquired of the housekeeper if she might speak with the princess's personal maid, Aimée Pain, the housekeeper looked disapproving, but conducted her into the foyer of the apartment and asked her to wait.

The housekeeper returned. "Follow me, please."

She led Cleo into a large, airy drawing room. Cleo was instantly captivated by the view over Parisian rooftops, the balconies with their window boxes overflowing with geraniums of pink and red, the ubiquitous Eiffel Tower in the distance. A small, elegant woman sat with her back to the window, her face in shadow.

This must be Princess Fahmy, the mistress of the maid who had found her.

"Madame, I have Cleo Davenport to see you."

"Oh, no!" Cleo turned to the housekeeper. "Wait, I—"

"Come in, Miss Davenport. You don't know it yet but it *is* I whom you wish to see."

Mindful of Philippe's warnings, Cleo hesitated, but this was too great an opportunity to pass up. She stepped farther into the room. "You know who I am?"

The woman opened her large, sad eyes wide. "But of course I know who you are. You are the child whom Serafina Davenport took under her wing." She spoke with great formality, as if rigidly holding to the standards of a bygone age. Not only that, the princess stared hard at Cleo, as if she wanted to drill right through, into Cleo's mind. "How you have grown."

"I rather expect I have," Cleo responded inanely, discomfited by the stare. She had never imagined the princess would take the slightest interest in her, much less invite her to tea.

"You have the look of him," murmured Madame Fahmy. "Indeed, it could not be better."

Before Cleo could ask what she meant, the housekeeper brought in the tea tray and the princess leaned forward to pour tea into two Meissen cups. She did not inquire about Cleo's preference but slipped a slice of lemon into each cup with a pair of silver tongs. She offered one cup to Cleo, who came forward to accept it, and obeyed her hostess's languid direction to sit down on the sofa opposite.

"Now, mademoiselle, what is it that you desire from me?"

This was the most important question Cleo had ever asked. She had rehearsed it over and over on the way to the apartment. "I heard from someone at Shepheard's Hotel that it was your maid, Aimée

Pain, who found me on the doorstep in the winter of 1919." Cleo leaned in. "I want you to tell me everything you know about me."

"You have come to the right place," said Madame. "I know *all* about you, my dear. In fact I wonder that I never thought of this before." This last was said almost to herself. Madame drew a deep breath through her nostrils. "Your story began during the Great War, right here in Paris."

Chapter Seven

MARGUERITE

Paris, France
Spring 1917

The first time she laid eyes on His Royal Highness, the Prince of Wales, Marguerite knew she must make him her next conquest. She was riding her chestnut gelding in the Bois de Boulogne when she noticed his slight, trim figure in the distance, also on horseback, coming toward her along the leafy avenue. Having eschewed his uniform while on leave in Paris, the impeccably tailored prince wore a smart tweed hacking jacket and fawn breeches and a brown bowler hat. He reined in and tucked his riding crop under one arm, sweeping off his hat to shake a fallen twig from its brim.

He was . . . dazzling. Dappled sunlight played over his golden head and gleamed on his tanned skin. He was lean and fit, and as perfectly groomed as the fine thoroughbred he rode. He was not above average height, if she judged correctly, but then she was tiny, so that didn't matter one bit.

And the prince's companion? He seemed familiar. Ah, yes. She'd seen that one a few times, at a soiree or two, perhaps at the opera in the company of her former client, the Duke of Westminster. One of His Royal Highness's countrymen, but she did not know his name.

As the gentlemen approached, a particular thrill ran through Marguerite that boded well. She became acutely aware of the gelding's solid flank against her thigh, the riding crop in her gloved hand, the light, cool spring breeze flirting at her cheek, and the tight fit of her waistcoat and jacket.

Like her friend Coco Chanel, Marguerite had her riding habits made by a tailor who catered for huntsmen and jockeys. Her costumes were as formfitting as possible without the bother of having to be sewn into them, as had been the practice of another courtesan in the previous century. There was no need for Marguerite to lift her chin or stiffen her spine at the prince's approach; courtesan or not, she had the finest seat on a horse of any woman in Paris.

The desire to meet the prince flamed inside her. Of course, one could not simply accost him. Marguerite did not meet royalty—or, indeed, any man worthy of becoming her client—without the proper introduction. She might have been the daughter of a coachman and a housekeeper but she had learned much from Madame Denart over the years.

But how to captivate such a prize as the heir to the British throne? According to report, the Prince of Wales had adopted a false name to visit the City of Light, while he kicked up his heels and tried to forget the horrors he'd witnessed at the Western Front. The attempt at anonymity was half-hearted and ultimately futile. The young prince was accustomed to recognition—and respectful adulation—everywhere he went.

Well, fawning was not in Marguerite's nature. Even if it had been, how would that sort of behavior make her stand out from the crowd?

As they approached, the gentlemen tipped their hats. Marguerite nodded, unsmiling, allowing her direct, assessing gaze to meet the prince's. In that instant, sky blue eyes ensnared her, making her light-headed, and her mannish necktie seemed to tighten around her throat. But before they might have noticed any crack in her stern facade, the gentlemen had passed by.

Marguerite gave a small smile of self-mockery as she urged her horse to a canter. Attraction aside, the unsettling vertigo she'd suffered at the mere sight of the man was not a good sign. She had always prided herself on her hardheadedness. From an early age, she'd harbored few illusions about the world and none at all about men, be they prince or pauper.

She gave a mental shrug. She supposed she might be forgiven for losing a touch of her composure in the brilliant presence of the most eligible bachelor on the planet. But it would not happen again. She needed to play her cards with cleverness and precision if she meant to ensnare such a prize.

As she returned home to prepare for her *cinq à sept* rendezvous that evening, Marguerite's mind was not occupied by the forthcoming interlude. Jean d'Astoreca, for all his mining millions and his house on the avenue Bois de Boulogne, could not compare with the heir to an empire.

Marguerite touched her riding crop to her lips. If he was on leave from the Army, he might be gone from Paris any day now. How could she contrive to meet the golden prince?

MARGUERITE'S MOTORCAR PURRED to a stop outside a *maison de rendezvous* in the exclusive 16th arrondissement. She told her chauffeur to wait and alighted, pausing to scan the street. How many of the respectable people who passed this address every day would guess the varied kinds of depravity that were routinely conducted behind the elegant facade? Well, perhaps a few. Parisians were practical about such matters, after all.

If working for Madame Denart had been a step up from life as a dancer at the Folies Bergère, a listing in the books at Sonia de Théval's residence in rue Bizet represented the pinnacle of the profession. It had taken Marguerite years to work her way up to this point, but now foreign pashas and aristocrats vied for her favors with wealthy bankers and industrialists. She was a rich woman in her own right, but there was always room in her jewel box for one more stunning piece. Several, in fact. One might always buy more jewel boxes, after all.

Clients would come to call at Madame de Théval's in the early afternoon and be conducted to a salon where they might look through albums full of photographs of the courtesans on Madame's list. The client would make a selection, the courtesan would be telephoned, and an appointment for later that day arranged. Either the rendezvous would take place in one of Madame's sumptuous bedrooms, or at the courtesan's apartment, usually between five and seven in the evening. Then the couple might go out to dinner and the theater or the opera afterward. A courtesan was never hidden away like a dirty secret, as was the practice in other, less civilized countries.

Marguerite had jeopardized her own coveted listing on Madame de Théval's books with a recent, unbridled display of temper. Ordinarily she saw no need to apologize for such outbursts and simply would have allowed a month or two to pass before reappearing at Madame's establishment, pretending nothing had ever happened to mar their happy—and lucrative—association. But with the Prince of Wales in town on leave, time was of the essence. She didn't have leisure to allow the incident to fade from memory. She needed to make amends.

Her fingers closed reflexively around the elegant gift box she carried. Ah, the burn to her pride—not to mention the pain in her pocketbook! Hmm. It was not too late to turn back. She hesitated, then sighed. She must remember the reason she was here. The prince was worth any humiliation, any price.

She paused to gather her strength like a thoroughbred gathers power before a jump, then tapped the ornate door knocker.

The door was answered, not by a maid this time, but by Ginette Folway, the *sous-maîtresse* of the establishment. Expressive eyes alight with curiosity, she grabbed Marguerite's wrist and pulled her inside, whispering, "I didn't think you'd be back. Madame is most upset."

"Still?"

"You slapped a client's face!" Ginette put her palms to her own cheeks—as if anything in the world had the power to make her blush. "In public, too. It's the scandal of Paris."

Marguerite shrugged. "He deserved it. Besides, he slapped me back." She'd been obliged to go into hiding immediately after that incident. Not out of embarrassment—it was just as well for everyone to know she was not a woman to be trifled with—but because her resulting black eye could not be concealed by any amount of powder.

"Well, you haven't been forgiven. I doubt she'll even see you."

Marguerite smiled grimly. "Oh, she'll see me. Tell her I brought a gift."

"It had better be something spectacular if you are to get back into her good graces."

"Pfft." Marguerite snapped her fingers. "I care *that* for her good graces. She knows no one is better at what I do than I am." Marguerite's repertoire encompassed all manner of elegant depravities, of course, but her specialty had always been the exquisite pain and rapture of a certain style of punishment. It was a talent hinted at in one of the photographs in Madame's book of her in masculine riding dress, light whip in hand.

In Marguerite's view, a public, physical display of temper could only enhance her reputation, and enliven interest from a certain sector of Madame's clientele. Madame had thought otherwise. "Whatever he might enjoy in private, a man does not wish to be made into a spectacle by his mistress in public."

"Ahh." A quiet voice came from the doorway. "And who have we here?"

Marguerite turned to the *maîtresse* and gave a slight nod. "Good morning, madame. I trust you are well."

A sniff was all the response Marguerite received to that. "I thought it would be months before you'd show your face again."

"Fortunately my bruise healed quickly." Deliberately misunderstanding the quip, Marguerite offered her gift.

The *maîtresse* took the beautifully wrapped package and tossed it onto a nearby table. She inclined her head and addressed the other woman without taking her eyes off Marguerite. "Ginette, bring us tea." Having dismissed her second-in-command, Madame viewed Marguerite with cynical amusement curving her lips. "I suppose I might guess the reason for this." She waved a careless hand toward the gift.

Marguerite nodded. If she'd known Madame would feign indifference and not even open her carefully chosen *cadeau* before deciding whether to grant Marguerite a favor, she would not have purchased such a valuable piece. Inwardly, she shrugged. It was an investment as well as a peace offering and bribe. Madame's connections were top-drawer. An expensive trifle from Boucheron might keep Marguerite uppermost in Madame's mind when her most distinguished clients came to call.

"I am sorry to disappoint you," said Madame, "but I haven't received a visit from the prince, nor am I likely to do so. I believe his friends made certain . . . arrangements for his entertainment on this visit." Her nose wrinkled with distaste. "They went to a common brothel, I believe. They did not come to me, *tant pis*."

Chagrin burned in Marguerite's chest. So she'd humbled herself for nothing! Well, perhaps not nothing. "*Vraiment*? Why didn't they come here?"

Madame shrugged, then leaned forward and spoke in a low tone. "Between us, it's said the prince is . . . inexperienced, shall we say. Perhaps they thought him too callow for one of my *poules de luxe*."

Nonsense, thought Marguerite. They probably did not think it worth paying through the nose for an experience that would likely be all too brief.

"Perhaps next time he is in Paris," said Madame, smiling and laying her hand on the present Marguerite had bought. "But a thousand thanks for my gift. I'm sure I shall have someone else for you very soon."

But no one else would do for Marguerite. As she returned to her motorcar, she ran through a list of the prince's acquaintances who might be in Paris at that moment . . .

She snapped her fingers. Of course! Why hadn't she thought of him before? The Comte de Breteuil knew the prince intimately, did he not? The prince had stayed with his family as a very young man and learned to speak French. The matter would have to be handled delicately, and she would put several other irons in that particular fire, but it was an avenue worth pursuing.

AS IT TURNED out, it was through her own connections rather than Madame de Théval's that Marguerite finally secured an introduction to the Prince of Wales. Marguerite's erstwhile association with the Duke of Westminster—known to his intimates as "Bendor"—had opened many doors. Marguerite had begun to hold *salons* at her own apartment, where she mixed acquaintances from all walks of life like a bartender mixed an excellent cocktail. She blended members of the aristocracy, industrialists, intellectuals, and sprinkled in a few artists to give the party a kick.

"The Prince of Wales, eh?" François, Comte de Breteuil lifted an eyebrow. A budding composer and the despair of his father, the marquis, François was a frequent visitor to Marguerite's salon, although they had never been lovers. "That is flying high."

Marguerite smiled. "Will you do it? He is young and a little shy, I am told. He must rely on you to guide him."

"I don't know about that," said the comte. "But I'll see what I can do."

She hadn't held out an awful lot of hope—this was just one of the many lures Marguerite had cast into the relatively small pond of Parisian high society, after all. But François had not failed her. She must organize a small concert performance of his work as a token of her gratitude.

As she approached the Place de la Concorde on the day of her introduction to the prince, Marguerite stared up at the sharp point of the obelisk and mentally rehearsed the conversational gambits she'd prepared. She was to meet François and Prince Edward for lunch at Les Ambassadeurs at the Hôtel de Crillon, one of the most elegant and fashionable restaurants in Paris. The building that now housed the hotel was originally commissioned by Louis XV; its magnificent frontage had been the backdrop to the execution of his grandson during the revolution.

Now bloodshed had come to France again, and there were uniforms and military vehicles everywhere. Marguerite thought about her short stint working for the Red Cross and shuddered. She was better at administering comfort to the healthy men on leave than at tending to the sick ones.

She checked her watch. *Quelle horreur,* she was running late. She had taken such pains with her appearance, she'd lost track of the time.

The dilemma of what to wear on this important occasion had sent her to her favorite couturier, Paquin, and the two of them had spent hours trying and rejecting various styles. At last, Marguerite wrung her hands in despair. "I simply can't decide."

Her maid spoke up. "I don't see what the fuss is about. He is English, and he is young. Surely he will not care what you wear, as long as you have the right equipment underneath."

"Don't be vulgar, Aimée," said Marguerite.

"Besides," said Paquin, "I hear the prince is very point-device in matters of dress. A trendsetter, according to newspapers."

Marguerite recalled the impeccably turned-out young man she'd encountered in the Bois de Boulogne and blanched. "Then *help* me!"

They settled on a square-necked cream day gown with an embroidered bodice and a wide-brimmed feathered hat. Marguerite's aim was always to look as if she might have been a gentleman's wife rather than his lover, only infinitely more chic. It was well-known that the courtesans, not the wives, were the fashion leaders of Paris.

"Aimée, the necklace!" The maid fastened around her throat a magnificent collar of emeralds and pearls. Marguerite closed her eyes and allowed herself briefly to dream of the jewels she might one day receive from the prince if she played her cards right.

Her motorcar seemed to crawl toward the hotel. "Hurry!" She leaned forward, as if that could make the traffic flow faster around the Place de la Concorde. "I cannot be late."

Marguerite entered the hotel restaurant later than the appointed time, but by some stroke of good fortune, she was earlier than Prince Edward and the comte. The head waiter at Les Ambassadeurs, informed beforehand of the prince's visit and of his spare eating habits, welcomed Marguerite warmly and showed her to the best table in the house.

Accepting this with satisfaction, Marguerite smiled and smoothed her skirt. The restaurant was in the former ballroom of the hotel. Its opulent rococo style might once have intimidated her; these days she scarcely noticed the high ceiling painted to look like the sky, nor the scintillating Baccarat crystal chandeliers suspended from it, nor the subtle gleam of gilding everywhere.

No, these days, Marguerite considered being entertained at such places her due. But she might as well admit it: she was nervous. If only she could be certain the prince would like her! She must exert every ounce of charm at her disposal to ensure that he did.

But her temper began to fray when, fifteen minutes past the designated hour, she was still sitting alone in the dining room of the Hôtel de Crillon. The recent face-slapping contretemps notwithstanding, it had been years since any man had dared to treat her with such impunity. She was not about to put up with this sort of thing—not even from a royal prince.

Surely he wouldn't stand her up altogether. No, François wouldn't allow that. But after another ten minutes, Marguerite had all but given them up. As she debated the dreadful dilemma of whether to slink away from the restaurant or perhaps telephone a friend to join her and save face, Marguerite's most detested rival, Bébé Latour, entered Les Ambassadeurs on the arm of her most recent conquest. Though tempted to lower her head and hide her face beneath the broad, feathered brim of her hat, Marguerite made herself look directly at the newcomers and curve her lips in a slight smile.

"*Oh, là là!*" crooned Bébé as she leaned down to kiss the air beside each of Marguerite's cheeks. "Has your swain left you all alone?" She glanced pointedly over her shoulder. "My poor, dear Maggie, come sit with us!"

"I am quite content, thank you," said Marguerite, putting out a hand to ward her off. Truly, Bébé should remember that less was more, even when it came to Jicky perfume.

"Henri won't mind." Bébé caught Marguerite's hand and patted it, smiling sweetly. "He loves old things."

It was such a well-worn insult, Marguerite could hardly be bothered to respond. She quirked an eyebrow at Bébé. "Evidently."

Natural color expanded the circles of rouge on the other woman's cheekbones but she countered, "Well, I hope you haven't been abandoned, *ma chère*. You know, once a man starts forgetting his engagements with you, it's already over."

Before Marguerite could reply, a stir in the doorway preceded gasps and a low hum of chatter from the other patrons. With a great bound of her heart, Marguerite caught sight of the prince, accompanied by François, Comte de Breteuil. The manager, bowing deeply, greeted the gentlemen.

Marguerite's gaze was fixed on the prince, but she heard Bébé's hoarse cry of surprise, which turned to spluttering as the manager led the newcomers toward them. Warm relief flooded Marguerite's chest, and excitement filled her head, light and exhilarating, like bubbles in champagne.

She hardly noticed Bébé slink away.

As the gentlemen were ushered to the table, Marguerite rose to her feet. She hoped her smile conveyed demure pleasure rather than the overwhelming triumph she felt. "Your Royal Highness." She curtsied deeply.

"Oh, no, please. N-none of that," he said earnestly, waving away the formality. "I'm not HRH in Paris. It's the Earl of Chester while I'm here. Traveling incognito, you know."

She did know; equally she was aware that everyone else knew it, too, and that her party was being watched by many of the other patrons of the restaurant with voracious curiosity. She suspected that the prince would have been affronted had she omitted such deference without his prior permission.

He didn't apologize for being late. It probably did not occur to him that he should. But Marguerite's furies always fizzled out as quickly as they built, and besides, her complete rout of Bébé Latour had put her in an excellent mood. She was prepared to overlook the prince's transgression. *This* time.

They ate a light luncheon—neither she nor the prince were hearty eaters. Indeed, he was so slim, she wondered how he managed to fill trenches, which is what he jokingly called his mission on the Western Front.

"Oh, how horrible!" said Marguerite, smiling into his eyes. "But now you are in Paris, sir. We must see what we can do to make you forget all of that."

The prince swallowed hard and tugged at his tie. "Ah. Smashing. Yes, I'd like that most awfully."

"Paris is a beautiful city," said Marguerite, teasing him a little. "Should you like to go for a little drive after luncheon to see the sights?" She lifted an eyebrow. "I am sure I can show you some things you haven't seen before."

Pity the young man; he nearly choked on his lobster. Later in the conversation, he excused himself for a moment. Watching his retreating back, François said to her, "Gently does it, *chèrie*. He is not at all what you might call an old hand at this game."

"I cannot think what you mean," said Marguerite, her eyes wide. But it was a timely reminder. She needed to proceed with caution.

When they'd finished lunch, François tactfully left the two of them alone and the prince escorted Marguerite out to his motorcar. It was a brand-new Rolls-Royce coupé and Marguerite exclaimed with delight as he proudly showed off his toy.

It certainly was a beautiful machine. And what could be better than riding around the wide boulevards of Paris in a luxury car with the top down, flirting with a royal prince?

"I saw you in the Bois de Boulogne one day," said Marguerite, allowing admiration to shine in her eyes. "You ride so well, sir. It's also a passion of mine. Would you like to see my stable? And perhaps, borrow one of my horses? We could try their paces tomorrow afternoon if you are so inclined."

"You ride?" He seemed to count that excellent news and added ingenuously, "I quite expected an elegant young lady like you wouldn't be up for sport of that nature. Do you hunt, by any chance?" He launched into a detailed and rather tedious account of a good run he had enjoyed the last time he'd ridden to hounds at Melton Mowbray, and Marguerite inwardly sighed and let her attention wander. He was so very young! She did not remember ever being that naïve. It drew out a protective side she'd never even guessed she possessed.

"I like the races," she said, when she could manage to get in a word. "We must attend Tremblay or Longchamp together when next you are in Paris." She would enjoy showing him off to her acquaintances.

He heaved a sigh. "Who knows when I'll be back?" He turned to her, and those bright blue eyes captured her completely. "But I'll write. I promise most faithfully. I'm an excellent correspondent, you know."

She beamed back at him. The wind whispered and gossiped in the plane trees that lined the boulevard. It was only after several honks from the vehicles behind them sounded that the prince remembered to drive on.

Paris, France
Spring 1918

MARGUERITE AND THE prince lay together in her boudoir late one afternoon, limbs tangled among the sheets. It was the anniversary of their first meeting—not that she'd expect him to remember—and Marguerite was surprised to feel none of the ennui that usually crept over her within six months of a liaison's beginning.

The Prince of Wales—David, he'd told her to call him, though she'd modestly declined the honor at first—was . . . different. But Marguerite knew better than to indulge in even the slightest affection for her clients. That way lay madness. Still, she did allow herself to enjoy intimate moments like this.

The prince stubbed out his postcoital cigarette and swung his legs over the side of the bed.

Marguerite raised herself on one elbow, letting the sheet fall away from her naked torso. "Is something wrong, sir?" Yes, she still called him "sir." He might beg her to subject him to all kinds of indignities in the height of passion, but she suspected he'd abhor any breach of protocol when they were done.

From his Army kit he retrieved something, and padded back to the bed.

The box was a large, flat square. Red leather. Gold detail and a tiny lock at the hasp. Cartier, without a doubt.

Her heart singing, Marguerite sat up. The Prince of Wales had spent every minute he could with her while on leave in Paris, canceling engagements and disappointing his friends. She'd dared to hope he would express his appreciation in jewels, but now she was genuinely overcome.

"I love you, Marguerite. I want to take care of you always." The prince sat on the edge of the bed and set down the box between them. Then he took her hand and kissed it. Turning her hand palm upward, he pressed a tiny key into its center. "Open it."

He held out the box to her. Marguerite nearly dropped the key, her hand shook so much as she tried to fit it into the lock.

She'd done it! She'd won the adoration of the most eligible bachelor in the world. What's more, she'd kept his interest when he could have had any woman in Paris and beyond. She'd worked so hard for this!

"You're trembling," said the prince, his voice tinged with affectionate laughter. "My dear girl." He kissed her temple and took the key from her hand. "Here, let me."

He unlocked the box and opened it, then turned it toward her, his gaze fixed on her face.

Marguerite gasped. A three-stranded choker of glittering diamonds with a great square emerald in the center, surrounded by more diamonds. The emerald must have been nearly thirty carats, if she was any judge. And she was. Madame Denart had seen to that.

She'd mentally rehearsed the reaction she'd give. Even if the trinket had been unimpressive, she would have treated it like the crown jewels. In this case, she didn't need to pretend. Marguerite put her hands to her cheeks. "It's magnificent! Oh, *thank you*, sir!" She met his gaze with a look that was half joy, half awe. "Will you put it on for me?"

"Of course."

She bunched up her masses of long, thick hair in one hand while he arranged the collar around her throat and fiddled with the clasp. The jewels were pleasantly cold against her skin, sending the most delicious shiver down her spine.

"There," said the prince. His fingertips lingered at her nape, then trailed to her shoulders. Gently he turned her to face him and held her at arm's length. "Let me look."

She was naked but for the necklace. His gaze roamed, turning hot and purposeful. His grip on her shoulders tightened. Inwardly she longed for him to go so that she could admire her reflection in the looking glass, then get out her jeweler's loupe and appraise the gems properly. But of course, the prince came first.

Marguerite leaned forward for a deep, sensual kiss. She'd been saving something special for just such an occasion, as a reward for good behavior. Her royal client was in for a night he'd never forget.

Mentally she calculated the approximate cost of the jewels that snugly clasped her throat. And as she used the most singular and addictive skills in her repertoire to drive the Prince of Wales to the brink of insanity, she knew she was worth every centime.

Paris, France
Autumn 1918

OF COURSE, THOSE halcyon days were never meant to last. Marguerite had been a fool even to hope that they might.

She took the prince's letter from the salver and dismissed the maid who proffered it. She squeezed her eyes shut and clutched the letter to her chest, her knuckles white. If only she might hold on so tightly to the prince himself.

They had enjoyed a delightful liaison. For weeks, as she sensed her royal lover drawing away from her, Marguerite had employed every stratagem and wile she knew to keep him by her side. But their meetings had been all too brief. Even princes could not get extended leave from the Army whenever they wished. David's love, so often and fulsomely expressed, was a shallow, transient thing.

He was so young . . . If she told him of the small life they had created together, he would surely spurn her, never darken her door again. He would bluster and say the child could not be his. She didn't think she could bear that.

This second pregnancy brought back the many nightmares

of the first. Pitiful, innocent, convent-educated Marguerite had been left pregnant and penniless at fifteen, sent away from the household she served without a reference. Her family had taken the baby but could not afford to keep the mother as well and given the choice between begging for their charity and prostitution, Marguerite had preferred to walk the streets. Despite her present, comfortable circumstances, with the growing life in her belly, the old fear returned.

But no. This time, it would be different. The prince would never acknowledge his love child but he wouldn't have to. She would travel to Egypt, birth the baby, and leave it there.

The end of the war came too soon for Marguerite. There was dancing in the streets of Paris but in her heart, there was only dread. The prince would leave France and forget her. It was the way of the world.

His final letter came when she was very low. She could not recall feeling this way with Raymonde, but that was a lifetime ago. She felt constantly ill, like the worst kind of seasickness. She couldn't eat. She couldn't ride. Her body was so fatigued at night, she only made it through each social engagement with the utmost effort and slept late the next day until her roiling stomach woke her.

She took a deep breath and turned the envelope over. Addressed in ink, not pencil. She looked at the franked envelope. He must have written it in England.

David had left France without coming to see her.

She reached for the wickedly sharp letter opener she kept beside the bed. In spite of her misgivings, hope waxed in her chest. But it waned at once, leaving an acid residue. She slit open the envelope and read until the nausea overtook her and she retched and ran to the basin.

He had written to break off their relationship. She'd expected this, hadn't she? Didn't a courtesan foresee the end of a liaison as soon as it began?

Well, she did not mean to let him go without his offering appropriate compensation. Wiping her mouth, Marguerite sat down at once to reply. She wrote a horrible letter, accusing him of playing her false, of lying and leading her on. She had kept his letters, of course, every indiscreet one. More fool he for the endearments he had sent her, for the many confidences he'd put on the page—not only about their intimate times together but about his loathing for his royal duties, about the British mismanagement of the war, and tirades about his father, the King.

An ugly business, blackmail. Such behavior was beneath her, and she took care not to mention the letters overtly. But how *dare* he simply dismiss her like that, without ceremony or apparent regret? Among her circle, these matters were settled more elegantly. The gentleman must present an appropriate parting gift: jewels, or perhaps an annuity if the relationship had endured for some time. A future king ought to know how these things were done.

The instant her letter was dispatched, Marguerite knew she ought not to have sent it. Threatening a prince was not good for business. If word got around, it might hurt the image she'd worked very hard to cultivate.

But her swift action bore fruit. A friend of the prince's paid her a discreet visit, offering a settlement of ten thousand British pounds. Not the elegant parting gift she'd hoped for, but after a short, internal struggle, Marguerite allowed avarice to overcome her pride. Making abundantly clear her disdain for the transaction, she accepted the offer.

As her pregnancy advanced and the nausea subsided, Marguerite began to feel more herself again. Never one to wallow in misfortune, she turned her attention away from lost opportunities and vowed to make the most of the time left to her in Paris before her pregnancy started to show.

On her passage to Egypt, she discovered delightful company in a wealthy Jewish businessman. By the time she arrived in Cairo, the prince, his letters, and his fleeting, flimsy love were firmly left behind.

Chapter Eight

CLEO

Paris, France
Spring 1937

And you gave birth to me in Cairo," prompted Cleo, when it seemed Marguerite had become lost in the past and might stay there for some time.

The older woman blinked, as if she'd forgotten Cleo was there while she narrated this incredible tale. "That's right. I went to stay with friends in Luxor, where I had the child—you—and then I returned to Shepheard's Hotel once I'd recovered from the birth."

"Then you arranged for Mademoiselle Pain to bring me to the hotel so I might be discovered." Cleo frowned over this. Why bring her to the hotel if Marguerite had meant to conceal her connection with Cleo? "Why not quietly arrange the adoption through other channels?"

There was a pause. "The adoption I had arranged through a lawyer in Cairo fell through at the last minute, so I had to improvise. You said you heard the story of how my maid discovered you on the doorstep. Well, I had fully intended to play lady bountiful and pretend to arrange for your adoption myself." She smiled thinly. "But then a bossy young British woman stepped in."

Serafina, thought Cleo. "So you intended to leave me in Cairo all along?" The thought made her heart give a painful twist, but she was determined not to show it. Marguerite's insensitivity was beyond Cleo's comprehension. How could she be so callous as to abandon her own child in another country without a second thought? How could she sit there now, calmly admitting to her past?

The courtesan shrugged. "Better for you and your adoptive parents to be far away from both me and the prince."

Cleo struggled to take all of it in. "So Serafina *didn't* know who my real parents were." And Cleo had a sister—half sister— Raymonde. And her father . . . *the Prince of Wales*? She could well imagine Brodie receiving the news with that skeptical quirk of his eyebrow and calling it quite the fairy tale. That sense of unreality she'd had when Mr. Costas had told her about the night she was left at Shepheard's struck her again.

Marguerite shrugged. "I certainly never told Serafina you were mine." She leaned forward and took Cleo's chin in a firm grasp, tilting her face toward the light. "You look like him," she said. "You remind me of him as he was then. A golden prince."

"Do I really?" She'd stared at the prince's photograph until she was cross-eyed but she could never see it. "I mean, obviously the coloring is similar, but I don't think . . ."

"It's not so much in your features, but in your air, my dear," murmured Madame. Her large eyes opened wider. "So. What do you mean to do about it?"

"Do?" repeated Cleo.

"Don't you want to get to know your father?" A bitter spasm

crossed Madame's features. "I'm afraid I can't make the introduction. His Royal Highness and I have lost touch."

Remembering the bored indifference of the King on the day of her presentation, Cleo's mind shied away from trying to meet him again. How on earth would she go about it? Bowl up to him at some social event and blurt out the good news?

She fixed the princess with her gaze. "Why don't I get to know you instead?" Cleo's lips pressed together, then trembled. *Maman.* She couldn't say it. How on earth could this exquisite, pampered, diamond-hard creature be her mother?

But Madame Fahmy did not seem to hear. She gripped one of the bracelets she wore and turned it around and around her thin wrist. The cuff was thick yellow gold and studded with gems that formed a glittering Maltese cross. Cleo recognized that it was a Chanel, the design by the Duke of Verdura. Then the princess snorted. "Had I known David would end up marrying such a creature, I might have played my cards quite differently. Have you *seen* the jewels he showers upon her?"

"Oh, yes, indeed," said Cleo. "They are truly marvelous. I am a student of Monsieur Lemarchand at Cartier, you know, and I saw his design for the engagement ring."

"*Vraiment?*" Madame eyed Cleo speculatively. "A student? Then, what? Do you mean to be a *jeweler,* Cleo? How odd."

"I want to be a designer. Or an artistic director, like Mademoiselle Toussaint," said Cleo.

Madame sniffed. "Design jewels for *other* women? You are beautiful and well-connected. Why not marry and have those jewels for your own?"

She sounded like Lady Grayson. Cleo smiled. "It's not wearing the jewels that interests me so much; it's the idea that jewelry can be a form of art. And art, you know, must be enjoyed by others, not hoarded all to oneself. Besides, as you can see, I am small and my figure is slight." She gestured at herself. "If I wear elaborate jewelry I look like an overdressed Christmas tree."

Marguerite, even smaller and thinner than Cleo, was looking baffled and affronted, as if she'd called *her* an overdressed Christmas tree.

Oh, dear! This wasn't going well. Desperation made her lick her lips. "I really am a very good designer, you know. Even Princes Fawzia of Egypt has admired my pieces." The instant the boast was out of her mouth, she flushed with embarrassment. *Bragging, Cleo? How low will you stoop to win this woman's approval?*

"Hmm." Madame pressed her lips together. "Perhaps you might bring me your designs next time. Let's see how good you are." She ran her fingertips over the large rope of pearls that looped twice around her neck. "Perhaps you might like to see my collection, too."

"I'll do better than that," said Cleo. "If you give me pencil, ruler, and paper, I will design something for you right this minute. It won't be to scale, of course, but we can refine it later."

The other lady drew back, as if Cleo had suggested an imposition. Cleo nodded encouragingly. "It won't take long."

Something in Cleo's demeanor must have persuaded the princess to relent. She rang the bell and ordered the implements Cleo had requested. Laying everything out before her, Cleo eyed the woman who was her mother, yet so utterly unfamiliar to her in every respect. "Now. Usually, I would design a piece around a particular jewel or a group of jewels. Do you have any you would like to use?"

"As it happens . . ." Madame rose and left the room, then returned some minutes later with the stone and handed it to Cleo.

"An aquamarine. Marquise cut. About ten carats," said Cleo,

turning it over in her hands so that it glinted in the sunshine. "Magnificent."

"An Indian prince gave this to me," said Madame. "But . . ." She shrugged.

"That clear azure shade does not suit your coloring," said Cleo, tapping her lips with her pencil. "But if we paired the aquamarine with stones that have a warm autumn tone—emeralds or tourmalines, topaz, perhaps, it could work. Let me see . . ."

She took paper and pencil and ruled sight lines, then sketched the aquamarine at the center, adding in a suggestion of the facets without going into too much detail. If she had her inks and paints with her, she could make it more interesting, but at this stage, she would have to manage without.

"A wide yellow gold cuff like the one you're wearing," she said. "The centerpiece will be the aquamarine. Then around the bracelet, emeralds and tourmalines in tones of sage or moss green set in the cuff like irregular paving stones. The muddy shade of the green stones will suit your skin tone *and* make the aquamarine shine."

"Oh, *no!*" said Madame when Cleo showed her the sketch. "Aquamarines should only be paired with diamonds and set in platinum. That is quite ugly."

Cleo tilted her head. "Well, it's unusual, certainly. But why have something designed for you that is like everything else? Diamonds and aquamarines . . ." She shrugged. "It's rather obvious, don't you think?" She took back the sketch. "Let me work on it a bit more, add in some color, and I think you will be surprised."

Madame eyed her for a moment. Then she said abruptly, "If you came here looking for a doting mother, you are destined for disappointment. I am not a maternal woman; I never have been. I'm sorry, but that's the truth of the matter."

The words struck her flesh like dagger points, but Cleo refused to let it show. "Frankly, the feeling—or lack of it—is quite mutual," she replied, folding the sketch and tucking it into her purse. "But I don't see why we shouldn't become better acquainted. We have a common interest in jewelry, after all."

"We do, at that." The princess thought for a moment. "Come visit me next week, then. And bring your sketches with you." She paused, sliding the Chanel cuff up and down her slender arm. "But you shouldn't expect anything from me, you understand. You will always end up disappointed."

A statement demonstrably true when Cleo arrived at the apartment the following week, only to be told the princess had left Paris for the summer and wasn't expected back until October.

CLEO LEFT MADAME Fahmy's apartment and stood on the landing with her back to the wall, clutching her portfolio to her chest and battling threatening tears.

How ridiculous! What had she expected? That the mother who had abandoned her without a thought eighteen years ago would now welcome her with open arms? That kind of ending only happened in novels.

The princess had been unforgivably rude to arrange to meet Cleo when she must have known she wouldn't be at home. That reflected badly on Marguerite, not on Cleo. There was no need to feel hurt by this; she'd been well aware when she'd pushed to see her mother again that Marguerite was reluctant to deepen their acquaintance.

No, Cleo shouldn't have allowed herself to hope. She'd been

looking forward to showing the princess her designs. Stupidly, she'd wanted Marguerite to be proud of her.

Well, Marguerite's behavior only made Cleo more determined. She would *make* her mother sit up and take notice.

Deep in thought, Cleo moved away from the wall and continued down the staircase with its fancy wrought iron balustrade. So Marguerite had left for the Riviera. Well, Cleo would be leaving with Lady Grayson for Cap d'Antibes soon. Perhaps she and the princess might cross paths there. She was almost certain that, given Lord Grayson's connection to the royal family, she could contrive to meet the King. Or no, not the King. He was the Duke of Windsor now, wasn't he? She couldn't quite get used to that.

Fear began to wrap its tendrils around her chest, but she refused to be intimidated. When all was said and done, the duke was just a man. And didn't his recent abdication to marry Wallis Simpson show that he had a loving heart beneath that polished exterior? That he valued personal relationships above everything? He might not reject Cleo's claim. He might even be moved by the sight of his daughter. A daughter who was said to resemble him, even if she couldn't see it herself.

Cleo tucked her portfolio under her arm and continued around to the Ritz, where she had promised to meet Lady Grayson for tea.

She approached the hotel via the rue Cambon entrance and paused in the corridor to inspect the showcases of jewelry and other luxury items from the nearby ateliers, then passed through to the lounge to await Lady Grayson's arrival. Cleo was early; she'd expected to spend an hour with Marguerite.

Having ordered coffee, Cleo opened her sketchbook. She'd work on another design for Marguerite while she waited. This time, a brooch in the shape of a flower—a marguerite, in fact—with a yellow diamond or citrine center and rock crystal for the petals, each petal traced with a glittering path of tiny diamonds.

Of course, she understood the message behind her mother's absence on a day she'd invited Cleo to visit. Marguerite was abandoning Cleo all over again. Well, Cleo did not mean to let that deter her. In fact, she would design, not just a few random pieces, but an entire parure for Marguerite. No woman who loved jewels as much as she did could possibly resist.

The soft murmur of guests and the tinkle of cutlery on china barely registered as Cleo filled page after page with concept sketches, carefully annotating them with the materials she would use. But despite her task, she couldn't stop her mind replaying over and over the moment her mother's housekeeper had shut the door in her face. It wasn't until someone called her name that she realized her eyes were full of tears.

"Cleo?" A deep voice penetrated her brain.

She came back to earth with a jolt, dropped her pencil, and looked up. "Brodie!" Hurriedly, she wiped her eyes with the back of her hand, hoping he hadn't noticed her distress.

But Brodie was bending to retrieve her pencil. Straightening, he held on to it. "Hello, there." His dark eyes were soft and luminous and faintly smiling.

Cleo stared up at him for a few moments before she found her voice. "What a surprise. H-how lovely to see you." And it *was* lovely, even though they'd parted on uneasy terms last time they'd met.

His gaze fell to her sketches and she hurriedly shut her book and jumped up. "Are you here to meet us? Lady G didn't breathe a word to me about your being here in Paris."

He shook his head. "Hang on." He took out a card, scribbled a note on it, and handed it to a waiter. "See that Mr. Skelton receives this when he arrives, will you?"

"Shall we get some air?" Brodie glanced at his watch. "Do you have time for a wee stroll before Lady Grayson arrives? You can leave your things with the waiter."

He had seen her crying. Feeling heat rise to her cheeks, Cleo tucked her hand in Brodie's arm and went with him.

Without speaking, they passed through the lobby and into the colonnade that ran along one side of the Place Vendôme. There were a million things Cleo wanted to say, but she was already off-balance from her mother's rejection. She didn't want the precarious balance she'd achieved to be completely overset.

After a while, Brodie said, "I hear you're leaving for the Riviera soon."

"Yes," Cleo replied. "A long overdue holiday, as far as Lady Grayson is concerned. The King's abdication stopped us going last winter."

"What a debacle that was." Brodie waited, but when she didn't break the silence, he sighed. "Come on. Out with it. What has you so upset, Cleo? It's not Philippe Santerre, is it? I hear the two of you have been getting close."

Cleo wrinkled her brow. "Philippe? He's a friend, nothing more." She looked up at Brodie. "What? Did he say something to you?"

Brodie laughed mirthlessly, shaking his head. "How can you be so oblivious?"

How can you? she wanted to retort but remained silent.

"So if you're not upset about Philippe Santerre, what is it?" Brodie asked.

Cleo glanced about at the passing traffic, the young men and women on bicycles, the smartly dressed Parisians window-shopping or heading for luncheon appointments at the Ritz, the luxury motor-cars pulling up outside the hotel. "Not here."

"Where, then?"

"Oh, never mind." What was the point in confiding in Brodie? He would only leave again. She checked her watch. "We'd better go back."

"If that's what you want," said Brodie. "But, Cleo . . ." He stared down at her with a furrowed brow, as if he were truly concerned for her. "About Philippe . . . Don't break the poor lad's heart, will you?"

This again! She rolled her eyes and turned to walk back toward the hotel entrance. "We are *just friends*."

"I heard he broke off his engagement."

If she were honest, she knew she was responsible for that. At least, Philippe's feelings for her were responsible for it. But she wasn't going to admit that to Brodie. "Well, that's nothing to do with me."

"Really? Then I think you ought to make that clear to Philippe."

"I have. Repeatedly. Ugh! Why is it so difficult to understand? A man and a woman can be friends, surely."

He gave a smile that went awry. "Not when that woman is you."

Cleo stopped walking and turned to stare at him. Did he mean she affected *him* the same way as he claimed she affected Philippe? "What—"

"Forget it." He started to move on, but she put a hand on his arm to stop him. He turned back to face her, his expression a careful blank.

"Brodie?" She read the denial in his face. He refused to admit he cared. She wanted to take him by the shoulders and shake him.

"Come on," he said, staring at a point just above her left ear. "Lady Grayson will be waiting."

That shining moment of possibility between them was over. They returned to the hotel in silence.

Chapter Nine

*I*n the year that followed, Cleo made no further progress in personal matters—neither on her quest to get to know her real parents, nor with Brodie. She had not set eyes on him since that meeting at the Ritz, and although she'd written, his replies had been impersonal and brief.

Several attempts to see Marguerite again bore no fruit. Cleo had even found out where Marguerite was staying in Biarritz and traveled down to see her, only to be denied an audience there, as well. Short of lying in wait outside her apartment building in Paris and waylaying her as she climbed into her chauffeured car, Cleo couldn't think of a way to get her mother to talk to her.

The Graysons were invited to the wedding of Wallis Simpson and the Duke of Windsor at a château near Tours. Cleo, who listened for news of the wedding on the wireless, felt the smallest leap of hope. Many of the duke's subjects felt bitter regret that their golden King had married That Woman, but Cleo didn't. She hoped the duke would be happy with the love of his life. She hoped that the people who criticized and disliked the duchess were merely prejudiced. And she hoped that an abdicated King who had married someone so eminently unsuitable would be more likely to accept an illegitimate daughter than one who had ascended the throne.

"She has been very affable," Lord Grayson said of the new duchess. "And a consummate hostess—saving your presence, my dear," he added in an aside to his wife.

"I don't know about that," said Lady Grayson. "*I* still say she's a schemer. But the two of them certainly can turn on the charm when it suits them."

Once the Windsors settled into their Paris apartment, Cleo had tried to angle for a visit, as the Graysons were sometimes invited to dinner there, but Lady G said, "I'm afraid the Windsors don't really socialize much with young people. Particularly not young, pretty females," she added. "Besides, I guarantee you would be thoroughly bored, Cleo. HRH played the bagpipes at dinner the other evening. Frightful racket! Bagpipes should be played in the open air outside a Scottish castle, *not* at dinner."

It was enough to drive one to accost the duke in the street and yell at him, *I am your daughter!* Imagine what a field day the press would have.

Of course, Cleo wouldn't do anything of the kind. The knowledge might complicate his life terribly—or, more likely, he would be completely indifferent. It was whispered that he had illegitimate children scattered all over the Commonwealth—all of them born to married women who could be counted on never to make claims on him. Cleo didn't wish for notoriety, nor to make things difficult for the duke, and she certainly did not desire to be rejected by him, either. But she longed to meet him, to get to know him a little. Surely that wasn't asking too much?

Stymied at every turn, Cleo retreated into her creative work, and once her classes began at Boulle, she had little time for anything else. Her instructors were exacting, but she had learned from the best. She quickly became one of the top students as far as design went. She found the fine art classes far more challenging, but doggedly, she persevered.

The truth was, Cleo was looking forward to a well-earned summer vacation. They were to leave again for the Riviera soon. She couldn't wait.

Lately, though, she'd been thinking more about what Marguerite had said and wishing she might further her acquaintance with the woman who had given birth to her, despite Marguerite's clearly communicated rejection. She decided to go ahead and complete the collection of jewels inspired by her mother. She would send her paintings of the major pieces to Marguerite with the promise of more to come, in the hope that it would pique her interest and provoke a meeting.

Cleo was finishing the colors on the sketch of Marguerite's necklace when Madame Santerre peeked over her shoulder. "Aquamarine, green tourmalines, citrines . . . I should not have thought to put that combination of stones together but *ma chère,* you have made it work to admiration. What an unusual piece."

Cleo beamed up at her. "I take that as a high compliment coming from you, madame."

"Who is this for?" Madame Santerre picked up the sketch and inspected it closely.

"Oh, no one in particular," said Cleo, feeling a twist in her stomach at the lie. "But if Monsieur Lemarchand likes it, perhaps it will go in my portfolio. He says he will show Mademoiselle Toussaint when I have enough quality pieces." For every one design Lemarchand approved, he dismissed hundreds of others, but that was all right. Cleo had learned to develop a thick skin when it came to critiques of her work. And there was no doubt that Lemarchand knew what he was talking about, so she never resented his criticism.

"Hmm." Like everyone else around Cleo, Madame Santerre did not approve of Cleo's desire for a career. "I hope you will set aside your sketches and have fun on the Riviera, *ma chère*. Meet some young men. Live a little. There will be time for work when you come back to Paris."

"But it's not work to me," protested Cleo.

"Well, at the very least, an artist needs to *experience* life in order to create. Besides," added Madame with a wistful smile, "you crave independence, but life can be hard when the only person you have to rely on is yourself. You don't see it now, but if you leave it too long, one day you will wake up and want someone but all of the good ones will be taken." It was the first time Madame had given any indication she did not relish her own freedom. Monsieur Santerre had died in the Great War, leaving Madame with two little boys to bring up alone. Well, alone if you didn't count a legion of servants.

"Have you ever been tempted to remarry?" Cleo asked.

Madame sighed. "I was too preoccupied with my boys during the best years of my youth. Later, it seemed as if men only wanted my money." She gave a dry laugh. "There is a golden time in a woman's life and it passes by all too quickly, *ma fille*. One only grows more cynical as the years pass, and less inclined to risk one's independence for love."

Madame Santerre spoke from experience. But what was Cleo to do? Her marriage was bound to mean giving up her dream of building her own jewelry brand. She didn't know who she would be without her creativity and her ambition.

"It's all Serafina's fault," commented Lady Grayson, who had been perusing the society pages. "No doubt she simply assumed you'd follow in her footsteps and remain a spinster."

"Well, you must admit that at least I have chosen a more lucrative profession than Serafina's," Cleo pointed out. "Potentially," she added when she sensed a mental eye roll from Lady G. "Scholarly articles hardly pay anything at all."

"Archeology is certainly a pursuit only suited to the rich or well patronized," Lady Grayson agreed. "But then, in a way, so is jewelry design. There are hardly any jobs for women in it, and if you want to set up your own business, you need financial backing. Otherwise how will you afford the gems and gold and such?"

It was a question Lemarchand had put to Cleo, too, but she'd decided to tackle the problem of her education first. Times were changing; it might not be too long before the larger jewelry houses hired more female designers. And she had an excellent mentor in Lemarchand, after all. No need to despair.

"I'll be your financier, Cleo." Philippe Santerre strolled into the room. He stood at her shoulder and leaned forward to pick up the sketch of Marguerite's necklace.

"Careful! The paint's still wet." Cleo turned to look up at him as he studied her work. "And thank you for the vote of confidence, but I'm not nearly ready to go into business for myself. Besides, it's never a good idea to mix business with friendship."

In the end, she decided to take Madame Santerre's advice. She would enjoy herself and take a break from her work, hoping to return to it after the summer all refreshed and full of ideas.

Cleo and Lady Grayson headed to the south of France on the blue train to join Lord Grayson at the Hotel du Cap. Lord Grayson had stayed in England while his wife visited Cleo and Madame Santerre for a few months in Paris. He met them at the Juan-les-Pins station with a smile lighting his eyes. "My dears! I've missed you both."

"It has been far too long," said Lady G, reaching up to kiss his cheek.

They really are in love, Cleo thought and suppressed a pang of envy.

"Indeed it has!" Cleo took the arm Lord G offered and squeezed it companionably. "How are Doris and Harry?"

He chuckled. "One might have expected those hellhounds would be your priority. As badly behaved as ever, I'm afraid. Harry chewed my best slippers last week."

"Surely he is too old to be doing that." Cleo frowned. "Perhaps he sensed you were about to leave and grew anxious. Oh, I do wish you could have brought them. I miss them so!"

Lord Grayson indicated to the porter that the trunks were to be taken by taxi to the hotel, then led the ladies to his automobile.

"What on earth!" said his wife, throwing up her hands. "A *sports* car, my dear?"

Cleo laughed. A yellow Hispano-Suiza awaited them, gleaming brighter than the Riviera sunshine. A vehicle hardly in keeping with Lord Grayson's dignity.

She had never seen this eminent member of the aristocracy look sheepish before. "Borrowed it from an old friend from my diplomatic days."

"Well, it's utterly outrageous," said Lady G.

Lord Grayson grinned, opening the door first for Cleo to climb into the backseat, then for his wife to tuck herself into the front. He took the wheel and tossed back at Cleo, "Hold on to your hat!"

Glorious! With the wind in her hair, Cleo lit up beneath the Mediterranean sun. The baking heat and the sparkling azure of the Mediterranean reminded her of holidays with Serafina.

Of course, for Serafina the summer months were spent writing up the research she had undertaken in the winter, but in Alexandria, Cleo had become part fish, spending half her time in the sea. Her toes tingled at the prospect of swimming again. She ought to buy a new costume or two while she was here. And a scarf to keep her hair from flying into the wild tangle she knew it would become by the time they arrived at the hotel.

But she couldn't forget her main purpose on the Riviera: to try to get close to her father, the former King.

When there was a lull in the conversation, Cleo leaned forward to shout over the wind, "I hear the Duke and Duchess of Windsor are holidaying down here."

"Yes, at the Château de la Croë," Lord Grayson called back. "Although they do come to the hotel frequently to dine with friends."

Lady Grayson shot Cleo an odd glance over her shoulder, so Cleo explained, "I want to see The Ring. I only saw sketches of it, and of course the photographs won't have done it justice."

"What?" Lady G cupped her ear with her hand, trying to hear over the wind and the roar of the engine. "This dratted motorcar!"

Cleo shook her head and sat back. "Never mind!"

She closed her eyes and tilted her face to the sun, enjoying the play of light and shadow, yellows and purples beneath her eyelids, the cool sea breeze on her face. Imagine the delight of trawling through the duchess's awe-inspiring jewelry collection. Say what you would about her, That Woman had taste.

Cleo opened her eyes and stared out at the bay below, as blue as Wallis Simpson's legendary eyes. Cleo often wondered about the duchess. Could she possibly be the conniving creature she was painted? What must it be like to be hated by an entire nation, hounded by the foreign press? Was it love or jewels that had motivated such a sacrifice? Or had Mrs. Simpson been trapped once the King gave up everything to be with her?

Cleo wrinkled her nose. Whatever the case, the duchess certainly would not be friendly toward Cleo if she found out who she was.

"Here we are!" They turned into a long, straight drive flanked by manicured lawns and trees. Ahead was a gleaming white château, with slate-blue roofs and shutters on every window. The main building was surrounded by a park of such lushness, the grass was an iridescent green. Glimpses of azure water peeked between the palm trees and in the distance, a pristine white yacht gleamed on the shimmering horizon.

Once they'd settled into their rooms, Cleo went off to explore.

The hotel backed on to terraced gardens and a swimming pool, then steps led down to a marina where there was a pretty teahouse. Pleasure craft were moored at the marina, presumably for the use of the guests. Perhaps another day, she would take one of those little boats out. Cleo's eyes widened when she saw a second swimming pool, this one blasted from the rock of the cliff-face and filled with seawater that lapped over its sides.

When she made her way back to the hotel, Cleo was delighted to receive a glass of lemonade made from freshly squeezed lemons. The drink was cool and sweet and refreshingly tart. She held the glass to her sun-kissed cheek and went out to the balcony.

Yes, Madame Santerre had a point. If one married well, one might spend every summer at the Hotel du Cap without a second thought about the cost. But would such a life make Cleo happy in the long run? She suspected not. Perhaps it was Serafina's influence, but even with all this beauty laid out before her, Cleo knew it would pall after a while. Sooner or later, she would need to create.

And not just to create, but also to be remunerated for her creations, and to be recognized for her skill.

That evening, Cleo and the Graysons drove over to Antibes to visit the Santerres. They arrived at Madame's villa to find that the electricity had gone out and it was not expected to be fixed that day.

"Candles!" cried Madame. "Candlelight is more flattering for the complexion. We'll eat on the terrace because it's so hot." The servants brought what seemed like hundreds of candles, setting them carefully along wide balustrades and on tables all around. As the long day slowly died, they ate with their fingers from platters of Serrano ham and fresh sardines, creamy goat's cheese, olives, chunks of tomato, and soft, crusty bread.

Cleo licked the honey-sweet residue of almond-studded nougat from her fingers. This was better than any fine Parisian restaurant: eating good food, drinking a little wine, and laughing in the company of friends as the crickets whirred and the sun sank in a flood of molten gold.

Servants moved in and out of the shadows, lighting candles, removing plates, refilling goblets with the local rosé wine—its refreshing chill welcome in the heat.

"Cleo?" She squinted up to see Philippe Santerre standing by her chair. "Would you care for a walk before it gets too dark?"

The balmy sea air whispered through the trees and made the candlelight around them flicker. Some of the lights snuffed out, giving off a whiff of waxy smoke. Cleo smiled. "I'd like that."

They picked their way along the stony ground to where a rough path wound along the cliff. Cleo skidded a little and was obliged to grab hold of Philippe's arm to avoid calamity. "I wish I'd worn my plimsolls! These shoes are pretty but entirely impractical."

He laughed, putting an arm around her to steady her. "Oh, but I don't mind at all."

Hmm. The conversation she had had with Brodie at the Ritz that day came back to her. She let go of Philippe and stepped away. "I think we'd best go back, don't you?"

"But wait," said Philippe, taking her hand in a firm grip. "We're nearly there." He led her around a bend. "Look."

The view merited the reverent tone in his voice. He turned his head to look back at her, his smile more dazzling than the setting sun. "See?"

"Oh, yes!" she breathed. In almost every direction, there was blue, the sea reflecting the sky so perfectly that the white ships on the horizon seemed to float like clouds in midair.

She met Santerre's gaze and it was as if the Mediterranean was in his eyes, too, a lucent sea of shifting blues and greens, surrounding a sunburst of yellow that radiated from the black pupil. The thick, black lashes and heavy brows made his eyes more brilliant. *Too much,* she thought. *You are altogether too much for any girl. Far too much for me.*

Gently she drew apart from him, wrapped her arms around herself. The wind had picked up and the sun was fast dipping below the horizon. "We'd best get back."

"Are you cold? Here." The silk lining of his jacket whispered against the voile of her dress as he settled it around her. His hands lingered a moment too long on her shoulders but he released her before she formed the words to protest.

She turned to go and for safety she had to accept Philippe's assistance as they picked their way along the top of the cliff. She wobbled as a loose rock shot from beneath her foot. He steadied her and she laughed breathlessly. "Curse these infernal shoes of mine! I'd go barefoot if the ground weren't so stony."

When they reached flatter terrain, Philippe bent and swept her up into his arms.

"What? Don't!" She hit his shoulder, but not very hard. He really didn't mean anything by it. "Oh, do put me down."

Deaf to her pleas, Philippe carried her the rest of the way, only halting and setting her on her feet when they came within sight of the villa. For one breathless moment in the gathering darkness, she felt his gaze searching her face. Then he bent his head and pressed his lips to hers.

His kiss was sweet from the nougat they'd eaten, and light and heady as wine. She felt something inside her soften and sway, and instinctively her fingers clutched the soft cotton of his shirt. But this was wrong. She gently pushed him away.

Philippe raised his head. "Cleo, you drive me mad."

"Gosh, *do* I? I don't mean to," she murmured shakily. Yes, it was wrong to be tempted when she didn't love Philippe. And yet his warmth, the feeling of his arms around her, the feeling of being wanted, for once in her life . . .

He laughed, a touch angrily, she thought. "No. You've no idea at all."

They returned to the terrace without speaking. Cleo shrugged Philippe's jacket from her shoulders and handed it to him. He'd made it sound like she was a temptress, an affliction he had to bear. She didn't like it.

It was with relief that she saw the Graysons getting ready to go.

THE INFORMALITY OF daily life on the Riviera suited Cleo. Since that kiss, Philippe seemed to have beat a strategic retreat, and reverted to his former role of amusing companion. Glad of his sensitivity, if that was what it was, Cleo tried to determine the exact nature of her feelings for Philippe. The only man she'd ever been utterly certain about was Brodie. While her head told her she was free to love elsewhere, her heart seemed always to hold her back.

Still, she enjoyed Philippe's company and life on the Riviera was sweet. When they weren't joining the other guests for a sun-bathe on the postage stamp of dark golden sand that served as the hotel's semiprivate beach, they went on hikes along the coastline, and vigorous swims in the seawater pool. In the hottest part of the day, Cleo would loll about on sun loungers in the shade, reading or dreaming of the next pieces in her collection.

Some evenings, Cleo and the Graysons would visit friends at their homes for meals and those were the gatherings she liked best. But on occasion it was necessary to attend a formal dinner or a ball, either at the hotel or at one of the palatial villas along the coast. Cleo took careful note of the jewels women wore on these occasions. Although she had vowed not to put pen to paper while on holiday, she couldn't help sketching them and making notes when she got back to her room.

One evening, they were at a party thrown by Daisy Fellowes when Lady Grayson murmured, "Will you look at that?" She gave a slight nod toward the staircase that flowed down to the ballroom.

Cleo searched the crowd. "You mean the cape? I believe Schia-parelli calls that color 'shocking pink.' *Oh!*" she added when the woman in pink stepped aside. "Oh, yes. I see."

Cleo's heart began to beat faster as the orchestra switched from a lively jazz number to "God Save the King."

Standing at the top of the stairs were the Duke and Duchess of Windsor.

"God save the King, indeed!" Lady Grayson muttered. "Look at them all, curtseying to *That Woman*."

Cleo stood, transfixed, as the noise of the music and the guests receded like waves from the shore. Here was her chance. But her chance to do what? She had rehearsed so many times what she might say to the duke should she ever meet him, but now the various gambits she'd once thought reasonable seemed stupid and gauche.

His Royal Highness looked impeccable as usual in evening dress, while his wife wore a silk gown of pale blue that made the color of her eyes even more intense. Around her neck and at her earlobes and wrist she wore aquamarines and diamonds. Everything about her was cultivated perfection.

When the couple reached the foot of the stairs, the duke caught sight of Lord Grayson and waved. "We are summoned." Tucking his wife's hand in one arm and Cleo's in the other, Lord Grayson led them over to where the former King held court.

"Ah! Grayson," said the duke. "Delighted, dear fellow!"

The introductions were made. Cleo curtseyed but even had her tongue not been tied into knots, she would not have had the opportunity to speak.

His Royal Highness wanted to tell Lord G about a racehorse he had just purchased from an Irish breeder. "A prime bit of horse-flesh, this one," said the duke.

Wallis gave a thin smile. "If you are going to talk about hands and furlongs and handicaps and all that, I shall excuse myself." She spoke with an accent that was not quite American, and without moving her mouth much, as if her jaw was permanently clenched.

"Yes, yes, Wallis. You'll only be bored silly, I daresay," agreed the duke, but the duchess had already turned away.

The duke's grudge over Lord Grayson's advising against his

marriage seemed long forgotten as the two men fell into a discussion so detailed and technical that Cleo found it difficult to follow. Lord Grayson promised to visit the duke and inspect the horse in question.

"You will be impressed!" said the duke.

"I have no doubt, sir."

"And bring Lady Grayson, and Miss Davenport, too," said the duke with a smile and a nod at the two women. His gaze took in Cleo properly for the first time and he surveyed her as he might inspect a piece of artwork. "Delightful!" he pronounced, his eyes twinkling. "You have that certain sort of something, as the chaps say."

Cleo flushed with pleasure at his praise. But before she could answer, the duke turned to Lady Grayson. "I've been spending hours and hours in the garden at the château, you know. You will like to see what I've done."

At this, Lady Grayson perked up. While horseflesh did not interest her any more than it appeared to interest the duchess, the prospect of sharing gardening advice was something within her purview. Cleo expressed her thanks also, grateful to be included in the invitation. She could see why people warmed to the duke. There was such charm and vivacity in his manner. When the light of his attention shone on her, even briefly, she found it difficult not to bask in the glow.

Chapter Ten

Cap d'Antibes, France
Summer 1938

*T*he Château de la Croë stood amid a twelve-acre estate, and it took some time once they left the road to wind their way through the park. They arrived at the garages, where a liveried servant flagged them down and bent toward the motorcar to speak with Lord Grayson.

"His Royal Highness is waiting for you in the cutting garden, sir." He gave Lord Grayson directions. They turned off the main drive and motored on a little farther, past what turned out to be a tennis court partly screened by flowering shrubs. Lord Grayson brought the car to a gentle stop and helped his wife and Cleo out.

Stands of Mediterranean pines shielded the garden from the strong sea breeze, and it seemed degrees hotter as they moved through to find the cutting garden laid out beyond the trees. Cleo's neck prickled with a light sheen of perspiration and her head beneath its fashionable hat began to feel uncomfortably hot. The nerves didn't help. This opportunity might not arise again. Everything seemed to rest on how she behaved today.

Lady Grayson exclaimed in pleasure as she looked about her. Purple bougainvillea rioted over the garden walls, and everywhere, there were flower beds, varieties grown specially to be cut and tastefully arranged to decorate the house. Flanking the stone balustrade that separated the area from the lower terrace, there were bright orange-and-purple birds of paradise, soft, scented lavender alive with bees, and aromatic rosemary. There were vast beds of roses in every color a rose could be: from black, to deep, velvety red, peach, pink, lilac, and white. Gazing at the pattern the roses made, a color scheme for yet another set of jewels began to form in Cleo's mind.

"Hallo, hallo! Welcome to la Croë!" The Duke of Windsor tramped toward them in his Wellington boots, beaming with pride. He was dressed in light brown tweed trousers and a white, open-collared shirt that was liberally smudged with dirt.

Despite His Royal Highness's claim to be a keen gardener, Cleo had expected the real work to be carried out by underlings trundling barrows and wielding garden forks. That the former King should enjoy getting his hands dirty—as well as the rest of him—endeared him to Cleo.

Alight with purpose, he showed them around the garden and chatted knowledgeably about plants with Lady Grayson. A lethal combination of nervous tension and boredom began to creep over Cleo. She was feeling a little faint by the time a servant came out to invite them in for tea.

Lady Grayson asked, "Is the duchess here today? I didn't have the chance to speak with her the other evening."

The duke's brow furrowed. "No, no. Wallis is out today. I asked you here *specifically* when she wasn't in because these sorts of things bore her silly."

Seemingly unaware of any offense he might have given, the duke added, "Won't be a mo'. Just dash up for a wash and change and then I'll be with you."

The servant who had come to fetch them continued on, leading them through a series of rooms that might well have graced Buckingham Palace to a drawing room with a view over the water. The château was perched on a cliff overlooking the Mediterranean and the view was truly spectacular. "It's like floating in a cloud up here, isn't it?" she murmured. "Like living in a dream."

Well, at least the absence of the duchess cleared up one dilemma—did one still address her as "Your Royal Highness," as the duke demanded, even though the royal family had refused to bestow the title upon her? Lady Grayson had said she would never do so and she wouldn't curtsey, either, but Cleo was relieved they didn't have to decide. She didn't like to offend the couple when she wanted to get to know them better. And what did it matter to Cleo what the duchess wanted to be called?

The interior of the château was furnished in a regal style but with an eye to mixing new pieces with old. Regardless of age, everything looked as if it had been there for centuries, even though the duchess had decorated it less than five years before. That Woman really did have immaculate taste and she had exercised it to splendid effect. Certainly it was a house fit for a king.

Lady Grayson complimented the duke on the interior design and he nodded enthusiastically. "Yes, Wallis is a magician. She had everything ready and waiting for us in no time at all. She is utterly magnificent. I could not live without her." He grimaced. "It makes it even more painful the way she has been treated by the royal family and by my former subjects, as well. I *cannot* allow her to set foot in England unless she is accorded the proper respect."

Cleo spoke up. "You must miss England, sir. I do hope you return soon."

"Yes, indeed." The duke looked wistful. "Things might have been so different. But I don't regret it. I would do it all ten times over to be with Wallis."

Lord Grayson cleared his throat and there was a lull in conversation while the tea things were brought. Despite the hour, no lunch was provided, not even a biscuit. Cleo was too nervous to be hungry, so she didn't mind.

"I wish you will have a word with him, John," said the duke, and there was a plaintive, almost petulant note in his voice that made Cleo squirm. By "him," the duke must be referring to his brother, the King. "I mean, I could be useful. I could do any number of things to assist the Crown but he won't have me anywhere near him." His brow darkened. "Or at least, Elizabeth won't. *She* is the fly in that ointment, mark my words. Hates Wallis, you know." He chuckled. "Wallis has the drollest nickname for her—"

"I've no doubt." Lord Grayson's gaze flicked to his wife and Cleo then back again. "Shall we discuss the matter while we take a look at your new acquisition, sir? I confess I'm impatient to see him."

"The horse! Yes, indeed!" said Lady Grayson as the two gentlemen rose. To the duke, she added, "Perhaps we might prevail on your steward to give us a tour of the house."

"Oh! Oh no, I don't think Wallis would like that *at all*." The duke plucked at his lower lip, then said, "We'll leave you ladies to, er . . ." He gestured vaguely toward the tea things, quite as if he expected them to clear the dishes. Cleo nearly burst into laughter at the look on Lady Grayson's face.

Cleo was disappointed not to be given a glimpse into the duke's stables, but despite the fact she and Lady Grayson had been invited along that day, the duke clearly wished to speak with Lord Grayson alone. Left to their own devices in the drawing room while the two men went to discuss the duke's bitterness and disappointment, the ladies blinked at each other.

"I wish he'd agreed to the tour." Cleo drifted around the opulent drawing room, with its mix of rococo and Louis XV furniture and pieces of memorabilia from the duke's travels tastefully displayed, and thought of the many rooms above. "Someone told me there is a solid-gold bath."

"I believe there is," said Lady Grayson. She threw a darkling glance at the doorway. "I can't imagine why he invited us. Ought we to play a game of 'I spy' while we wait?"

Cleo was saved from answering, her attention caught by the sound of clicking heels that stopped at the drawing room threshold. Wallis Simpson—the Duchess of Windsor, rather—stood frozen in the doorway, as if she were a deer in hunting season attempting to blend into the trees. Cleo's stepmother? How odd that seemed!

Aware that Lady Grayson had risen to her feet but that she had done so out of Cleo's line of sight, suddenly Cleo couldn't remember whether they had agreed to curtsey to the duchess or not. She compromised with something that might have been interpreted as a curtsey or perhaps just an inelegant wobble. Either way, it was an awkward moment in the presence of a woman who, say what you would about her, was the epitome of style and poise.

The duchess wore a brown suit with a blue blouse and a blue hat, and a pretty sapphire and diamond brooch on her lapel. Cleo wished she could get a closer look.

"Your Grace," said Lady Grayson, thus firmly establishing herself in the anti-Wallis camp. No doubt her failure to call the former Mrs. Simpson "Your Royal Highness" would be reported to the duke in due course.

Those cornflower blue eyes lit with amusement but the thin mouth twisted to show that the nature of her amusement was cynical. Her attention wandered indifferently over Lady Grayson, then switched to Cleo, her gaze snagging on the brooch at Cleo's breast. "That is a stunning piece," she said, coming farther into the room. "Belperron?"

Cleo shook her head. "No, ma'am. My own design."

The duchess's thin eyebrows rose. "*Yours?*" Her tone clearly communicated disbelief.

Stung, Cleo was tempted to answer baldly, *Yes*. Instead, she explained, "I have been studying jewelry design under Monsieur Lemarchand of Cartier and at l'École Boulle."

A gloved hand shot out, palm upward. "May I see?"

"Of course!" She was especially proud of this piece, but it hadn't occurred to her that the great Duchess of Windsor would comment on it. Cleo hurried to unpin the brooch from the lapel of her dress. She closed the catch over the pin so as not to accidentally stab the duchess and handed it over.

The platinum brooch was in the shape of a uraeus snake, head reared to strike. Its sinuous body wrapped around a large, pearl grey rock crystal, then tapered to a tail below, concealing the hasp. The snake's skin was patterned with pavé diamonds and pink tourmalines, and she'd chosen dark pink rubies for its eyes.

"An unusual arrangement," the duchess said, inspecting the brooch closely. Her gaze flickered to Cleo.

"I like to mix gems and semiprecious stones. Of course, I know I'm not the first to do so."

"You are in excellent company," Wallis commented. "I have a few pieces by Belperron and Verdura myself."

"Expanding the materials I work with makes for an interesting palette, for different finishes and textures," Cleo agreed. She could hardly believe she was conversing about jewelry with the woman who owned one of the world's most interesting and expensive collections.

The duchess handed the brooch back to her. "Fine work. You have an eye."

Giddy with delight, on impulse, Cleo said, "Please. Would you like to have it?" Seconds after the offer left her lips, Cleo realized the duchess might think her impertinent. She flushed and stammered an apology. "Of course you wouldn't. Forget I said it."

To her relief, Wallis smiled, and this time it seemed genuine. "What a generous girl you are. But you keep it." She closed Cleo's hand over the brooch and patted it. "Cleo Davenport," she repeated, as if committing the name to memory. "I shall watch your progress with great interest."

"Thank you, ma'am." Cleo couldn't quite believe that her creation had received the duchess's stamp of approval. Wait till she told Lemarchand!

She caught Lady Grayson's expression—partly aghast at Cleo's blurting out her passion for design and partly relieved at not having to carry the conversation herself, if Cleo guessed correctly. She would apologize later. For now, she only felt exhilarated. That such an arbiter of taste as the Duchess of Windsor had admired one of her designs surely meant she was on the right path.

The duke and Lord Grayson joined them then, and the duke's anxious gaze did not stray from Wallis from the second he set eyes on her until Cleo and the Graysons left the château. He was like a schoolboy caught in mischief by a stern parent.

It wasn't until they were saying their farewells that Cleo remembered again with a jolt: that man was supposed to be her father. She still couldn't believe it.

Well, whether she believed it or not seemed to make very little difference to whether she could do anything about it.

If only she could ask someone for advice! She didn't want to hurt the Graysons by explaining the situation to them and she rather suspected Lord Grayson would dismiss Marguerite's wild tale as fabricated, in any case. More than ever, Cleo longed for the comfort of Brodie's presence. Too bad he was off traveling somewhere in Europe with friends, yet again.

MADAME SANTERRE'S PALE pink villa with its free and easy style of living was a welcome contrast to the Windsors' stiffly regal establishment. Whenever she had a surfeit of sun and sand at the hotel, Cleo persuaded the Graysons to visit or asked Philippe to bring her back with him.

"You should learn to drive," said Lord Grayson one afternoon as the yellow Hispano-Suiza climbed up to the Santerres' eyrie. "I'll teach you."

"I'd love that." She relished the idea of getting behind the wheel and driving along the stunning Riviera coastline by herself, the wind in her hair, a scarf fluttering behind her. Just like someone from the movies.

The sea air was cool against her cheeks, the sun hot on her bare head. The sky that met the blue of the Mediterranean was almost white.

She didn't often spend time with Lord Grayson on their own like this, but his wife had gone on a day trip to see friends in Cannes and both Lord G and Cleo had elected to stay behind.

"I'm sure you'll say it's none of my business, but how was your discussion with the King?" Cleo asked. The visit to la Croë had been playing on her mind for some days now. "The duke, I mean. I must get used to calling him that."

"Oh, there was nothing much more than variations on the theme you already heard," said Lord Grayson. "It is a terribly difficult adjustment for him to make. He wants a purpose, a significant role. But of course, the royal family want him to stay away. The new King doesn't stand a chance with his brother outshining him everywhere he goes."

"Are you still of the same opinion regarding the duchess?"

"Hmm." Lord Grayson seemed to be choosing his words with care. Unlike everyone around him, he never criticized the duchess, even in private. "She has been placed in a difficult position."

"Yes, I don't envy her, despite the jewels and the clothes and everything." Cleo wrinkled her brow. "The duke adores her, doesn't he? Worships her, even." She didn't say it, but she hadn't liked seeing the man who had once been ruler of the British Empire so . . . was "subservient" the right word? "I wonder how she does it. After all, the duchess is no beauty."

"She is charming and stylish," said Lord Grayson, as if determined to give the devil her due. "She can be witty."

"Hmm. I think it must be more than that, don't you?" There were rumors about the duchess, many of which were discussed avidly by the sun-kissed crowd at the hotel beach. Cleo tried to reconcile the salacious things they said with the woman she had met briefly at the château and failed. "Anyway, I thought she seemed brittle. Hard, but vulnerable in some way. I expect she feels as if she's always on show and people are forever looking for things about her to criticize."

Lord Grayson was quiet for a moment. "I've no doubt you're right." He turned his head and his eyes were warm. "You have a rare understanding of other people, Cleo. I wonder where you get it from. *Not* Serafina. She barely notices that other people exist."

She warmed at the compliment, and the sudden, overwhelming need to blurt out the whole, sorry truth of her parentage made her take the plunge. "Before I left Egypt, I begged the staff to tell me how I came to be left there as a baby." She hesitated.

"Wait a moment." Lord Grayson pulled over to the side of the road and cut the engine. Then he gave her his full attention. "And?"

"They didn't say much, but the little I found out led me to a certain lady in Paris. A Marguerite Meller, I believe her name was, at the time of my birth."

Lord Grayson frowned. Either he was a good actor or it was the first he'd heard of Marguerite. "You went to see her?"

"Yes." Cleo swallowed. "She told me she was my mother." Her voice trembled and she was afraid she might burst into tears. "But she doesn't want to have anything to do with me, I'm afraid."

Lord Grayson was silent for some time. Then he said, "That is her loss, Cleo. Some women do not wish to be mothers and are forced into the role, or perhaps their circumstances don't allow them to be good ones."

Cleo nodded and fought not to cry. She couldn't look at him or she would come undone.

"You are very precious to Lady Grayson and me, you know, Cleo." Lord Grayson's deep voice was gentle. "We have grown to love you and Brodie as we would love our own children." He cleared his throat. "I know that's hardly adequate, but—"

"Of course it is," said Cleo, reaching for his hand and gripping it. "It means the world to me!" Then why did she still feel like there was a deep fissure inside her, one that could only be filled with the love of her real parents?

She wouldn't receive that kind of love from Princess Fahmy. It was too much to hope for from the Duke of Windsor. She'd be miles better off accepting the kindness the Graysons showed her and forgetting all about the accident of her birth and the people whose sole tie to her was blood.

"Really, I'm fine," said Cleo. She wouldn't mention the Duke of Windsor. She wasn't ready to face the advice she was certain Lord Grayson would give: that she should never speak of it to anyone. "Let's not talk about it anymore and enjoy the day."

After regarding her for a few moments, Lord Grayson nodded and put the car in gear. They drove the rest of the way to the Santerres' residence in silence, each deep in thought.

As they pulled up on the drive outside the villa, Cleo thought how lucky she was to have Lord Grayson. Her fondness for him seemed to have crept up on her, unawares. She'd miss him when he went back to England.

"You should come back with us to Paris," she said, as he opened the car door for her to get out. "I—"

The breath was sucked out of her and a sudden, hard pulse beat in her ears.

In the doorway of the villa stood Brodie.

Chapter Eleven

Cap d'Antibes, France
Summer 1938

Cleo's throat closed over and her heart began to race. Maybe if she hadn't been feeling so melancholy after her conversation with Lord Grayson, she would have acted as if she didn't care. But she had never been good at pretending, particularly not with her child-hood friend. "Brodie!" Cleo dropped her bag and flew to meet him. "What are you *doing* here?"

She was reaching toward him when she noticed that his arm was in a sling. The blue blazer he wore was draped loosely over it so that at first, she had not seen the bandaging beneath. Cleo stopped abruptly, skidding on the gravel driveway in her flimsy espadrilles. Brodie caught her elbow to steady her and gave a grunt of pain.

Cleo gasped. "Sorry! I'm so sorry. Did I hurt you?"

The space between his eyebrows was pinched and his lips were pressed together tightly. Then he smiled. "Cleo. It's good to see you."

He slung his uninjured arm around her shoulders in quite the old way and hugged her awkwardly. Then he released her and shook Lord Grayson's hand.

"Been in the wars, have you, m'boy?"

"What have you been doing with yourself, Brodie?" Cleo demanded before he could answer. "I hope there's nothing seriously wrong."

Brodie glanced at Lord Grayson. "Come into the house and I'll tell you."

They followed him into the villa and continued through to the wicker chairs and occasional tables set out on the terrace that overlooked the sea. From below them on the next tier of the garden, they could hear splashing in the swimming pool, talking and laughter from several voices.

"Have we interrupted a party?" asked Lord Grayson.

"Hippolyte brought several guests with him to stay," said Brodie. "Including me."

"Really?" said Cleo. "We had no idea that he was coming down. I'm sure Madame Santerre did not mention it."

"It was a last-minute decision," said Brodie. "He thought I should come here to recuperate, rather than return to an empty house in London, and Madame Santerre insisted I'd be more comfortable here than at the hotel. And I must say," he added, gesturing toward the view of the bay and marina below, "it is a wonderful location for rest and relaxation."

"But what are you recuperating *from*?" Now that Cleo really looked at him, she noticed how drawn he was. He had dark smudges beneath his eyes and the golden tan of his skin had turned a sickly grey.

"As to that . . ." He glanced again at Lord Grayson. "You'll be furious with me, I daresay, but—"

He broke off as Madame Santerre flew into the room like the mistral and kissed cheeks with Cleo and Lord Grayson. "Brodie, what are you doing off the sofa? These boys!" She threw up her hands. "I suppose he told you what they've been up to."

"No, and we are quite on tenterhooks to find out," said Lord Grayson mildly.

"If someone doesn't tell me soon, I shall scream!" said Cleo. "*What?*"

"They've only been off fighting in Spain," said Madame, shaking her fist a little at Brodie and baring her teeth. "And very lucky neither suffered worse."

Cleo stared at Brodie, who stared back at her with a mixture of defiance and defensiveness in his dark eyes. "D'you mean to tell me you were *shot*?" she demanded. "In a *war*?"

"Is Hippolyte injured, too?" Lord Grayson seemed to be taking the news with almost devastating calm. Cleo watched him anxiously. She had never seen him lose his temper but he would be justified in expressing his anger at this news.

"He's fine." Brodie swallowed, the bob of his Adam's apple making him appear much like his younger self. Perhaps he, like Cleo, found Lord Grayson's calm ominous.

"I'm glad to hear it." Lord Grayson contemplated Brodie for a moment, before he said, "Brodie, do you feel up to a stroll in the garden? Cleo, madame, will you excuse us?"

Cleo wanted to protest, partly to save Brodie from whatever unpleasantness was to follow, and partly because she longed to know more about his adventures in Spain.

While the men headed toward the olive grove at the side of the villa, Madame filled Cleo in on the details. Of course Hippolyte and Brodie had fought for the republicans, as had so many other youthful idealists who were keen to hold back the tide of fascism that seemed to be engulfing much of western Europe.

"Not a word to me, of course!" Madame said. "And no contrition

at all for scaring me half to death over it when they came home."
She put her hands up to her cheeks. "My greatest concern is that
they will insist on going back. I depend upon Lord Grayson to talk
them out of it."

"Can't he simply forbid it, in Brodie's case? He holds the purse
strings, after all."

Madame shook her head. "He would disdain to employ such
crude methods. And Brodie is too proud to be swayed by money,
in any case. Lord Grayson is all too aware that he has no claim over
the boy beyond affection."

Cleo gazed off in the direction the two men had taken. "I do
hope both of them see reason. If anyone can persuade them, surely
it's Lord Grayson."

The two men rejoined them presently but did not speak of the
matter again. Cleo longed to pepper Brodie with questions about
what it had been like to go to war in a foreign country, but even
she could see that such an interrogation would not be welcomed
by anyone.

The rest of the party arrived in dribs and drabs onto the terrace, laughing and chattering Spanish. Philippe, who was wearing bathing trunks and nothing else, came up from the swimming
pool. His chest and arms were lightly muscled and tanned so
evenly that one might conclude he had spent most of his vacation
sans shirt. He shook his head and droplets of water showered over
him, glistening on his flawless skin. Several of the young women's
admiring gazes strayed to Philippe every now and then, and they
seemed to take any excuse to touch his arms. Cleo rolled her eyes.
It was lucky she felt no romantic attachment for Philippe or she'd
be annoyed at the way he flirted.

Upon catching sight of Cleo, Philippe paused in the act of toweling dry his hair and a smile lit his face. He made a beeline for her. "You're here! I'd given up on seeing you today."

Cleo became aware of Brodie's attention upon them. "Hello, Philippe. Oh!" she said as he bent to kiss her—not in the French way, but in the manner of a man greeting his lover. "You are very damp." Cleo pulled away, conscious that Brodie was watching them with an air of cynical amusement.

She shot the words like bullets in his direction. "Brodie, it's been so long. Can we have a talk? Just the two of us?"

"Later, maybe."

"I think now would be better." She stood and held out her hand. "Come and get some sunshine. You look like death warmed up."

He flinched. Did he see that as an unflattering comparison between his appearance and Philippe's godlike perfection? Right now, she didn't care.

"Your Majesty," Brodie said softly, and slowly rose to follow her.

They descended the sandstone steps to the now deserted lower terrace, where evidence of the young people's fun was all around. The pool still rippled with small waves that bent the sunlight into warped diamonds, and the flap of its skimmer box knocked in rhythm as the choppy water passed through. There were small puddles of water here and there, wet towels draped on the sun loungers, and a few pairs of sandals scattered around. A whiff of ubiquitous coconut oil overlaying the pungent base note of chlorine briefly stirred Cleo's senses. She turned one sun lounger side-on, sat down on it, and patted the space beside her.

Brodie took the place she indicated. They stared out across the pool to the spectacular view beyond, blue sea and sky, and below them, a glittering bay edged by a crescent of beach. Climbing up the cliff were ice cream–colored buildings in shades of apricot, strawberry, and peach, with their red-tiled roofs—all shimmering in the late afternoon sun.

"Why did you go off to fight in Spain without telling me?" Cleo asked. It seemed as if, these days, she held little importance to him. The knowledge hurt.

"You would have insisted on coming along."

She snorted. "I'm not that brave. Not that foolish, either."

That made him frown. "Foolish?"

She waved a hand. "To think of war as some sort of big adventure."

He stared at her. "You think that's why I went?"

She worked at her temples with her fingertips. "No, of course not. I'm sure you went because you thought the cause was right. Only I don't think it's in me to risk my life for a principle. I would fight for my country, of course . . ."

"And which country would that be?"

She smiled ruefully. "Good point." France? England? She hardly knew. Egypt? But who was she to fight for Egypt? She'd lived such a sheltered, otherworldly existence at Shepheard's Hotel.

Cleo scrunched her toes. "There is so much for us to catch up on, I don't know where to start. Tell me all about what you've been doing first."

His gaze searched her face. "I'd rather hear about you."

He seemed sincere, so she told him about her London season, the friends she'd made, about the King's abdication and all the trouble Lord G had over it, about her lessons with Lemarchand and at l'École Boulle. She wanted to confide in him about Madame Fahmy and the duke, but something held her back. Fear of his skepticism, perhaps.

"You are staying in Paris indefinitely, then?" said Brodie.

She nodded. "I'm going to be the next Suzanne Belperron." But of course he wouldn't know who that was. "I want to start my own jewelry brand. Like Cartier or Boucheron."

"Philippe mentioned some of this to me." Brodie stared straight ahead. "Going into business is risky. Wouldn't you prefer to get married?"

"Why? Are *you* proposing?" Cleo said it flippantly, but her heart gave a sharp pound.

Brodie hesitated. "I'm asking what it is you really want. Why do you need to make a business out of selling your creations? Isn't it better to do it as a passion, something you love? You don't need to work for a living."

Cleo plucked at the scarf around her throat. "I want to be independent. Surely you understand that."

"Hmm. To a point, I suppose I do." He clasped his hands together. "I just never . . . I mean, I suppose I expected you to be engaged by now."

Was he trying to find out what was between her and Philippe Santerre without appearing jealous or declaring his own feelings? She wanted to punch something. "Why does it matter to you whether I get married or not?"

He didn't give her an answer. His position hadn't changed, then. He wanted to make something of himself, whatever that meant. Until then, he wouldn't even admit he cared.

Impatience welled up inside her, but she understood the reason he hesitated. Pride. It was simply a part of who he was. What could she do but accept it? She couldn't drag a confession out of him. "Why don't you tell me about yourself. Not Spain, if you'd rather not, but your studies, your travels."

When he saw that she was interested and not just being polite, he told her much more than his letters ever revealed. As they talked, she could feel their old connection warming, glowing, strengthening, like steel tempering in a forge. She half resented him for it. To say what was in her heart would only make things harder for him. But really, if he hadn't wanted her to feel this way, he oughtn't to have gotten himself shot.

"Can I see your wound?" she asked.

"What, now?" There was exasperation in his voice, but amused recognition and a suggestion of relief, too. As if he was pleased to find she was the same old Cleo he'd always known.

She lifted the blazer he wore to peer at his bandaged arm beneath. "I suppose it wouldn't be a good idea to unwrap it now. But when the dressing is changed, can I be there? I've never seen a bullet wound before."

"You're a revolting wee lassie," he said equably, removing his jacket from her grasp. "I am not going to show you my wound. Next question."

"Will you tell me what it was like in Spain?"

He grimaced. "I'd rather show you my wound."

She smiled. The constraint that had developed between them seemed to have lifted, at least for the time being. She was happy simply to be with him again, even if she was furious at him for nearly getting himself killed.

Impulsively, she said, "There's something I've been wanting to tell you. I finally found my mother."

WHEN CLEO HAD explained, Brodie said, "The *Duke of Windsor*? So you're the daughter of the Duke of Windsor now, are you?" He shook his head and gave an odd, mirthless laugh.

"According to Madame Fahmy," Cleo said. "But I'm not sure if I believe her."

"Fahmy . . ." He frowned. "That name rings a bell."

"They're an Egyptian family," said Cleo. "You might have heard of them in Cairo, perhaps."

He cocked his head, as if still uncertain. "That might be it."

"Anyway, on that day you saw me at the Ritz, I was feeling rather low because Madame Fahmy had asked me to visit and then left town without telling me." Cleo drew a shaky breath and willed the tears to stay back. "She doesn't want to know me, you see. And it's been quite . . . impossible to raise the subject with the duke, as you might imagine."

Brodie looked aghast. "Cleo! You weren't thinking of telling the former King of England this cock-and-bull story, were you?"

His words struck Cleo like a blow. She'd expected him to be skeptical, but to hear him speak so harshly about it hurt. It drove her to say, "I don't see why I shouldn't! He might be a royal duke but he's flesh and blood, after all. He might like to know he has a daughter, even if I *am* . . ." She waved a hand. "You know." She'd never said the word before. "Illegitimate."

But Brodie was staring at her as if she'd just painted her face blue.

Cleo plaited her fingers together and gazed down at them. "I just want to know my mother and father. Is that so much to ask? But they don't want to know me."

There was a pause. Then a large hand settled on her shoulder. "I'm sorry, Cleo."

She wished he would hold her, but even if he had the use of both arms, she sensed he would refrain. "I'm glad you're here, Brodie," she whispered, putting her hand up to squeeze his. "I've missed you terribly."

He didn't answer. She looked up to see him gazing into the distance. His throat worked as if he found it hard to swallow. After a pause, he drew his hand away.

Had Brodie missed her all this time? Not enough. Not half as much as she'd missed him. "I can't believe you went off to fight without a word to anyone," she muttered, scuffing the tile with the toe of her shoe. "You could have been killed. And we wouldn't have had the least idea where you were."

"I left a letter, in case," Brodie said.

She turned her head and glared. "A *letter*? If you weren't wounded, I'd hit you."

His gaze shifted beneath hers. "You're right," he said. "I'm sorry. I thought it was for the best."

Ever since they'd left Cairo, he'd been trying to distance himself from her. He'd never promised her anything and she had no right to expect it. He wanted to travel the world studying wildlife, that's what he'd told her. There wasn't room in his life for her.

Abruptly, she jumped up. "I smell dinner cooking. They'll wonder where we are."

His eyebrows drew together. "Cleo? I—"

It took a great effort to smile. "You've turned into such a scarecrow. We need to feed you! Come on."

He had no choice but to follow her upstairs. As they emerged onto the next level, Philippe called out to them, "There you are! Finally." He seemed watchful, poised to start an argument. Oh, dear heaven, not now! Cleo shot him a forbidding look. Did he think he owned her? He was very much in the wrong about that.

Cleo was too preoccupied to be conciliating. She ignored the accusation in his tone and joined the others. She soon realized that Hippolyte's guests were refugees he'd rescued from internment on the French-Spanish border. Her personal concerns seemed petty and wrong, and that made her more miserable than ever.

Someone produced a guitar and strummed a stirring and complicated melody. Extra tables and chairs were brought to accommodate everyone, and the evening took on a spontaneously festive air.

Madame beamed upon the gathering. She loved nothing more than to be surrounded by young people, and to have her two sons with her was icing on the cake. She pinched Brodie's chin. "Do not ever frighten us like that again, do you hear? I hope you apologized to the *bon papa*."

Brodie glanced at Lord Grayson. "He was more understanding than I had any right to expect."

"He loves you, dear boy. As do we all." The words were spoken with a sly, significant glance at Cleo that made her feel utterly wretched.

One of Hippolyte's guests, a young Spanish man with a limp and a shy smile, had cooked them a feast. It was served all at once, rather than in courses—a variety of dishes with piquant flavors and enticing, savory smells: local olives warmed with oil and garlic, a spicy sausage in a dish that reminded Cleo of French cassoulet, eggplant in a rich tomato sauce, and succulent lamb roasted with lemon, rosemary, and thyme.

After dinner, the guitarist took up his instrument again and played a wistful lament that made Cleo want to throw herself off the promontory where she'd shared that kiss with Philippe. Many around the table joined in the chorus, their eyes glistening. The republicans had all but lost to Franco, and everyone knew it.

Lord Grayson murmured to Cleo, "I'd best be going, but if you want to stay . . ."

"No. I'm ready." Cleo shot to her feet, hoping she hadn't sounded as eager to be gone as she felt. In the darkness, she sensed Lord Grayson regarding her with concern. She collected her things, thanking Madame, the cook, and the guitarist for a wonderful evening.

Brodie came over to them as they said their farewells. "Cleo, we need to talk. Can I see you tomorrow?"

"Oh! I—I'm afraid I must go to Cannes tomorrow. Perhaps another day. I'll come up and visit." She was a coward, but she couldn't bear to be hurt by him again. Not when the pain of her mother's rejection was still raw.

She turned, to find Philippe at her elbow. He slid his arm around her waist in a gesture that could not be mistaken for mere friendship. "Come, *ma belle*. I'll see you out."

She felt Brodie's gaze upon her as she allowed Philippe to escort her to the front drive. In the shadow of the open doorway, Philippe said, "*À demain*. I'll pick you up at ten." He bent and kissed her, just below her ear.

"Stop it, Philippe." She pulled away from him. "There's no need for you to collect me. I'll take the train."

His eyes glittered. "You are different tonight. It's him, isn't it? Just when we were . . . He has come back and ruined everything."

There was nothing to ruin. Why couldn't she make him believe that? "You must understand . . . We grew up together." And why should she justify anything to Philippe?

"What I understand is that you did not take your eyes off him the whole night." He made a scoffing sound in his throat. "He has hardly been near you for years and yet he turns up like this out of the blue, crooks his finger, and you come running. I thought you had more pride."

His words stung like salt on an open wound. "Let go of me." She wrenched her arm free and ran down the steps, and out to the waiting motorcar, where Lord Grayson was putting the roof up to guard against the evening chill.

"What was that about?" Lord G glanced toward the villa as she got in beside him.

"Nothing."

His lordship eased the Hispano-Suiza down the steep driveway. "Hmm. Let me know if Philippe bothers you, Cleo. I'll have a word."

If only Lord Grayson could fix everything for her, simply by "having a word." She brooded for some time in silence, before she blurted out, "I hope you gave Brodie a piece of your mind, sir. I can't believe he would go to war without even telling us." That she was channeling her unreasonable anger into a perfectly rational complaint did not escape her. She glanced at her companion. "He said you were pretty decent about it. How could you have been?"

"Well, Cleo, what good would it have done to scold him? I can imagine no better way to drive him back to Spain. Besides, I've no claim on Brodie, nor any right to tell him what to do."

"Does affection—*love*—not give one any claim? Quite apart from all you've done for him—"

"Well, he never asked for that, after all, did he?" Lord G shifted gear. "Brodie is a grown man, free to make his own decisions." The motorcar slowed as they descended a steep, winding road. "You will be happy to hear he intends to return to Oxford in the autumn." He glanced at Cleo. "At any rate, a war with Germany will put all of our plans on hold."

"You think it will really come to that?" Cleo hated the thought that there might be a repeat of the Great War, an entire generation of young men slaughtered for no good reason.

"I am certain of it," said Lord Grayson. "According to Brodie, the Germans provided weapons and personnel to Franco in Spain. That means they're testing their capabilities. Make no mistake, Cleo. The government might have their heads in the sand but those who are keeping an eye on developments in Germany are in no doubt. There will be war in Europe. It's simply a question of when."

CLEO'S INSTINCT WAS to avoid Brodie as much as possible after their meeting at the Santerre villa. Philippe's words came back to her. *Pride*. She had very little of that when it came to Brodie.

But Philippe had been wrong about the reason for Brodie's absence. It wasn't because he'd assumed she'd always be there waiting. Brodie had said he'd been prepared for her to marry someone else. That hurt more than the idea of his taking her for granted. That meant he had made peace with his sacrifice.

The worst of it was, she couldn't rail at him about it because he was only doing what everyone around them expected. He thought he was doing the right thing by letting her go.

Logic told her she shouldn't be hurt and angry. But logic did not seem to matter to her unruly heart.

So in the months that followed, she kept Brodie at a distance.

She tried not to be alone with him without making her efforts obvious, and Philippe was eager to aid her in this aim. Mercifully Philippe seemed sensitive to her mood and stopped pushing her into a romantic relationship with him; for the time being he seemed willing to return to their previous camaraderie. Obviously Philippe had his pride, too, because he began to flirt with other girls. The fact Cleo felt not an atom of jealousy over this told its own tale.

Cleo succeeded in avoiding Brodie well enough while he was an invalid tied to the villa, but once he'd healed he often turned up unexpectedly, when she was least prepared.

On the beach in front of the hotel, Cleo was stretched out on a towel wearing a swimsuit as yellow as the Hispano-Suiza, her tanned skin covered in coconut oil. Most of the patrons had already retired after a morning swim but Cleo had stayed, sunning herself and reading a book, her face shaded beneath a red-and-white-striped umbrella.

"Thought I'd find you here," Brodie said, looming above her, his shadow thrown across her body.

"You're in my sun." Ignoring the way her heart suddenly kicked in her chest like an unbroken colt, Cleo put down her copy of *Tender Is the Night* and gestured for him to move. "Sit down, will you?" She jerked her head to indicate the raffia bag she'd brought. "There's another towel in there."

"That's all right," he said, dropping to the sand beside her and stretching out his legs. "Lord and Lady G about?"

"No, they went back up ages ago. Did you want them?"

"Definitely not." He huffed a laugh. "They mean well, but . . ."

"They are coddling you to an inordinate degree," said Cleo. From the corner of her eye, she watched as he unbuttoned his pale blue shirt, noting he wore swimming trunks beneath. She transferred her gaze to the sea. "Not to join in the nagging, but ought you to be swimming yet?"

"My wound has healed." There was a large plaster on his shoulder, but that was more to conceal the raw, ugly scarring there from prying eyes than for medical reasons. He shrugged. "I won't be breaking Olympic records but I can swim."

"Off you go, then." Cleo reached again for her book.

He grinned at her and stood up. "Lazy bones. Aren't you coming?"

"You interrupted me at the exciting part," she answered, determinedly flicking the pages to find her place. She was aware of Brodie standing with his back to her, rolling his shoulders and stretching, the muscles in his back rippling beneath his tanned skin. He had been thin when he'd arrived back at the villa, but in the ensuing months, Madame Santerre had taken care of that. All to the good, Cleo thought. He appeared in the peak of health and would be well enough to return to Oxford soon, just as she would return to Boulle.

She took her sunglasses off the top of her head and slid them on. That way, she could pretend to read while also keeping an eye on Brodie. For safety, of course. She needed to be sure he wasn't overdoing it. If anything went wrong, she'd alert the lifeguard.

Yes, she thought, admiring the lines of his body as he waded into the water, then made a shallow dive. Safety. She needed to be vigilant.

As she watched him carve through the calm waters, Cleo felt the urge to join him and propose a race out to the pontoon, but she restrained herself. Racing would not be good for him, and it might well be dangerous for her to get so close. These days, she was aware of him as a man in a way she never had been before.

The two of them would only be in the same place for another couple of weeks. Brodie had said nothing further about Cleo's future or marriage prospects or given any indication he felt more than friendship toward her. Perhaps he'd interpreted her relationship with Philippe as a serious one and retired from the lists. Several times, she'd wanted to yell at him that he was a coward, that he'd hurt her terribly when he stayed away. But he'd made his position clear.

Cleo tried very hard to have fun in those dying weeks of summer. But the champagne sparkle of life on the Riviera had dimmed.

Like the beach scene through her sunglasses, she experienced everything at a distance, and through a filter of a painful emotion she couldn't quite name. Disappointment? Sadness? She was a person who needed to love with her whole heart and with glorious abandon. She was a person who needed that kind of love in return. That Brodie could accept she might marry another man meant he did not love her enough.

Those years without him had hurt. Not only because she'd missed him, but because he'd proven himself just like all the rest. Everyone left her in the end.

What if he had died in Spain? What if she had to go on without him for the rest of her life? Had he given her feelings a second thought when he'd gone off to fight?

Cleo wanted a love that knew no limits. She wanted a man who would put her ahead of everything else. Yes, that was selfish, perhaps, but she might as well be honest about it. She'd prefer to remain alone than to compromise. She wanted someone to love her with as much abandon as she knew she would love him.

Every time she saw Brodie, she felt the pain of the approaching void, when they'd both go back to their normal lives. But she only had to endure for another couple of weeks. Very soon, she'd be in Paris. Then she'd focus fiercely on her work and try very hard to be happy without him.

Chapter Twelve

Paris, France
Autumn 1939

*G*o back to England? Why would you do that?" Philippe Santerre regarded Cleo with shocked concern. They had come to Angelina for one last hot chocolate before Philippe returned to the Army. He had enlisted well before France declared war on Germany, but he seemed surprised to learn that Cleo intended to serve her country, as well.

When Germany invaded Poland, making a mockery of the peace Chamberlain had so proudly brokered, Cleo was forced to accept that her dreams of becoming a jewelry designer in Paris must be put on hold indefinitely. She had not finished her course at Boulle before Lord and Lady Grayson came to fetch her back to England.

"It's all hands on deck, my dear," said Lady Grayson. "You'll have to decide what you want to do. Most young girls I know are joining the FANYs or the WAAFs."

"But what about your studies?" demanded Philippe.

Cleo shrugged. "I'll have to defer my training, of course." The truth was, she hadn't been enjoying the course at l'École Boulle lately. She felt as if she'd learned all she needed to know. Was a formal qualification really necessary?

"Britain might have declared war on Germany but nothing's actually happening over there yet," Philippe protested.

"Still, it's where I need to be." More accurately, she needed to be useful, and unlike the French, the British were keen to employ women in all kinds of roles. She might even be given a posting in Cairo if she played her cards right.

Philippe didn't understand. "But why leave Paris when the home of fine jewelry is here?"

"There's a war on," said Cleo. "I think my ambitions in that direction will have to wait."

"But no," said Philippe. "Cleo, don't you see? I was serious about backing you financially. You can go into business for yourself here in Paris. You are immensely talented. Everybody says so."

Cleo smiled. "That is a high compliment. But really, dear Philippe, even if the timing was right, I couldn't accept such a generous offer."

Philippe leaned toward her, his face alight with zeal. "If you were a man, Cartier or Boucheron or one of those would have snapped you up by now. But *I* am astute enough to see what they cannot. You will set the fashion and those others will scramble to follow your lead."

She couldn't help laughing at the grandiose pronouncement. "You exaggerate, my friend. Even if that palaver were true, I don't feel ready. I don't know the first thing about running a business."

"That part is easy," said Philippe. "I'll take care of all the details. You will simply create."

That sounded so enticing, Cleo had to mentally shake herself out of the dream. "I can't," she said firmly. "I value your friendship too much ever to contemplate going into business with you. Please don't mention it again."

Philippe fell into silence and Cleo finished her hot chocolate. Glancing around her, she thought back to the first time she'd been to Angelina with Brodie and Madame Santerre. "How I shall miss Paris." With surprise, she realized she'd said the same of Shepheard's Hotel. Paris had become part of her, too.

"Let's hope the war is over quickly," said Philippe. Hippolyte had already left for his posting, but Philippe had a few more days' leave.

As they stood to go, Cleo saw a small, richly dressed woman enter the tearoom in the company of a middle-aged gentleman.

Cleo froze. After all this time, seeing her mother came as a shock.

Philippe noticed her hesitation, glanced at the newcomer, then said in Cleo's ear, "Keep walking."

Princess Fahmy's sad green eyes looked through Cleo, as if she were made of air. Then she turned to her companion and made some remark. Cleo made herself pass by Marguerite without acknowledging her.

Suddenly Cleo and Philippe were outside the tearoom and she had no memory of how she came to be there. She gasped as if she'd just come up for air and turned her head. "I have to go back."

Philippe caught her elbow. "She doesn't want to see you, Cleo. She didn't even seem to recognize you. Besides, it's not a good look, you know. Young ladies like you shouldn't associate with women like that."

"Women like that?" Cleo repeated icily. "That woman is my mother."

Philippe's eyebrows snapped together. Then he hustled her toward the street and hailed a taxi. "Come on. We can't talk about this in the middle of the sidewalk."

Hurt and angry as she was at Philippe, Cleo knew he was right. She couldn't go back in there and confront her mother. Marguerite must have recognized her, which meant she'd deliberately pretended she hadn't. How could anyone be so cold toward her own flesh and blood?

When they arrived home, Cleo told Philippe everything, including the details of her one and only meeting with Marguerite, although she omitted mention of the Duke of Windsor. "And that's the first I've set eyes on her since!"

Philippe listened to her, open-mouthed. "But . . . You said it was the maid. That she was the one who found you on the doorstep as a baby."

"That's true, but it was all a pretense."

"But . . ." Philippe ran a hand through his dark hair until it stood up in short tufts. "Cleo, do you know who that woman is?"

"Yes, of course I do! She told me she was a courtesan. Do you think I care about that?"

"No, no, there is more to it than that. Damn it, Cleo, if I'd known . . . But I *did* warn her off . . ." He seemed to be talking to himself. "*Mon Dieu,* what an escape!"

"What?" Cleo sat up straight. "Warn her off? Who gave you the right to do that?"

But Philippe was pursuing his own line of thought. "You seemed so different after your visit to her, I thought something must have happened, but you wouldn't confide in me. I wanted her to know you had powerful friends, in case . . . And my instinct was right. She's trying to ensnare you in her schemes. This tale about your birth . . . How can that be true? That woman—"

"I don't want to hear it!" Cleo interrupted sharply. "No matter what she's done, she's still my mother, Philippe. I won't listen to a word against her." She was breathing hard as she shot to her feet. "It was wrong of you to warn her off like that. How *dare* you interfere in my business, without even telling me? No wonder she won't see me again."

It all made sense now. The princess hadn't *wanted* to shun Cleo; she'd been given no choice.

Cleo wrote Marguerite a long letter, explaining the situation and begging to see her, but received no response. She visited the apartment in Place Vendôme several times more but got no further. In the end, Cleo was obliged to leave Paris without seeing her mother again.

MARGUERITE

Paris, France
Spring 1937

THE INSTANT CLEO left her apartment after her first visit, Marguerite began to make plans. First, she needed to gather all the intelligence she could find. About Cleo, about the family into which she'd been adopted, about her associates in Cairo and her friends and acquaintances now.

She also needed to establish a timeline of her own and the Duke of Windsor's movements in the year preceding Cleo's birth. One incorrect statement or recollection could sink her. After all, who would believe a courtesan's word over that of a former king—unless the courtesan was very clear and unequivocal about the matter? Unless she had proof.

Since beginning her career as a courtesan, Marguerite had kept a coded appointment book. While that helped somewhat with the dates and times of her assignations with the duke, it was a terse record.

She took out a leather-bound scrapbook. It was a compendium of men, their biographies, vital statistics, interests, dislikes, fetishes, and habits—everything she might have learned about them in the course of a liaison which might prove useful. This book did not mention dates but it contained ticket stubs and newspaper clippings.

A pity she didn't have the letters the duke had written her. They would have helped to prompt her memory about the specifics. Ought she to send for the copies? But she couldn't trust such sensitive correspondence to the post—nor to anyone else, for that matter. Her fingers worked at her pearls like prayer beads as she pondered.

Tabling that question, Marguerite wrote to her lawyer and to other contacts in Cairo and to old friends in England and Paris. She spent hours composing a letter to Serafina Davenport, care of Shepheard's Hotel. She made several attempts to convey her meaning but her language was so circumspect, she couldn't be sure that Serafina would understand. It was like smuggling sensitive information past wartime censors. One might end up using such veiled terms as to be incomprehensible to one's correspondent—particularly as Serafina was English and Marguerite wrote in French.

This was turning into a very large headache. To put her plan into action, Marguerite needed to be sure of her facts. She couldn't commit anything to writing that might throw doubt onto her claim.

Letters made excellent blackmail material. Moreover, they

contained evidentiary weight. No one knew that better than Marguerite.

She inspected the photographs of Wallis Simpson that had been splashed all over the papers, which she had carefully cut out and pasted in her scrapbook. One showed the King's mistress, as she had been at the time the photograph was taken, wearing a spectacular necklace of rubies and diamonds.

Marguerite coveted that necklace. It was precisely the sort of gift the young prince ought to have given Marguerite when they parted. By all accounts, the twice-divorced Wallis was no better than a courtesan herself. Had the King wished to marry a commoner— and such an unsuitable one, at that—why couldn't it have been Marguerite?

Admit it, she is cleverer than you ever were. That might be true, but Marguerite had a card up her sleeve that Mrs. Simpson did not. If she played it well, at the very least, the duke would pay her a handsome sum to go away. A sum she would only accept in jewels fit for a queen.

She rose from her desk and stood looking out the long window of her apartment, over the slate-blue rooftops of Paris. Marguerite narrowed her eyes. She could threaten to go to the press, but anyone might guess the threat was an empty one. Such publicity would severely hamper her ability to earn income in the future. No other man would touch her if she embroiled a former King in scandal, and no matter how large the recompense might prove to be for hushing up Cleo's existence, she was not ready to retire. Besides, once the story was common knowledge, her leverage would be gone.

No. She would carry out her due diligence, then she would contact the duke and begin to play her hand.

It all seemed so obvious, she wondered why she had not thought to employ this tactic sooner. Perhaps because she truly had put the former King out of her mind until his recent engagement.

Had David done the dutiful thing and hitched himself to a European princess, ascended to the throne, and kept Mrs. Simpson as his mistress on the side, Marguerite might have shrugged and carried on. But the knowledge that he had not been so far out of her reach as she'd thought when first they'd met fueled her ambition now.

Jewels. The duke showered upon Wallis Simpson the best jewels money—or credit—could buy. Surely he could be persuaded to spare just one stunning piece as a final parting gift for the mother of his child.

If only Cleo herself had an ounce of Marguerite's guile, she could have played a significant role in this operation. But one meeting with Cleo showed she was a romantic and an idealist, two words that Marguerite could barely contemplate without a shudder.

Marguerite had planted the seeds. The logical next step for Cleo was to pursue her other parent: the duke. But would she have the boldness or the connections to inveigle her way into that circle? Well, they would see.

Marguerite made a decision. She returned to her desk, picked up the pile of carefully worded letters on her escritoire, and threw them into the fire.

She would seek out all of her sources face-to-face, first traveling to England, before visiting her lawyer and Serafina in Cairo. Best to have all of the information at her disposal before she pursued this plan. She had tangled with the powerful machine behind the British royal family before. They could crush her if she wasn't careful.

Might Cleo ruin everything by pursuing her own agenda at

cross-purposes with Marguerite? She thought hard about it but she couldn't see how. Certainly Cleo might alienate the duke by accosting him and tactlessly blurting out the tale Marguerite had told her. But how could the duke gaze upon that young woman's piquant, fair face with its pretty blue eyes and golden skin, so like his, and her delicate frame, also like his, and not see the resemblance? The duke, being vain to a fault, might become irrationally enamored of this miniature, feminine version of himself. He might take her up as his pet, although he would probably face stern opposition from Wallis if he tried.

Worst case: he would spurn Cleo cruelly, and then Marguerite could make her move without compunction. He might even make Cleo angry enough to help.

The doorbell interrupted her musings. She turned in her chair, surprised. She was not expecting callers today.

Her housekeeper came in, bearing a visiting card on a silver salver. "A Monsieur Santerre, madame."

She looked at the card, then tapped it on the arm of her chair. Santerre. An old and venerated family. Unusual for him to visit her, rather than to seek an introduction through mutual friends. Ordinarily she would not entertain any gentleman who had not been formally introduced, but a spark of curiosity made her say, "Admit Monsieur Santerre."

The gentleman was young, and very attractive. He strode into the sitting room as if he owned the place and baldly refused her invitation to sit and take tea.

Marguerite's eyebrows rose. He was gauche. Coldly, she said, "Then perhaps you will come to the point, monsieur. I have a pressing engagement."

"It's Cleo," said Santerre. "Mademoiselle Davenport. I know she had business with you here today. Your maid, rather. I was hoping to speak with her."

That took her by surprise. Did he know what kind of business? "You were right the first time. Mademoiselle Davenport's business was with me, as it turned out. But you have not told me how that concerns you." She waited, a bland look of inquiry on her face. She would not play any cards before she saw his hand.

"With you, was it?" The young man's jaw tightened. "Then I want to be sure that you know, madame, that Cleo Davenport is under my protection—the protection of the Santerre family. Not only that, but her sponsors in London society are none other than the Marquess of Grayson and his wife."

"Indeed?" Cleo had omitted these salient facts. "But my dear sir, I think you are under a misapprehension. Mademoiselle Davenport sought me out. I did nothing to encourage her." She tried to read him. Did he know what her relationship was to Cleo? Evidently he was in love with the girl. "And does Mademoiselle know you're here?"

He frowned. "She doesn't. Let's keep it that way, shall we? Mademoiselle Davenport is innocent. Too innocent to realize the danger she courts in getting tangled up with you." His lips pressed together. "To be blunt, I haven't told her of your brush with the law, madame. But I will have no compunction in doing so if you seek to entangle her in some intrigue. If you toy with Cleo, you take on two very powerful families. I'll see to it personally that you are destroyed."

Fury boiled up inside Marguerite. She gripped the arms of her chair hard in a supreme effort to contain her ire. When she had sufficient command over herself, she said evenly, "There is no need for such histrionics, sir. I have no intention of continuing the acquaintance." She picked up the little silver bell at her elbow and rang it. "My housekeeper will see you out."

When Santerre had gone, Marguerite let out a howl of rage. She snatched up a glass paperweight and hurled it at the wall. But instead of smashing into a thousand glittering shards, it ricocheted off the wall and rolled under a nearby chaise longue. Balked of that release, Marguerite paced the floor, thinking furiously.

She had intended to use Cleo as a pawn in her game with the Duke of Windsor. Marguerite might be impulsive but she wasn't foolhardy; she had no intention of sacrificing the life she'd built for whatever she might get out of the duke. Santerre had made it clear that if Marguerite sought to bring shame upon Cleo by association, she would find the might of two influential houses of England and France ranged against her. And that was quite apart from what the House of Windsor might do.

Reluctantly she decided not to meet with Cleo again in person for the present. She could very well carry out her plan without Cleo's cooperation. The softhearted girl might turn out to be a hindrance rather than a help, in any case.

Marguerite sat down at her desk again to prepare for her trip. She hadn't enjoyed visiting Egypt since her marriage to Ali had ended with such explosive suddenness.

Again, her dreadful temper! It had always been her besetting sin.

Chapter Thirteen

Cairo, Egypt
Summer 1922

*I*n the years following her romance with the Prince of Wales, Marguerite became a very wealthy woman. She owned a magnificent collection of jewels, and slept with a revolver under her pillow each night to protect them. She owned a chauffeured car and a stable full of horses.

But no matter how much wealth she acquired, it was never enough. Like the jewels in her bedroom safe, it could all be taken away from her at any moment.

In 1922, Marguerite decided to marry again. Her longstanding lover, Jean d'Astoreca, did not seem likely to oblige her. There was only so far she could get with some men; like the Prince of Wales, most never remotely considered her in the role of wife. Paradoxically, the fact that mistresses (or more accurately in her case, courtesans) were so much a way of life and accepted in Parisian society made it that much more difficult to cross the line into the category of "wife." Marguerite looked about her for another likely candidate.

Prince Ali Fahmy was absurdly young, ridiculously wealthy, and utterly besotted. Marguerite had not exercised her talents unduly to bring him to this point; he had seen her one evening on a previous visit at the Semiramis Hotel in Cairo and immediately, she had become his obsession.

He sent her a message that night, offering to hold a Venetian fête on board his yacht in her honor. Intrigued but already committed to another man for her stay in Cairo, Marguerite declined. She would find out more about her admirer before she agreed to spend time with him.

Marguerite did her research and liked what she discovered. Although called a prince in Europe, Ali was in fact nothing of the kind. He was the son of a pasha who had been given the title "bey." His inheritance from both parents had been invested wisely in cotton fields, the value of which had skyrocketed due to the high price of cotton during the Great War.

At twenty-one, Ali owned a palatial mansion in Zamalik, a wealthy suburb of Cairo, a villa in Luxor, and an office building in Cairo. Addicted to racing, he collected fast cars as if they were toys and owned a speedboat in which he would zoom up and down the Nile, to the consternation of everyone else on the river. A sumptuous, steam-powered yacht, called a "dahabeeyah," was the vehicle for more luxurious and leisurely travel. Ali (nicknamed "Baba" after "Ali Baba and the Forty Thieves") spent much of his time careering from one European pleasure haunt to the next, a lifestyle that appealed strongly to Marguerite.

With this knowledge under her belt, Marguerite remained purposely elusive while Ali pursued her to Paris, then to the seaside resort of Deauville, and back again.

When she judged him completely ensnared, Marguerite allowed

herself to be formally introduced to Ali at the Hotel Majestic. A whirlwind courtship followed, and Ali showered her in expensive gifts, including fabulous jewels from Cartier.

She returned with him to Cairo, where the renovations to his palace in Zamalik were finally complete.

Marriage to Ali Fahmy would bring security, and his status as a diplomat would give Marguerite an entrée to higher levels of European society than had opened their doors to her until now. There was the matter of religion—Ali was, of course, a Muslim— but what did that matter, if they could be together? And as long as Marguerite could convert to Islam and still wear Parisian couture.

Besides, she rather liked Ali. It was impossible not to like him; his love for her made him so generous. Uninhibited by the European upper class's distaste for vulgar displays of wealth, Ali loved to throw his money around. While pretending to aristocratic disdain, Marguerite reveled in his extravagance, especially when directed toward her.

Now she glanced around the Moorish dining room at Shepheard's Hotel in Cairo, where the tinkle of a fountain accompanied the sweet strains of a French orchestra. Yes, Shepheard's would be the perfect venue for the wedding celebrations. Let Ali's sour sisters shun her if they liked; she would invite the cream of Cairene society to the reception.

She returned her attention to the prospective groom, who had been fidgeting with the salt cellar for some time. "What is it, Baba?" she asked sweetly, laying a hand over his fidgeting one.

"You won't like this." He hesitated. "But I hope it will not put you off marrying me."

"Oh, dear," she said, widening her eyes as if in alarm. She had hired an Egyptian lawyer to make sure there were no surprises for her in the marital negotiations, so she wasn't overly worried.

"I mean," continued Ali, "I know what a devout Catholic you are."

Marguerite barely managed to refrain from rolling her eyes. Perhaps he had been fooled by the repertoire of devotional songs that she trilled away at, looking very fetching and innocent, while accompanying herself on the piano. It was all part of the illusion she worked so hard to create.

"What is the matter, *mon chèr* Baba?" she teased. "Are you worried for my soul?"

He was a handsome young man, if a little on the delicate side for her taste. His earnest dark eyes seemed to swallow his face whole. "Under the terms of my mother's will, I must marry a Muslim woman to keep my inheritance."

Marguerite knew this already, of course. "Oh, no! Oh, Baba, truly?" She only wished she was wearing the beautiful cross Jean had given her so that she might clutch it with suitable drama. "But however can I let you go?"

"No, no!" His voice edged toward panic. "You can convert, you see. It's a simple process. I will have my sisters explain it to you."

They would rather scratch my eyes out, Marguerite thought. "Well, I don't know . . ." She cast down her gaze and feigned reluctant confusion. Ali responded with pleas and desperate cajoling, and promises of every material thing her heart could desire, if only she'd agree.

Marguerite allowed him to turn both himself and his pockets inside out to persuade her. She was a born negotiator; by the time they'd finished their *poires belle Hélène* she had wrung several gifts from him in return for a concession she had been prepared to make from the beginning.

They were about to leave when Marguerite caught sight of a familiar face. Was it . . . ? Yes, she believed it was. Serafina Davenport. Did she still live at the hotel or was she merely wintering here, like Marguerite?

Serafina wore an opera cloak of bottle-green taffeta, and for once her unruly curls were rigorously tamed. Around her throat glittered an emerald and diamond necklace Marguerite herself would not have disdained to own.

She bowed slightly as Serafina swept past but the other woman didn't seem to notice. Marguerite stared after her, wondering whether to be affronted.

True, in Serafina's shoes, she might see Marguerite as a threat. But if Marguerite was to spend more time in Cairo, she would be bound to run into Serafina often. Briefly, she allowed herself to wonder about the child. She would invite Serafina to the wedding reception as a gesture of goodwill. One never knew when such a connection might prove useful.

THE RECEPTION MARGUERITE held at Shepheard's Hotel following the civil wedding ceremony had been a great success, if not nearly as raucous as the New Year's Eve party that followed it. Serafina Davenport had attended the reception but her manner gave no indication that she recalled their previous acquaintance. Marguerite decided to let the matter rest. She had too much else to think about—not least of which was the jealousy and volatile temper of her young husband, which seemed to grow worse with every passing day.

The couple spent time in Luxor before returning to Cairo for the religious wedding ceremony in February.

The evening before the religious ceremony, Marguerite sat at her dressing table preparing for bed. Her bedroom in Ali's palace at Zamalik was decorated with furnishings that had once belonged to King Peter of Serbia, a First Empire fantasy of blue and gold silk. The en suite bathroom even boasted a solid silver bathtub. By now she felt she'd earned every last fixture and fitting. Dealing with the insecure Ali required endless reassurances and the exercise of great tact, not to mention keeping her unruly temper in check. Thank goodness she did not have to keep up the pretense much longer.

She'd scarcely finished the thought when Ali stormed in, waving a piece of paper. "You must sign this."

"What is it?" She bent her head to read, then stared hard at Ali's reflection in the looking glass. "You want me to renounce my ability to divorce you? Even if you are cruel to me, or neglectful, or leave me for another woman?"

"Yes." He jutted out his chin. "That's exactly what I want!" Ali looked as if he had pumped up his courage and needed to blurt out his message before it deflated again like a punctured tire.

She observed him for a moment, then gave a slow blink. "And if I refuse?"

He slammed a pen down on the toilette table, making her accouterments jump. "Sign it, or I won't go through with the ceremony tomorrow."

Refusing to be rattled, Marguerite continued to stare.

"If you love me, you will do it." Ali was breathing hard, his eyes fierce.

Marguerite sensed another hand at work here and asked, "Have your sisters been saying horrible things about me, Baba?"

"I take no notice of them," he responded, dismissing his female relatives with a wave of his hand. "They are mere women, and jealous."

Then it was Said Enani, Ali's private secretary, who had put him up to this. The older man had a powerful influence over Ali. Said, in turn, employed a secretary of his own who followed them both around. Some wit had once called Said "the shadow of the light" and his secretary, "the shadow of the shadow of the light." Marguerite felt the shadows closing in.

Stalling, she countered, "If you loved me, you would not ask me to renounce anything."

She picked up her hairbrush and ran it slowly through her hair. It was one of a set Ali had commissioned for her: hairbrushes and combs and scent bottles in tortoiseshell and gold, with "M" picked out in diamonds on each piece.

He did not perform the service for her as he had often done in the past, but the steady motion of the hairbrush calmed her sufficiently to apply reason to the problem. She must not panic or rush into anything. She thought back to her meetings with her lawyer. The wily Maître Assouad had said that her civil marriage contract allowed her to divorce Ali, and that overrode any religious arrangement. What remained unclear was her right to the dowry of six thousand pounds Ali had promised her, and her right to alimony should they indeed divorce.

Reluctantly she decided to give in to Ali's demand this time. He was increasingly volatile and she didn't want to give him any cause to call off the marriage altogether. She cut off his protestations with, "*Bien,* if it will make you happy and since I love you so much . . ." She heaved a sigh. "I will sign."

The couple spent the weeks following the wedding sailing up the Nile to the Winter Palace at Luxor, where a crowd had gathered to await the opening of the inner chamber to Tutankhamun's tomb.

Despite the tedium of the voyage, during which Ali's steampowered dahabeeyah ran aground on several sandbanks, Marguerite was delighted once they had reached their destination. She was in her element, lavishly entertaining all the attending dignitaries aboard her husband's yacht.

Marguerite mixed with Howard Carter, the famous archeologist who had discovered the tomb, Lord Carnarvon, his sponsor, General Sir John Maxwell, the Maharaja of Kapurthala, and various other local luminaries besides. It was precisely the sort of event over which Marguerite loved to preside, reveling in her new social status as Ali's wife.

Despite the frustrations of the trip up the Nile, it was an auspicious beginning to their honeymoon. They rode donkeys to Karnak and the Valley of the Kings to visit the inner chamber of King Tut's tomb. Marguerite, laughingly assisted by Ali, climbed into an open sarcophagus and had her photograph taken—only to be scolded by one of the archeologists for tampering so callously with the artefact. She apologized but secretly remained unrepentant. How many people could say they'd lain in the same sarcophagus as ancient Egyptian royalty?

But on the voyage back to Cairo, the trouble began.

"You are determined to make a fool of me," Ali sulked. "I saw you flirting with all of those men back there in Luxor."

Ali's brooding bordered on petulance, an exceedingly unattractive quality. "What if I was? Where's the harm in flirting? Are you saying you never *flirt* with the girls at those clubs you frequent?"

"How dare you question my actions?" Ali responded hotly. "I

cannot let you out of my sight or you are lifting your skirts for other men."

Quicker than thought, Marguerite slapped Ali so hard in the face that her palm smarted. Icily, she said between her teeth, "I do not 'lift my skirts' for anyone. I indulged in a little harmless banter, that's all—just as you did with that redheaded *salope* at the Winter Palace." It was in her nature to be flirtatious, as Ali well knew. She would not change her ways simply because she was married.

She'd unleashed this tirade in a rapid spray of French. Ali, astonished at having been assaulted by a woman, and Marguerite at that, stared at her with wide eyes, his hand pressed to his cheek.

Then he seemed to gather himself. She braced for it, but when he hit her back, the blow was so hard she spun away from him and fell against the ship's rail. He grabbed her by the arm and dragged her to her cabin, where he locked her in. A muted conversation and heavy footsteps told her he had posted a guard outside.

Marguerite went to the mirror and stared at the angry patch of red on her cheek. With a grim smile, she went to her little desk and snatched up paper and pen to write to her lawyer. "Send witnesses to see how my husband handles me," she wrote. "I am documenting everything, just as you told me to do. But for this, I need a witness."

With a burning sense of righteous wrath, she wrote a hasty account of her argument with Ali and hid it among her other papers. She inspected her face at frequent intervals over the next few days of her incarceration, observing how the livid mark turned purple-black, then grew a greenish tinge, until it gradually faded to bilious yellow. She was not let out of her cabin until they docked in Cairo.

Their row upon her release brought her fresh bruises. With bitter satisfaction, Marguerite drew the attention of several onlookers to her injuries, and later showed them to the doctor at the Continental Hotel. She sent her account of Ali's treatment of her to her lawyer along with a list of witnesses. But was it enough? Quite a lot of lenience was given to husbands who physically mistreated their wives.

Soon Ali began to go out alone more often, visiting dance halls and cafés where the lower forms of entertainment were on offer, and returned smelling of hashish and other women. Furious, Marguerite went out alone, too, provoking more rages on Ali's part.

One evening, she accepted another man's escort in a taxi ride home. When they arrived at the palace, they found an irate Ali waiting for them. "What the hell do you think you're doing?" he roared, pacing up and down beside the taxi, from which Marguerite's escort had cravenly refused to get out.

She left the taxi door open so the driver couldn't immediately move off. "Baba, stop it! I will not be lectured by you about a perfectly innocent outing."

She made as if to push past him but Ali grabbed her by the collar of her dress and roughly yanked her back. "Look at me when I'm talking to you!"

Marguerite squared up to her husband, speaking through gritted teeth. "And where have you been tonight, hmm?" He smelled of smoke and liquor and another woman's perfume—a cheap, obvious scent that mingled sickeningly with the patchouli he always wore.

But Ali wasn't listening to her. "My sisters were right. You look down on me. On all of us! I was a fool to have married you."

"You *begged* me to be your wife!" Marguerite hissed. "And what did I get in return, hmm? A *little boy,* totally incapable of keeping a woman like me s—"

She didn't get the final word out before he'd swung his fist into her face.

Pain exploded in her jaw. Warm blood filled her mouth with rust. The pain throbbed over one half of her face and reached fiery tendrils into her skull. When her vision cleared, Marguerite was lying on the ground, her palms scraped and bloody, her face a tight mask. She raised herself to her elbows, and through the open door of the taxi, her gaze met the shocked eyes of her escort. She turned her head away.

Another witness. Marguerite licked her bloody teeth and laughed.

Chapter Fourteen

CLEO

London, England
Spring 1940

The outbreak of war was a devastating blow. Lord Grayson had been predicting the calamity for months but Cleo had always held out hope that peace would reign. Brodie came home after another extended absence dressed in the uniform of the Scots Guards, and the sight gave Cleo a terrible jolt of fear. When she first saw him in the foyer of the Graysons' London house, he was laughing at something Lord G said, his arm slung casually around Lady Grayson's waist, as if he had just emerged from her fond embrace.

How things had changed between them over the years. Lady Grayson's discovery that Brodie was a distant cousin of *the* Scottish Gordons had something to do with it, but the great thaw in her attitude had more to do with Brodie himself.

Cleo's shoes clicked on the marble floor and he looked up, the laughter falling from his eyes, the crinkles around them smoothing, his lips flattening into a line. She might have thought he was angry at her, but she'd done nothing wrong.

"Hello, Cleo."

"Hello." She'd seen him seldom since that summer they'd spent on the Riviera. She no longer hugged him impetuously when they met. Somewhere along the way, she had crossed the threshold to womanhood and there was no turning back. There was no pretending that an embrace between them could be innocent.

In spite of her resolutions to keep a cool head in his presence, Cleo drank Brodie in greedily. He seemed to have grown since she saw him last, in height, perhaps, but certainly in breadth. In his khaki uniform he looked like a man capable of leading other men into battle.

Fear came in a freezing rush through her veins. It hurt—physically hurt—to think of him going off to fight, perhaps to die, in this war.

Brodie promised Lady Grayson he would write, but Cleo set little store by that. Even absent the vagaries of battle, Brodie had never been a regular correspondent.

She participated little in the conversation at dinner until Brodie addressed her directly. "You're in uniform also, I see."

"Just the FANYs," Cleo said. "Pretty tame so far."

Lord Grayson nodded as he cut into a pink slice of Spam. "I've been keeping an eye out for a foreign posting so that Cleo can use her linguistic talents." Lord Grayson himself was due to leave shortly for an unspecified destination. He was not eligible for active service, of course, but he meant to make himself useful.

"Do you think they might send me to France?" she asked.

Brodie's eyebrows drew together. "No."

"Certainly not," said Lady Grayson. "They don't send women behind enemy lines. What on earth are you thinking of, Cleo?"

"You'd never make it as a spy, anyway," said Brodie. "Everything you think and feel is written all over your face."

She turned to him, put her elbow on the table, and cupped her chin in her hand. "Oh? What am I thinking now, then?"

Brodie grinned and reached for his wine. "Something I'd better not repeat in front of Lady G."

"*I'm* thinking of Portugal, actually," said Lord Grayson.

"But I don't know any Portuguese," Cleo objected. "I'd be far more useful in Cairo."

"You're not going on a Cook's tour, Cleo," said Brodie. "You don't get to pick and choose."

"Well, what would I do in Portugal?" she objected. "They're not even in the war."

"No, but Lisbon is a hub of intelligence activity," said Lord Grayson. "All sorts of interesting things going on. Work at the British Embassy, that's the ticket. I know a chap. But I can only get you an interview, mind. You'll have to do the rest."

"No rationing in Portugal," put in Brodie. "You can eat all the custard tarts you want."

She eyed him scornfully. "As if that matters!" She turned to Lord Grayson. "You're not just trying to get me out of London because of the bombing, are you? I'm not going to sit out the war in safety while our brave young men go into battle." Her voice wavered on those words but she managed to hold herself together. It was the duty of all civilians to send off their troops with a smile. "What about you, Lady G?"

"I'm staying right here," she answered calmly.

"Now, Lyddy," her husband began.

"*No!*" The word seemed to explode into the quiet room. Lady G placed her fingertips carefully on the edge of the table as if to calm herself and continued in a modulated tone. "Cleo's right. We shall not hide in our little mouse holes while you men head into danger.

I'm staying right here in London, come what may." She smiled at the three of them. "And you will always have a place, ready and waiting, to come home to."

Lord Grayson's eyes warmed with pride. He reached over to put his hand on hers. "Quite right," he said softly. "Quite right, my dear."

The Graysons departed for the opera when dinner was over, leaving Cleo and Brodie alone together.

A silver cigar box sat on the dining table by the port decanter. Brodie poured Cleo a glass of port, then he selected a cigar, clipped the end, and slipped the cigar into his breast pocket.

"Shall we go out and sit in the garden?" The long twilight was softening to dusk. The air was warm, and while she and Brodie both had other engagements later that night, she didn't want to let him go.

They took their small cut crystal glasses of port and sat together, listening to the chirrup of crickets and smelling the sweet scent of jasmine that still climbed along the garden wall. The perfume reminded her of Shepheard's.

Brodie had been back, but Cleo never had. "Did you see Serafina the last time you were in Cairo?" she asked.

"We had tea together. But I didn't spend much time with her."

"How is she?"

"Oh, you know. Cursing the war and the suspension of work on her archeological digs. She's terrified the fighting will destroy the important sites."

Cleo kicked off her evening slippers and tucked her feet beneath her. She watched as a lone firefly danced in and out of the yew hedge that bordered the garden. The lawn had been dug up to plant vegetables long before.

"I'm going to get back there," said Cleo. "I need to be there now."

Brodie slowly shook his head. "It's all a mirage, you know. Shepheard's. It belongs to a different time. The Egyptians want true independence. And when the time comes that they get it, there will be no place for the likes of us at Shepheard's Hotel."

She sighed. "I know you're right, but I feel sad, all the same." Despite her failure to return in the past few years, the hotel still felt like a safe harbor, forever waiting for her to sail in. It was her childhood home, after all. She eyed Brodie. "Don't you miss Shepheard's?"

He shrugged, puffing on his cigar. The scent of it, spicy and exotic, was a pleasing contrast to the crisp night air. "You and I shared some good times there, true, but I can't say I'd miss the place." He contemplated his cigar. "I was practically a servant, not a guest, remember."

It was a sore point, so she changed the subject. "Lord Grayson told me your regiment might well see action soon."

"You know I can't talk about that."

"I wish you didn't have to fight." Cleo said. "But in your shoes, I suppose I'd want to be in the thick of it."

"If I'd ever had any romantic illusions about what war is like, Spain shattered them all. But I've seen how the Nazis fight, Cleo. They firebombed Spanish villages full of civilians just to test the capabilities of their weapons. It was . . ." He expelled a harsh breath. "I've never seen anything like it, and hope never to again. Hitler must be stopped."

And Brodie might well die trying to do just that.

He cleared his throat and set down the cigar. "I've got something to tell you— Hey, are you crying? What is it?"

She wiped at her eyes with a trembling hand. "Oh, I don't know. Nothing ever seems to go according to plan."

"We're at war, Cleo. Very hard to lay plans at a time like this. Hey," he said again, more gently this time. Rising, he took her hands and drew her to her feet and put an arm around her shoulder. She turned into him, and after a slight hesitation, he put his other arm around her, too. She smelled smoke and the sharp, clean scent of his cologne, and pressed her cheek against his chest, not caring that his uniform was rough beneath her skin.

"I wish we could stay like this. I want to be like this with you forever." She shouldn't say it, but it was true.

"Cleo, I—"

She hugged him more tightly, then looked up into his eyes. In the deepening darkness they glittered and the planes of his cheekbones and jaw were sharply defined. Her hands seemed to move of their own accord, smoothing his lapels, reaching up behind his head, settling on his nape, urging him down to her. But her lips had not touched his before he drew back, hands clamping over her wrists.

"No, Cleo. This isn't right." He was breathing heavily, just as she was, but he avoided her gaze. "You're feeling sentimental and it's our last night together before I ship out. But this . . ." Releasing her, he stepped back. "Let's not become a cliché."

She'd fallen from her horse once and landed so that the wind was knocked out of her. She felt like that now, as if she'd tumbled from a height and her stomach hurt and she couldn't breathe. She couldn't bear it.

Somehow she managed to speak. "What are you saying, Brodie?" It might be the last time they ever saw each other. How could he stand on principle? Unless he didn't want her. "Don't you want to kiss me?"

"More than anything." His voice roughened on the words. "But

I can't ask you to wait. I can't ask you to marry me, not as things are. I'm not going to take advantage of you like that—certainly not under this roof."

"*Advantage?*" Cleo put her fingertips to her temple and turned away. "Do you know how patronizing you sound?"

"Cleo. This feeling . . . it will pass, believe me."

"That's just the trouble," she whispered. "I know it won't." She squeezed her eyes shut and opened them again. She must not let him see her cry.

"I'm sorry, Cleo."

She didn't answer. There was nothing more to say.

Lisbon, Portugal
Summer 1940

TRUE TO HIS word, Lord Grayson secured Cleo an interview for a secretarial job in Portugal. Soon enough, she was posted to the British Embassy in Lisbon, where she had graduated from the intensive Portuguese immersion course with flying colors. She'd wanted to go to Cairo but there were no openings there, or so his lordship had told her. She couldn't help but feel he had another reason for keeping her away from home.

Cleo certainly could not complain about the lifestyle in Portugal, however. There was a vibrancy there that was lacking in London, where the effects of rationing made everyday life for its citizens increasingly grim. Refugees from all over Europe flooded into the city of Lisbon, desperately trying to secure American visas or perhaps permission to stay in Portugal itself.

Cleo worked for David Eccles at the Ministry of Economic Warfare, which entailed masses of paperwork, liaising with other departments, and appointment-keeping. Eccles was waging his own war on Germany, persuading and sometimes bribing the locals to prevent Spanish minerals and Portuguese wolfram from falling into German hands. In addition to her duties for the ministry, Cleo was taking a course in wireless transmission on the side as she'd heard they needed wireless operators and cipher clerks at Middle East General Headquarters in Cairo.

The frantic activity of her role was a blessing to Cleo. She didn't want to think about Brodie and the way they'd left things back in London.

At first, she couldn't stop going over and over that horrible night they had said goodbye. But she was so busy in Lisbon that the memory speared through her mind only once or twice a day now. That felt like progress. On one level, she knew that keeping herself so occupied was only delaying the inevitable. The day would come when she had to *feel* his loss, but she would put it off for as long as she possibly could.

One day in late June as the heat simmered in the narrow, winding Lisbon streets and made people fan themselves with their panamas in the outdoor cafés, Mr. Eccles called Cleo into his office. Sitting at the desk opposite Eccles was an unassuming type, also not in uniform.

"Close the door and take a seat," said Eccles, indicating the other chair pulled up to his desk. A friend of Lord Grayson, Eccles had been delighted to take Cleo under his wing. A handsome man in his midthirties with brushed-back dark hair and a cleft in his chin, he was well-connected and amusing, though his wit sometimes had a vicious bite. He had certainly not stinted on Cleo's workload despite the family connection, and she was apprehensive about what this meeting might add to the stacks of paper on her desk.

Cleo set her chair at a slight angle so that she could face both men. What was this about? There was an air of constraint in the room.

She looked inquiringly at the stranger, who coughed and murmured, "Good to meet you, Miss Davenport. My name's Smith."

That seemed unlikely, but Cleo accepted this without showing her disbelief.

Eccles leaned forward and clasped his hands together on his desk. "Now, what we are about to tell you is top secret, Miss Davenport. A matter of national security. You've signed the Official Secrets Act, haven't you, so that's all right and tight."

"Oh, absolutely," said Cleo, resisting the urge to childishly cross her heart and hope to die.

"If I may . . ." Smith uncrossed his legs and leaned toward Cleo, fixing her with an earnest gaze. "We've received word that at this moment, a VIP is on his way to Lisbon."

"A *V*-VIP, wouldn't you say?" interposed Eccles, his eyes alight with mockery.

"Could hardly be more 'V,'" Smith agreed, his expression as bland as cream. "We have it on good authority that this person and his entourage will be staying at a villa in Cascais," he continued. "The villa is owned by a banker called Dr. Ricardo do Espírito Santo e Silva."

The colorless Mr. Smith pronounced the name with such a flawless accent that Cleo blinked.

"You are fluent in French and German, aren't you, Miss Davenport?" said Eccles. "A smattering of Arabic, too, I hear."

She nodded. That had been one advantage of having a German

nanny and a French governess. The Arabic, she'd learned during the summer months she'd spent in Alexandria, where she'd played with the local children.

"And your Portuguese is as good as anyone's around here," added Eccles.

"Thank you."

"Excellent," said Smith. "Well, I'll be frank with you, Miss Davenport. It is of the utmost importance that we keep abreast of this personage's movements while he and his wife are in Portugal."

"The Espírito Santo estate is large, heavily wooded, and faces the sea, so it's bally difficult to defend," said Eccles. "We are most concerned about a commando assault from the water to kidnap the couple."

"Gosh!" Cleo didn't like the sound of this.

"The Portuguese secret police are in charge of their protection. We will have agents stationed all around, but we don't have anyone on the inside. Now, we want to put you on the VIP's staff and have you report back on the VIP's social engagements, conversations, correspondence, anything and everything he says and does."

"If he blows his nose, we want to hear about it," said Eccles, clearly enjoying himself.

"You mean you want me to work undercover there as a maid or something like that?" said Cleo. She wasn't sure how she would do as a spy. Subterfuge wasn't in her nature, generally speaking, and eavesdropping on people in their own home seemed like dirty work. She wasn't sure whether she could convincingly work as a maid, either, but that was beside the point.

Smith spoke. "We thought it might be best to offer your services as a social secretary and interpreter for the wife. Answer the telephone, make appointments, accompany her if she goes out, that sort of thing. They are required to have an armed escort wherever they go and, really, the Portuguese don't want them going anywhere at all, so I don't think there'll be too many excursions. They are, quite frankly, in protective custody at this point."

"All right," said Cleo. She'd be glad of the prospect of leaving behind the mountain of paperwork she had to get through every day, though she was a little anxious that said mountain might grow to unscalable heights in her absence. "May I ask? Who is this VIP? Ah, I mean V-VIP?"

"The Duke of Windsor," said Eccles. "I believe you are acquainted. Lord Grayson has sent a telegram to the duke to recommend you."

"The Duke of . . ." Cleo stopped, her heart beating hard and fast. "Yes," she said weakly. "I am a little acquainted with the duke."

Eccles nodded. "I've fixed everything for you, and Grayson has added his mite. Well!" He clapped his hands together, rising to his feet. "That's settled, then."

Suddenly her mission took on a different color. She was going to spy on the man who might well be her own father. It was too much.

Mr. Smith smiled at her reassuringly. "You'll be fine. We'll have you installed at the Boca do Inferno before the happy couple arrive."

Boca do Inferno. The "jaws of hell." Good grief, Cleo thought. What exactly was she letting herself in for?

DR. ESPÍRITO SANTO'S pink stucco villa was situated on a wooded estate on the outskirts of the coastal fishing village of Cascais. As Cleo discovered, the estate was named after a place nearby, where the sea had carved a tunnel through the rock, and waves crashed and flowed beneath the natural arch into a deep pool, pounding its walls and creating a devil's cauldron of the sea.

The eighteenth-century town of Cascais was not far from Estoril, with its famous casino and the opulent Hotel Palácio by a sandy stretch of beach. Mr. Smith told Cleo that the Windsors had tried to get a suite at the hotel but had been refused. The Palácio was at full capacity.

Refugees from all over Europe had flooded into neutral Portugal, applying for entry to other countries like the United States and Canada. Somehow they must pass the time while the paperwork was processed and their visas issued. The queues grew ever longer, the waiting time increased, and the casino at Estoril teemed with anxious gamblers desperate to forget their troubles in the turn of a card or the roll of the dice.

Into the heart of this confusion, the Duke and Duchess of Windsor arrived. Their entourage comprised the ducal couple in a Buick along with the duke's comptroller, Gray Phillips, and three cairn terriers. This was followed by a Citroën containing a British couple who turned out to be Captain and Mrs. Wood, with yet another small dog whose breed Cleo did not recognize, and the duchess's maid. The Citroën towed a trailer packed with luggage.

Along with their hosts and several others, the British ambassador, Sir Walford Selby, was at the villa to greet the Windsors. "A telegram from the prime minister, sir." He handed the cable to the duke, which the duke tucked into an inner pocket of his coat.

"I cannot believe I left my swimming costume behind at the chateau!" the duchess lamented as they went inside. "I'm sure I told you to pack it, Jeanne."

"Which costume is that, Wallis?" The duke, who surely must

have more important things on his mind, looked concerned. "Not the blue?"

"The eau de Nil. I never liked any swimsuit half as much." The duchess frowned. "Somebody will have to go back and get it, that's all."

Go back to Vichy France? For a *swimsuit*? Forgetting her nerves, Cleo stared at the duchess.

"I'll speak to Tiger about it," said the duke. "He will know just what we should do." He pulled at his lower lip. "Maybe the Americans can send it in a diplomatic bag."

Cleo listened in disbelief. The Germans had marched on Paris and set up a puppet regime in the South of France. The British invasion had been a disaster, albeit followed by a gallant retreat from Dunkirk. Brave men were dying in the air, on the land, and at sea, not to mention the dead and injured civilians wherever the bombs rained down—and the former King of England and his wife were worried about a swimsuit!

With a sense of unreality, as if moving through a dream, Cleo stepped forward and recited the introduction she'd prepared. "Good evening, Your Royal Highness. I trust everything at the villa will be to your satisfaction. My name is Cleo Davenport and I've been sent to assist you in any way I can with your social appointments and act as a guide and translator should you need my services."

"Davenport?" The duke put a finger to his lips.

"I visited you at la Croë with Lord and Lady Grayson one summer," Cleo supplied. "I believe Lord Grayson sent you a telegram to say I was meeting you here."

The duchess clicked her fingers. "The jeweler! Yes, I remember you." She quirked an eyebrow. "Here to keep an eye on us, are you?

Yes, well. As you can see, we are woefully short-staffed. I don't know *why* we have had to go about all this in such a pitiful way. We should have stayed in Madrid."

The Spanish, though technically neutral, were hand in glove with the Germans, so that would not have been advisable at all. It seemed odd that the duchess should not realize this when it was plain even to Cleo.

Cleo said brightly, "I'll do all I can do to make your stay here agreeable." She wondered how long it would be before they were on their way again. On the latest information Eccles had given her, the British government hadn't made up its mind what to do with its erstwhile King.

The duchess checked her watch. "I won't have time to rest before dinner."

"Who is it tonight, Wallis?" asked the duke.

"The Espírito Santos, of course, the Spanish ambassador and some others. I'd better check on arrangements." The duchess clicked her fingers as if calling to a dog. "Come, Miss Davenport. We have work to do."

The duke waved a hand. "Espírito Santo will have taken care of all that, surely."

The duchess smiled. "I always find it best to start as I intend to go on. You know how I am, my dear."

The duke chuckled indulgently. "None better. Well, then, Wallis, I believe I'll take a wander in the grounds." He whistled for his dogs, who came scampering up.

Cleo crouched to make a fuss of them, scratching behind their ears and beneath their shaggy chins. She looked up. "I miss having dogs! How lovely to have them here with you."

The duke smiled down at Cleo and it was as if the sun had entered the room. Cleo blinked and smiled back. She straightened, brushing a little at her skirt.

"Look after the duchess, won't you, Miss Davenport?" he told her. "This whole business has been quite a trial, you know."

"I will do my best, sir."

As she left the room with the duchess, Cleo glanced back. The duke had taken the prime minister's telegram out of his pocket and was reading it. His eyebrows slammed together and his face reddened beneath its tan.

What had the telegram said? If it was from the prime minister, presumably Smith would have another way to discover its contents. She needn't worry about finding out. She hurried to keep up with the duchess's brisk stride.

The duchess's standards were as exacting as any true queen's, although in fact Cleo doubted any British monarch would concern herself with such matters as replacing the host's table linen with her own, requiring it all to be unpacked, aired, and pressed in record time, or rejecting the butler's choice of wines and sending to the Hotel Palácio for a selection of the best French vintages from the hotel's well-stocked cellars.

"The table setting is all anyhow," she told the butler, frowning. "You need to measure the distances precisely, like they do at Buckingham Palace. His Royal Highness is most particular. I can't *imagine* why you weren't provided with the proper instructions in advance of our arrival."

She rattled off measurements, from the distance the chairs should be placed from the dining table, to the space between the place setting and the table's edge, and Cleo translated, couching the duchess's orders in more polite terms. Looking shaken, the butler bowed and went off to find an appropriate measuring stick.

The duchess sent the crystal back to the kitchens to be polished but seemed happy enough with the sparkling cutlery and plates.

When everything was to her satisfaction, Wallis turned to Cleo. "Tell Jeanne to order my bath and then go get dressed for dinner. Come to my room in three quarters of an hour."

As Cleo passed the front hall, she saw a visitor hand his hat to the butler. "Don Miguel Primo de Rivera y Saenz de Heredia to see His Royal Highness." What a mouthful! She repeated the name over and over under her breath until she could find pen and paper to write it down.

Cleo knocked on the door to the duchess's bedroom at the appointed time. The duchess was dressed in a slip and stockings, her makeup and hair immaculate, as ever. Cleo wondered if she simply woke up every day with every strand of dark hair already in place.

The gown the duchess had chosen was a violet silk patterned with tracings of silver. Her necklace was sapphire and diamond and she wore a bracelet and earrings to match. Jeanne held out the gown for the duchess to step into, careful not to crush the delicate fabric. As the maid fastened the tiny buttons up the back, the duchess murmured, "What do you think of this necklace, Cleo? Not too much for a dinner at home?"

"Not at all," said Cleo. The sapphires were magnificent, as all the duchess's jewels were. She didn't recognize this particular parure. Perhaps it hadn't been purchased at Cartier. She noticed, however, that the duchess still wore her Cartier bracelet with nine crucifix charms dangling from it. A gift from the duke on their wedding day, Lemarchand had told Cleo, each cross inscribed with a significant event of their courtship.

Monsieur Lemarchand had returned to Paris before the war. Cleo wished he hadn't stayed there. He insisted he had nothing to fear, but he was a rebel at heart, accustomed to going his own way. She hoped he would be sensible and not do anything to provoke the occupiers.

Would Cartier remain open in the City of Light? She had heard that Jeanne Toussaint and the Cartiers had fled south to the Basque region. The great Louis Cartier himself was recently in Lisbon, waiting for passage to America.

Cleo didn't expect to learn much of interest at the dinner. Surely there would be little indiscreet talk with the Spanish ambassador there.

However, even before they were summoned to the table, the duke had launched into complaints about the British treatment of him. "Received the most impudent telegram from Churchill. Even he has turned against me."

The duchess ignored this, or at least, she pretended not to have heard, holding court with the Spanish ambassador and his wife.

Later in the evening, as the duke drank steadily and often, he became even looser in his talk. "Bomb the blazes out of London and they'll soon come to their senses. War . . ." He shook his head. "Germany is too strong, too powerful. Britain must sue for peace at any cost."

Cleo felt the blood rush to her head. What sort of talk was this for any Briton, much less for a former King? Winston Churchill was adamant that nothing but force would stop the Nazis. Anyone who had watched Hitler ride roughshod over Europe could see that. Why on earth should he treat Britain any differently?

Surely it was the brandy talking. The duke couldn't truly think like that, could he? Uneasily Cleo wondered what other loose talk she'd be obliged to report back to Mr. Smith.

Chapter Fifteen

*O*ne evening in the company of the Windsors showed Cleo why she'd been given the task of monitoring them. Out of loyalty to the duke, she had given him the benefit of the doubt, but the dinner with the Spanish ambassador had convinced her that it was her duty to tell Smith everything she'd heard.

The duchess had given Cleo the afternoon off because the Windsors were going to lunch with David Eccles and some others from the embassy, so Cleo telephoned the number Smith had given her and made an appointment, then drove her little hunter green Fiat back to Lisbon and let herself into her apartment.

Mr. Smith was there waiting for her, sitting in her favorite chair and reading the *Jornal do Comércio*. She jumped, her heart pounding. "Gosh, you gave me a fright! How did you get in?"

"Sorry." He folded his newspaper and set it aside, ignoring her question. "What do you have for me?"

Cleo rattled off a list of the guests at dinner and recited the duke's indiscretions. There had been many, and she'd caught the Spanish ambassador exchanging a knowing look with one of his countrymen.

"It's almost as if he wants Hitler to win!" said Cleo.

"Oh, I don't think so," said Smith. "But he was greatly affected by the horrors he witnessed in the last war, you know. I think he believes Britain will never win, and we would do better to negotiate while we are still in a position to do so. It's defeatist, of course, and not what we want spread about. But he certainly doesn't *want* Germany to win."

Mr. Smith sat staring into nothing for a few moments. Then he tapped a fingertip on his folded newspaper. "Perhaps it would be best if I explain the situation a little further. Why don't we go for a walk outside?"

The heat was stifling in the apartment, which had been shut up for the past two days, so this was a welcome suggestion. "I'll just get my hat," said Cleo. She chose a straw panama with a shiny blue bandeau and joined Mr. Smith. They went down the winding staircase that led to the foyer of Cleo's apartment building and out into the shimmering bright summer's day.

"This heat is quite oppressive isn't it?" Mr. Smith took his hat off and fanned his face with it.

"I am fairly accustomed to it, having grown up in Cairo," said Cleo.

"Cairo?" Mr. Smith raised his eyebrows. "Ah, yes. I seem to recall your mentioning you spoke Arabic."

"I have a knack for languages although I never studied ancient ones the way my guardian did. Serafina Davenport. Have you heard of her? She is quite a well-known scholar."

"Hmm. Can't say I've had the pleasure."

"She tried very hard to educate me but when it became clear that I would never reach her standards of learning and my interest in Egyptian tombs and mummies and things like that was minimal, she gave up on me. But that's all right. She found a new protégé."

What was Brodie doing now? Wherever he was, she prayed he was safe.

"I would like to be posted to Cairo," she continued. The more people she told, the more likely it was that when a posting came up, they would think of her. "I feel I could be of most use there. I'm taking a wireless operating course, too."

"Why do I get the impression that you have another reason for returning home?" said Mr. Smith. "Is there a man, perhaps?"

"Goodness, no!" She'd been out with a couple of young men, but nothing serious, and no one at all since she'd come to Lisbon. No one to help her forget Brodie.

"I see." Smith stopped by a kiosk selling newspapers and magazines. Briefly he perused the front page of that morning's *O Século*, but did not buy anything.

The suspicion that Mr. Smith was a spy popped into her head once more. Didn't intelligence operatives make dead drops at newspaper kiosks all the time?

As they moved on, Mr. Smith took Cleo's hand and drew it through the crook of his arm, responding to her automatic recoil with, "No, don't pull away. It's better to appear as if we are a couple, don't you think? It will explain our continuing acquaintance."

"Well, you might have warned me what you were going to do before you did it," said Cleo. "What's all this about?"

"There are spies everywhere in this city. They might take an interest in the movements of a young lady in a position such as yours. In fact, don't look, but there's someone from the Portuguese secret police following us now. You'd think they'd have better things to do."

Cleo forced herself not to check behind them. "And do they take an interest in your position?" she asked. "What *is* your position, exactly?"

"Ah! Here we are." They had come to an ice cream shop with a red-and-white-striped awning that had a long queue outside it.

"Care for a *gelado*?" asked Smith, quite as if he hadn't just been warning her about cloak-and-dagger intrigue. "There will be quite a wait but trust me, it will be worth it."

Cleo nodded, but she was becoming more confused. As they chatted about Cairo and Shepheard's and Cleo's childhood there, she studied her companion carefully. Behind the horn-rimmed glasses, he had rather fine eyes, a silvery grey with dark lashes that made them seem almost translucent. His skin was tanned, which seemed to belie his claim to be unaccustomed to hot climates. She wondered whether he always spoke the truth about himself, or any truth at all.

"Remember, everyone has their own agenda," Lord Grayson had told her before she'd accepted the Lisbon posting. "Follow your own instincts and make your own judgments about people. Safest not to trust anyone too far."

She supposed Smith must be all right because Eccles had vouched for him. Still, was it necessary to pretend to be lovers? Was he doing that for the mission or because . . . well, she supposed that was terribly vain of her, wasn't it? Better to take what he said at face value.

They arrived at the head of the line for ice cream and Smith looked down at her. "Will you let me order for you?" Without waiting for an answer, he ordered two cones.

Cleo stripped off her gloves and put them in her purse, then accepted the sour cherry cone from him. She took a tentative taste. Tart and sweet. The perfect balance. They walked on until they came to Parque Eduardo VII. The air was noticeably cooler as they moved into the shade of the silky oak trees along the patterned walks but the path was on a steep incline, so Cleo was glad when Smith headed for a bench not far away. It was too hot to climb hills today, even though the view from the top was spectacular.

Cleo licked at her ice cream, which was melting in the heat. She would make it her mission to try every flavor before the summer was out.

"What do you think?" Smith watched her with a smug expression.

"Generally speaking, I prefer to order for myself," said Cleo. "But this is delicious. Thank you."

She held it out to him. "Care to try?"

For the first time, he smiled at her. "Please." Smith encircled her hand with his to hold the ice cream steady and bent to taste.

Cleo felt an odd fluttering sensation in her stomach. He was flirting, but it was all part of the act, wasn't it? When Smith lifted his head, there was a smudge of red at the corner of his lips, as if he'd been kissing a lipsticked mouth. She knew an urge to wipe it off with her thumb, but that might be taken as real flirtation rather than the pretend kind.

"You're dripping," she told him, indicating his own ice cream, which was now weeping beige rivulets onto his hand.

He didn't immediately break eye contact. "Am I?"

Flustered, Cleo held out her ice cream to him. "Take this." She opened her purse and took out her handkerchief, then exchanged it for her cone.

He seemed amused and wiped at his hand. "Thank you. I'll

have this laundered and returned to you. Would you like some of my *gelado*?" He made a face. "Although I suppose it's not quite so appealing now."

She declined. "I'll order hazelnut next time."

He dumped the rest of his ice cream in a trash can, then rejoined her on the bench. "Now, let me tell you all about the Windsors."

After war broke out, the duke had been stationed in Paris with the British military mission to France. However as the Germans swept all before them, he became concerned about the duchess. The duke took the duchess down to Biarritz and saw to it that she was comfortable, then he returned to Paris.

However, soon afterward, he left his post without warning or permission from his superior officers, and traveled back to Biarritz, collected his wife, and took her to the Château de la Croë. From there, they packed up and went back along the coast, into Spain, stopping at Madrid.

"Now, this is where it gets interesting," said Smith. "Madrid is crawling with Nazis and Nazi sympathizers. So you would think the duke might be keen to leave that city for Portugal as soon as possible."

"I should rather think so, yes," said Cleo. "But the duke doesn't seem to see the Germans as the enemy at all."

"What you must remember is that he has family in Germany. I mean, the Windsors—the Saxe-Coburg and Gothas, as they were called until they changed their name during the Great War—were German originally, after all. The duke spent the happiest time of his life in that country with his cousins, away from the harsh criticism of his father. The outbreak of the Great War was a tragedy for the Prince of Wales, as he then was. He loves Germany, speaks the language fluently. His stance on achieving peace at all costs has not wavered. Even now, after Chamberlain's humiliating failure to read Hitler's intentions and the turning of the tide of opinion in Britain, the duke still wants us to throw in our lot with Herr Hitler."

"But why?" Cleo stared. "Surely he doesn't think Hitler will reinstate him as King."

"Give the lady a prize," murmured Smith. "That is precisely the carrot that will be dangled before him. He'd be a puppet king, of course."

"And Wallis Simpson would be queen," murmured Cleo.

"She is the one you need to watch closely," said Smith. "The duchess has, er, shall we say connections in high places among the German command. She and the former ambassador, Ribbentrop, were . . . close."

This was frightful. "I'm glad you explained it all to me," said Cleo. "I had felt guilty and a bit ashamed of agreeing to spy on them until now. But I quite see how vital it is."

"Well, do what you can easily get away with but don't take any risks, will you? After all, they are not the enemy and if they are given clear evidence that the intelligence services are monitoring their movements, it might push them into action we don't want them to take."

Cleo finished her *gelado*, and Smith handed her his handkerchief. "I don't see the duke as a traitor or as a man who would act purely out of self-interest at his country's expense. I think he genuinely believes Hitler's vision is best for Europe, if not for Britain. It's certainly not a line of argument sanctioned by the British government. His public indiscretions on the subject are becoming a problem."

"I can see that," said Cleo, thinking about the previous evening. "Has there been any word on what role they will allow him to play in world events? He is champing at the bit to be 'of use,' as he calls it. The telegram he received from Churchill made him furious."

Smith shrugged. "Churchill has recalled him to England, but I feel he would do considerable damage there. The royal family probably feels as I do—Queen Elizabeth has no love for her brother-in-law, and less for his spouse. Churchill will do what he can for him, however." Smith smiled grimly. "As if the prime minister doesn't have enough to do without soothing the pride of a petulant former King."

"So what do you think will happen?" Cleo watched as the pigeons fought over some torn pieces of *carcaça* an old lady was scattering for them over the path. In England, where rationing had hit the populace hard, such a waste of precious bread would be frowned on. In Paris, the birds had fled the city altogether, driven off by the awful smell of burning that preceded the Nazi advance.

"Whatever position he is offered, the priority is plain. We need to get the duke out of Europe as soon as possible," said Smith. "The P.M. must be almost at the end of his tether. He sent a telegram to the duke that he must return to England immediately and reminded him that he is still under orders and subject to court-martial for disobedience."

Cleo gasped. "No wonder the duke was so angry!"

Smith regarded her with those grave eyes of his. "If the Germans don't succeed in persuading the duke to join them, they might resort to kidnapping. The longer he stays in Europe, the greater the risk. He might not be King any longer, but it would be the height of folly for us to leave such a valuable piece on the board."

"GOVERNOR OF THE Bahamas!" The duke was fuming, pacing the floor. Then he stopped at the window and stared out to sea. "Put simply, it's exile. The St. Helena of 1940. It's an insult! I can't believe Winston would serve me such a trick."

The duchess went to him and put her hand on his shoulder. She must be equally furious, but her first priority was to calm her husband. "I am sure it is not his doing. Let us think about this, my dear. Let us not be too hasty." In a low voice, she added, "Do you think they know? Might they have guessed who you've been in talks with?"

"I've hardly made any real secret of it," said the duke. "But my one wish is for peace. Can't they see that? I've been to war. I *know,* Wallis. I know what a hell on earth it is."

"Of course you do, David," said Wallis, as if calming a child. "Of course. But at a time like this they see everything in black and white, don't they? Any talk of appeasement is considered tantamount to treason."

He looked at her. "Do *you* think I've been unpatriotic? Honestly, Wallis, your opinion is all that matters to me."

She took his hands. "You are the greatest patriot, and only an idiot would fail to see it."

There was a long silence. Then the duke said, "If only I had an ally left in Britain. But I fear Winston is against me now, too." His shoulders slumped. "I'll accept the post. I must. You know how it will look if I don't."

"But the Bahamas!" The duchess threw up her hands. "What on earth will we do in such a place?" She hesitated. "Let's not rush to accept. Let's see what else might be on offer first."

"No, no. I can't delay. I said I'd telegram my acceptance after lunch." The duke sighed. "I promised I would serve anywhere in the Empire. And this is where they send me. It might as well be the South Pole."

"At least that wouldn't be so hot," said the duchess.

Cleo had been standing silently in the drawing room doorway, watching this exchange. Footsteps approached along the corridor behind her, so she quickly tapped on the open door, drawing the couple's attention. "It's time for your manicure, Your Royal Highness," she said to the duchess.

"Is it? Thank you, Cleo."

As she left the drawing room, Cleo's mind raced with speculation. Was the duke truly reconciled to leaving for the Bahamas, or did he have an alternative plan? Of course he would take the appointment as an insult, but she hoped for his sake that he'd accept his fate gracefully. As Smith had said, the longer the Windsors remained in Europe, the more dangerous it would be.

THE WINDSORS DID not leave for the Caribbean straightaway. The duke spent the weeks leading up to his departure in a manner that made it seem as if he didn't have a care in the world: swimming in the villa's pool, playing at the Estoril Golf Club, holding lunch parties and dinners for friends and dignitaries now residing in Lisbon.

For her part, the duchess moved into organization mode. She was renowned for her ability to transform a house into a bastion of style and good taste, and she was determined that the governor's residence in Nassau would be no exception. She had managed to contact the chef from la Croë, inviting him to work for them there. To the chef and his wife, the duchess had given the task of loading up a van full of the Windsors' belongings from the château in Antibes and driving with them all the way to Lisbon. The Windsors' plan to go themselves to oversee the removal had been vetoed by the British.

A man called Tiger Bermejillo came as emissary from Spain and stayed for several days. He was a lively fellow, and both Windsors seemed to cheer up in his presence. His main function, however, was to help the duchess retrieve her possessions from France and he undertook to obtain the necessary visas and permits for the operation.

The Windsors had sent Wallis's maid back to Paris to retrieve as many valuable items from their apartment in the boulevard Suchet as she could reasonably transport through occupied France: the silver, china, linen, paintings, and furniture, not to mention the duke's collections of mementos from his travels throughout the Commonwealth. Unofficially, Mademoiselle Moulichon had been given safe passage through France by the Germans. Having secured the relevant visa, the maid had traveled to Paris and packed the Windsor valuables into a van. Sometime after her departure in the lorry the Windsors had rented for the purpose, Jeanne had been abducted by the Germans. She was now nowhere to be found.

At breakfast one morning, the duke frowned over a telegram. "The Germans have taken Jeanne into custody. Why on earth would they do such a thing?"

"More to the point, what has happened to everything she was supposed to bring back from the Paris apartment?" The duchess lit a cigarette and began to pace the floor, smoking furiously. "At this rate, we'll have to set sail with only the clothes on our backs."

The duke shot out of his chair. "Telephone the German embassy, Phillips," he told his comptroller. "Get Hoyningen-Huene on the line. This must be sorted out immediately. We want our possessions returned. If one solitary pillowcase is missing . . ." His hand clenched into a fist.

"I'm sure it's just a misunderstanding," said the duchess. "Tiger will sort it out."

As the days wore on and the precious cargo failed to arrive, Cleo could see that the couple had little concern for the maid, but rather an overabundance of concern for their possessions. But the fact that they seemed to regard the enemy as bound to fall in with the duke's wishes on the matter was more shocking still.

This fretting over their belongings went on for the rest of the Windsors' stay in Portugal, which was to last almost a month. The American ship that was to take the couple to the Bahamas was due to depart on August first.

The duke had just enough self-awareness to prevent a photograph of him playing a round at the Estoril Golf Club to make the papers, but not quite enough to eschew his favorite pastime altogether.

But the golf games came to a halt when odd things started happening at the villa.

A warning arrived from a so-called friend that the British meant to get the Windsors out of Europe so that they could assassinate them. Stones were thrown against the windows and strange figures appeared outside during the night, then ran away. Security around the duke tightened. He was no longer permitted to leave the estate.

To Mr. Smith, Cleo said, "I know the Portuguese secret police are determined to keep the duke safe, but I'd feel much better if there was a British presence in the house. I keep jumping at shadows."

"These scare tactics do rather seem almost comically amateur-ish, though, don't they?" said Smith. "I shouldn't think there is anything to worry about from these characters. Still, I suppose you ought to be on your guard. Sometimes fools succeed by accident." He eyed her for a moment. "There is no need for you to engage in any heroics. Leave that to the professionals."

"Don't worry, I will," said Cleo.

"Sensible woman." Smith guided Cleo to a park bench and they sat to eat their *gelados*. Almond for Cleo and milk coffee for Smith.

There was little more news to report. The duke and duchess continued to lament the loss of their possessions and their concern for the maid who was to shepherd them safely to Lisbon quickly turned to exasperation. If Jeanne did not arrive soon, they would be obliged to leave for the Bahamas without her. She would be left to make her own way to the Caribbean.

On the day before the couple's departure, finally Cleo made a decision. She would talk to the duke about her relationship with him, and about Marguerite. She would make it clear that she wanted nothing from him. She understood that public acknowl-edgment was not possible. For her, that was neither necessary nor desirable in any case. She had no wish to be gossiped about in so-ciety or the newspapers. She did not even wish for further contact unless the duke wanted it. She just needed him to know.

Cleo was well aware how hard this disclosure would be. The Windsors could be charming when they wished—in fact there was no one more charming in the world than the duke when he was at his best—but they were both materialistic and self-centered to a point that was incomprehensible to Cleo.

Ordinarily Cleo would have reveled in the duchess's extravagant shopping sprees but even their trip to the most famous jeweler in Lisbon, Leitão & Irmão, did not inspire her with anything but deep disquiet.

The dire contrast between her own previous existence and the horror of what so many faced in this war made Cleo ashamed of the comfort of her position. Some of the men she'd known at Boulle had been taken prisoner by the Nazis and were now performing forced labor in German camps. Parisians like Monsieur Lemarchand and Madame Santerre, having refused to leave their beloved city, now watched miserably as the Nazis overran it. Lady Grayson in London was dealing with power cuts and food shortages. And that was only the people she knew.

The brave Royal Air Force were battling the Nazi Luftwaffe in the skies. In North Africa, the Italian Army had captured a strategic entry point to the Sudan, forcing a British retreat. Reluctantly, the British had scuttled the ships of the French Navy to prevent them falling into German hands, provoking retaliation in the Vichy French bombing of Gibraltar. The British Channel Islands had fallen to the Germans, and it was thought that the Germans were now preparing to invade Britain itself.

With all of this going on, and in view of the duke's own protestations that his influence and talents were being wasted, the petty concerns that seemed to occupy most of the Windsors' waking moments beggared belief. Cleo came to suspect that the duke only liked the *idea* of being the monarch, not the actual work involved.

The nation had wept when Edward VIII had abdicated his throne. Now Cleo wondered whether it was just as well that he had.

Given their attitude, Cleo was not sanguine about the Windsors falling in with British plans to get them off to the Bahamas without delay. Many tense discussions went on behind closed doors at the villa. Many appointments were made with personages believed to be conduits to Germany.

The duke seemed to be vacillating right up to the point of his departure, only breaking off scheming to lament that his treasures still had not arrived from Paris. Poor Jeanne had not returned, and no one knew where the maid was, or why the Germans had taken her.

Of course, Cleo was being selfish—perhaps on a similar scale to the Windsors—by seeking to disclose her relationship to the duke now, with the world at war and the duke himself at dangerous odds with the British government. Her concerns would seem petty to him, no doubt.

But with the couple departing for the other side of the world, who knew when or whether they would return? She might never have this chance again.

Chapter Sixteen

$\mathcal{A}$s Cleo agonized over how to raise Marguerite's claims of paternity with the duke, the days at the villa slipped by with increasing speed. The duke was never alone and she couldn't seem to work up the nerve to ask for a moment of his time.

When the Windsors' final morning before they set sail for the Bahamas arrived, she still hadn't approached him. "Coward!" she told herself. "Brodie would laugh if he could see you now." She sighed. Brodie would tell her she had bats in the belfry to even think of speaking to the duke about such a wild and improbable story as Marguerite had told.

But Cleo knew she'd never forgive herself if she didn't at least try to discover the truth.

"I'll be glad to get out of this prison!" The morning of his departure, the duke came into the drawing room, where Cleo was writing letters for the duchess.

"Oh, it's you, Miss Davenport." The duke crossed to the sideboard and poured himself a liberal glass of whisky. "All I wanted was a walk in the woods with my dogs," he complained. "They sent out a search party! And then lectured me about it as if I were a truant schoolboy." He took a deep swallow of his drink.

Not the most auspicious mood to find him in, true. But for the first time, the two of them were alone together. That wouldn't last long. Cleo took it as a sign. She drew a deep breath. It was now or never.

She approached the former King. Her father. "Sir, perhaps I might have a word?"

He looked at her properly then, his eyebrows raised. "Oh? Yes, of course. Sit down." He gestured to the armchair opposite his.

Cleo joined him but remained standing. "Sir, there is no easy way to say this, so I think I must simply blurt it out. I have been told by a certain lady, a lady of your acquaintance, that I am your natural daughter, sir."

The duke dropped his glass, which landed with a thud and rolled from side to side, spilling its golden-brown liquid over the rug. His head reared back as if she'd punched him. "*What* did you say?"

Rapidly losing confidence, Cleo rattled off an edited version of the story Marguerite had told her. As the expression on the duke's face turned from thunderstruck to furious, it took all of her courage to stand her ground.

She spread her hands palm outward, as if to calm a wild animal. "I don't expect anything of you. Really. I'm not going to tell anyone. I just . . . I just wanted you to know, that's all." Her throat caught on a sob, which she forced back. "I'll go."

She turned and hurried toward the door, but he said, "Wait. Now wait one moment, Miss Davenport."

Cleo halted, her heart beating wildly.

"Come back here and sit down."

As Cleo obeyed, he muttered, "That bloody woman! She's like malaria. You think she's gone away, then she comes back, more vicious than ever."

"I beg your pardon, sir?" She'd heard the words but she didn't understand what they meant.

"Never mind. Look, Miss Davenport, clearly you are very young and innocent in the ways of the world. I know you mean no harm. But I must tell you that you've been cruelly deceived by that hateful woman. I am not your father."

There was a rock of ice in her chest. Had she expected him to admit it? But then his muttered aside indicated he had enjoyed a liaison with Marguerite at one time or another. How could he be positive he hadn't fathered a child?

As Cleo was trying to think how to phrase her question tactfully, the duchess erupted into the room, a greeting card in one hand and a bouquet of roses gripped tightly in the other. She carried the bouquet upside down, without a care for the violent bobbing of the perfect blooms, nor the dark red petals they shed on the floor behind her like drops of blood. "Will you get a load of this!"

"What is it, Wallis?" Immediately Cleo and the question of her paternity were forgotten. The duke was on his feet. "Flowers, Wallis? Who are they from?"

"Not the flowers. This!" She thrust the greeting card out to him. "Read it and tell me if I'm not right to be scared."

He perused it, his frown deepening. He turned it over. "It's not signed."

"Threats like this rarely are, I believe!" Cleo had seen the duchess give others the sharp side of her tongue but she'd never seen her lash out at the duke. The urgency and depth of the upset penetrated Cleo's fog, eclipsing her own troubles. She stood and edged her way toward the door.

The duke bent his gaze again to the card. "Not a threat, but a warning that we're in danger. How frightened you must have been to receive it. Oh, my poor, dear Wallis."

He went to put his arm around her but she shrugged him off, flung the bouquet across the room in a shower of red petals, and started to pace, arms folded across her thin chest. "They say we cannot trust anyone, least of all the British. What if they're right?"

"My dear . . ."

Too distraught to eavesdrop on any more of this conversation, Cleo turned and hurried from the room.

Lisbon, Portugal
Summer 1940

CLEO WATCHED THE duke and duchess board the *Excalibur*, a small ship of the American Export Line, which had been searched from top to bottom several times over following the threat the duchess had received.

In the frenetic activity that had preceded the Windsors' departure, Cleo had forced her emotions into abeyance. Now she felt adrift. She hadn't ever truly believed she was the duke's child, had she? It had always seemed like a fantasy, particularly when Princess Fahmy had given such a detailed account of her liaison with her golden prince. Even when Cleo had become part of the Windsor household in Cascais, there had been a disconnection. She'd felt as if she was watching a play with actors, not real flesh-and-blood people. Real people didn't behave that way.

Had Marguerite lied to her, as the duke said? Would Cleo ever know the truth?

There was no getting near the duke after the drama of the bouquet that had delivered the warning to the duchess. He was quickly surrounded by a human wall of security. Out of diffidence and fear, Cleo had left it too late to speak with him, and now she might never hear his side of the story. She doubted he would ever agree to see her again.

The duke hadn't been angry with her for blurting out what she thought was the truth of their relationship. If she hadn't been well-acquainted with his character by now, she would have concluded that he had deliberately avoided her before he'd left. But knowing him as she did, she suspected their conversation had completely slipped his mind. Cleo was less important to him than the duchess's eau de Nil swimsuit. He didn't care enough to explain himself, or even to be angry with her.

"Sad to see them go? You surprise me," said a voice beside her. She jumped, put a hand to her chest, and saw that Mr. Smith was holding out a handkerchief—her own—to her. She took it automatically but didn't use it. "I'm not crying."

"No?" Smith gripped her shoulders and turned her to face him. He studied her for some moments, then said, "No tears. But you do look so very sad. Care to tell me about it?"

"Not really," said Cleo. She turned away from the dock and took his arm the way she had done all those times when they'd met for ice cream and a walk in the park. She'd expected to feel a degree of relief once the Windsors were safely aboard and bound for the Bahamas after all the intrigue and demands of the past weeks but she simply felt empty.

"What shall you do now?" Cleo asked Smith as they headed toward the car park. "Are you based in Portugal for the time being?"

He squinted into the distance, as if looking to the future. "Only another few weeks. But I hope you will still meet me for *gelado*." He opened his car door for her. "Come on, I'll take you home."

When they arrived at the apartment, Cleo hesitated before getting out of Smith's car. Loneliness welled up inside her like the swelling waters of the Boca do Inferno. A deep tidal pull of need made her turn to him and say, "Would you please kiss me, Mr. Smith?"

For once, Smith did not step lightly around their mutual attraction. His expression was sober, yet the air between them crackled. "Are you sure?"

Doubts scurried about in her head, but she drove them out as a beater drives grouse from the undergrowth in hunting season. She didn't want to think. She needed only to feel.

For an answer, Cleo leaned over the gear stick and softly kissed Mr. Smith on the lips. "I'm sure."

He would be gone soon. She didn't even know his real name. All that mattered was his warmth, his closeness, and the instinctive certainty that he would not expect any more from her than she was willing to give.

MARGUERITE

Paris, France
Winter 1938–Summer 1940

MARGUERITE SPENT MANY months and traveled great distances to amass the evidence she needed to prove she was Cleo's mother. A few romantic digressions along the way delayed her further; despite her mission, she was not prepared to dismiss a wealthy protector when one offered to keep her in style. There was a businessman in Cairo, in London, an earl who owned half of Dorset, a Greek shipping tycoon.

Those detours notwithstanding, she succeeded in most of what she had set out to do.

But supporting her claim that she was Cleo's mother was one thing. Establishing the Duke of Windsor's paternity was a different matter. That could not be done definitively, but the faithful Aimée Pain had written a statement that in those final months of her liaison with the young prince, Marguerite had consorted with no other man.

Whether or not that statement might be disproven was almost immaterial. One only had to look at Cleo to see the truth Marguerite sought to reveal—she possessed the right coloring, the right build. She looked like the duke. In short, she was perfect.

How to get David alone in order to give him the news was the problem. One could not simply call at a royal duke's residence without an invitation. Mutual friends like Bendor and the Comte de Breteuil had cut Marguerite's acquaintance long ago.

Marguerite began haunting all the places the Duke of Windsor might be, and that took many more months with nothing to show for her efforts. The French and British had declared war on Germany months before, and she wasn't sure how much longer the duke would remain in Paris under those circumstances.

As rumors began to fly that the Germans had managed the impossible and crossed the Maginot Line, Marguerite's quest became urgent. The time for trusting to luck was well past.

She sent her maid to strike up conversations with the Windsors' servants during their time off. According to her staff, the Duchess of Windsor was an acerbic, exacting mistress who kept a notepad by her place at dinner to note down every tiny detail that might be wrong with the meal or the service. They called it her "grumble book." Despite expecting perfection, the Windsors were amazingly stingy when it came to bonuses or presents at Christmas. Marguerite wasn't surprised.

In exchange for a generous bribe, Aimée obtained a copy of the duke's diary for the following two weeks from a house maid. Now Marguerite had a way to see him. Whether she could get near enough to give him the note she had spent hours composing was another matter.

The duke was shadowed wherever he went. Even if she could make it past the bodyguard from Scotland Yard, the duke was always flanked by Fruity Metcalfe or Gray Phillips or one of the others in his inner circle.

Those men appeared easygoing, but they were quick to shield him from anyone who might impose. And of course, there were the women, who were even more vigilant on his behalf. They had penetrated the inner circle; they would defend their position from all intruders. And Marguerite certainly did not wish to tangle with Wallis, who was a "tough cookie," as the Americans would say. Marguerite smiled sourly. The Duke of Windsor had a taste for women who dominated him.

After all of that planning and stalking, Marguerite finally managed it. She planted herself in the duke's path during dinner and dancing at the Ritz as he left the restroom.

Marguerite prided herself on not having aged much since those halcyon days they'd spent together. Would he remember her? She snorted. Of course he would. After she'd dragged him, kicking and screaming, into the Fahmy affair, how could he not? Or had there been all too many women since? Either way, she wouldn't let anything stop her. He'd remember her, all right, by the time she was done.

He was coming toward her, dapper as ever in a dinner suit, his blond hair brushed back from his forehead. His skin was wrinkled around the eyes, as if a cartoonist had drawn careful circles around them. Unlike her, he looked old beyond his years.

She said one word in her low, husky voice. "David." That got his attention. Only his intimate friends and family called him by that name. She handed him the note that hinted delicately at blackmail and requested an audience.

Marguerite retreated from his presence before he had time to react. She would allow him to digest her demand, to imagine the possible consequences if he failed to accede.

She'd done it! Finally her plans would be set in motion. Satisfaction humming through her veins, she went home and waited, and waited some more.

Nothing.

Had he misunderstood? Maybe she ought to have been more explicit in the note, but she didn't want written evidence of her crime. Must she go to greater lengths to force the duke to speak with her?

Before she could think what to do next, the duke joined the British Military Mission and became less accessible than ever.

By July, the Windsors had left France, and later sailed off for the Bahamas, thousands of miles out of her reach.

Chapter Seventeen

CLEO

Cairo, Egypt
Autumn 1941

The journey back to Cairo was a long and circuitous one, due to German blockades. Cleo boarded a Dutch ship bound for Sierra Leone. From there, she managed to get herself to Lagos for a flight across the Sudan and up the Nile, and finally to Cairo. Seeing the pyramids from the air as they flew in brought her an almost mystical feeling of peace.

"I'm home. I can't believe it. I'm *home!*" Alighting from the cab outside Shepheard's, Cleo scarcely waited for her luggage to be unloaded before she took flight. Feeling like a little girl again, heedless of the officers and ladies sedately drinking tea or reading newspapers on the terrace, she dashed up the steps. She waved to the dragomen who sat in their privileged seats by the entrance, patted the head of the Sakkara sphinx by the door, and strode into the lobby of Shepheard's Hotel.

Mr. Meyer, the Swiss porter, was still at his post and greeted her warmly. Mr. Mansoor was busy with a customer in his shop. The Egyptian dancers still guarded the staircase, albeit slightly worse for wear, having been the subject of so many thefts and practical jokes over the years. But the hotel's clientele had changed markedly. The establishment was full of uniforms. Cleo headed up the stairs to Serafina's suite.

It had taken just over a year for Cleo to talk her way into a position in Cairo, but the mysterious Mr. Smith had remembered her expressed wish to work in her home city and arranged for her transfer. The coveted position as a wireless operator had not eventuated, however. She had persuaded and cajoled and even demanded, but the British Army seemed determined to put her where she would be of least use: in charge of payroll at Middle East General Headquarters.

Cleo reached Serafina's door and looked about. Where was Taaleb? Had he gone off to fight?

She knocked, but there was no answer. She had written to say she was coming but received no reply. Lady Grayson had frequently urged her sister to abandon Egypt. It was too dangerous with Rommel on the rampage. If she wouldn't come home to England she ought to travel to South Africa, where she would be safe. Had Serafina given in and left?

Cleo went back down to reception and inquired about Serafina's whereabouts. The receptionist was new and unacquainted with the Misses Davenport, but just then, Mr. Costas emerged from the staircase leading down to his domain.

"Mr. Costas!" Cleo ran over and threw her arms around him. "It's so good to see you. It's been far too long."

"Well! Well, well," said Mr. Costas, clearly flustered by this onslaught. "Cleo! Is it really you?" He cleared his throat. "Miss Davenport, I should say."

"No, you certainly *shouldn't* say! I will always be Cleo to you. It is so wonderful to be back. But where is Aunt Serafina?"

"Ah." Mr. Costas removed his spectacles and dusted them with his handkerchief. "She went to Palestine, I believe. She left a letter."

He went himself to the reception desk and found her key as well as Serafina's letter and pressed them both into her hands. "You will come down to see Mrs. Costas and have coffee with us, won't you?"

"You have real coffee? What luxury! Yes, of course I will." Cleo gave his squat form another hug and followed the porter upstairs.

Having tipped the porter, Cleo slowly removed her hat and gloves, looking about her in surprise. The room was bare. Completely devoid of the detritus Serafina had commonly strewn about the place. No maps, charts, notes, books, or artefacts littered the tables, chairs, and floors. In fact, one could walk from one end of the sitting room to another without tiptoeing around or stepping over anything.

"I have a *system*," her guardian had said often, furious when one of the maids moved anything from its place.

Serafina's letter explained her absence. She'd gone to work as Colonel Drayton's secretary in Palestine. In her spare time, she was volunteering for the Red Crescent, as she had during the Great War. She trusted Cleo would go on well without her, and she was welcome to take the train up to stay with the Draytons whenever she could get leave.

"Well, that's that, I suppose." Cleo was disappointed, but she refused to let Serafina's absence spoil her homecoming.

Gosh, but she was exhausted! The suite was very hot and close. She opened the French doors and stepped out onto the small balcony that overlooked the dance floor and gardens, and breathed in the spicy, dry air. Then she threw herself on her bed, fully clothed, and slept until dark.

She awoke to a rap on the door accompanied by feminine laughter. "Cleo? Open up!"

Recognizing the voice, Cleo opened the door.

"Pat!" She'd met Patricia Lomax on the boat to Sierra Leone. They'd traveled the rest of the journey together, which was only broken by a stint in the hospital at Sierra Leone where Pat suffered from terrible boils and Cleo had nursed her through the worst. Upon parting at the train station Pat had promised to come and find Cleo at Shepheard's.

Cleo hadn't expected a visit quite so soon. Pat was neat and thin with a blond pageboy haircut. She introduced her companion as an old school chum, Liz Radleigh, a striking brunette.

Patricia held a champagne bottle aloft like a trophy and waggled it. "Let us in, quick! We stole this from some officers and we need to drink the evidence."

Laughing and shaking her head, Cleo stepped back and allowed them to enter. She turned on lamps and went to Serafina's cocktail cabinet to fetch glasses. Suddenly she felt ravenous and rang down for fruit and cheese to be sent up.

Pat was flipping through Serafina's record collection and grimacing. "Gracious, what a load of dirges. Isn't there anything by anyone who's still alive and kicking?"

"Wait a minute." Cleo went and opened all of the windows, letting the music from the orchestra in the gardens below drift through. The girls danced around the room to "Begin the Beguine," holding their coupes aloft and singing their hearts out to the music.

How different from the quiet, studious evenings spent in Serafina's company, fearful of disturbing the great mind at work. As she got older, Cleo would become equally absorbed in her designs but in her early years, she remembered longing for Serafina's attention, only to run up against the invisible force field of Serafina's powerful concentration.

Ah, but she was becoming maudlin. "More champagne!" She held out her glass to Liz, who was now swigging from the bottle and leaving lipstick marks of Victory Red.

A knock on the door and Taaleb stood there, beaming, a tray of food in his hands. Not only the fruit and cheese Cleo had ordered, but a selection of sweet treats from that evening's dinner menu.

"Taaleb!" Cleo wanted to throw herself at him and hug him as she had done with Mr. Costas, but she knew that would embarrass him. "Come in! Come in! It's so good to see you."

The other girls stood wide-eyed, clearly in awe of Taaleb's majestic height and breadth.

"Princess," he said, his smile wide. "It is good to see you, too."

When she had inquired about his health and his family, Cleo asked him the question uppermost on her mind. "Taaleb, have you seen Brodie?"

"Brodie?" Pat raised an eyebrow. "And who might *he* be?"

"A friend," said Cleo, hoping she wasn't blushing.

"I have not seen him, princess. Not for weeks now."

She knew Brodie had been promoted to second lieutenant. As an officer, he was entitled to stay at Shepheard's and occasionally availed himself of the privilege when on leave. She'd left a message at reception to be given to him upon his return. She was impatient to see him.

When Taaleb left, the three women fell upon the food. "You don't get anything like this in London these days," said Pat. "I *almost* feel guilty."

"I don't." Liz leaned forward to select a plump fig from the cheese board. "I've been starving for *years*!"

"Liz has been doing something incredibly hush-hush in England," said Pat. "And now she's doing something incredibly hush-hush out here."

"Only here I shall be much better fed," said Liz, licking fig juice from her fingers. "Where are you, Cleo?"

"Middle East General Headquarters," she replied. "Payroll." She made a face. "I trained to be a wireless operator and they stick me in accounts, of all things."

"Oh, the Army here won't put you where you'd be most useful," said Pat.

Liz laughed and raised her glass in a toast to military incompetence. "No fear of that!"

Cairo, Egypt
Winter–Spring 1942

CLEO'S JOB AT MEGHQ was disappointingly mundane. She had little responsibility and no opportunity to use her linguistic skills. The workday began at nine o'clock and ended at one in the afternoon, and as far as she could see, the officers in her section spent the rest of the time at the races, playing polo or golf or going sailing. The evenings were for dining and attending the opera or cabarets or one of the many balls and parties at the various hotels.

Cleo wanted to be more useful but when the Army refused her request for a transfer, she decided to volunteer. As had happened during the Great War, the Heliopolis Palace Hotel had been converted into a hospital. The grandeur of the establishment with its chandeliers and marble staircases and columns of granite contrasted starkly with the suffering of the men who occupied the rows and rows of beds in its reception rooms and ballroom.

Cleo took to spending her afternoons with the wounded men, washing them, and making beds and removing waste. Her duties were menial because the one thing she wasn't trained in was nursing. However, Cleo put her secretarial skills to good use. She would spend hours every day, taking shorthand dictation from soldiers who wanted to write letters home. Then she would type them up on an old typewriter she'd unearthed in the basement of Shepheard's.

She never grew accustomed to the horrible, tragic sights and smells, but she learned to mask her horror behind a bright smile. This could be one of the boys she'd met during her London season, she would think. It could be Brodie, or Philippe or Hippolyte. Many of the men were afraid that they were so disfigured, their own families would not want them back. Sometimes, she needed to shut herself away in a bathroom stall and bawl.

Serafina, who was working as a secretary for Colonel Drayton in Palestine, had written giving permission for Pat and Liz to move in with Cleo.

Liz had become great friends with various members of the Special Air Service Brigade during her short time in Cairo and she'd agreed to meet them for a drink one evening. Having heard about the exploits of these commandos and their risky missions out in the desert, Cleo was curious to meet them and agreed to go along.

The SAS Brigade itself had been partly conceived at Shepheard's, and they'd taken their winged parachute motif from the Egyptian ibis of Isis design that proliferated around the hotel. When the moon was down, these men would be dropped by parachute behind enemy lines near German landing grounds and ammunition dumps to plant explosives. The Long Range Desert Group would drive into the desert to collect the SAS men at the rendezvous point in roofless Chevrolets fitted with Lewis machine guns. For a small force, their record was impressive.

"Who dares wins," murmured Cleo, quoting their motto. She liked the sound of that.

The most popular watering hole among officers at Shepheard's was called the "Long Bar," and people joked that was because you had to wait so long to get a drink. The bartender, Joe Scialom, had established quite a reputation. Fluent in many languages, he was the consummate bartender, lending a sympathetic ear to a patron's troubles or defusing volatile situations as they arose between officers of different nationalities and backgrounds.

Women had only just been admitted to the bar due to the war. Whether they were altogether welcome was another matter, as Cleo gathered from a few frosty stares she and her friends received from the older officers as they entered and queued for their drinks.

"I'll have a Suffering Bastard, please," said Liz. She winked at Cleo. "And this shall be the last drink I pay for tonight."

Pat ordered a gin and tonic and Cleo chose whisky.

"What's that when it's at home?" Cleo asked, gesturing to Liz's drink. "It sounds like a hangover cure."

"Quite the reverse," said Liz. "Makes a fellow forget *all* his troubles." She held up her drink. "Cheers!"

Pat said to Cleo, "Our Liz broke it off with her boyfriend."

"Oh, no!" Cleo squeezed Liz's shoulder sympathetically. "What happened?"

"I don't want to talk about it," said Liz. "I want to drown my sorrows in expensive liquor and cheap men." She took a long, deep sip.

Pat waved. "There's David Stirling."

Stirling was tall and handsome, with thick, straight eyebrows and an air of restless energy. He stood with a group of other men in uniform, their sand-colored berets folded and tucked into the back pockets of their trousers.

Liz waved, too. "Who's that with him? I haven't seen him before."

Cleo knew instantly. "*Brodie*." She couldn't do much more than whisper his name. Was he in the SAS, now, too? She hated the very thought.

"You know him?" Pat sent him an admiring glance. "I say, he is a dish, isn't he?"

Cleo didn't answer. The relief of seeing him standing there, alive and apparently unharmed, held her transfixed. She couldn't seem to get her legs to work. The tension she'd carried ever since he'd shipped out drained, leaving her limp and light-headed.

"Cleo?" Liz waved a hand in front of her face. "Are you in there?"

Cleo blinked and gave a shake of her head. "Sorry. It's just seeing him like this, all of a sudden. He's . . . he's very special to me, you see."

"Like that, is it?" Liz sighed and rolled her eyes. "Why are all the good ones taken?"

By now, Pat had managed to catch Stirling's eye and he indicated to his group that they ought to join the women. That was when Brodie turned and saw Cleo.

For a long moment he held her gaze and her insides turned warm and liquid. She'd tried very hard to stop loving him in the time they'd been apart. But what was the use? One look and she was lost.

He surveyed her companions, then returned his gaze to her. Setting his half-drunk glass on the bar, he gave a slight jerk of his head toward the door. Without a word to her friends, Cleo was on her feet and moving toward the exit.

"Hey! Cleo, where are you going?" called Liz, who seemed to have perked up now that she was surrounded by men. "The party's just getting started!"

Cleo hurried to catch up with Brodie's quick stride. In the corridor, she looked around.

"Over here." In the shadows, Brodie stood waiting for her.

She put out her hands and found his, gripping them tightly. "I was hoping you'd come! What are you doing here? Where are you staying?"

"I'm putting up in a friend's room while he's off fighting." He hesitated, looking down at their joined hands. "They told me you were using Serafina's suite."

"Yes, I'm living there with two other girls. But you . . . You look . . ." She checked him over, what she could see of him in the dim light. "You're in one piece."

He huffed a laugh. "So far I am largely unscathed. I've got a few days' leave before I head back out again. Will you sit with me for a while? I want to hear everything you've been up to."

"If you're with Stirling's men, I gather you've had a much more interesting time than I have," she replied. "But I suppose you can't talk about it."

"It's not all that interesting, believe me."

"I wish we could go to your room," said Cleo. "There are things I want to say that I can't say in public."

"How about a ride in the desert tomorrow? It will be quite like old times."

"I'd love to, but we don't have any horses. Serafina's were requisitioned by the Army."

"Let me take care of that," said Brodie with a grin. "I'll call in a favor."

"Truly?" Her heart lifted at the thought. She hadn't been riding at all since she'd arrived in Cairo and in Lisbon there had been little time for leisure.

"Shall we go outside?" she suggested.

"Good idea."

It was a clear night and the air was soft and warm. The band played a slow song and couples danced, clinging together dreamily in the moonlight. The setting was romantic, but that only brought back in full force the humiliation she'd felt when Brodie rejected her on that awful night.

She'd forgotten all of that in the joy of seeing him again. Now constraint descended on her like a cloak. She smoothed her hands over the pristine white tablecloth. "Brodie, I—"

"Something to drink, sir? Miss?" A waiter stood beside them, head tilted in inquiry. Brodie shook his head and Cleo also declined, although she regretted her refusal as soon as the waiter bowed and moved away. She could have used some false courage.

"Let's go for a stroll, shall we?" Brodie rose from the table. Perhaps the awkwardness was getting to him, too.

Cleo let him lead her away. They exchanged news as they walked in the gardens, which were softly lit and dotted with other couples taking an evening promenade. "Have you seen Serafina since you came back?" Brodie asked.

Cleo shook her head. "I haven't been able to get away. Have you?"

"I stayed with her at the Draytons' a while back. She seems to be keeping busy."

"She's certainly not one to sit about bemoaning her lot," said Cleo. "I wonder if things will ever be the same. It seems like a lifetime ago that the three of us were here together." She turned to him. "I suppose it must seem quite extraordinary to return to Shepheard's after surviving out in the desert for weeks at a time."

He grinned. "I barely manage to get the sand out of my hair before I'm back there again. But I wouldn't change it. We've a fine band of men. The finest."

Cleo had heard all about their exploits from Pat and Liz and she felt an equal measure of pride and fear when she thought of the danger he courted on every mission, not only from the enemy but from the harsh desert conditions. She wanted to beg him to be careful, but she knew that would be futile.

"I understand from Lord G that you had some excitement of your own in Lisbon," he said.

"The Windsors. Yes." The scent of jasmine wafted to them on the gentle breeze. She told him what had happened in Lisbon. That she, against all wisdom, had confronted the duke with his paternity. That he had recoiled from the very idea.

"He denied everything, of course. But he did seem to know Princess Fahmy, and I don't doubt it's true that he did have a liaison with her."

They came to a stone bench in a small alcove and sat down. "I'm sorry, Cleo."

She shrugged. "At least, now I know he doesn't want to have anything to do with me. I won't run after him again. Can't, anyway. He's on the other side of the world."

She seemed to spend her life running after people who didn't want her. "At all events, there's not much more I can do about either of my parents."

"Cleo, about your mother—"

"No." She cut him off. "No, *really*. I don't want to talk about her or the duke, or any of it anymore. You're on leave and we need to make sure you enjoy yourself to the full while you're here."

WHEN CLEO RETURNED from work the following afternoon, Brodie was waiting for her in the lounge, reading a newspaper. "I've got us some horses. They're stabled over at Mena House."

Her spirits soaring, Cleo hurried upstairs to change.

They took a taxi to Mena House and went around to the stables, where their borrowed horses awaited them, all saddled and ready. Brodie tipped the groom and cupped his hands to throw Cleo into the saddle.

She slipped her boots into the stirrups and gathered up the reins. "I managed to get some leave, so I'm all yours for the next couple of days."

"Then I'll have to make the most of it," said Brodie. As they walked their horses out of the stables, they approached a man in a galabeya with a monkey on his shoulder. The monkey suddenly gibbered as they passed, causing Brodie's grey to snort and sidle. He brought the gelding under control. "Are you settling in all right to the new posting?"

"Oh, it's routine stuff, really," said Cleo. "I've been angling for a job translating or as a wireless operator but there's none to be had at the moment."

Mena House stood on the edge of the desert, affording its guests a magnificent, uninterrupted view of the pyramids from its terrace. She gazed out toward the massive peaks, a human-made marvel that might soon bear witness to death and destruction. "There are rumors about moving GHQ to Palestine." She turned her head to look at Brodie. "Will it really come to that?"

His mouth set in a grim line. "It might. Word is that Rommel has already picked out a suite at Shepheard's."

The thought of Nazis overrunning the beautiful old hotel disgusted her. She prayed that Rommel would be stopped.

"Come on!" Brodie broke into her thoughts, jerking his head toward the open space. "Let's blow the cobwebs away."

The desert was a stony wasteland, bleak and grey, but to Cleo that afternoon, it was paradise. As they galloped and raced, she forgot her troubles and gloried in the sun on her skin, the wind and grit in her eyes and mouth, the tangle of her hair as it tumbled free of its pins. She felt wild and daring, reckless in a way she hadn't felt for years. The war, her worries over Marguerite, and all of her anguish over Brodie fell away. The years rolled back and it was just the two of them again, the only two people in all the world.

"You beat me!" The finishing post was a lone, arthritic tree that seemed to have been there since the beginning of time. Brodie had crossed it several lengths ahead of her.

He reined in, laughing in a carefree way she hadn't seen him do since they'd last ridden in this desert together. "It's a new world, Cleo. I won't hold back with you anymore."

His smile died and a serious look took its place. Suddenly shy, Cleo lowered her gaze and brought her sidling mare to a halt. "I'm parched. Let's stop for a minute." She slid down from the saddle without waiting for Brodie's help and they tethered their horses to the finishing post. Cleo put her hands on her hips until she brought her breathing under control, then she drank from the flask she'd slung by its strap across her body.

But Brodie was staring at her as if he had never seen her before. A little unnerved, she busied herself unclipping the canteen from its strap. "Want some?" Brodie nodded, took it from her, and tilted it to his lips.

Cleo wiped at her forehead with the heel of her hand. "Ugh, I need a wash."

"You look fine to me." Brodie held out the canteen to her, but as she reached for it, he gripped her hand instead and pulled her into his arms. "More than fine."

"What? Are we . . . ?" She searched his eyes but his gaze was on her lips. "What are we doing?"

He smiled. "What we've both wanted to do since we met last night."

"I don't. You . . . I *have not*!"

He bent his head. "Liar," he said through his smile, and stole her gasp with his kiss.

The canteen dropped with a hollow clatter to the stony ground. After the initial surprise of his mouth, hot and demanding on hers, Cleo responded with equal urgency. She strained to get closer, to tell him with her body the things she'd never had the courage to put into words. That kiss was everything in the universe, the only thing.

"Cleo, I love you," Brodie murmured into her ear. "I was a fool not to say it long ago."

They were the words she'd longed to hear, but . . . She cradled his face in her hands and drew back, searching his expression. "I don't understand," she said. "In London, you said you couldn't ask me to wait."

"I've had a promotion, Cleo. I'm a second lieutenant now. The pay's not brilliant, but I'll work hard and I'll do my damnedest to make you happy." He kissed her again.

Cleo couldn't have cared less about his finances or his status, but she didn't argue. She was too happy that finally, after all these years, Brodie was hers.

CLEO AND BRODIE spent a blissful weekend together. They drove to the Nile delta for a picnic one day; on another, they went walking among the pyramids like tourists, then drank orangeade on the terrace at Mena House, and danced together into the night.

Maybe the happiness Cleo had experienced these past few days was heightened and pure because she knew it would be fleeting. Every now and then, the intensity of her feelings would overcome her, and she would break off in midsentence and simply drink him in. She wanted to impress every small detail of him on her memory.

Neither of them spoke of his leaving. She wanted him to remember her with a smile on her face, even if sometimes her eyes glistened with tears.

"Cleo," Brodie said gently one evening. "There's something I have to tell you before I leave. It's about Madame Fahmy."

Chapter Eighteen

MARGUERITE

London, England
July 1923

Marguerite spent the final few months of her marriage in the exhilarating state between excitement and terror. Every sense on the alert, she anticipated the next fiery argument with Ali.

She had always been quick to anger and prone to the occasional violent quarrel with her lovers, but the fact that she was trapped in marriage with Ali made it worse. His boasts that he would "school" Marguerite to be an obedient wife made her boil with rage whenever she thought of them. That he, a mere boy several years her junior, should have the temerity to seek to control her simply because his ring was on her finger showed just how stupid he was.

Ali might be young, foolish, and weak-willed, but the beatings he gave her hurt just the same. She was heartily sick of him and his petty jealousies. He'd known all along who and what she was. Did he expect her to change for him?

She was not afraid of him. She *refused* to be afraid of him. When he swore on the Koran to be avenged on her with murder, she'd shrugged. He didn't have the nerve.

But then he had threatened to take her jewels—*all* of them, not just the ones he'd given her—away from her. From that day on, the weapon beneath her pillow was no longer a revolver. It was a .32 Browning semiautomatic.

They moved to London in July of 1923, into an apartment that was the epitome of luxury in a complex adjoining the Savoy Hotel called Savoy Court. Their suite boasted a marble bathroom and a spectacular view over the Thames, toward Waterloo Bridge.

The increasing volatility of their relationship was made worse by spending so much time together, Marguerite was convinced of that. Because Ali would not let her out without him, she had no choice. They went out every night, to the ballet, the opera, and to see Fred and Adele Astaire dance at the Shaftesbury Theatre. The summer was a hot one, but that made no dent in their daytime activities, either—the Henley Regatta, tennis at Wimbledon, cricket at Lords.

Despite pursuing this hedonistic existence, Marguerite did not love England. She couldn't speak or understand the language, for one thing, and the English remedy for her incomprehension was simply to speak English at her more loudly. She needed a translator even to go shopping, and the only one available to her was Said, Ali's private secretary—hardly congenial company.

She longed to return to Paris. If possible, without Ali.

They'd brought staff with them but there was only room in the suite for her and Ali, whom Marguerite relegated to the smaller of the two bedrooms.

Marguerite had with her Aimée Pain, her maid, although Aimée shared accommodation with other servants of the guests on the eighth floor of the hotel. In addition, there was Eugène Barbary, her personal chauffeur. She felt better knowing he was in London—strong, handsome, and loyal to her and her alone. And of course her little dog, Mitzi. She could not go anywhere without her. Between Mitzi, Barbary, her own iron will, and the fully loaded weapon under her pillow, Marguerite felt as safe as it was possible to feel from her husband.

Ranged against her small army were Ali and his secretary. Wherever Ali went, Said followed like the shadow everyone called him.

Aimée handed her a letter. It had been posted in London and had no return address. "Ah. Thank you," said Marguerite. She tossed the letter onto her desk, unopened. She didn't need to read it; she had sent it to herself, after all, an anonymous warning of the danger of marriage to Ali. She checked her pistol was loaded and put it in her bedside table drawer before she left.

Marguerite put the letter into her purse along with her lipstick and powder compact, then scooped up her little dog. Mitzi squirmed in delight, tail wagging madly. "Shall we go for a little walk, *chérie*? Shall we? Yes?"

Marguerite tucked Mitzi under her arm and left the suite. But when she stepped out onto the pavement, the sultry air swamped her. Ugh. Summer in London was foul. The humidity seemed to be building each day. Surely it couldn't get any worse! Perhaps an evening storm might bring some relief.

Eugène Barbary was waiting for her by the car, his exquisitely chiseled face shadowed beneath his chauffeur's cap. Marguerite took a moment to admire his wide shoulders, the tapering waist that looked so smart in the livery she'd designed for him.

"Why don't we drive to the country today?" said Marguerite, walking past him to the waiting Rolls-Royce, slanting a glance back at him beneath her eyelashes. "I feel the need for a little fresh air." After a pleasant interlude with Barbary, she must pack for her return to Paris. A new wardrobe was definitely in order. "Then to Selfridges this afternoon, I think."

"*Oui,* madame."

ALI WAS THE most frustrating man! Just when Marguerite wanted him to argue with her, he became mild and reasonable. She did her best to pick a fight with him at dinner and then again after the theater, where the musical playing was *The Merry Widow.* She was wearing a floor-length Chanel gown of pearl-embroidered white satin and long white gloves, a poor choice at these temperatures; the fabric, made heavy by its embellishments, seemed to stick to her skin, refusing to let her breathe. This infernal heat! It was like a fever that seemed to have climbed inside her and infected her brain.

After the opera, with thunder rumbling in the distance, she hurried up to the suite and locked the door behind her.

A few minutes later, the door handle jiggled, and there came a knock.

"Munira, let me in." Munira was her Muslim name, and Ali knew she hated it. That wasn't likely to persuade her to do his bidding.

Shoulders pressed against the door, heart pounding, Marguerite didn't answer. The darkened suite pulsed with the white flare of lightning, and a second later the companion crack of thunder split the air.

Ali, his temper rising to match hers, pounded on the door and demanded to be let in. She didn't answer. Would he give up and go away? Or was this going to be the night? She had already booked her ticket back to Paris.

The rain seemed to gather itself for a stronger onslaught. She'd left the window open to try to cool down the suite. The scent of rain filled the air. Another rumble in the heavens ratcheted up her tension.

Her husband was working himself up to a similar rage. "I'll kill you!" he yelled through the door. He sounded like he meant it this time.

Eyes wide with fear, Marguerite flew to the bedroom and fumbled with the drawer of the bedside table. She picked up her gun, felt the reassuring heft of it as she moved silently back to listen at the door.

A quieter voice spoke into the lull between Ali's shouts. "May I be of service, sir?"

That was probably one of the hotel staff. The porter, maybe, come to deal with this embarrassing guest.

A witness. This was it.

Holding the pistol behind her, Marguerite slowly opened the door.

Ali barreled into the suite, sending her stumbling back. The door slammed behind him and he stared at her, wild-eyed, as if he had been smoking hashish. He snatched up a bottle from the sideboard and wielded it like a club.

Marguerite backed up quickly as he came toward her, until she was in the sitting room. Through the open window, she heard traffic even at this late hour, and faintly, the music from a nearby night spot.

The pistol was a heavy weight in her hand. She remembered it with a start. She didn't have anything to fear.

The storm had reached a crescendo, and the curtains billowed around her, droplets of rain pelted her back. Ali moved toward her, and she brought the pistol up, ready to fire.

He stopped. "Ha! You'd never fire that thing. You wouldn't have the nerve."

Deliberately, Marguerite pointed the pistol out the window, aimed for the blackened night sky, and fired.

The kick of the pistol sent her stumbling back. The noise had nearly shattered her eardrums, but had anyone else heard it above the storm?

Desperate now, Marguerite managed to steady her stance. She pointed the pistol at her husband. "Touch me and you die."

"You . . . You *woman*! You fiend! Why did I ever marry you? I'll kill you! I'll smash this bottle in your face!" He gave a bullish cry of rage and charged.

IN HER PRISON cell, Marguerite had time to reflect on her actions on the night of Ali's death. At first, her mind had been confused. She'd needed Said to translate. She couldn't remember what she'd told the porter, or the police.

They arrested her, took her away. She remembered, belatedly, not to say anything more until her solicitor arrived.

Marguerite wished very much that Maître Assouad, her lawyer in Cairo, was here. He would know what to do. Shooting Ali in a London hotel had not been part of the plan.

Now that her head had cooled, she was well aware what a fix she was in. She'd been found with a gun in her hand and bullet wounds in her husband. Witnesses knew the two of them fought like cats and dogs. Said would supply the details. He would tell the court that if she'd divorced Ali, she would have walked away with nothing.

It was, as they say, an open-and-shut case. Marguerite claimed self-defense against the brutality of her spouse, but that was belied by the number of times she had shot him. She had wanted to finish him off. That was clear. Incredibly, he'd still been alive when they'd rushed him to hospital. However, he'd died shortly afterward, and the charge became murder.

One thing stood in her favor. She was in England. In England, she had leverage.

Shortly after her arrest hit the papers, she received a visit from a representative of the royal family. Major Bald was not employed at the palace, but he had obviously been selected for the role because he was discreet, an intimate of the royal family, and he spoke excellent French. In addition, he had always been an habitué of Parisian *maisons de rendez-vous*. He was a friend of both the Prince of Wales and Marguerite's other erstwhile lover, the Duke of Westminster. Best of all, Marguerite had known him since before the war.

What a relief to explain everything in her native tongue. One might convey with subtlety things that would undoubtedly be lost or blunted in translation. She told the major her demands, expressed in the politest possible terms.

Bald listened gravely. He acted as if anxious to help her, which didn't fool her for an instant. "Yes, yes, of course. We will do what we can. But the royal family cannot influence trials of this nature, you know. It simply can't be done."

"Why do I find that hard to believe?" Marguerite had developed a cough in the damp cells of Holloway. Even the interview room in which they sat at a cheap pine table was riddled with mold. Her voice rasped. "The letters that are in my possession . . . I'm sure you're aware that the prince was most confiding, most indiscreet. It's not just the love talk that might embarrass his family, but his discussion of the war and the way it was bungled, his many rages against his father, the King . . ." She knew some of those passages by heart and had no trouble quoting them.

"And you needn't send agents to search my belongings for them, either," she said. "They are safely in the possession of my lawyer in Cairo." Not *all* of them, but she would not mention that part. She had no intention of relinquishing all the letters David had sent. He wouldn't remember well enough to make inventory. There were enough in the bundle she offered the prince to make it appear that the collection was complete.

"The world is changing, madame," said the major, rubbing at his creased forehead with finger and thumb, as if the entire business was a headache. "Monarchs have to be very careful not to be seen to abuse their power."

"They also have to be careful to maintain their reputation, do they not?" said Marguerite sweetly. "David is their future King, and the British public loves him. It would be such a pity if that were to change."

And so, over the ensuing weeks, they eased closer and closer to agreement. Major Bald promised to do what he could if her Egyptian lawyer surrendered the inflammatory letters to the British High Commission in Cairo. Marguerite wrote to Maître Assouad and instructed him to comply.

Meanwhile, Marguerite remained clapped up in Holloway, awaiting trial. Those early days of hunger and deprivation, always hovering at the edges of her existence, returned in full force to haunt her. She would get out of this place if she had to bring down the entire British monarchy.

When the trial began, Marguerite maintained her dignity. She portrayed herself as an innocent, ill-used wife. On top of the beatings for which she had several witnesses, she hinted at "depraved, Oriental sexual practices" in which Ali liked to indulge. She alleged further that these practices had given her an embarrassing medical complaint, the evidence of which her doctor was happy to provide.

Despite her displays of emotion in the dock, Marguerite managed to keep a cool head while she waited for her letters to make their way from Cairo to England. They would need the prince himself to verify the letters. She'd heard he was at Balmoral now. Would there be time for him to read the letters that had been brought from Egypt before the trial ended? What would happen to them then? He'd burn them, she supposed.

Major Bald seemed to have ensured that no mention was made of Marguerite's past as a courtesan by the prosecution. The accused presented to the public as a respectable lady who had suffered unimaginable indignities at the hands of her brutish husband, whose depraved sexual practices might be accepted in the East, but certainly not in jolly old England.

The judge's summing up was weighted heavily in Marguerite's favor—perhaps again because of Major Bald's intervention. The prejudice of the jury did the rest.

Acquitted.

She was free.

She had fired three shots at her husband, at point-blank range. She hit him in the back as he ran from her, then again in the side of the neck in the corridor outside their apartment, felling him to the floor. A third time in the left temple for good measure, as he tried to crawl away.

And this British jury had found her "not guilty."

She could not believe her luck.

Chapter Nineteen

CLEO

Cairo, Egypt
Spring 1942

Cleo couldn't speak for several minutes after Brodie finished the story of Marguerite's murder trial. Eventually she managed to ask, "How do you know all of this?"

"When you mentioned the name 'Fahmy' I knew I'd heard it before. I was only a bairn at the time, but it was a huge scandal. The Egyptians were outraged. I did some digging and found out the story."

And they'd all known it, too. Mr. Costas, Madame Santerre, Philippe . . . "No one told me." No wonder Philippe hadn't wanted her mixed up with the princess. But he had tried to explain, hadn't he? She remembered now that she'd refused to listen.

But it was all quite surreal. Hoarsely she said, "That tiny little woman killed her husband? Murdered him in cold blood?"

"Perhaps not quite in cold blood. That part is in dispute. Marguerite said she fired at him in the heat of the moment, not knowing what she was doing. Clearly she was afraid of what her husband might do to her. There was evidence he had assaulted her on several other occasions."

"There are women, I believe, who are so badly abused by their husbands that one day they snap," said Cleo. "I think they deserve compassion rather than to be clapped up in jail." Her poor mother, trapped in a violent marriage, with no other means of escape. She must have been desperate to have resorted to murder.

"Without question," said Brodie. "But in Egypt there was a feeling that the entire thing was a setup from the beginning. That Marguerite intended to dispose of Ali to get her hands on his money, and that it was the anti-'Oriental' sentiment of a prejudiced jury that truly exonerated her, not the facts. On the facts, she ought to have been convicted three times over."

"But to shoot him in front of a witness like that . . ." Cleo shook her head. "She must have known she couldn't get away with it. That doesn't seem like it was calculated to me."

"Unless she knew no British jury would convict her," said Brodie.

"What do you mean?"

He shrugged. "It helps to have friends in high places."

She stared at him. "You think she dragged the duke into it?" He would have been the Prince of Wales at the time.

"She was desperate, and charged with murder, and she knew one of the most influential men in the country. I think it's pretty likely, don't you? She might well have resorted to blackmail."

So now her mother was not only a courtesan and a murderer but a blackmailer, as well. Nauseated, she pressed her fist to her lips and inhaled heavily through her nose. That delicate, impossibly elegant woman! What a nightmare.

Her mind buzzed with speculation. She didn't know what to believe. It was such a fantastical series of events. She needed to speak to the Fahmys. She needed to find out the truth. They would hardly be sympathetic to Marguerite, but until Cleo could return to Paris she wouldn't have an opportunity to get her mother's side of the story. Until she had, she refused to believe the worst.

"It's a lot to take in." Brodie pulled her into a gentle hug. She stood there, her arms by her sides, half wishing he hadn't told her all of this. She was appalled at the horrible experience Marguerite had been through. Was it any wonder that she'd been hardened by life and reluctant to welcome a daughter into it?

Even the feeling of Brodie's arms around her didn't help. She'd missed him for so long, worried about him every day of this terrible war, but even so, she couldn't bring herself to return his embrace. She eased herself free.

"I'm sorry, Cleo." His voice sounded rough and raw. "I wish I could have spared you, but I thought you'd want to know."

"Of course," she responded automatically. "You did the right thing." And now she'd have to come to terms with the idea that her mother might well be a murderer, on top of everything else. "I think I ought to speak with the Fahmys if I can. I don't want to upset them but I need to hear their side of it."

"Here." He put a hand in his pocket and brought out a scrap of paper with an address on it and handed it to her. "The family will probably refuse to see us. They're highly sensitive about the business and still in litigation with Marguerite. But I found Ali's secretary, Said Enani. Maybe he will agree to talk."

AFTER SUCH A turbulent evening, sleep was impossible. Cleo was still lying on her bed fully awake when she heard someone sneak back into the suite. Something clattered on the floor. "Whoops!" That was Liz.

Cleo got up to see if her friend needed help. "Liz? Are you all right?"

Caught in the act of tiptoeing in stockinged feet to the bathroom, Liz saw Cleo and lifted the shoes she carried as if in a toast. "Evening! Didn't think I'd see you back here tonight."

"Do you need help?" said Cleo, ignoring the truly excessive eyebrow waggling from Liz.

"Nope. Everything's tickety-boo." Then Liz lurched and gagged, clapping a hand to her mouth. Dropping her shoes, she made a dash for the bathroom and slammed the door behind her.

Cleo listened at the door in case she was needed, but eventually she heard Liz brushing her teeth. Concluding she wasn't required to hold back Liz's hair while she lost her supper, Cleo returned to her room. She perched on the window seat, her legs tucked under her as she'd done as a child and stared out at the moon that glimmered through the tall palms.

She couldn't get the idea of Marguerite's suffering out of her head. To be treated so cruelly by the man she loved that she resorted, in the end, to shooting him . . . She must have been utterly desperate. How could the shooting have been calculated? Marguerite couldn't possibly have been certain her former liaison with the Prince of Wales would be the key to exonerating her. It was a gamble no one in her right mind would take.

No, Ali's violence and abuse had caused Marguerite to snap. There was no other rational explanation.

It seemed an eternity and yet no time at all before the birds began their morning chatter to greet the rising sun. Dawn was breaking, the muezzin would soon be calling the faithful to prayer, and she would have to face another day.

The thought of discussing Ali's murder with someone who had

been there at the time made Cleo feel sick with apprehension. She made herself sit at her desk and write to Said, scribbling several drafts before finally deciding that brevity was best. She only tied herself in knots when she tried to explain her relationship to Ali and her interest in his death. She asked to meet him and suggested a time and place, addressed the letter, and propped it against the mirror on her vanity, ready to take down to the post office later. She blew out a long breath, feeling better for having taken the next step.

For the moment, that was all she could do.

TEA AT GROPPI'S had always been a post-cinema treat for Cleo on excursions with Fifi, but although she'd sneaked Brodie sweets from the famous coffee shop over the years, she'd never been there in his company before. His exclusion from these outings had been a source of hot contention between her and Fifi, who refused to go anywhere with a mere "stable boy."

Cleo had appealed to Serafina over it, without success. Irritated to be pestered with such trivialities, Serafina refused to upset Fifi. "It's difficult enough to get a governess prepared to put up with your headstrong ways, Cleo. Mademoiselle Faubert has lasted longer than any of the others. Just do as she says."

The café was light and airy, with apricot marble walls, black wrought iron chandeliers, and enormous windows framed with leadlight and stained-glass borders. Cleo and Brodie chose a table by the window and waited for the third member of their party to join them.

The heavenly scent of roasting coffee and fresh pastries usually delighted her but today, Cleo was too nervous to take more than a cursory look at the menu. She pleated the apron of the apricot linen tablecloth and smoothed it out again and began to wish she hadn't suggested this meeting.

Brodie tried to rally her. "Shall we order roast beef sandwiches or skip directly to dessert?"

She wasn't hungry. "Dessert, I think." But her heart wasn't in it.

"We don't have to do this," said Brodie. "We can leave now and you won't have to think about it again." He held out his hand and Cleo clasped it, thankful that he understood her anxiety.

"I hope he hasn't decided not to come," said Brodie, when they'd waited half an hour, lingering over their drinks—an espresso for Brodie and a lemon squash for Cleo. "Shall we go ahead and order?"

There was a host of exotic-sounding pastries and desserts and they pored over the descriptions for some time. "I can't decide between the peach melba and the *sfogliatella* flavors," said Cleo, sure she wouldn't eat a bite, but she was determined to keep up a good front for Brodie's sake.

"Order both and we'll share."

Deliberating over gelati flavors reminded Cleo of Lisbon and her covert meetings with Mr. Smith during the Windsor affair. She wondered where he might be now, and mentally toasted her erstwhile contact. Their light romance had ended with his departure from Lisbon and without regret on either side. To her surprise and deep gratitude, Smith had later arranged for her to be posted to Cairo, just as she'd always wanted. She had him to thank for the fact that she was sitting here with Brodie right now.

Their orders had already arrived when a small man dressed in a well-tailored blue suit walked in. After a cursory glance around, he approached them. "Lieutenant Gordon? And Miss Davenport. How do you do?"

"Mr. Enani? Do join us." Cleo gave him a tentative smile but the secretary didn't return the gesture. She was glad his English was so good. Her Arabic was very rusty.

Said Enani ordered coffee. Cleo's stomach was in knots. She didn't want to launch into the reason for this meeting straightaway. That would be rude, particularly in Egypt, where the preliminaries could go on for some time. But Cleo was too anxious and upset to make small talk.

As if he sensed her turmoil, Brodie drew Enani into conversation, inquiring after his health and the health of his family, and so on, until Enani had finished his coffee and been served another, and the waiter had moved away.

A discussion of Enani's continued employment with the Fahmys turned to the unpleasant business of Ali's death.

Finally Cleo spoke. "Mr. Enani, please understand that I'm not here to spy for Madame Fahmy. I simply want to know what happened on the night Fahmy Bey died."

The secretary's dark eyes filled with sadness and a hint of anger. It left Cleo in no doubt that he'd had genuine affection for his employer. "A tragedy. He should never have married that woman, of course."

Cleo sensed Brodie's concern but she didn't look at him. She'd braced herself for this meeting and she was determined to get through it without faltering. "Did you counsel him against it?"

"Madame Fahmy was after Ali's money from the very beginning. Anyone could see it, but he was obsessed. His sisters told him, I told him, time and again, but he didn't listen." He shook his head. "But no one suspected her true motives. No one thought she'd go that far."

Cleo's entire body trembled. Her ice cream sat untouched in front of her. "So you think it was murder, then."

"There is absolutely no doubt in my mind." He waved a hand that sported a heavy gold signet ring. "They are still fighting it out in the courts, but the Fahmys are determined Madame will get nothing from Ali's estate."

Cleo remembered Brodie saying that under Sharia law Marguerite was unlikely to inherit from a husband she had shot and killed. "It seems she is bound to lose that battle."

"That woman will stop at nothing," said Enani. "She even lied about being pregnant with Ali's child just so that she could inherit his fortune."

Cleo stared at him. The ruse sounded sickeningly familiar. She looked at Brodie, who said, "This is a story we had not heard about. How and when did this happen?"

Chapter Twenty

MARGUERITE

Paris, France
Autumn 1923

After all the trouble Marguerite had taken to ensure she inherited her widow's share of Ali's estate, after her time in prison and the murder charge she'd beaten, she might have been forgiven for thinking it would all be plain sailing from there.

Maître Assouad wrote with the bad news. Yes, as Ali's widow she ought to be entitled to the sum he had settled on her in their marriage contract, a sum she would not have received had they divorced. However, just because she had been acquitted of murder in England did not mean she would be deemed innocent under Sharia law. And Sharia law governed the disposition of Ali's fortune. A wife who killed her husband could not inherit his wealth.

In the eyes of Fahmy's family, Marguerite was a murderer. They would fight with everything they had to stop her seeing a penny of Ali's money.

If there had been a son from the marriage, it would have been different, of course.

Furious that all her scheming had left her in a worse position than if she'd simply divorced Ali, Marguerite dashed off an impetuous note in reply.

Thinking furiously, she paced the floor of her apartment, rubbing the pearls of her necklace between finger and thumb. There was no way she could be pregnant with Ali's son, but his family weren't to know that.

She telephoned Maître Assouad, who had come to Paris to confer with her about the details of her claim on Ali's estate and explained what she wanted.

He had known her for many years now, but even he was taken aback. "A baby?"

"Yes," she snapped. "But it must be a newborn boy. As new as can be. And I'll need it"—she flipped through her diary, calculating dates—"in April."

Assouad's eyebrows knitted. "I believe there are adoption services, but . . ." He was clearly out of his depth.

"No, no, I can't go through official channels." When he still looked bewildered, she added impatiently, "I need a baby boy I can pass off as my natural son. Mine and Ali's."

She would have to go into hiding for months while supposedly pregnant. That would be tedious, but she could wait a few months yet, blame her still slim figure on the lack of nutrition in prison.

Where might she go to wait out her fake pregnancy? Somewhere no one knew her. Her mind slipped from the contemplation of the child she didn't want but must have, to likely spa resorts.

Maître Assouad put her in touch with Cassab Bey, a Syrian

moneylender who was also in Paris at that time. He told her that a real child was not necessary for the fraud she intended to perpetrate. By sleight of hand, it would be possible to register a fictitious baby's birth, followed by his death a few days later, thus providing an heir to a larger portion of Ali's fortune than Marguerite would ever stand to inherit on her own. By the laws of succession, that portion would then be passed on from her dead child to her.

But like so many of Marguerite's wilder schemes, this one came to nothing in the end. As difficulty followed delay, she became paranoid that she was likely to be implicated in the ensuing investigation if the scheme were discovered. Unable to stand waiting any longer, she reported Cassab to the authorities. In the end, Marguerite was obliged to explain in a court of law that she had been duped by Cassab but had soon put a stop to the fraud when she realized what was going on. Miraculously the court accepted her version of events, despite her having announced her pregnancy publicly the previous October.

From that point, Marguerite was forced to accept that there was no easy way to win the fortune she saw as her due. The press had a field day with this latest development. She decided to remove herself from Paris for a while to let the gossip die down. The spa town Carlsbad was nice this time of year.

Well, Marguerite might be down, but she wasn't out. Once she'd enjoyed a well-earned holiday, she would set about pursuing her legal claim against her dead husband's estate.

She'd invested a lot of time and effort and suffered much hardship to get her hands on Ali's wealth. She wasn't going to give up without a fight.

CLEO

Cairo, Egypt
Spring 1942

"MADAME FAHMY BACKED down," said Enani, "but even before she admitted the truth, we knew she was lying about the baby." He looked at Cleo, then at Brodie. "A detective the Fahmys hired discovered that Madame had surgery late in 1917 that rendered her infertile."

From his briefcase, he took a document and laid it next to Cleo's dessert. It was an affidavit sworn by a doctor from the American Hospital of Paris. Cleo didn't understand the medical terminology but the effect of the procedure was stated clearly.

"Can we keep this?" Brodie asked.

"I have an unsigned copy here." Enani handed it to him.

Infertile. Then Marguerite Fahmy cannot be my mother. Cleo heard nothing more. The men's conversation flowed over and past her, words and more words pooling around her like the puddle of melted ice cream in her bowl.

Finally she felt Brodie's hand settle on her shoulder. She heard him, as if through a glass wall, say, "Come on, Cleo. Let's get out of here."

Unsure her legs would carry her, she struggled to her feet.

Marguerite was not her mother. She couldn't be. Cleo had been conceived in 1918, at a time Marguerite could no longer conceive a child. The knowledge was like a stone sinking in a vast, deep ocean.

One day it would hit the ocean floor and she would be able to as-similate the information. Now she simply couldn't.

Somehow Brodie got her back to Shepheard's and up to her room. At the sight of them together Taaleb uncrossed his massive arms and opened the door, a worried look in Brodie's direction.

"She's had bad news," said Brodie. "I'm going to sit with her awhile." His tone brooked no argument and Taaleb did not protest.

Cleo looked around. Thankfully there were no signs of Liz and Pat, who were both working that day. When the door had shut be-hind him with Taaleb outside it, Brodie scooped her up, holding her tightly against his chest.

"I can walk," protested Cleo.

"Let me do this." He strode to her bedroom, kicked open the door, then laid her gently on top of her four-poster bed. "What can I get you? Water? Whisky?" He straightened and dashed a hand through his hair. "I know I could do with a drink after that."

Without waiting for an answer, he went out again. She heard the *shush* of the water siphon and the clink of crystal glasses. He came back in with a tray of drinks and a small dish of nuts and dried apri-cots. Setting the tray on the bedside table, he said, "You'd better eat something. You look like you're about to faint."

She blinked. "Marguerite is not my mother. The duke cannot be my father." The words played over and over in her head.

He didn't answer, just offered her the glass of whisky, and sup-ported her while she sipped. When he laid her back on the pillow, Cleo stared up at the brass hoop and the cloud of mosquito netting that hung from it. She swallowed hard, but tears leaked from the corners of her eyes, rolling down her temples, dampening her hair.

After a few moments, she felt the mattress dip and then Brodie was on the bed beside her, gathering her in his arms. She turned

into him, and pressed her cheek against his broad, solid chest, un-
utterably thankful he was there. She stayed that way, listening to
the timbre of his voice, but not taking in the meaning of his words,
until darkness fell and oblivion finally claimed her.

Cairo, Egypt
Winter–Summer 1942

THE MONTHS THAT followed Brodie's first departure for the desert were a time of high anxiety, terrible lows, and magnificent highs
for Cleo. She struggled to come to terms with the fact that Marguerite had lied to her, not only about the Duke of Windsor, but about
the fact that she was Cleo's mother in the first place. That level of
callous cruelty was incomprehensible to Cleo.

When she thought of the way she herself had confronted the
duke, Cleo was filled with shame.

It was almost with gratitude that she worked ever longer hours,
both at headquarters and at the hospital at Heliopolis. If she kept
herself busy, there was less leisure to think. Less time to worry
about Brodie and the dangers he faced, as well.

Brodie never talked about the SAS and their nighttime raids,
but their small force had become legendary for their toughness
and daring. After weeks in the desert, Brodie would return, gaunt
and sunburned, every part of him full of sand, to the safety and
luxury of Shepheard's. Cleo treasured every second she spent
with him until he had to go out into the desert again.

When Brodie was away the days dragged painfully. Cleo developed insomnia, and after a week of nights spent lying awake and

staring into the darkness, worrying, she finally said, "Enough." If she couldn't sleep, she might as well do something useful. Something to take her mind off things she couldn't control or change.

She'd neglected her design work for almost the entirety of the war, but once she sat down and made herself work on some sketches, the urge to create returned in full force.

When she mentioned her designs to Mr. Mansoor, he snapped his fingers as if she'd triggered an idea. "More and more, I'm being approached by clients who at present are short of ready cash," said the antique dealer. "They want to break up their heavy jewelry, have it pared down and redesigned and sell the spare gems. Usually I send them to a manufacturing jeweler whose work is very fine, but he has little in the way of design skills. I'd be happy to recommend your services if you like."

The war had resulted in a shortage of both materials and people with the money to purchase fine jewels, but Mr. Mansoor's commissions took care of both. Cleo's habit of incorporating semiprecious stones in her designs was a cost-saving innovation, as well.

Until now, she'd always created in a vacuum; true, Lemarchand was an exacting critic, but he wasn't going to wear her pieces. By working for Mr. Mansoor, she learned to adapt her designs to a client's taste. Each successive woman became Cleo's muse, and she found herself continually inspired, not just by their appearances, but by their stories, as well.

Cleo's workload increased as word of mouth spread. Instead of frequenting parties and nightclubs after long days divided between work and the hospital, Cleo sketched feverishly through the night, mindful of the skills she'd honed and techniques she'd learned in her years at Boulle.

Something in her rebelled against the art deco style that had been all the rage at the design school, however. She preferred flowing, sensual lines and naturalistic subjects. She used everything and anything she could study and sketch around the hotel: the animals in the zoo, the birds that flocked to the hotel gardens to be fed, feathers and shells, dragonflies, leaves, flowers, the abstract patterns in nature. She developed her own palettes and sinuous sculptural shapes, and many women who had been previously mired in the traditional became converts to her modern style.

This frenetic activity eventually took its toll. Her superior officer, remarking on her thinness and the dark circles under her eyes, ordered her to take leave. With Brodie away goodness knew where, Cleo decided to visit Serafina and boarded the train to Palestine. It wouldn't be the first time they'd met since she'd arrived in Cairo but it was the first time since she received the news about Marguerite's machinations. She needed to tell Serafina the whole story but she hated to think of what her guardian's reaction would be.

If only she'd listened to Serafina in the first place, she would have been saved all of this heartache. She hoped Serafina would refrain from reminding her of this fact. She felt awful enough as it was.

Palestine was greener than Cairo, and more colorful. More German, these days, too. Cleo was disconcerted to hear German spoken around her, and the menus full of sausage and sauerkraut. "German Jews, most of them," commented Serafina when they'd finished their meal. "And no friends of Hitler. But you can spot the Nazi spies a mile away. They're so badly dressed!"

As they drove out to Colonel Drayton's house, where Serafina was working as a secretary, Cleo wondered how to broach the subject uppermost in her mind. She might not have an opportunity to get Serafina alone again during her overnight stay and she didn't want their conversation overheard.

"You seem to have something on your mind," said Serafina, surprising her with sudden insight. "Well, out with it. I'm sure it can't be as bad as all that."

"You won't like it, I'm afraid." Cleo explained about finding Marguerite and related all that she'd heard about her from Brodie and from Mr. Enani, as well.

"So it seems I've been played for fool," said Cleo finally. Shame washed over her anew. The pain of discovering the truth still lodged deep inside her, but uppermost now was humiliation. Every time she remembered her encounter with the Duke of Windsor, Cleo physically cringed.

She fully expected Serafina to be furious with her and braced herself. But Serafina was silent for some time after she'd finished her story. Then she reached across the gear box and laid her hand on Cleo's. It was a fleeting touch, the necessity of shifting gears requiring use of the hand again, but it was everything to Cleo. "Good people must never blame themselves for expecting only good in return," Serafina said. "You've never encountered the likes of Marguerite Fahmy before." Grimly, she added, "And I hope you never will again."

Cleo bit her lip, forcing herself not to dissolve into tears. Serafina was practical, logical, rarely sympathetic. How had she managed to say exactly the right thing?

One good thing had come from hearing the true story behind Marguerite's lies. "I have to say I'm relieved she's not my mother. I don't know how anyone with the least claim to a conscience could use someone like that."

They pulled up outside the house. Serafina made no move to get out but turned to Cleo, her gaze troubled.

"Hello! Hello!" The colonel came outside and was moving toward the car to greet them.

Whatever Serafina had been about to say was lost as the colonel wrenched open the door to let Cleo out. As she went to retrieve her valise from the trunk, Cleo thought back to the girl she'd been before the war. She'd been so determined to find out her origins, as if the identity of her parents was the key to her whole life. But Brodie was right. The war had changed things. She'd learned to count her blessings and see every moment spent with the people she loved as precious. It made the mystery of her parentage less significant.

"Let me take that, my dear." Colonel Drayton had a red face and a burly build with a shock of red-blond hair and a luxuriant moustache. He looked like the type to yell at his troops while pacing up and down with a swagger stick, but Serafina had assured Cleo that he was an excellent fellow, so Cleo reserved judgment.

At the door, Mrs. Drayton welcomed them with a warm smile and said, "Do come out to the garden, where it's cool." They drank lemon squash in the shade and the conversation soon turned to Rommel and the likelihood of his storming into Cairo at any minute.

"Plenty of room for you here, Cleo," said the colonel. "I can arrange a transfer, keep you out of harm's way."

"You could volunteer for the Red Crescent," said his wife. "We always need bright young things like you at the hospital."

Cleo sipped her lemonade. "Thank you, but I'll stay where I am until they decide to evacuate. All the women at GHQ were made to enlist in the Auxiliary Territorial Service, so if we're captured we'll be prisoners of war." Liz had kicked up quite a stink about it, insisting that she be made an officer in the ATS, rather than a private. Cleo hadn't cared.

"Well, we must all hope the decision to evacuate isn't made too late." The colonel gestured at Cleo. "You'd be no good to anyone if Rommel stormed into Shepheard's Hotel. Tiny little thing!"

That was probably true. "I have been learning how to shoot a gun." Cleo had persuaded one of the officers to take her out to an old quarry and teach her while he was on leave, but she hadn't got very far with it yet.

"Don't be silly, Cleo." Serafina was back to her old self. "What's that going to achieve?"

Cleo tilted her head. "It's not about Rommel so much. There are stories of rape and murder happening all the time around Cairo, these days. But I'm not a very good shot. I haven't had much chance to practice."

"Personal protection, eh?" said the colonel. "Quite right. Well, as it happens, you've come to the right place."

Ignoring Serafina's objections, Cleo drove with the colonel to the police station in the Jaffa Road. He gave her a preliminary briefing, then they went to the range, where Cleo spent two grueling hours practicing her shooting with the colonel's Smith & Wesson.

The colonel taught her how to load the ammunition, how to cock the pistol, how to sight her target.

"The gun must become a part of you, your aim automatic," he said. "Hold the gun like you're holding an orange. Squeeze the trigger. Almost. Try again."

Cleo shot the gun several more times, wincing as the noise blasted her eardrums.

"Now, see the dummies we've got rigged up here?" The colonel gestured at eight figures dotted around the range. "I want you to try to hit them."

He made her shoot with her right hand, her left hand, with both hands together, in the dark and with the light on. By the end of the session, he gave a grunt she interpreted as expressing satisfaction. "By tomorrow, you'll be shooting the pips out of playing cards."

She returned to the house with a pleasant exhaustion flooding her body and a deep yearning for a hot bath. But when they went in, she saw Serafina, a telegram in hand, pacing the front room. Lady Drayton started and leaped to her feet as they came in.

A telegram. Bad news. Cleo couldn't speak. She simply looked at her guardian.

Serafina, her eyes wide with shock, said, "Cleo. It's Brodie."

Cairo, Egypt
Summer 1942

AT THE MIDDLE East General Headquarters of the British Army, ashes whirled and danced through the air like a dirty snowfall and lay in drifts shin-deep on the ground. Top secret files were burning. Rommel's German troops were advancing rapidly, now just miles from Cairo.

Everywhere, people were packing boxes, rummaging through desks and file cabinets, dumping papers. "We've been ordered to evacuate!" an officer yelled at some newcomer over the din of activity. "Moving lock, stock, and barrel to Palestine."

They'd been expecting the order in the past few days but somehow, Cleo hadn't registered the urgency of the situation. She was numb.

The news that Brodie had not returned from one of his recent raids still hadn't quite penetrated to the reasoning part of her brain. She kept waiting for him to arrive at Shepheard's in a taxi, his head full of sand, his beard long, and his eyes haunted and weary.

But he wasn't coming back to Shepheard's. Not before Rommel stormed Cairo, anyway. Perhaps never. She didn't know if he'd been killed or captured, or even which army he'd fought.

The Germans executed commandos found behind enemy lines. If he'd been captured by them and not the Italians, she might never know what happened to him. The Italians would be the better proposition. She knew women whose husbands were in Italian prison camps and they'd been treated quite well.

Logically she knew she must obey orders but she hated the thought of leaving Cairo without knowing where Brodie was. What if he'd managed somehow to survive in the desert, or if captured, to escape? What if he returned starving and broken—injured, perhaps—and she wasn't there to take care of him?

She had to get hold of herself. Someone would send word to her if he was alive. Then she'd go to him.

Clearing out headquarters was exhausting work, which was just what she needed, and Cleo kept at it long after her colleagues were told to go home and pack. There were smuts on her face from trips to the incinerators and her hands were black with soot. There was ash in her hair, on her clothes, in her mouth and nostrils. She had paper cuts that needed tending—the slightest abrasion in the desert was always a possible source of infection—and she hadn't eaten since breakfast. But she couldn't seem to stop.

One of the officers pulled up short when he saw her and barked out, "You were supposed to be on the train to Palestine an hour ago."

"Yes, sir. I'm off now, sir." But she wasn't leaving until she made sure her boys at the hospital were all safe.

From GHQ she went directly to Heliopolis to help evacuate the wounded. Some of the men were too injured to move. What would become of them? Cleo sat with each one in turn until eventually she dropped to sleep from exhaustion. She woke disoriented, her mouth and eyes gritty.

She scarcely remembered packing and boarding the train for Palestine.

A sense of unreality carried her through the ensuing days of chaos as they established the new GHQ. Before too long, the panic that had led to the evacuation of Cairo eased. The Allies had managed to cut Rommel's supply lines and force a German retreat.

But Cleo felt little satisfaction that everything had turned out all right. Until she heard from Brodie she couldn't feel anything at all.

"I'd know if he was dead," she murmured to herself many times a day. "I'd feel it. I'd *know*."

Then the news came: Brodie had been captured by the Italians and transported to a prisoner of war camp in Italy. "Oh, thank God!" Cleo fell to her knees, clutching Lord Grayson's telegram in her hand. "He's alive!"

It certainly wasn't the best news but it wasn't the worst. The story behind his capture—or a heavily censored version of it she heard from the other SAS men—was that Brodie had been separated from his men in a melee and the others had been forced to retreat, leaving him behind. He had escaped capture that time, and spent three weeks in the desert, using every survival skill he knew, drinking water out of the radiators of derelict vehicles along the way.

Picked up by an Italian patrol, he'd been dehydrated and half-delirious and his recovery had been slow. The Italians had failed to list him among their prisoners by an oversight and by the time Lord Grayson received notice from the Army as next of kin, Brodie had already arrived in Italy and written to Cleo.

She fell upon his first letter greedily, scarcely able to believe he truly was alive and well enough to write. He told her of his adventures, adding, "The only thing that kept me going at all was the thought that I had to get back to you, darling Cleo. When this bloody war is over, I don't ever want to be parted from you again."

Chapter Twenty-One

Cairo, Egypt
1942–1943

*H*eadquarters did not return to Cairo, so Cleo was in Palestine when the Axis powers in North Africa finally surrendered in May 1943. There were wild celebrations everywhere, but Cleo could not join in with a carefree heart. Brodie had so narrowly missed the end of the fighting.

The war might have ceased in North Africa but there was still much work for Cleo, both at the hospital and at GHQ. Liz and Pat felt they could be of more use in England, so they applied for transfers.

"I can't believe we're going home!" said Pat, as they drank to their time together. "I really will miss this place."

"I'll miss the food," said Liz, slinging an arm around Cleo and planting a smacking kiss on her cheek. "And you."

"Yes! Cleo most of all," said Pat. She bent to look into Cleo's face, a little owlish but serious now. "And you must write the minute you hear from Brodie, understand?"

Cleo prayed for Brodie every night and waited anxiously for his next letter. But toward September of 1943, with the Italians in complete disarray and surrendering to the Allies, the Germans took over many of the Italian prison camps. Brodie's letters ceased and she heard nothing more.

By late November, she and Serafina were back at Shepheard's. Cleo had been transferred to a nursing home in Cairo. She worked long hours helping to rehabilitate wounded soldiers, but nothing could keep her mind off Brodie. She hadn't heard from him since July.

One evening when she was alone in Serafina's suite and inching ever closer to despair, a knock fell on the door.

"Lord Grayson!" She was half laughing, half crying, so delighted to see him standing on the threshold that she threw herself into his arms and hugged him tightly. "What are you doing here? Did you come for the conference?" All of the bigwigs were in town for a summit, including Winston Churchill.

"That's it." He patted her gently and said, "It's good to see you. I've missed you, my dear."

"Tell me everything!" Cleo drew him into the sitting room and peppered him with questions. Lady Grayson was holding up well, considering. Their London house had the glass blown out of its windows and had to be boarded up because there was no glass to be had to replace it, but everyone in the household was safe and sound. The list of casualties among their family and friends was soberingly long. Hippolyte had joined the Free French and died in action at Bir Hakeim. Several servants from the estate had perished, as well.

"Can I get you a drink, Lord G?" Taaleb managed to keep her well-stocked with gin, although recently, the hotel cellars had run out of French champagne and wine.

"Allow me." Lord Grayson moved to the drinks trolley and fixed them a double gin and tonic each. He handed her a glass and sat down.

Unable to resist, she asked the question that never left her mind. "And Brodie?" But if Lord Grayson had heard anything, he would have told her straightaway.

"Brodie is alive and well and already back in active service," said Lord Grayson. "I only just heard the news and came straightaway to tell you."

Cleo nearly dropped her drink. "*What?* Why didn't you say so? But . . . but how? Last I heard, the Germans had taken over the camp he was in."

"He and some other men escaped into the Apennine Mountains shortly before the Italians abandoned the camp. It took him some time, but eventually he made his way south to join the Allied forces. And so, here we are." Lord Grayson's eyes crinkled at the corners. "You know, I really think you ought to have that drink now."

He was right. Cleo sipped her gin. It was bracingly strong. The instant the alcohol hit her bloodstream, she felt the tension leave her body. Brodie was alive. He was free. She hadn't even dared to hope for news like that. "Where will he go now?" With the fighting over in North Africa, he wouldn't return to Cairo.

"I'm not privy to details but I expect he will be deployed some-where in Europe. Perhaps France," said Lord Grayson. "I'm sorry to say this, but I don't suppose we'll see him again until the war is won."

"Let's hope that's very soon," said Cleo.

Lord Grayson raised his glass. "I'll drink to that."

Chapter Twenty-Two

Scotland
Winter 1945-1946

*W*hen her war service came to an end in late 1945, Cleo arranged to spend Christmas with the Graysons in Scotland. Despite her dislike of Scottish winters, Cleo was beside herself with excitement. Brodie was coming home.

The Special Air Service had officially disbanded, but Brodie and a group of others had been busy searching all over Germany and beyond for their fallen comrades. The Nazis had been excellent record-keepers except in one respect: they had deliberately obliterated all trace of what happened to commandos and spies. Cleo remembered well the agony of the months she'd spent not knowing what had become of Brodie. She couldn't imagine experiencing that uncertainty for the rest of her life.

To Cleo's surprise, Serafina decided to come with her. "It's years since I've been back. I suppose it's the war. One grows sentimental."

The journey to Scotland was far less circuitous than Cleo's trip out to Cairo from Lisbon. She'd thought she remembered the cold of a highland winter, but the bitter weather made her feel as if she would never be warm again. Honestly, why anyone would want to live there was beyond Cleo.

She was busy with an arrangement of clean-scented fir branches and holly for the mantel of the massive open hearth, when a voice behind her said, "What? No mistletoe?"

"Brodie!" Greenery scattered and holly berries bounced on the floor as Cleo whirled around and ran to throw herself into his arms. He stared down at her, his lean, lined face alight with laughter, and then he was kissing her until she couldn't breathe.

"Marry me, Cleo. I want you to be my wife."

"Oh, yes, yes. Yes!" She took his face between her hands and kissed him in between each "yes." It was so wonderful to have him back again, she would have agreed if he'd proposed an expedition to the South Pole.

The thought of expeditions made her say, "I know you'll be traveling the world and I can't always be with you, but—"

"I have good news," said Brodie. "My grandfather has decided to reinstate me as his heir. He was impressed with my war record, maybe. Anyway, if I agree to live on the estate and learn how to manage it . . ." He broke off, as Cleo stared at him, horrified. "Don't you see, Cleo? Now we can afford to get married. I . . . I thought that was what you wanted, too."

"But what about becoming a famous naturalist? What about traveling the world and having adventures?" This about-face was bewildering. She'd never dreamed Brodie would settle for the life of a country gentleman. She couldn't imagine it.

His brow furrowed. "But I thought you'd be pleased."

Pleased? At the prospect of his giving up his passion, his dream, to marry her? At the idea that she must live out the rest of her days in Scotland, the only place she'd ever been that she utterly detested. Well, no, not detested, precisely, but every time she stayed here it felt like the cold would slowly kill her.

And what about his study, his research? "You'd give up everything you've planned, everything you've worked for, for me," said Cleo.

He frowned, searching her face. "It's not like that."

"That's what it amounts to." And with a sudden jolt, she realized he would expect her to give up her dream of building a jewelry business, too. The idea chilled her more than the blizzard brewing outside.

"We all need to grow up some time," said Brodie. "Travel, adventures . . ." He sighed. "Those ambitions seem to belong to another life."

"But Oxford . . . Your field research. The hard work you put in . . . All of that was for nothing?" She might have been talking about herself.

"Not *nothing*," said Brodie. "Of course not." He ran a hand over his closely cropped head. "Look, Cleo, I have to go back to Berlin next week. But I wanted to show you the manor while we're here, introduce you to my grandfather. The property is not on the scale of this place but it's very comfortable. And you'll put your own touches on it, I'm sure."

"*Stop!*" Cleo could hardly believe things between them had gone awry so quickly. "This isn't what I want. It's not what you want, either." The look on his face made her falter. "Is it?"

He was quiet a moment. Then he said simply, "I've never had a home to call my own." He shook his head. "No, it's more than that. That estate was my father's birthright but he was disinherited because he fell in love with the wrong woman. Having it passed down to me feels like a vindication, somehow. I think my mother would have been proud to see me there."

"I just . . ." She made a helpless gesture. "This kind of life. Farming in Scotland. With you. It never even occurred to me."

He frowned. "Cleo, are you saying *you* don't want to live in Scotland?"

Five minutes before he'd walked into the room she would have said she'd happily live with him on the moon. "Yes," she blurted out. "That's what I'm saying. The climate is just dire, Brodie. And how am I to build a jewelry business in the Scottish Highlands?"

His face was paler than before. "After all we've been through to get here, I thought this part would be simple. You. Me. Together at last."

When he put it like that, she felt awful. Hadn't she always wanted him to consider the world well lost for love? And now here she was, balking at their proposed living arrangements. But she knew that being the wife of a farmer—even a gentleman farmer—was a full-time occupation. Not to mention the babies that would follow. If she was forced to stay in Scotland, she'd hate it. Worse, she would grow to resent him. She half resented him already.

When she'd dreamed of their future together, she'd imagined his long absences exploring foreign jungles while she designed her collections. Then she would join him on his travels or have him with her in Paris while she worked and he took a break or wrote up his research. It wouldn't have been ideal for most people, but she could see herself loving that life.

Had his thirst for nature and travel really belonged to youthful daydreams? She didn't think so. She thought he was compromising because he wanted to be a good husband and provider. Because he wanted to prove to the rest of his family that he was good enough.

That wasn't the man she'd fallen in love with. That wasn't the life full of passion and adventure they'd always longed for.

She took a deep breath. "Brodie, I love you. More than anyone or anything in the world. But I simply cannot be your wife. Not if it means us both giving up our dreams."

"I can't believe I'm hearing this." He looked as shocked and hurt as if she'd shot him. "You can't mean it."

It was so wrenching to see him like that, she nearly gave in, but she had to fight for the life they'd always wanted. Didn't they both deserve it after all they'd been through during the war? "It's not something I would say lightly, Brodie. You know how I feel about you. This idea of settling down on a farm . . ." She made a helpless gesture. "It's just not you."

"Cleo, truly, I've had my fill of adventure. Believe me."

The more he justified the decision, the more convinced she became that she was right. "You've spent years at war. You're battle-weary and longing for home comforts. I understand. But you are healthy and strong and have all of your faculties. It won't be long before you are itching to be out there again, seeing all the marvels of this world. I *know* it." She was desperate for him to understand, but he seemed not to really hear her. "You've hardly had a chance to catch your breath. Give yourself a little time to decide what you really want."

He gripped her shoulders and stared into her eyes. "Don't you think I know my own mind?"

"Perhaps you do." She hesitated. "But I'm holding on to my dream, Brodie. And I simply can't pursue it here."

He let his hands fall to his sides. He didn't belittle her ambition or give her an ultimatum, which might have made it easier for her to hold steady. He looked shattered.

As if sleepwalking, he slowly turned and headed to the door.

"Please," she called after him, her voice trembling. "Try to understand." But he didn't answer and he didn't look back.

In the excruciating days that followed, both Lord and Lady Grayson and even Serafina tried to persuade Cleo to accept Brodie's proposal. Thinking of what life would be like without him, Cleo was tempted to give in several times, but she forced herself to remain firm.

As she watched Brodie drive away, bound for his new home, she knew she'd made the right decision. Maybe in time he'd realize he'd made a mistake and throw in the sensible, stable life for the one he was meant to have. And if he didn't, and he transformed into the kind of man who was content to live on a small Scottish estate, then he'd be better off marrying one of those county girls who had been brought up to be chatelaines of such establishments. Not a half-tamed girl from Cairo who would always pine for Paris and the life of creativity and color she might otherwise have had. The thought of him settling down with another woman was like a knife through the heart.

One more reason to loathe Scotland. She was never, *ever* coming here again.

Paris, France
Winter 1946

CLEO LEFT FOR Paris as soon as she could persuade Serafina to go. Brodie had politely included her in the invitation to the Graysons to tour the manor house but she had declined. She couldn't bear to see the place that had caused their rift, nor to meet his horrid grandfather.

Misery constantly shadowed her but she did her best to hide her heartache. After experiencing war, one's personal troubles never seemed to loom as large or have the power to incapacitate. Her prayers had been answered and Brodie had come home safely. That was the greatest gift she could ever expect.

It was a relief to arrive in Paris, but at the Santerres', Cleo and Serafina found a household weighted with grief. Madame had survived the war but she was broken by the loss of Hippolyte. Philippe, after a stint at a German labor camp, had successfully navigated the German occupation to emerge from the war even wealthier than before. He had been accused of collaboration until it came out that he had been part of a resistance circuit run by the British from Baker Street in London.

The reunion was bittersweet. "*Ma pauvre petite,* it is good to see you! And Serafina, too. It's been too long." Madame looked gaunt, the dark shadows under her eyes standing out starkly against her pale skin.

Wordlessly Cleo embraced her and felt her frail body tremble. The four of them sat for some time, drinking the South African wine Serafina and Cleo had brought and listening to Madame's stories of Hippolyte.

When Madame retired, Philippe took his mother upstairs, then came down again. He sat next to Cleo and took her hands in his. "Thank you, my dear. She loves to talk about him. But it's been years now, and most people don't want to hear. They expect her to move on."

Cleo sought out her other friends from her time in Paris but it was an exercise full of sorrow. Many had died in camps or been incarcerated, beaten and starved under the harsh Nazi regime.

Some of the young women at Boulle who had taken up with German boyfriends had been cruelly vilified by their own countrymen after the war.

One person who had survived relatively unscathed was Monsieur Lemarchand, who had returned to Paris before the occupation and had settled back into his studio in Montparnasse. "It was a close-run thing," he told Cleo. "I designed this little jewel, you see." He flipped through his sketches and came up with the right one. It was a bird in a gold cage. For the bird, Lemarchand had defiantly used the French *tricouleur*: a red coral breast, blue enamel wings, a white gold head, the feathers beautifully rendered, and a sapphire for the eye. The bird spread its wings but could not take flight. It was trapped in a gilded cage.

"Mademoiselle Toussaint and I were taken in for questioning over it." He chuckled at Cleo's horrified gasp. "Clearly a work of subversion, the Bosche said. Mademoiselle coldly explained to them that the caged bird was a recurring motif at Cartier, and there was no subversion intended. We were lucky that Coco Chanel intervened or we might have been shipped off to a concentration camp and Cartier shut down altogether."

He found another sketch and showed it to Cleo. "Liberation," he said with satisfaction. This time, a bird released from the cage and poised to take flight. It made Cleo's heart lift to see it.

"How is business, these days?" she asked.

"Terrible, as you can imagine," he replied. "No one can afford to buy the best pieces anymore. The largest, most beautiful gems must be cut down. It's a travesty. I don't know if we'll ever reach those heights again."

Of course, Cleo had realized already there was little likelihood of her getting a job as a designer at one of the top jewelry houses now. Even had business been booming, after the war, all the available jobs went to men, with women being sent back to domestic duties. The time had come to strike out on her own.

She needed to land one or two prominent clients, trendsetters who would wear a Cleo Davenport creation once and cause a sensation. Even a positive review in one of the major fashion magazines would be something. But to attract this kind of publicity, she needed to build a collection. To do that, she needed capital. But she couldn't accept Philippe Santerre's offer and the banks would never lend to a single woman with no collateral.

Still she refused to give up. She'd brought her designs to show Lemarchand. Together, they pored over them. "Many of these are excellent, but for a collection, you need a theme." He deliberated over the cuff she'd designed for Marguerite. Cleo had all but forgotten her determination to win Marguerite's admiration by creating a complete parure for her.

"Not that one," she said, moving to take it from him.

"No, I think it should be this one," he said, ignoring her outstretched hand. "What made you put the cool blues together with the autumn tones here? It shouldn't work, but it does. This piece is special. It speaks."

Cleo remembered how inspired she'd been with all kinds of hopes and dreams when she'd created that piece.

"And this." He selected the double choker of jade beads with a large daisy clasp, its petals made from diamond-crusted rock crystal, the center picked out in yellow citrine.

"But these are pieces I designed before I even went to Boulle," said Cleo. "Have I learned *nothing* since then?"

Lemarchand shrugged. "Learning a craft requires concentrated effort and attention to technique. But you need to forget what you've learned in order to truly create."

She frowned. "I don't understand."

He waved a hand. "In the untutored amateur, the imagination runs wild; it doesn't know any better. There is the spark of genius but not the skill to turn it into something great. In the student, the imagination is tamed, reined in, curbed at every turn because in order to implement the rules, the student must be *conscious* of everything they do. It's only after the principles and techniques of design become innate that the artist can truly flourish, let her imagination run free."

"So all of the work I've done in the past years was just practice?" She thought of all those feverish hours she'd spent late at night or squeezing in her work between clerical duties and volunteering at the hospital.

"*Oui, c'est ça.*" Lemarchand gave a decisive nod. "None of it wasted, mind you. Choose a new theme for your collection or take the Marguerite designs and perfect them with the knowledge and techniques you now have." He held up his hand as if in blessing. "You have served your apprenticeship, my dear Cleo. Now you must set yourself free."

SERAFINA AND CLEO'S stay in Paris stretched into months while Serafina wrote her book and Cleo designed her new collection.

Cleo rejected the idea that her best work was on the pieces she'd designed for Marguerite and set about searching for inspiration. But Europe was battered and depressed in the aftermath of the war and Cleo's spirit was scarcely less so. All her life, she'd felt the need to create, a single-minded obsession. Despite the importance of her war work in Cairo, she'd often chafed at the lack of time to pursue her designing career.

Now that she had the time to create, she seemed to have lost the drive.

Deciding that she needed to release the death grip on her creative muse, Cleo took the day off and persuaded Serafina to join her. They had never spent the day together like this before.

Somehow Cleo managed to persuade her guardian to visit all her favorite haunts. They were sitting in a smoky café sipping crème de cassis when Serafina asked, "What are you going to do with yourself now, Cleo? Have you decided to go back to Boulle?"

"Monsieur Lemarchand says I'm ready to design my first collection. But well, there's the problem of working capital. The banks won't lend to me, of course. Philippe Santerre has offered to be my financial backer, but that would place me in a difficult position."

Serafina raised her eyebrows. "I suppose it never occurred to you to ask me."

It never had. Cleo's mouth fell open in shock. "But you've done so much for me already. I couldn't."

"Nonsense!" Serafina waved a hand. "You have talent. I've never doubted it. You've got training. You have quite a great deal of persistence. I'd expect you to pay me back, of course. And I want to see a proper plan, and a budget and costings. If you don't know how, ask Philippe to teach you. When you arrive at the figure you need, double it, and I will lend it to you. We'll draw up a repayment plan, as well."

Cleo opened her mouth. Closed it again. "Aunt Serafina! I—I don't know what to say."

She chuckled. "Cleo Davenport, lost for words. Now, *that* I never thought I'd see."

"But it will be quite a sizeable sum." Cleo bit her lip. Perhaps Serafina didn't realize what it took to finance a business like hers. "Forgive me for being blunt, but can you afford it?"

Serafina tapped the side of her nose. "I might have inherited money, but I've been remarkably astute with my investments, if I do say so myself. You just work on getting all the pieces in your collection made. As long as you satisfy me that you have a good plan for how my money will be spent, you won't have to worry about capital."

Cleo couldn't bring herself to admit that she didn't even have the beginnings of a collection to work with yet. But she couldn't let the opportunity pass. She must find a way.

Chapter Twenty-Three

*A*fter months of creating and rejecting designs, reluctantly Cleo decided to take Lemarchand's advice and work on the "Marguerite" collection. Serafina might grow cold on providing her with initial working capital if she didn't come up with a concrete plan soon.

Cleo's inspiration board soon filled with sketches and photographs she cut from newspapers and magazines. Once she focused on a particular motif, she saw it everywhere. The daisy was not considered to be a noble or romantic flower but to Cleo, it meant spring—new beginnings. She'd begin anew, leave the real Marguerite far behind.

Once she had some concept designs, she would have to source the gems. One of her former colleagues at Boulle put her in touch with a dealer, and Lemarchand gave his stamp of approval, so she went to work, negotiating prices and setting out her costings and budget, as well as a business plan, which she nervously produced to her guardian.

Serafina asked a few pointed questions, Cleo made some changes, then Serafina handed over the money without further quibble. They both signed the repayment plan, which would only be triggered when Cleo was turning a certain figure in profit. Cleo was determined to make this business work, but she was doubly determined because of Serafina.

"I'm so grateful you've put your trust in me like this," she said, throwing her arms around her guardian and hugging her tightly. "Thank you."

"Don't mention it," said Serafina a little gruffly. She patted Cleo on the back—whether out of affection or as a prompt to let her go, Cleo couldn't decide. "As I said, you've got talent. And what use is money if it isn't spent?"

Cleo still needed raw materials, which were in scarce supply. She began to join in the social round with Lady Grayson and mentioned her desire to purchase quality gold and platinum jewelry to a couple of the most talkative of Lady G's friends. They could look at her askance if they wished; she needed gold.

Word spread, and discreet inquiries came from some of the women whose families had been hit hard by war.

Eventually Cleo moved back to Paris permanently and rented a small studio. Through Madame Santerre and her friends, she found many women wishing to sell the jewels they'd smuggled out of occupied countries with them. They were women accustomed to luxury forced to live as poor refugees, and Cleo had to exercise every ounce of tact she possessed to close the transactions.

She bought some pieces she didn't want and each time paid more than they were worth. Reluctantly she had to forgo some truly spectacular pieces, which she couldn't justify purchasing, given her budget. Even so, Lemarchand shook his head over her buying practices. "You cannot afford to be softhearted in business, Cleo."

"If making a profit means I must take advantage of other people's suffering, I'd rather go under," retorted Cleo. "But I'm well within budget, and my generous prices mean all of the best pieces come to me." From one of the cabinetmakers she'd known at Boulle, she had bought a little cabinet with shallow drawers in which to sort and store the gems she extracted from their settings, before sending the gold to her manufacturing jeweler to melt down.

When finally she had all the materials she needed, she reworked her designs, modifying them to accommodate the size and color of the gems she'd sourced. "Sometimes constraints are the mother of invention," said Cleo, showing Lemarchand the bib necklace that had transformed from not-quite-right to absolutely perfect because she'd been obliged to substitute amethysts for the emeralds she'd intended to use.

She suffered several setbacks, of course. Advertising was an expense she had included in her budget but it cost far more than she'd anticipated to place ads in the major magazines.

"Well, I simply can't afford it, that's all," she told herself. "I'll have to get word out some other way."

There were several glitches with the manufacturing process. When Cleo received the first piece, a simple brooch in an abstract design, it didn't look right. She went back to her design and compared them. Yes, she'd specified the correct dimensions. But while the gems were the correct size, they seemed crowded together, rather than surrounded by thick swirls of gold. She measured the brooch. She was right. It was too small.

The manufacturing jeweler dealt with much more important customers than Cleo, and it took more than two weeks for him to make time to see her. When she explained the problem, he waved a dismissive hand. "There is no mistake. We worked with the dimensions stated in the brief. Now, if you don't mind, I'm busy."

Monsieur Prideaux was middle-aged, bald on his head but hairy where his rolled-up sleeves exposed meaty forearms. He wore a heavy gold signet ring and a scowl.

Cleo stood her ground. "This isn't good enough, monsieur. You must get it right or I will be forced to take my business elsewhere." It was an empty threat. He was the best and she needed the best. But she couldn't let him ride roughshod over her. Who knew how her collection would end up if he continued to allow these mistakes?

"Be my guest," said the jeweler.

Cleo blinked. This wasn't going the way she'd imagined when she'd walked in full of righteous anger.

"But," added the jeweler, "you'll find we have a contract. So you will be liable for the expenses already outlaid, plus a penalty if you walk away now."

All right. She could work with this. She smiled at him. "You must understand that I don't *wish* to go elsewhere. You are the best and the best is what I must have. But how can I continue to send you my work if I cannot be certain it will be carried out to my specifications? Please, monsieur, look at my design and then look at this brooch. It's not right."

Prideaux studied her exhibits. He grunted.

Interpreting that to mean he was prepared to listen, Cleo said, "You have an excellent reputation, monsieur. I am building mine. I fully intend to be the next Belperron. But how am I to do that if such costly mistakes are made in the manufacturing process?"

She waited expectantly but received no answer. Cleo persisted, "I really am asking you, monsieur. How am I to turn a profit if I must pay twice for a piece? Because this brooch must be done again and I don't think it should be at my expense."

"As I said, mademoiselle, you are free to go elsewhere."

She sighed and opened her purse. "I was reluctant to do this but

I see I have no choice. I have a letter of demand here from my lawyer." It was Philippe's lawyer and she couldn't afford to pay him to do more than to write this letter but she wouldn't tell Prideaux that.

She shrugged. "I had hoped we could remedy this amicably, monsieur, but if I must resort to relying on the contract, as you were so quick to do, then I will. Under clause three of our agreement, you are obliged to manufacture jewels to the exact specifications I give you. Failure to do so, and subsequent refusal to rectify upon request at no cost to me, is grounds for termination of the contract. And *you* will be liable to compensate *me*." She held the letter out. "As I said, I didn't want to do this. Now. Shall I give you this letter? Or shall we discuss the matter further?"

Philippe laughed when he heard about her meeting. "Bravo! We will make a businesswoman out of you yet."

She'd expected to loathe the business side of things but because she was negotiating for something she believed in with her whole heart, she found it stimulating rather than tedious. Her strength did not lie in the numbers, however, and on Philippe's advice, she hired a bookkeeper to help her. Another expense she had not anticipated. How right Serafina had been, advising her to double her estimate!

But Giselle Thièrry was smart and didn't treat Cleo like an idiot or a little girl. She took a collaborative approach, as if she had a personal stake in Cleo's business. The bookkeeper had recently gone into business for herself, as well, having been turned off from an accounting firm when the male employees returned from the war. Giselle's story made Cleo determined to hire only females in her business and work with female contractors where she possibly could.

As Giselle so often reminded her, while there was a lot of money going out at this early stage of the business, there wasn't any coming in. Sometimes Cleo despaired of ever repaying Serafina. But as the pieces began to come in from Prideaux's—with no more mistakes— her heart lifted. She had rented the perfect space to show her collection. Now she needed to persuade people to come.

"An unknown *créatrice joaillière* will need to make a big splash to catch the eye of the right people," said Lemarchand.

Cleo considered this. "You mean, I need some sort of gimmick or stunt?"

"Or someone famous to wear your creations."

Philippe had been studying her accounts. "But remember that if you make a splash and get lots of orders, you will need the capital to fill those orders."

"Best to start small," said Cleo. Part of her longed to create a sensation along the lines Lemarchand suggested but she knew Philippe was right. No one paid a deposit when they ordered a piece; once she'd sold the pieces she'd already manufactured she would have to front the cost herself. According to Giselle, lack of sufficient funding was the number one way most fledgling businesses failed. If she built gradually, remained exclusive until she made a name for herself, she would be better able to survive.

"All right," she decided. "Here's what we'll do."

She would personally hand-paint reproductions of her designs on invitation cards for all the major players in the fashion industry. Even if they tossed the invitation away, they would at least glimpse a color representation of her work and perhaps be intrigued. Catalogs were necessarily photographed in black-and-white. Jewelry appeared that way in magazines, too. This was a way to lift her collection out of the ordinary. It took a lot of time, and halfway through the list of eighty guests she'd compiled, she wished she hadn't begun, but when the cards were finished she couldn't help but be hopeful.

"These are works of art!" said Giselle, who had taken to staying on at Cleo's studio for a glass of wine after she'd gone through her accounts. She sipped at her Bordeaux. "You should frame and sell them, not give them away."

Cleo laughed, grabbing the wine bottle with a gouache-daubed hand. "Who would want to hang a picture of a necklace on their wall?" She surveyed the paintings that were pegged on washing lines to dry. "But I'm glad you like them. I hope they're intriguing enough to attract some of the press to my show."

Paris, France
Spring 1947

WHEN EVERYTHING WAS finally ready for her première, Cleo put her hands on her hips and gazed around her, relieved the hard work was over and everything had gone to plan, but anxious about what the evening held in store once the guests arrived.

Against everyone's advice, she'd decided to launch her collection in the spring. In the fashion world, one always showed a collection with the following season in mind. However, she wanted her guests to feel the fresh promise of spring when they saw her creations, and she wasn't trying to interest department store buyers in her pieces, so she didn't need to be concerned with lead time.

Giselle's comment about her paintings being works of art stuck in Cleo's mind. Rather than show her jewelry in vitrines or on mannequins, she'd decided to display them in a gallery, as the works of art they were.

Each parure was mounted on a separate plinth and arranged like a sculpture, supported by clear Perspex stands Cleo had designed and ordered specially. Included in the display was a card describing the inspiration behind each piece.

The different color palettes in the collection were each developed from a different colored daisy but Giselle had objected to Cleo saying that. "If you're going to present it as serious art, you need to show serious inspiration. Hmm." She eyed the chalcedony, blue sapphire, and yellow diamond necklace. "Why don't you say something like . . . 'This piece came to Cleo in a dream . . .' Wait. No, that's not right . . ."

She opened her notebook and grabbed a pen to scribble some notes. "A dream?" Cleo's smile went awry. "Lately my dreams would lend themselves more to surrealist art." Her nights had been troubled with visions of Brodie, nightmarish scenarios where she was searching for him through a field of wounded soldiers, calling his name. She still ached for him, longed for him every day.

"What do we want to *feel* when we wear your creations?" Giselle tapped her pencil on the table, bringing Cleo back to the present. "I think we can take a leaf from Monsieur Dior, don't you? Women want to feel feminine again."

"Then why can't I talk about the daisies?" said Cleo. "Monsieur Dior had his flower gowns, didn't he? Besides, I've no patience for people who say if it's beautiful it can't be art. Hmm." She tilted her head, reviewing her collection in her mind's eye. "Feminine, yes. Maybe. But I want to appeal to the modern woman with these pieces."

"All right. Yes, I see." Giselle kept scribbling. She was a little older than Cleo, wore her dark hair short and dressed always in black. Viewed objectively, she was not beautiful but no one ever noticed. She had something that transcended beauty, a timeless chic that only Parisian women ever truly achieved.

Cleo waited, but Giselle kept writing, crossing out, and writing again. Cleo shrugged and went back to her painting. She'd been working hard on her next collection and nearly had those designs ready for production. Seeing her sketches come to life in three-dimensional form at long last had been just the creative spur she'd needed.

Now, with her big gala opening upon her, Cleo skimmed the lines Giselle had written describing the chalcedony necklace, and smiled. Her bookkeeper had proven herself more than just a bean counter. She had an evocative turn of phrase. Giselle came up to her, slipped her hand into Cleo's, and gave it a squeeze. "Here we go!"

The Santerres and Lemarchand had arrived already, and the Graysons weren't far behind. "I'm so glad you came," Cleo said to Lord Grayson, standing on tiptoe to kiss his cheek. His hair was threaded heavily with silver now and she thought he looked pale. She tilted her head. "Is everything all right? Are you well, sir?"

"Of course, of course." He chuckled. "All the better for seeing you, my dear. Now run along. I'm sure you have things to do."

It was true that she had wanted to double-check on a few details but she hadn't seen him for such a long time, and he looked so ill, that she was reluctant to leave him. She hoped they'd have time for a proper talk later.

"Right. Attention everyone!" Philippe, who seemed to have appointed himself master of ceremonies, gestured to the small group, who all gathered around. At a signal from Philippe, a waiter brought a tray filled with flutes of champagne. "The guests will begin to arrive soon. But first, let us drink a toast. To a woman who throws herself, heart and soul, into everything she does. We wish her every success tonight and well into the future. To Cleo!"

"To Cleo," everyone murmured.

Cleo made a short speech, thanking each of them sincerely. She only wished Serafina could be present for this special night, but she'd broken her ankle and was laid up in hospital in London. "This is a dream come true. I couldn't have done it without each and every one of you. If Aunt Serafina were here, I would—"

"Who says I'm not here?" Serafina, her foot in a cast and a walking stick in hand, hobbled in. "Beelzebub and all his minions couldn't keep me away."

Cleo laughed and her vision blurred. This event represented all the hard work she'd done, not just on this collection but for many years before that. Best of all, she was surrounded by the people she loved, even if they weren't related to her by blood. Whatever happened next, she'd count the evening a success.

THE POSITIONING OF Cleo's work as art might well have back-fired had she made the claim overtly. But the clever way Giselle had phrased the description of each piece, Cleo's artwork on the invitations and in the catalog, and the atmosphere of the gallery space she'd rented all operated as subtle cues on those who attended the showing.

"It is not mere 'bijoux' or even '*joaillerie*,'" commented one pundit within Cleo's hearing.

"It's sculptural," agreed another.

"Wearable art" became the catchcry of the evening, as it had been when Elsa Schiaparelli revealed her collaborations with Dalí and Cocteau. Giselle, who had been fielding inquiries from prospective buyers, said to Cleo out of the corner of her mouth, "They are enraged that these are all one-off pieces. I thought one of them would start a riot."

To the other compliments on her work, the words "bespoke" and "limited collection" were added. Cleo had deliberately not priced the jewelry in the catalog, and her decision turned out to have been wise. The response she'd received that evening justified the same percentage markup Lemarchand had told her Cartier made on their creations. While that might well turn out to be hubris, the price of art lay in what people were willing to pay, after all.

Her family had congratulated her and left, and the evening was nearly drawing to a close when Cleo became aware of a stir in the corner of the room, by the piece that had begun the collection: the yellow gold cuff she'd designed for Marguerite. She'd been obliged to substitute a topaz for the aquamarine and use fewer gems, but in essence, the design had remained the same.

She moved to a small clump of what seemed to be journalists if the notebooks they held at the ready were anything to go by. Who were they interviewing? Cleo couldn't see through the crowd, but she heard a familiar voice. "And of course, my daughter is very talented, you know. You can tell where her sense of style comes from. Her father might be quite the trendsetter but this *entire* collection was inspired by me."

Marguerite! After years of silence, she'd turned up here at Cleo's show. The courtesan's tiny form was obscured by the huddle of reporters and photographers, but who else could it be?

Cleo froze. She couldn't seem to make herself move. It was as if she'd been gilded and fixed to the spot, her mind a complete

blank. She could only watch helplessly as the press ate up Marguerite's story. Flashes started going off. Where had those photographers come from? They hadn't taken pictures of Cleo's jewelry;
they seemed to have sniffed out Marguerite's sensational news like
bloodhounds. Or had Marguerite called them here herself?

Philippe strode over, as if determined to deal with Marguerite
by force, if necessary, but Cleo put her hand on his arm. "No. Don't
give them more fuel for the fire."

Giselle came up to them and peered at the crowd. "What's going on?"

"I'll explain later." Cleo gave Giselle a hug. "Thank you both for
everything. I think it's best if I leave. I can't risk them demanding a
photo of us together."

"Most of the guests have left, anyway," said Philippe. "I'll wrap
up here. You go."

Cleo slipped out of the gallery and, finding herself suddenly in
the fresh air of the street, she felt lost. Instead of hailing a taxi, she
decided to walk for a while. As the shock of Marguerite's outrageous behavior waned, fury swept over her like a firestorm. The
rosy lights along the Seine failed to enchant her; the river's inexo-
rable flow did not restore her calm. She walked to the middle of the
Pont Neuf, turned and braced her hands on the balustrade. Then
she let out a long, loud scream.

"THAT ARTICLE COULD have been worse," said Giselle, tossing
the tabloid newspaper down on her desk. "It mentions Princess
Fahmy but points out that her claim was false." Cleo had employed

Giselle full-time since her little business had taken off, but they had yet to settle on a title for her position. Giselle was accountant, financial officer, and marketing director all rolled into one.

She had helped Cleo word a stern denial of Marguerite's claims. Later, she had leaked to the press that Marguerite had undergone a medical procedure which made it impossible for her to be Cleo's mother, and that Cleo was within her rights to sue for defamation if these articles continued to appear. No doubt the royal household quickly acted to scotch the story, as well.

The damage was largely done, however. Cleo had become notorious through Marguerite's claims. Ironically, the scandal brought her even more clients, but she'd have preferred to gain that publicity through her hard work and creativity rather than through Marguerite.

Tempted though she was to confront the princess, Cleo had decided to ignore her. Yet again, Marguerite's ploy had backfired. She had lied so often in the past, no one believed her now. Still they wondered why Marguerite, who was clearly becoming a fantasist, had chosen Cleo as the subject of her latest scheme.

No smoke without fire, as they say. Cleo thought of the Duke and Duchess of Windsor, now living in an *hôtel particulier* in the Bois de Boulogne, and wondered what, if anything, they'd made of the business.

She was soon to find out.

The Duchess of Windsor summoned Cleo to her home one day. And it was a summons, not an invitation. "She's got a nerve," said Giselle, who did not hold with royalty or duchesses, for that matter. "Treating you like a tradesman!"

"The duchess would never deal directly with a tradesman," said

Cleo with a feigned look of hauteur. "Hmm. I wonder what she wants. Do you think she'll scold me over the scandal with Princess Fahmy? I could hardly have helped that, could I?"

But as it turned out, the duchess was not interested in the wild claims of the princess but in Cleo's designs. "Miss Davenport," she said, turning to retrieve a box from the table at her side. "I want you to create something for me." She opened the box to reveal a heavy diamond necklace that might have belonged to Queen Mary—and probably had.

Cleo's mind raced with possibilities. She'd always been drawn to colored stones principally, so the diamonds would be a new challenge. "What did you have in mind?" she asked. "My inclination would be to break it up and design several pieces, but—"

"Yes. Yes, let's do that." The duchess might have been discussing state secrets to judge by her earnest concentration.

They spent two hours discussing what the duchess wanted, with Cleo sketching out possible designs. By the end of their meeting, Cleo's mind was flourishing with inspiration. She already knew how to expand the designs for the duchess into a completely new collection.

The possibility that the Windsors wouldn't expect to pay for her work occurred to her, but even if she made an initial loss, the duchess's stamp of approval would see her popularity skyrocket.

As she got up to leave, the duchess said, "I admit, I got you here with no other thought than to publicly stamp out those stupid rumors, once and for all. But I'm looking forward to seeing what you can do, Miss Davenport. Impress me."

Chapter Twenty-Four

Paris, France
Autumn 1951

From the moment the duchess was photographed wearing Cleo's carved rock crystal cuff with the diamond inlay, Cleo's success was assured. She now employed enough people to run her small business—all of them women—but she refused to expand too much or move into mass production. Cleo preferred to keep the list of her clientele exclusive and her jewelry bespoke.

Eventually Giselle left her, ironically to go into business with Philippe. Giselle had always been destined for bigger things and Cleo was happy for her. She watched the romance blooming between her two closest friends with satisfaction and a touch of relief. She couldn't have succeeded without either of them, and she hoped they'd found their reward in each other.

The deep sense of pride when Cleo finally repaid Serafina every penny, plus interest, was only equaled by the reflection that far from needing a husband to pay for her jewelry, she had designed most of the items in her jewelry box herself. She might have reached this peak of success sooner had she accepted Philippe's generous offer all those years ago but she'd been right to tread this path. Cleo was proud of the business she'd built, and proud to have been given her start by another independent woman.

The confidence Serafina had shown in her had been the greatest reward of all.

Cleo was back in her studio, clearing out and filing away the designs from her previous collection, when the telephone rang. It was Philippe. "Cleo, I have bad news. I'm sorry. Maman just received a telegram. Lord Grayson has taken a turn for the worse."

CLEO COULDN'T REMEMBER hanging up or making the travel arrangements, or anything else. She only seemed to wake from her trance when she found herself in the foyer of their London home, enfolded in Lady Grayson's embrace. "I'm so glad you came. Go straight up. I think he's been waiting for you."

At the showing of her first collection, Cleo had noticed Lord Grayson didn't look well. He had managed to keep his diagnosis secret from her until six months ago, but after she'd spent some weeks with him, he'd seemed to rally, and he'd insisted she return to Paris for the showing of her new collection.

She never should have left.

Cleo dropped her bags and hurried upstairs to Lord Grayson's bedroom. She'd never set foot in there before but she scarcely took in her surroundings. Her attention was focused on the man in the four-poster. He lay flat on his back with the covers pulled up to his chest, and perhaps it was the effect of the enormous bed, but for the first time in her life, he seemed small. He looked ashen-faced and weary from the fight.

Startled, Cleo realized Serafina was sitting in a chair by the bed.

"You're here," said Serafina, getting up. "Good. Perfect timing." She turned to Lord Grayson. "Can't abide funerals, I'm afraid, so I won't stay. Must get back." She smiled as if to take the sting out of her words and bent to kiss his cheek. "Goodbye, old friend."

She turned and hesitated, awkward as ever in a situation that clearly called for human touch. She patted Cleo gingerly on the shoulder and left.

Lord Grayson had the strangest expression on his face. Cleo couldn't blame him. What an abominable lack of tact! "Just when I think Serafina is becoming vaguely human," she remarked, trying to infuse a little laughter into her voice. She sat on the edge of the bed and put her hand to his cheek. "Lady G said you've been waiting for me."

"Yes." He swallowed convulsively. "Well . . ."

"Are you thirsty?" said Cleo. "Shall I fetch you something to drink?"

"No. Thank you. Listen, Cleo, there's something I must tell you. But that *wretched* Serafina . . ." He closed his eyes. "How to begin?"

Cleo waited. What had Serafina done? Cleo had been surprised to see her at her brother-in-law's bedside. She'd never thought of them as terribly close.

And then he told her precisely how close the two of them had been, many years ago.

"It was the war," he said. "I was stationed in Cairo and Serafina was volunteering at Heliopolis hospital, just as you did. We . . . well, it was wartime and I daresay you can guess. We hit it off. Fell in love, actually. But when I had to leave, she refused to come with me. It was her dream to be an archeologist, you see, and she was desperate to get back to the field. I had responsibilities to the estate in Scotland that I couldn't escape. We realized we wanted different things from life and parted—not without much soul-searching and a great deal of regret, I might add. What I didn't realize was that by then, *you* were on the way."

So that was it. Cleo felt no shock, nor even much surprise. She felt acceptance, a sense of completion, as if this knowledge had been buried deep inside her for a very long time.

She could see it all. Or most of it. "But how on earth did Marguerite become involved?"

"Yes," said Lord Grayson. "Well, as I understand it, Maggie Meller, as she then called herself, had struck up an acquaintance with Serafina. She noticed Saffy's condition and offered to help her. Maggie knew of somewhere discreet in Luxor where Serafina could live until the baby was born." His eyes moistened, as if the thought pained him. "Serafina must have felt so very alone, to have accepted help from someone like that."

"So Marguerite was the one to suggest 'finding' me on the doorstep and had her maid do it to divert suspicion from Serafina," said Cleo. "That makes sense. I don't see what she stood to gain from it, though. She's hardly the type to help out of the goodness of her heart."

Lord Grayson shrugged. "Perhaps for once in her life, she did a good deed. Or perhaps she thought Saffy would prove useful in the future. Anyway, while all of this was going on, I was in Paris, and having the time of my life, I'm ashamed to say. In Cairo, Serafina had introduced me to Alain Santerre as an old family friend . . ."

"Alain? You mean Madame Santerre's husband?"

"Yes. He and I rapidly became quite close, as one does in wartime. Poor chap was killed in the Sudan. I had some personal effects of his to deliver to his widow in Paris." A smile lit his eyes. "And that's where I met Lydia."

"Of course," said Cleo. "And it was for Lady G that Aunt Serafina kept it secret all these years."

"And for my sake, too, I feel," said Lord Grayson. "I have been so very happy with my Lyddy. But I wish . . . I wish she'd told me. And it wasn't fair for you to grow up not knowing the truth."

Cleo could understand why Serafina hadn't told anyone. Lord Grayson might have insisted on leaving Lydia to marry her. Or if he hadn't, the secret would have always weighed on his conscience. And if Cleo had known, she wouldn't have been capable of concealing the truth. For Lydia's sake, Serafina couldn't risk it.

Cleo had spent a good part of her life yearning for real parents. Despite understanding and even agreeing with the reason Serafina hadn't told her the real story, she couldn't help being hurt by the years she'd lost. She'd secretly yearned for Serafina's love—or perhaps more precisely, the expression of that love—yet never felt entitled to demand or even hope for it. She bitterly regretted not knowing that such a fine man as Lord Grayson was her father.

But she'd come to understand that regret was a profitless emotion. She'd learned to appreciate what she had, and she'd had a wonderful life, both with Serafina at Shepheard's Hotel, where she had so many dear friends, and with the Graysons and the Santerres, too. A patchwork quilt of a family that when stitched together gave her all the warmth and comfort she'd needed.

"I think it's best if we keep this from Aunt Lydia," said Cleo. She didn't like to say it, but Lydia would need Serafina more than ever when her dear husband was gone. The old Cleo would have insisted on bringing everything into the open. The old Cleo would have chased after Serafina, accusing her of ruining her life.

But life wasn't all black-and-white. She understood why Serafina had never given her the truth. She'd done her best to raise Cleo without compromising her own dreams. It was an example Cleo realized now that she'd followed, albeit unconsciously.

"Oh, Lydia must never know," agreed Lord Grayson, his voice growing fainter. A lone tear trickled from the corner of his eye and slipped down the side of his wasted cheek. "It would break her heart. She was utterly distraught not to have a child of her own. To hear that Serafina and I . . . *No*. But you have been such a blessing to us both, my dear. When Serafina told me, I could not have been happier. It's as if all along, deep down . . ." He closed his eyes.

Cleo whispered the words. "We *knew*."

Cairo, Egypt
December 1951

FOR THE FIRST time since the early years of the war, Cleo left her sketchbook closed, and her pens and paint brushes lay idle. Usually in times of trouble, she found comfort and escape in her art. In the months after Lord Grayson's death, she simply couldn't.

Sometimes people talked about the creative well running dry. Cleo thought of her creativity as a golden lightstream that hovered just beyond conscious thought. Usually if she worked hard and pushed herself, she could tap that golden light as a doctor might tap a vein. However, since Lord Grayson died, no matter how hard she pushed herself to find that light again, all she encountered was darkness.

"It happens," Lemarchand said. "Don't force it. That is the absolute worst thing you can do."

She resisted taking his advice. She was a professional, after all.

Determined to meet her commitments, Cleo slogged away in darkness until she'd completed what should have been a pivotal piece for her new collection. With a leaden heart, she showed Lemarchand the design, hoping she was wrong, that she didn't need that feeling of transcendence to achieve something worthy. Slowly he shook his head.

"Well, what would *you* know," Cleo muttered as she unlocked her studio the next day. Lemarchand wasn't *always* right. Part of reaching maturity as an artist was making her own judgments about her work.

But when she viewed the piece after only twelve hours away from it, she saw what he meant. She ripped up the painting and crushed the pieces in her fists, her shoulders slumped.

Lemarchand was right about something else, too. She needed a break. She needed to get away. A letter from Serafina gave her the perfect excuse. She had decided to leave Cairo for good.

The political situation in Egypt had troubled Cleo for some time. The British had never ceased to interfere in the nation's government and now the Egyptians were rising up in protest. From the Turks to the British, the Egyptians had suffered foreign rule for far too long. Change was coming. Cleo could only hope that if revolution occurred, it would be quick and bloodless.

Against everyone's warnings about the frequent demonstrations and unrest in Cairo, Cleo returned to Shepheard's Hotel to help Serafina pack. Serafina was going to live with Lydia and try—albeit in her own, inimitable fashion—to be a comfort to her sister through her grief.

Cleo's mother—how strange it was still, to think of her like that!—had achieved her dream of publishing her life's work, and it was time to leave Egypt for good. Serafina's opus was a hefty tome entitled *Reflections on Hieratic Funerary Papyri,* and Cleo felt guilty every time she laid eyes on it. Although she was proud of Serafina, there was no way she was ever going to wade through the first page, much less the entire book.

"That's all right," said its author when she tactfully expressed her regret. "I don't wear your jewelry, do I?"

Cleo conceded that this was true. "I wish you hadn't ordered so many copies of this to be delivered here if you were only going to have to move them all again. The porters will break their backs trying to carry this lot. We'll have to scatter them throughout multiple trunks."

She went down to seek out a porter to ask for more packing cases. While she waited at reception, Cleo looked around her. The interior of the grand hotel was as exotic and luxurious as ever. Mr. Mansoor had retired, but the manager, Mr. Elwert, and Mr. Meyer, the head porter, remained at their posts. Yet despite its air of time-lessness, the Shepheard's she had known was fast becoming a part of Egypt's past, or soon would be. She had to accept that it was now a cherished part of hers.

But she wasn't quite ready to let go completely. Now that her business was well-established, she could see her way clear to spending less time on its running day-to-day. It might even be possible to spend part of the year in dreaded Scotland. A month ago, she had written to Brodie and begged him to meet her here. Perhaps it was too late for them. It was almost certainly too late, of course. But she needed to know.

When they'd shipped most of their belongings and Serafina was ready to depart, she patted Cleo's cheek. "Take your time. I know you wanted to say a proper goodbye to this place." She looked around her and nodded. "It's been good to us, but it is well past time that we left."

Cleo watched Serafina's diminutive figure get into a taxi with the last of her luggage and drive away. For the first time in her life, it struck Cleo that Serafina looked lonely. It was a good thing she would be with her sister soon.

As Cleo wandered around the hotel, she found echoes of her past self. So much of her young life had been spent longing and hoping. For her real parents, for Serafina's attention, for Brodie's love.

Maybe it wouldn't work out between her and Brodie. Maybe they were each too set on their own path, just as Serafina and Lord Grayson had been. But Cleo had to try to find out, one way or the other. She still loved Brodie. She probably always would. She wanted to find a way to share her life with him. She didn't want to sacrifice *everything* else for her dream.

BRODIE WASN'T COMING. That was hardly a surprise. Cleo had spent three weeks at Shepheard's and still received no word. Had she really thought he'd drop everything and come all this way to see her?

She spent her final days in Cairo exploring her old haunts one last time. She rode in the desert early in the morning, went to a film at the Princess Theatre, ate ice cream at Groppi's and kebab at the Parisiana. She walked among the pyramids with the tourists and rode a very bad-tempered camel to see the Sphinx. She took tea at Mena House with the Draytons, who had settled in Palestine but were staying at the hotel for New Year.

She wandered idly through Shepheard's, remembering the enchanted adventures of her childhood. At night, she sat in the window seat of her suite, humming to the music and watching the dancing below.

All of those beautiful, glamorous women . . . Were any of them wearing Cleo Davenport? She gave a wry smile. Would Cleo Davenport create another collection, ever again?

She lifted her face to the breeze. The stars burned white-hot in a sky of deep onyx black. The wind in the palm fronds told the band below "hush . . . hush." The moonlight picked out the men's collars, a bright white against their black tailcoats.

A tiny glimmer of inspiration winked from the dim recesses of her brain. Black and white. Clean, elegant, almost masculine lines to emphasize the wearer's feminine beauty. A necklace of onyx and diamonds, a bracelet of obsidian and mother-of-pearl . . . Cleo jumped up and hunted around for her sketchbook and pencil.

In the morning, Cleo woke late, to the eerie cries of a kite wheeling overhead in search of prey. The corner of her sketchbook was digging into her cheek and she was still clutching her pencil.

She closed the sketchbook and set it aside. She wouldn't look at what she'd done because if she didn't like what she saw, she might suffer yet another setback. It was enough that last night, she had struck that golden vein again, and the light had poured into her and through her, turning hours into minutes while she filled page after page.

With a yawn and a luxuriating stretch, Cleo got up and padded to the bathroom, hopeful about her design work for the first time since Lord Grayson's passing.

Egypt had restored her. She was a bit rusty, and she'd probably overdone it, staying up all night. But she had nowhere to be today, so she might even break the habit of a lifetime and take a nap after lunch.

Cleo breakfasted late and lingered over her orange juice. Now that she had done everything she'd come to Cairo to do—well, almost everything—she was ready to bring this chapter of her life to a close.

She went down to the basement and found Mr. and Mrs. Costas to tell them of her decision to leave Shepheard's for good. Over a tiny cup of strong coffee, Mrs. Costas said, "You'll come back one day. People always come back to Shepheard's."

"One moment." Mr. Costas went to the storeroom and returned with a pink-and-white-striped hatbox. "Your aunt Serafina left it for you."

"My baby box," said Cleo, taking it and smoothing her hands over the satin finish of its lid. "I was wondering where that was. Thank you."

Cleo hesitated. It felt strange not to explain to the couple about her true origins, that "Aunt Serafina" was really her mother. Mr. and Mrs. Costas had helped her investigate her birth, after all, despite Serafina's prohibition. But she'd keep the secret, even from those she loved. The only person Serafina had given her permission to tell was Brodie.

Cleo set the box on the old steamer trunk they used as a coffee table and lifted the lid. Inside were little keepsakes from her childhood: a photo album, a scrapbook, a delicate, lacy christening shawl. There was a silver rattle, engraved with what she now knew was her real birth date, and a small gold ring with a heart on it that had been a gift from Aunt Lydia when she was small.

She opened the scrapbook and turned the pages until she came to the newspaper cutting of the photograph of her and the Prince of

Wales—a painful reminder of the way Marguerite had deceived and used her, and of her own humiliating conversation with the duke in Portugal. She considered tearing out that page, but she supposed that every experience, even the bad ones, was a part of who she was now. She closed the book and returned it to the hatbox.

When she emerged from the basement, Cleo sensed something in the air. Something wrong. She smelled burning and there were shouts in the street. She hurried into the foyer. Looking outside she saw a sea of protestors marching past.

"What's happening?" she asked a passing guest, but he shrugged. "The usual carry-on. Nothing to worry about."

Cleo wasn't so sure. She took the elevator and climbed the stairs to the hotel's rooftop. The view made her blood turn to ice. Black smoke plumed upward from several buildings, but she couldn't identify which ones. A fire engine raced past the hotel, bell clanging.

A couple of streets over, she could see young men dragging items out of the Victoria Palace Hotel. Priceless Persian carpets, paintings, sofas, and mattresses were hurled into a pile and set alight.

She'd seen independence demonstrations before but this was different—and far more frightening. At least the looters didn't seem to be harming anyone, but the destruction and mayhem—not to mention the fires—would produce many incidental casualties, no doubt.

Would Shepheard's be safe?

Cleo went down to the lobby again, where Mr. Elwert was asking everyone to remain calm and stay near the exits.

One of the men, a journalist, judging by his notebook and pencil at the ready, commented to his colleague, "These attacks are targeted and professional. It's definitely a well-orchestrated affair."

The other responded, "Rumor has it that it's not part of the protest march at all. It's a ploy by King Farouk to bring down the government."

"What are the police doing?" a querulous voice demanded. "They're conspicuously absent in all this, as if they've been told to stand down. I think it's the British."

Another voice. "Surely not! Oh, no, I don't think it can possibly be us."

Why were they all standing around debating the matter? Cleo hurried up to Mr. Meyer. "Shouldn't we evacuate? The situation out there can only get worse. They might come for Shepheard's next."

The head porter replied, "The main thing is not to panic the guests. For now, the situation is under control."

As if to dispute his words, a bundle of cotton alive with flame sailed into the foyer. It rolled and unraveled almost at their feet. Mr. Meyer ran forward to stamp the fire out. Gingerly he uncovered what was inside the bundle. A grenade! Cleo felt the blood leave her head. She couldn't move. All she could do was wait for the explosion.

"Don't worry. It's not live," said Mr. Meyer. He covered the grenade quickly before anyone else saw and took it away.

Don't worry!?

Cleo raced down to the basement to alert Mr. and Mrs. Costas to the situation and insisted they leave their work and return upstairs with her. Back in the lobby, the staff were still telling people there was no cause for alarm. Hardly reassured by this after the grenade incident, Cleo decided to take matters into her own hands. She went up to her floor and started knocking on doors and calmly asking everyone to come downstairs.

She'd managed to alert half of her floor when the lights went out, plunging the corridor into darkness. The smell of smoke was stronger now but she couldn't tell where it might be coming from.

Had a fire broken out inside the hotel? The darkness was so complete, she couldn't see her hand in front of her face. Cleo forced down the urge to panic. Struggling to get her bearings, she set off in what she thought must be the direction of the stairs, feeling her way along the passage wall until she rounded the corner and saw the outline of the stairwell ahead.

The crash and splinter of glass breaking spurred her on, going down the stairs as fast as she dared. In the lobby, youths were running about with fistfuls of cotton waste and using them to set the curtains alight.

Cleo recoiled in horror and hurried to join the guests who were moving with remarkable calm toward the garden.

Then she saw Brodie.

Chapter Twenty-Five

Cairo, Egypt
Winter 1952

Is everyone out?" Cleo heard Brodie demand of the manager.

"Not quite," Mr. Elwert replied. "There are still some guests upstairs."

Brodie swore. "If you'd bloody well evacuated when I told you to, this wouldn't have happened."

"Brodie?" Cleo croaked, her voice husky and broken from inhaling all of that smoke. "Brodie!"

His head jerked up and his wild gaze locked with hers. With a muttered exclamation, he strode over and gripped Cleo by the shoulders. "Thank God you're safe. I've been looking for you everywhere." Glass shattered behind them and Brodie pulled her out of harm's way. "You'd better get out of here. Go into the garden and stay well clear of the building."

Without waiting to see if she obeyed, he turned to the porter. "Is there a safe way to get up to the floors above? Someone said the staircase is on fire."

"The service stairs. There's an entrance from the garden that we can access," Cleo answered him. "But it's dark up there. I'll get a flashlight." She dashed over to reception and found a small one with the first aid kit. They also needed to soak cloths in water to put over their mouths. Serviettes. There'd be some in the dining hall.

When she raced out to the service door entrance in the garden, Brodie had already gone.

Cleo wrenched open the service door, intending to go after him, but a hand grabbed her and pulled her back. It was the porter. "It's too dangerous, miss. And what are you going to do anyway? You can't lift anyone or drag them out. You'll be dead from the smoke before you've done any good."

Cleo hated to admit he was right. "Where's Brodie?"

"He went in. But he asked me to tell you to stay put. Told me to knock you out cold if you try to go after him."

Too concerned to be annoyed by this high-handedness, Cleo didn't respond. She was forced to stand by and wait on tenterhooks for Brodie to come back.

MARGUERITE

Cairo, Egypt
Winter 1952

SHEPHEARD'S WASN'T WHAT it had been in the twenties, that was for sure. Marguerite had returned to Cairo for yet another hearing in the interminable battle for Ali's inheritance but things were looking grim. Stubbornness made her persist with the lawsuit but even the faithful Maître Assouad was discouraging about her chances of success. Typical. Men. They were always against her.

She'd lain down for her noon repose and woke to a terrible racket that seemed to be coming from downstairs. Or was it in the street outside? Marguerite looked out the window and saw black smoke blanketing the city like a thunderhead. Coughing, she closed the window. Then she turned to see smoke seeping beneath her door.

Galvanized, she fumbled for her shoes and purse, coughing as the smoke invaded her lungs and made her eyes sting. Her hair was loose but there was no time to make herself presentable.

The jewels! She'd been out late last night and hadn't returned her jewel box to the hotel safe. Marguerite stumbled to her dressing table, breaking off for a paroxysm of hard coughing. She needed to get out.

The lights weren't working, and between that and the smoke, she could hardly see. She snatched up her jewel box and the gun from her bedside table, because the first was no use without the second to protect it. Shoving both in a small shopping bag, Marguerite stumbled across the room. She wrenched open the door and plunged into blackness.

Someone—a man—grabbed her arm and said something in English, then pulled her in the other direction.

"*Français,*" she managed, coughing. Marguerite clutched the bag with her belongings tightly and let herself be drawn swiftly along. The man switched to French, his words muffled, as if he wore something over his mouth. "A couple of paces forward, and you'll find the stair rail on your left. Hold on to it and go slowly."

He didn't join her but went back the way he'd come. By degrees, she felt her way down the two flights, pausing now and then for fits of coughing.

When she reached the gardens where the guests were assembled, she breathed in relatively clean air and looked down to check the contents of her bag. Then she realized. She had taken with her not her jewel case, but the chased silver tissue box from her bedside table.

She gave an animal cry of fury and hurled the tissue box into the garden. Gritting her teeth, she started toward the hotel again. She'd go back the way she'd come. It wouldn't be easy but she'd manage.

Just then, the crowd gave a ragged gasp, making her look back. They were all tilting their faces to the sky. Marguerite looked up to see a man climbing out of a top floor window using knotted sheets. A woman cried out as the flames licked at the top of the makeshift rope.

Marguerite pushed past several of the gawkers, opened the service door, and went in. The door slammed shut behind her. The dark was absolute, the smoke worse than before. She started to feel her way along the wall.

She jumped as the service door opened behind her. Automatically she felt in her shopping bag for her gun.

"Hello? Ma'am, please come out. It's not safe here." It was a woman and she spoke in English. She had a flashlight. Its beam dazzled Marguerite's eyes.

The owner of the flashlight came toward Marguerite and grabbed her by the elbow, trying to drag her back out. "Let go of me!" There was no time for this.

"Madame! I'm sorry but you can't go back in. It's not safe." The young woman had switched to French. She was stronger than Marguerite, whoever she was.

"Let me go up and get my jewels," said Marguerite. The .32 felt heavy and cold in her hand. "I'll be back in no time."

"It's too dangerous," said her unwelcome savior. "I'm afraid I can't let you do that."

They were both coughing by now, and Marguerite was nearly

at snapping point. "Dangerous!" she snarled between hacks. "The longer you delay me, the more dangerous it gets." The flashlight's beam bobbed wildly as Marguerite struggled to get free.

"*Princess Fahmy?*" The grip on her arm slackened, then tightened once more. "Madame, it's Cleo. Madame, please. Your jewels are not worth your life."

Furious, Marguerite spoke through gritted teeth. "You are mistaken. My jewels *are* my life." She swung up her free arm and fired. The flashlight beam veered wildly then skittered along the floor. Marguerite scooped it up. Then she moved toward the staircase, climbing swiftly now that she had the light to guide her.

CLEO

Cairo, Egypt
Winter 1952

CLEO CAME TO her senses with a gasp. There was a ringing in her ears and a vise crushed her skull. She was on the ground, half sitting, half lying, propped against someone's chest. Slowly she opened her eyes, and turned her head to see that Brodie, his face covered in soot, was cradling her in his arms.

"Thank God," he murmured, his hand coming up to rest against her cheek. "I was nearly out of my mind."

Cleo tried to speak, but she jackknifed forward to cough, which hurt her head so much, she had to turn and retch into the grass.

Brodie gently rubbed her back. When her paroxysms subsided, he offered her a water canteen. "Sip slowly."

She did as she was told, and after a few more bouts of coughing, interspersed with swigs from the canteen, the paroxysms seemed to subside. She rinsed out her mouth and then drank again.

"Easy does it." Brodie took the canteen and set it aside, then gathered her back into his arms and rested his cheek against the top of her head. "You hit your head and passed out. Lucky I saw you go in."

Cleo looked up to see flames curling skyward through the hotel windows, acrid smoke billowing out like puffs from a giant dragon. The fire raged beyond control through the grand old building, and even at this distance, she could feel the heat coming off it in waves. There was no going back in there now for anyone, and still no firefighters in sight.

"Madame Fahmy . . ." Cleo pressed the heel of her hand to her forehead and struggled to think. "She went back to get her jewels. That's why I went in after her. Did you see her?"

"So that's why." He exhaled a long breath. "I didn't see her." His arms tightened around Cleo. "You should never have gone in."

"I have to look for her." Cleo tried to sit up but her head swam. With a cry of frustration, she sank back.

Brodie's chest felt so solid and warm against her. "Rest," he said. "Whether she came out or not, there's nothing you can do for her, not in this state." He shook his head. "*Jewels*. What possessed the woman?"

How to explain the almost mystical power jewels held over some women? Brodie would never understand. Cleo wasn't at all sure that she did, herself. She was awed by the beauty and artistry of fine jewels, and put her soul into creating them, but she'd never been acquisitive in that way. And although she could be obsessive at times about her work, she knew without doubt that she'd never put her role as *créatrice joaillière* before the people she loved.

Marguerite had worked, married, connived, and murdered for jewels. In the heat of that struggle in the service stairwell, she'd been prepared to kill Cleo. Marguerite's words came back to her: "My jewels *are* my life!"

Then the flash in the dark, the earsplitting shot. It must have gone wild. At least, sometimes people in shock didn't feel any pain . . . She froze. "I'm not wounded, am I?"

"No, you're fine, sweetheart. You're safe now." She felt his lips press softly against her temple. "You're safe." He seemed to be reassuring himself as much as her.

She turned her head to gaze up at him, hardly believing he was there with her at last. No longer the strapping lad she'd grown up with, Brodie was battle-hardened, lean and tanned, with laughter lines fanning from the corners of his eyes, deep grooves on either side of his mouth. "I love you quite dreadfully, you know. I always have."

He swallowed hard. "I know."

She settled back against him, grateful for his strength. The clang of a firetruck grew steadily closer. She hoped it was stopping outside Shepheard's, though what they could possibly do to control the blaze now, she didn't know.

Slowly Cleo became aware that the other guests were moving, filing out of the gardens via the street exit. "The police have arrived to escort us to safety," she heard Mr. Elwert say. "Come, ladies and gentlemen. All of us must go."

Brodie helped her to her feet and gripped her elbow as she wobbled. "Shall I carry you?"

"I can walk." She was a little shaky at first, but his arm around her waist was a steady support.

Cleo turned her head to look back at Shepheard's Hotel, at the great tongues of flame licking through the gaping windows, at the black smoke roiling into the sky, and felt an overwhelming sadness. She'd been ready to close this chapter of her life, but the destruction of the beautiful old building that had been her childhood home was difficult to bear.

Whether or not the protestors had in fact been responsible for the fires throughout Cairo that day, full independence for Egypt would come soon, she was sure of it. She only prayed it might be achieved without bloodshed. They'd all experienced far too much of it for one lifetime.

As she and Brodie made their way out to the street with the other guests, Cleo shivered. "Someone said the riot was too well-orchestrated to be a spontaneous protest. Do you think it could possibly have been the British who did this?"

"I wouldn't put it past them," said Brodie. "But then you're asking a Scot. Still, I can't see the British sacrificing Shepheard's, can you?"

"Maybe it was King Farouk, then." They might never know.

She and Brodie stood in silence. They were supposed to wait for a car to arrive to take them to the station. Given the number of hotel patrons to be transported, that might well take some time.

There'd been no opportunity to think about anything but the present crisis, but now that it was over, Cleo had to ask. "Brodie?"

"Hmm?"

"What are you doing here?"

He was weary and sweat-stained and his face was smudged with soot, but his smile lit the world. "I came for you, of course. Didn't you write, asking me to meet you here?" He grinned. "It was good timing. I'd just come back from a research trip to Madagascar."

"*Madagascar?*" For the first time, she felt real hope. "Then you're not going to be a farmer anymore?"

"None of it meant anything without you." He squinted at the sky and tugged at his earlobe. "And . . . loath as I am to admit it, you were right. I'm not cut out to be a farmer. I broke it to my grandfather as gently as I could."

"Did he take it badly?" Cleo asked.

He blew out a breath. "Oh, yes. I am well and truly out of the will."

"Thank goodness for that," said Cleo. She didn't mention it but she had money enough for them both. Her business was turning a handsome profit, and, like Serafina, she had invested her money wisely.

"Granddad might be repeating his mistakes but I refuse to repeat my father's," said Brodie. "I won't let the old man shut me out of his life or make me cut ties with the rest of the family. He's a tough old curmudgeon but I expect he'll come around."

"Hmm." Cleo pursed her lips. "I suppose that means we must visit Scotland occasionally."

"You'd do that?" said Brodie, smiling. "You must see the manor. It's a beautiful place."

"Short visits, mind," said Cleo. "And *only* in the summer."

He laughed, and his teeth looked very white against his soot-ridden face. He stole an arm around her and lifted her against his chest, then bent his head and kissed her.

"I love you, Cleo," he said softly. "I'll love you for the rest of my life. Marry me?"

She laughed and nodded, and he kissed her again. He set her on her feet and dug in his pockets for something. Then he frowned and looked back at the hotel. "The ring! I must have dropped it in the hotel somewhere."

He looked as if he was about to charge back into the fire to get it. Cleo grabbed his elbow to stop him. Then she reached up and put a hand to his cheek. "I don't care about the ring, Brodie. All I've ever cared about is you."

Wrapped in each other, it was some time before they noticed that a police car had pulled up beside them and they were the only hotel guests left.

"How about Paris for the wedding?" said Brodie as he opened the car door for her.

Eyes shining, Cleo nodded. But she didn't mind about the ring or the wedding, or even about Paris. Their future together would be full of interest, passion, and love. And that was more than enough.

Author's Note

In writing this story, I drew inspiration from several, disparate sources that had been percolating in my brain for years: the luxurious and eccentric Shepheard's Hotel in Cairo; Edward VIII and Wallis Simpson and their strange interlude in Portugal during the Second World War; the brilliant and brave commandos of the nascent Special Air Service; and finally, high-end jewelry and the history of Cartier.

As I delved deeper, I found serendipitous connections between these elements. The almost forgotten mistress of a young Edward VIII (or Prince of Wales as he then was) had stayed at Shepheard's Hotel on several occasions, both before and after her marriage to Ali Fahmy—she even held their wedding reception there.

Marguerite Fahmy was as fond of fine jewels in real life as she is shown to be in this novel, and lived above the famous jeweler Van Cleef & Arpels near the Paris Ritz.

Unsurprisingly, there was a connection between Wallis Simpson and Cartier—an intimate one, as Cartier was commissioned to make not only Wallis's engagement ring, but several other love tokens exchanged between the couple: most notably Wallis's crucifix bracelet and a rose-gold cigarette case Wallis gave the duke with a map showing all the destinations the couple had visited together marked out with precious stones.

The SAS was practically born at the Long Bar at Shepheard's Hotel and took their winged parachute design from the Egyptian ibis of Isis symbols that proliferated around the hotel.

I first read about Shepheard's Hotel in the marvelous Amelia Peabody mysteries by Elizabeth Peters. The hotel played host, not only to prominent archaeologists, but to all kinds of famous people, from Lawrence of Arabia, who often disguised himself as a sheikh and ducked out the back way if reporters came looking for him, to Rita Hayworth and the Aga Khan, Winston Churchill, Josephine Baker, and Mark Twain.

When I stumbled upon the bizarre story of French courtesan Marguerite Meller and the prince who would later become Edward VIII, I felt compelled to write about her. For readers who wish to discover more about Marguerite's extraordinary story, I recommend Andrew Rose's two excellent books on the subject, *The Prince, the Princess, and the Perfect Murder* and *The Woman Before Wallis*. I was fascinated to read reports of the trial and the judge's extremely biased summing up. (As a former lawyer, I love any excuse to delve into the legal world.) With all these ingredients thrown into the melting pot, I began to imagine ... *What if ...?*

In real life, Marguerite did engage in an ill-conceived plot to pretend she'd given birth to Ali Fahmy's son. What if she had done a similar thing to Edward VIII in order to blackmail him? Surely with a mind as devious as Marguerite's, if a young woman turned up on her doorstep who was of the right age and who happened to bear a resemblance to the former King, how could she resist?

There is little doubt the affair between Marguerite and the Prince of Wales, as he then was, took place. Although the prince seems to have ripped out the pages of his diary that pertained to his interlude with her, there still exists a letter from him to a friend, which refers to the end of their liaison, and a "filthy" letter she sent him, as well as the amount of money the prince thought it would take to buy Marguerite's silence.

It is unclear whether a procedure Marguerite underwent during the war left her infertile—I adapted this circumstance to suit my plot. She never claimed to have been made pregnant by the Prince of Wales, as far as I'm aware.

The bargaining over the cache of letters in Marguerite's possession might or might not have taken place. Andrew Rose makes a good argument for the former, but his theory is based largely on circumstantial evidence, so it should perhaps be taken with a grain of salt. However, because it suited my purposes, I adopted that theory in this book.

Whether the palace interfered directly with Marguerite's murder trial is not certain. One could well imagine the prosecution being reluctant to delve into Marguerite's sexual history in court, even in the absence of any overt request from the royal family that her liaison with the Prince of Wales be suppressed. There is also a fascinating documentary in which Marguerite's grandson is interviewed, entitled *Edward VIII's Murderous Mistress*, which can be found on YouTube.

Marguerite is not a very likable character; she is not meant to be. I wrote her as I saw the real person emerge from the accounts of those who knew her and wrote about her. She was larger than life, a woman of unabashed avarice and ungoverned temper. I saw her as hardened by terrible experiences when she was very young, constantly living in fear of being forced to return to that degrading life. So perhaps, even if we cannot like her, we might understand why she behaved as she did.

I think it quite possible Marguerite suffered from mental illness of some kind, because her behavior seemed so illogical, erratic, and extreme. One might have thought that if she was planning to murder Ali for his money, she would have gone about it in a way less likely to end in her conviction for murder. A rational person couldn't have been certain those letters from the Prince of Wales would save her. It is also possible that although she saw herself as in control of Ali, in fact, his rages and physical abuse took a mental toll of which she herself was only dimly aware. Perhaps she really did snap when he threatened to kill her that night at the Savoy.

Marguerite's encounter with Cleo is fictional, as are her machinations trying to prove Cleo was her daughter by the Duke of Windsor. Marguerite was not at Shepheard's Hotel during the fire that burned the hotel down in 1952 and she lived to a ripe old age.

The incident where Marguerite mistakes a tissue box for her jewelry box is based on the experience of the guest prima donna of the Italian Opera Company, who escaped the Shepheard's fire in a negligée, bedroom slippers, and a fur coat, holding a box of Kleenex instead of what she'd thought was her jewel case—yet another serendipitous discovery that tied in so well with Marguerite's obsession with jewels.

The interlude before the Duke and Duchess of Windsor left Europe for the Bahamas has been well-documented and analyzed, with some historians claiming the duke had no intention of throwing in his lot with Hitler, and others dubbing him an outright traitor who was waiting for his chance to return to Britain as King under Nazi rule. For more discussion of this subject, please see *Traitor King: The Scandalous Exile of the Duke & Duchess of Windsor* by Andrew Lownie and *17 Carnations: The Royals, the Nazis, and the Biggest Cover-Up in History* by Andrew Morton.

Cleo and Brodie are fictional, as are Serafina, the Graysons, and the Santerres. (Noting here that usually a marquess would not have the same surname as his title, but to save confusion, I only gave the Graysons the one name in this book.)

Many of Cleo's experiences in Cairo during the war years were inspired by accounts of the adventures of Hermione Ranfurly in her wonderful memoir *To War with Whitaker*; of Barbara Skelton in various books, including *The Secret Listeners* by Sinclair McKay; and of author Graham Greene's sister, Elisabeth Dennys, in Jeremy Lewis's *Shades of Greene: One Generation of an English Family*.

Mr. Meyer, Mr. Mansoor, and the Costases were real people. They said that Winston Churchill left a book of poetry at Shepheard's in World War I and Mr. Costas promptly returned it to him when he arrived at Shepheard's again during World War II.

Pierre Lemarchand was the designer of Wallis Simpson's famous flamingo brooch from Cartier, decorated in the style that was, at the time this book was set, called *pierres de couleur*. Later, the colorful style was dubbed "tutti-frutti." Lemarchand was also responsible for designing the poignant and highly subversive liberty bird brooch, which saw him and Cartier's creative director, Jeanne Toussaint, hauled in for questioning by the Nazis.

The culprits behind the burning of Shepheard's Hotel on what came to be known as "Black Saturday" on January 26, 1952, were never discovered. There are theories that the attacks were too well-orchestrated to have been the work of the protestors who were marching that day, and might well have been perpetrated by King Farouk or even the British themselves. In any case, the riots heralded the end of an era. A few months later, a military coup brought Gamal Abdel Nasser to power and far-reaching political reforms followed, marking the end of British influence over the government of Egypt.

Acknowledgments

Each time I first hold a copy of my new book, it feels like a small miracle. That a story from my imagination will be shared with readers all over the world is the greatest gift for a writer to receive. To the chief miracle-worker, my editor, Lucia Macro, thank you for your boundless enthusiasm, guidance, and editorial expertise, as well as everything you do to shepherd my novels through the publishing process. My immense gratitude also to my fabulous literary agent, Kevan Lyon, for your wise counsel and staunch support and for championing my books with such skill and determination.

There are so many people without whose hard work my novels would not reach the shelves. Heartfelt thanks to the marketing and publicity teams at William Morrow, in particular, the amazing Amelia Wood and Danielle Bartlett; to Asanté Simons, who is always so responsive and helpful; to the crack team in sales; to the art department who make my beautiful covers; and to the many dedicated people at William Morrow who take part in the book's production and distribution. To the magnificent booksellers and librarians the world over, thank you for the hard work and love you pour into your vocations and into sharing my stories. To my readers, I can't tell you how grateful I am that in the era of streaming services and gaming, you continue to love and read books and to support me as an author.

To Lucy and Jason, Vikki, Ben, and Yasmin, thank you for your friendship and for cheering me on when the going gets tough. I couldn't do this without you! All my love to my sons, Allister and Adrian, who have become such fine young men—I'm so very proud of you. To my parents, Ian and Cheryl, and to my brother, Michael, I am so very lucky to have you and I'm forever grateful for your love, interest in my work, and unfailing support.

READ MORE BY
CHRISTINE WELLS

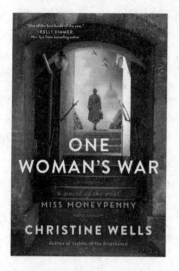

ONE WOMAN'S WAR
A Novel of the Real Miss Moneypenny

From the author of *Sisters of the Resistance* comes the story of WWII British Naval Intelligence officer Victoire Bennett, the real-life inspiration for the James Bond character Miss Moneypenny, whose international covert operation is put in jeopardy when a volatile socialite and Austrian double agent threatens to expose the mission to German High Command.

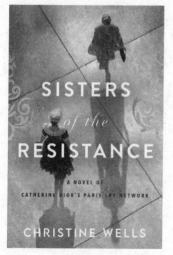

SISTERS OF THE RESISTANCE
A Novel of Catherine Dior's Paris Spy Network

Two sisters join the Paris Resistance in this page-turning new novel inspired by the real-life bravery of Catherine Dior, sister of the fashion designer and a heroine of World War II France—perfect for fans of Kate Quinn and Jennifer Chiaverini.

12/23.